Agnes Strickland

The Queens of England

A series of portraits of distinguished female sovereigns, by eminent artists. With

biogr. and historical sketches.

Agnes Strickland

The Queens of England
A series of portraits of distinguished female sovereigns, by eminent artists. With biogr. and historical sketches.

ISBN/EAN: 9783337321390

Printed in Europe, USA, Canada, Australia, Japan

Cover: Foto ©Raphael Reischuk / pixelio.de

More available books at **www.hansebooks.com**

THE

QUEENS OF ENGLAND:

A Series of Portraits

OF

DISTINGUISHED FEMALE SOVEREIGNS.

DRAWN AND ENGRAVED BY EMINENT ARTISTS,

WITH

BIOGRAPHICAL AND HISTORICAL SKETCHES,

FROM

AGNES STRICKLAND

A NEW EDITION.

NEW-YORK:
D. APPLETON & COMPANY,
443 & 445 BROADWAY.
M.DCCC.LXI.

NOTICE.

THESE pages contain portraits of Queens of England, from the earliest period of the monarchy to the present day. In this number are those of many who were unsurpassed in their personal charms, and in the lofty and heroic traits of their character; whilst all have been distinguished by the elevation of their rank, and the incidents of their career. Notwithstanding these circumstances, it has been designed to place the highest claim of the work to a favorable reception, upon the eminent skill and taste of the Artists which it should display. For this purpose, all these portraits have been painted and engraved only by such artists as were distinguished in their profession. That their labors might be surpassed in excellence and perfection need not be denied; but that such an attempt would place them far beyond the limits of a just expenditure, is equally apparent.

The biographical sketches are confined strictly to the personal history of each queen; and whilst they delineate the

striking events of their lives, they are intended likewise to
portray equally the grandeur of the queen, the attachments
of the wife, the affection of the mother, and the charms and
the infirmities of the woman.

Contents.

6   CONTENTS.

List of Plates.

QUEENS OF ENGLAND.

MATILDA OF SCOTLAND,

QUEEN OF HENRY I.

THIS princess, the subject of our present biography, is distinguished among the many illustrious females that have worn the crown matrimonial of England, by the title of "the Good Queen;" a title which, eloquent in its simplicity, briefly implies that she possessed not only the great and shining qualities calculated to add lustre to a throne, but that she employed them in promoting the happiness of all classes of her subjects, affording at the same time a bright example of the lovely and endearing attributes which should adorn the female character.

Matilda the Good received her earliest lessons of virtue and piety from her illustrious mother, and of learning from the worthy Turgot, the preceptor of the royal children of king Malcolm and queen Margaret of Scotland.

To this great and good man did Margaret, at the time of her death, consign the spiritual guardianship of her two young daughters, the princesses Matilda and Mary, and her younger sons. Turgot has preserved

2

the words with which she gave him this important charge; they will
strike an answering chord on the heart of every mother.

"Farewell!" she said; "my life draws to a close, but you may sur
vive me long. To you I commit the charge of my children. Teach
them, above all things, to love and fear God; and if any of them should
be permitted to attain to the height of earthly grandeur, O then, in an
especial manner be to them a father and a guide. Admonish, and if
need be, reprove them, lest they should be swelled with the pride of
momentary glory, and through covetousness, or by reason of the prosperity of this world, offend their Creator, and forfeit eternal life. This,
in the presence of Him who is now our only witness, I beseech you to
promise and perform."

Adversity was soon to try these youthful scions of royalty with her
touchstone; and of the princess Matilda, as well as her saintly mother,
it may justly be said,

> "Stern, rugged nurse, thy rigid lore
> With patience many a year she bore."

Soon after the disastrous defeat and death of her royal father and eldest
brother, Donald Bane, the illegitimate brother of Malcolm Canmore,
seized the throne of Scotland, and commanded all the English exiles, of
whatsoever degree, to quit the kingdom, under pain of death. Edgar
Atheling, Matilda's uncle, then conveyed to England the orphan family
of his sister, the queen of Scotland, consisting of five young princes, and
two princesses.

The princesses Matilda and Mary were placed by their uncle in the
nunnery of Rumsey, of which his surviving sister, Christina, was abbess.

Matilda thus became an inhabitant of the same abode where the royal virgins of her race had always received their education.

It was the express desire of the queen, her mother, who survived
that request but a few hours, that she should be placed under the care of
the lady Christina at Rumsey.

While in these English convents, the royal maid was compelled to
assume the thick black veil of a votaress, as a protection from the insults
of the lawless Norman nobles. The abbess Christina, her aunt, who
was exceedingly desirous of seeing her beautiful niece become a nun

professed, treated her very harshly, if she removed this cumbrous and inconvenient envelope, which was composed of coarse black cloth or serge; some say it was a tissue of horse-hair. The imposition of this veil was considered by Matilda as an intolerable grievance. She wore it, as she herself acknowledged, with sighs and tears, in the presence of her stern aunt; and the moment she found herself alone, she flung it upon the ground, and stamped it under her feet.

During the seven years that Matilda resided in this dreary asylum, she was carefully instructed in all the learning of the age. Ordericus Vitalis says she was taught the "*litteratoriam artem,*" of which she after-wards became, like her predecessor, Matilda of Flanders, a most munifi-cent patroness. She was also greatly skilled in music, for which her love amounted almost to a passion. When queen, we shall find her some-times censured, for the too great liberality she showed in rewarding with costly presents, the monks who sang skilfully in the church ser-vice.

The superior education which this illustrious princess received dur-ing these years of conventual seclusion, eminently fitted her to become the consort of so accomplished a prince as Henry le Beauclerc. Robert of Gloucester, and Piers of Longtoft, and, above all, Eadmer, a contem-porary, assert that the royal pair had been lovers before circumstances admitted of their union.

According to the testimony of the ancient chroniclers, especially the chronicle of Normandy, this princess was remarkable for her beauty. Matthew Paris says she was " very fair, and elegant in person, as well as learned, holy, and wise." These qualities, combined with her high lineage, rendered her doubtless an object of attraction to the Norman princes.

Henry was regarded by the people of the land with a greater degree of complacency than the elder sons of the Conqueror, from the circum-stance of his being an English-born prince.

Henry was in his thirty-second year, when the glancing aside of Wat Tyrrel's arrow made him king of England. The chroniclers of that era record that, from whatever cause, omens, dreams, and predictions of the death of the Red King, were rife in the land, immediately preceding that event. He promised every thing that could reasonably be demanded of

him, and set about reforming the abuses and corruptions that had pre
vailed during the licentious reign of the bachelor king, and completely
secured his popularity with the English people, by declaring his resolution of wedding a princess of the blood of Alfred, who had been brought
up and educated among them. Accordingly he demanded Matilda, the
daughter of Malcolm, king of Scotland, and Margaret Atheling, of her
brother Edgar, king of Scotland. The proposal was exceedingly agreeable to the Scottish Monarch; but great difficulties were opposed to the
completion of this marriage, by those who were of opinion that she had
embraced a religious life. The abbess Christina, Matilda's aunt, in particular, whose Saxon prejudices could not brook the idea that the throne
of the Norman line of sovereigns should be strengthened by an alliance
with the royal blood of Alfred, protested, "that her niece was a veiled
nun, and that it would be an act of sacrilege to remove her from her
convent."

Henry's heart was set upon the marriage, but he would not venture
to outrage popular opinion, by wedding a consecrated nun. In this
dilemma, he wrote a pressing letter to the learned Anselm, archbishop
of Canterbury, who had been unjustly despoiled of his revenues by
William Rufus, and was then in exile at Lyons, entreating him to return,
and render him his advice and assistance in this affair. When Anselm
heard the particulars of the case, he declared that it was too mighty for
his single decision, and therefore summoned a council of the church at
Lambeth, for the purpose of entering more fully into this important
question.

Matilda made her appearance before the synod, and was closely inter-
rogated by the primate Anselm, in the presence of the whole hierarchy
of England, as to the reality of her alleged devotion to a religious life.

The particulars of her examination have been preserved by Eadmer,
who, as the secretary of the archbishop Anselm, was doubtless an eye-
witness of this interesting scene, and, in all probability, recorded the
very words uttered by the princess.

The archbishop commenced by stating the objections to her marriage,
grounded on the prevailing report that she had embraced a religious life,
and declared "that no motive whatever would induce him to dispense
with her vow, if it had already been given to Almighty God."

The princess denied that there had been any such engagement on her part.

She was asked "if she had embraced a religious life, either by her own voice or the will of her parents;" and she replied, "Neither." Then she was examined as to the fact of her having worn the black veil of a votaress in her father's court, and subsequently in the nunneries of Rumsey and Wilton.

"I do not deny," said Matilda, "having worn the veil in my father's court; for, when I was a child, my aunt Christina put a piece of black cloth over my head; but when my father saw me with it, he snatched it off in a great rage, and execrated the person who had put it on me. I afterwards made a pretence of wearing it to excuse myself from unsuitable marriages; and on one of these occasions, my father tore the veil and threw it on the ground, observing to Alan, earl of Bretagne, who stood by, that it was his intention to give me in marriage, not to devote me to the church."

She also admitted that she had assumed the veil in the nunnery of Rumsey, as a protection from the lawless violence of the Norman nobles, and that she had continued to wear that badge of conventual devotion against her own inclination, through the harsh compulsion of her aunt, the abbess Christina. "If I attempted to remove it," continued Matilda, "she would torment me with harsh blows and sharp reproaches: sighing and trembling I wore it in her presence; but as soon as I withdrew from her sight, I always threw it off, and trampled upon it."

This explanation was considered perfectly satisfactory by the council at Lambeth, and they pronounced, that "Matilda, daughter of Malcolm, king of Scotland, had proved that she had not embraced a religious life, either by her own choice or the vow of her parents, and she was therefore free to contract marriage with the king." The council, in addition to this declaration, thought proper to make public the most cogent reason which the Scottish princess had given for her assumption of the black veil, on her coming to England.

According to the Saxon chroniclers, Matilda, notwithstanding her repugnance to the consecrated veil, exhibited a very maidenly reluctance to enter the holy pale of matrimony with a royal husband. It is certain that after the council at Lambeth had pronounced her free to marry,

Matilda resisted for a time the entreaties of the king, and the commands of her royal brother and sovereign, to accept the brilliant destiny which she was offered.

All who were connected with the Saxon royal line importuned Matilda, meantime, with such words as these: "O most noble and most gracious of women, if thou wouldst, thou couldst raise up the ancient honor of England : thou wouldst be a sign of alliance, a pledge of reconciliation : but if thou persistest in thy refusal, the enmity between the Saxon and the Norman races will be eternal; human blood will never cease to flow."

Thus urged, the royal recluse ceased to object to a marriage, whereby she was to become the bond of peace to a divided nation, and the dove of the newly-sealed covenant between the Norman sovereign and her own people. Henry promised to confirm to the English nation their ancient laws and privileges, as established by Alfred, and ratified by Edward the Confessor—in short, to become a constitutional monarch; and on those conditions the daughter of the royal line of Alfred consented to share his throne.

Matilda's demurs, after all, occasioned little delay, for the archbishop Anselm did not return to England till October; the council at Lambeth was held in the latter end of that month, and her marriage and coronation took place on Sunday, November 11th, being St. Martin's day, just three months and six days after the inauguration of her royal lord at Westminster, August 5th, 1100; which we may consider quick work, for the dispatch of such important business, and solemn ceremonials of state

We give the singular scene of the marriage, in the very words of one who was a contemporary, and most likely an eye-witness.

"At the wedding of Matilda and Henry the First, there was a most prodigious concourse of nobility and people assembled in and about the church at Westminster, when, to prevent all calumny and evil report that the king was about to marry a nun, the archbishop Anselm mounted into a pulpit, and gave the multitude a history of the events proved before the synod, and its judgment, that the lady Matilda of Scotland was free from any religious vow, and might dispose of herself in marriage as she thought fit. The archbishop finished by asking the people in a loud voice, whether any one there objected to this decision, upon which they answered unanimously, with a loud shout, ' that the matter was rightly settled.' Accordingly the lady was immediately married to the king, and crowned before that vast assembly." A more simple yet majestic appeal to the sense of the people, in regard to a royal marriage, history records not.

To this auspicious union of the Anglo-Norman sovereign Henry I. with Matilda of Scotland, a princess of English lineage, English education, and an English heart, we may trace all the constitutional blessings which this free country at present enjoys. It was through the influence of this virtuous queen that Henry granted the important charter which formed the model and precedent of that great palladium of English liberty, Magna Charta; and we call upon our readers to observe, that it was the direct ancestress of our present sovereign-lady, who refused to quit her gloomy conventual prison, and to give her hand to the handsomest and most accomplished sovereign of his time, till she had obtained just and merciful laws for her suffering country, the repeal of the tyrannical imposition of the curfew, and, in some slight degree, a recognition of the rights of the commons.

Matilda's English ancestry, and English education, rendered the new king's marriage with her a most popular measure with the Anglo-Saxon people, of whom the great bulk of his subjects was composed. By them the royal bride was fondly styled Matilda Atheling, and regarded as the representative of their own regretted sovereigns. The allegiance which the mighty Norman conqueror, and his despotic son, the Red King, had never been able to obtain, except through the sternest measures of compulsion, and which, in defiance of the dreadful penalties of loss of eyes, limbs, and life, had been frequently withdrawn from these powerful monarchs, was freely and faithfully accorded to the husband of Matilda, Henry I., by the Saxon population. All the reforms effected by his enlightened government, and all the good laws which his enlarged views of political economy taught that wise monarch to adopt, were attributed, by his Anglo-Saxon subjects, to the beneficial influence of his young queen.

The invasion of duke Robert, Henry's eldest brother, on his return from the Holy Land, took place in the second year of Matilda's marriage. King Henry's fleet being manned with Norman seamen, and, of course, under the influence of Norman chiefs, revolted, and, instead of guarding the coasts of England from the threatened invasion of the duke, swept across the narrow seas and brought him and his armament in triumph to Portsmouth, where he was joined by the majority of the Anglo-Norman baronage. Robert had also his partisans among the English: for Edgar Atheling so far forgot the interests of his royal niece, queen Matilda, as to espouse the cause of his friend Robert against the king her husband.

Robert landed at Portsmouth, and marched direct to Winchester, where queen Matilda then lay in with her first-born child William the Atheling. When this circumstance was related to the duke, he relinquished his purpose of storming the city, with the observation, "that it never should be said he commenced the war by an assault on a woman in childbed, for that would be a base action."

Matilda duly appreciated this generous consideration on the part of her royal brother-in-law and godfather, and exerted all her influence to negotiate a peace between him and her lord, in which she was assisted by the good offices of the archbishop Anselm: and this formidable crisis passed over without the effusion of a drop of blood. These are Harding's words on the subject:

> "But Anselm archbishop of Canterbury,
> And queen Matilda, made them well accord:
> The king to pay three thousand marks yearly
> To duke Robert, who thus more desired."

After this happy pacification, Henry invited Robert to become his guest at his court, where the easy-tempered duke was feasted and entertained, greatly to his satisfaction, by his royal god-daughter Matilda, who, in her love for music, and the encouragement she bestowed on minstrels, or trouvères, quite coincided with the tastes of her sponsor and brother-in-law, "for," says Malmsbury, "every poet hastened to the court of Matilda to read his verses to that queen, and to partake of her bounty." So much did Robert enjoy his sojourn at Henry's court, that he stayed there upwards of six months, though his presence was greatly required in his own dominions.

Matilda's eldest son, prince William, (or the Atheling, as he was more generally styled by the English,) was, in the year 1115, conducted by the king his father with great pomp into Normandy, where he was presented to the states as the heir of the duchy, and fealty was sworn to him by the barons and freemen.

Matilda passed the Christmas festival of the same year, in the company of her royal husband, at the abbey of St. Alban's. The existence of a portrait of queen Matilda is certainly owing to this visit; for in a rich illuminated volume, called the Golden Book of St. Alban's, (now in the British Museum,) may still be seen a miniature of the royal benefactress. The queen is attired in the royal mantle of scarlet, lined with white fur; it covers the knees, and is very long. The mantle is square to the bust. A cordon of scarlet and gold, with a large tassel, passes through two gold knobs: she holds the cordon in her left hand. She wears a tight kirtle of dark blue, buttoned down the front with gold. Her sleeves fit close to the arms, and are scarlet like the mantle. A white veil is arranged in a square form on the brow, and is surmounted by a gold crown, formed of three large trefoils, and gold *oreillettes* appear beneath the veil, on each side of the cheeks. The veil flows behind her shoulders with lappets. Matilda is very fair in complexion: she has a long throat, and elegant form, of tall proportions. She displays with her right hand the charter she gave the abbey, from which hangs a very large red seal, whereon, without doubt, was impressed her effigy in grand relief. She sits on a carved stone bench, on which is a scarlet cushion figured with gold leaves. The cushion is in the form of a woolpack, but has four tassels of gold and scarlet. A piece of figured cloth is hung at the back of her seat. There are no armorial bearings— one proof of the authenticity of the portrait. " Queen Matilda gave us Bellwick and Lilleburn," is the notation appended by the monks of St. Alban's to the portrait.

Unbounded hospitality was one of the social virtues of this peaceful reign, especially at this peculiar era, when the benignant example of the good queen had, for a period of nearly seventeen years, produced the happiest effect in softening the manners of the haughty and powerful Norman families, who were at that time the magnates of the land.

3

A fresh revolt in Normandy deprived Matilda of the society of her husband and son in 1117. The king, according to Eadmer, returned and spent Christmas with her, as she was at that time in a declining state of health; leaving prince William with his Norman baronage, as a pledge for his return. His sojourn was, of necessity, very brief. He was compelled, by the distracted state of affairs in Normandy, to rejoin his army there, and Matilda never saw either her husband or her son again.

Resigned and perfect in all the duties of her high calling, the dying queen remained, during this trying season, in her palace at Westminster, lonely, though surrounded with all the splendor of royalty; enduring with complacency and patience the separation from her beloved consort and children, and affording to the last hour of her life, a beautiful example of piety and self-denial.

She expired on the first of May, 1118, passionately lamented by every class of the people, to whom her love and wisdom had rendered her inexpressibly dear.

ELEANORA OF AQUITAINE,

QUEEN OF HENRY II.

THE life of the consort of Henry II. commences the biographies of a series of Provençal princesses, with whom the earlier monarchs of our royal house of Plantagenet allied themselves, for upwards of a century. Important effects, not only on the domestic history of the court of England, but on its commerce and statistics, may be traced to its union, by means of this queen, with the most polished and civilized people on the face of the earth, as the Provençals of the twelfth and thirteenth centuries indisputably were. With the arts, the idealities, and the refinements of life, Eleanora brought acquisitions of more importance to the Anglo-Norman people, than even that great "Provence dower" on which Dante dwells with such earnestness.

The grandfather of Eleanora had been gay and even licentious in his youth; and now, at the age of sixty-eight, he wished to devote some time, before his death, to meditation and penitence, for the sins of his early life. When his grand-daughter had attained her fourteenth year, he commenced his career of self-denial, by summoning the baronage of Aquitaine, and communicating his intention of abdicating in favor of his grand-daughter, to whom they all took the oath of allegiance. He then opened his great project of uniting Aquitaine with France, by giving Eleanora in marriage to the heir of Louis le Gros. The barons agreed to this proposal, on condition that the laws and customs of Aqui-

taine should be held inviolate; and that the consent of the young princess should be obtained. Eleanora had an interview with her suitor,
and professed herself pleased with the arrangement.'

Louis and Eleanora were immediately married with great pomp, at
Bourdeaux; and, on the solemn resignation of Duke William, the
youthful pair were crowned duke and duchess of Aquitaine, August 1,
1137.

On the conclusion of this grand ceremony, duke William, grandsire
of the bride, laid down his robes and insignia of sovereignty, and took
up the hermit's cowl and staff. He departed on a pilgrimage to St.
James's of Compostenella, in Spain, and died soon after, very penitent,
in one of the cells of that rocky wilderness.

At the time when duke William resigned the dominions of the south
to his grand-daughter, he was the most powerful prince in Europe.
His rich ports of Bourdeaux and Saintonge supplied him with commercial wealth; his maritime power was immense; his court was the
focus of learning and luxury; and it must be owned, that at the
accession of the fair Eleanora, this court had become not a little
licentious.

Louis and his bride obtained immediate possession of Poitou, Gascony, Biscay, and a large territory extending beyond the Pyrenees.

They repaired afterwards to Poictiers, where Louis was solemnly
crowned duke of Guienne. Scarcely was this ceremony concluded,
when Eleanora and her husband were summoned to the death-bed of
Louis VI., that admirable king and lawgiver of France. His dying
words were,

"Remember, royalty is a public trust, for the exercise of which a
rigorous account will be exacted by Him who has the sole disposal of
crowns and sceptres."

So spoke the great legislator of France, to the youthful pair whose
wedlock had united the north and south of France. On the conscientious mind of Louis VII. the words of his dying father were strongly
impressed, but it was late in life before his thoughtless partner profited
by them.

Eleanora was very beautiful; she had been reared in all the accomplishments of the south; she was a fine musician, and composed and

sang the *chansons* and *tensons* of Provençal poetry. Her native troubadours expressly inform us that she could both read and write. The
government of her dominions was in her own hands, and she frequently
resided in her native capital of Bourdeaux. She was perfectly adored
by her southern subjects, who always welcomed her with joy, and they
bitterly mourned her absence, when she was obliged to return to her
court at Paris; a court whose morals were severe; where the rigid rule
of St. Bernard was observed by the king her husband, as if his palace
had been a convent. Far different was the rule of Eleanora, in the
cities of the south.

The political sovereignty of her native dominions, was not the only
authority exercised by Eleanora in "gay Guienne." She was, by hereditary right, chief reviewer and critic of the poets of Provence. At
certain festivals held by her, after the custom of her ancestors, called
Courts of Love, all new *sirventes* and *chansons* were sung or recited before her, by the troubadours. She then, assisted by a conclave of her
ladies, sat in judgment, and pronounced sentence on their literary merits.
She was herself a popular troubadour poet. Her *chansons* were remembered, long after death had raised a barrier against flattery, and she is
reckoned among the authors of France.

In the year 1150, Geoffrey Plantagenet, count of Anjou, appeared
at the court of Louis VII. Geoffrey did homage for Normandy, and
presented to Louis his son, young Henry Plantagenet, surnamed Fitz-
Empress. This youth was about seventeen, and was then first seen by
queen Eleanora. But the scandalous chronicles of the day declare, the
queen was much taken by the fine person and literary attainments of
Geoffrey, who was considered the most accomplished knight of his time.
Geoffrey was a married man; but queen Eleanora as little regarded the
marriage engagements of the persons on whom she bestowed her attention, as she did her own conjugal ties.

About eighteen months after the departure of the Angevin princes,
the queen of France gave birth to another princess, named Alice. Soon
after this event, Henry Plantagenet once more visited Paris, to do
homage for Normandy and Anjou, a pleuritic fever having suddenly
carried off his father. Queen Eleanora now transferred her former partiality for the father, to the son, who had become a noble, martial-look-

ing prince, full of energy, learned, valiant, and enterprising, and ready to undertake any conquest, whether of the heart of the gay queen of the south, or of the kingdom from which he had been unjustly disinherited.

Eleanora acted with her usual disgusting levity, in the advances she made to this youth. Her beauty was still unimpaired, though her character was in low esteem with the world. Motives of interest induced Henry to feign a return to the passion of queen Eleanora; his mother's cause was hopeless in England, and Eleanora assured him that if she could effect a divorce from Louis, her ships and treasures should be at his command, for the subjugation of king Stephen.

The intimacy between Henry and Eleanora soon awakened the displeasure of the king of France, and the prince departed for Anjou. Queen Eleanora immediately made an application for a divorce, under the plea that king Louis was her fourth cousin. It does not appear that he opposed this separation, though it certainly originated from the queen. Notwithstanding the advice of Suger, Louis seems to have accorded heartily with the proposition, and the divorce was finally pronounced, by a council of the church, at Baugenci, March 18, 1152; where the marriage was not dissolved on account of the queen's adultery, as is commonly asserted, but declared invalid because of consanguinity.

The celerity with which the marriage of Eleanora followed her divorce, astonished all Europe; for she gave her hand to Henry Plantagenet, duke of Normandy and count of Anjou, only six weeks after the divorce was pronounced. Eleanora is supposed to have been in her thirty-second year, and the bridegroom in his twentieth—a disparity somewhat ominous, in regard to their future matrimonial felicity.

Henry was busy, laying siege to the castle of one of his rebels in Normandy, when the news of Stephen's death reached him. Six weeks elapsed before he sailed to take possession of his kingdom. His queen accompanied him.

Eleanora and Henry were crowned at Westminster Abbey, December 19, 1154, "after England," to use the words of Henry of Huntingdon, "had been without a king for six weeks." Henry's security, during this interval, was owing to the powerful fleet of his queen, which commanded the seas between Normandy and England, and kept all rebels in awe.

The coronation of the king of England, and the luxurious lady of the south, was without parallel for magnificence. Here were seen in profusion mantles of silk and brocade, of a new fashion and splendid texture, brought by queen Eleanora from Constantinople. In the illuminated portraits of this queen, she wears a wimple, or close coif, with a circlet of gems put over it; her kirtle, or close gown, has tight sleeves, and fastens with full gathers, just below the throat, confined with a rich collar of gems. Over this is worn the elegant pelisson, or outer robe, bordered with fur; with very full loose sleeves, lined with ermine, showing gracefully the tight kirtle sleeves beneath. The elegant taste of Eleanora, or, perhaps, her visit to the Greek capital, revived the beautiful costume of the wife of the Conqueror. In some portraits, the queen is seen with her hair braided, and closely wound round the head with jewelled banks. Over all was thrown a square of fine lawn or gauze, which supplied the place of a veil, and was worn precisely like the *faziola*, still the national costume of the lower orders of Venice. Sometimes this coverchief, or kerchief, was drawn over the features down below the chin; it thus supplied the place of veil and bonnet, when abroad; sometimes it descended but to the brow; just as the wearer was disposed to show or conceal her face. Frequently the coverchief was confined, by the bandeau, or circlet, being placed on the head, over it. Girls before marriage wore their hair in ringlets or tresses on their shoulders. The church was very earnest in preaching against the public display of ladies' hair after marriage.

The long hair of the men likewise drew down the constant fulminations of the church; but after Henry I. had cut off his curls, and forbidden long hair at court, his courtiers adopted periwigs; indeed, if we may judge from the queer effigy on his coins, the handsome Stephen himself wore a wig. Be this at it may, the thunder of the pulpit was instantly levelled at wigs, which were forbidden by a sumptuary law of king Henry.

Henry II. made his appearance, at his coronation, with short hair, mustachios, and shaven chin; he wore a doublet, and short Angevin cloak, which immediately gained for him from his subjects, Norman and

English, the sobriquet of Court-mantle. His dalmatica was of the richest brocade, bordered with gold embroidery. At this coronation, ecclesiastics were first seen in England dressed in sumptuous robes of silk and
velvet, worked with gold. This was in imitation of the luxury of the
Greek church : the splendor of the dresses seen by the queen at Constantinople, occasioned the introduction of this corruption in the western
church.

Such was the costume of the court of Eleanora of Aquitaine, queen
of England, in the year of her coronation, 1154.

The Christmas festivities were celebrated that year with great pomp,
at Westminster Palace, but directly the coronation was over, the king
conducted his queen to the palace of Bermondsey, where, after remaining some weeks in retirement, she gave birth to her second son, the last
day of February, 1155.

The English chose to regard Henry II. solely as the descendant of
their ancient Saxon line. "Thou art son," said they, "to the most
glorious empress Matilda, whose mother was Matilda Atheling, daughter
to Margaret, saint and queen, whose father was Edmund, son to king
Edmund Ironsides, who was great-grandson to king Alfred."

Queen Eleanora brought her husband a princess in the year 1156;
this was the eldest daughter, the princess Matilda.

The next year the queen spent in England. Her celebrated son,
Richard Cœur de Lion, was born September 1157, at a palace considered
one of the finest in the kingdom, called the Beau Monte, in Oxford.

Eleanora of Aquitaine, in some passages of her life, appears as one of
the most prominent characters of her age: she was very actively
employed, either as sovereign of her own dominions, or regent of Normandy, during the period from 1157 to 1172.

Henry sent for his queen to Normandy in 1160; she went in great
state, taking with her prince Henry and her eldest daughter, to meet
their father. The occasion of her presence being required, was the marriage of Marguerite, the daughter of her former husband Louis VII. by
his second wife, with her young son Henry. Chancellor Becket went,
with a magnificent retinue, to Paris, and brought the little bride, aged
three years, to the queen at Rouen. Both bride and bridegroom were
given, after their marriage, to Becket for education; and this extraordi-

nary person inspired, in their young bosoms, an attachment to him, that ended but with their lives.

From the time of the marriage of her daughter Matilda to the Lion of Saxony, Eleanora had not visited England. The coronation of her eldest son, and the murder of Beckct, had occurred while she resided in her native province. She had seen her son Richard, in 1170, crowned count of Poitou, with all the ceremonies pertaining to the inauguration of her ancestors. But king Henry only meant his sons to superintend the state and pageantry of a court; he did not intend that they should exercise independent authority; and Richard's will was curbed, by the faithful Norman veterans pertaining to his father. These castellans were the real governors of Guienne; an order of affairs equally disapproved of by prince Richard, queen Eleanora, and their Aquitanian subjects. The queen told her sons Richard and Geoffrey, that Guienne and Poitou owed no obedience to a king of England, or to his Normans; if they owed homage to any one, it was to the sovereign of France; and Richard and Geoffrey resolved to act as their Provençal forefathers of old, and pay no homage to the king of England.

All these fermentations were approaching a violent crisis, when Henry II., in the summer of 1173, arrived with his son, the young king, in Guienne, to receive the long-delayed homage of count Raymond of Thoulouse, and to inquire into the meaning of some revolts in the south, against his Norman castellans, evidently encouraged by his wife and prince Richard.

It was part of the duty of a feudal vassal, to give his sovereign advice in time of need; and when Raymond of Thoulouse came to this part of his oath of homage, as he knelt before Henry II., he interpolated it with these emphatic words:—

"Then I advise you, king, to beware of your wife and sons."

That very night the young king, although he always slept in his father's bedroom, escaped to the protection of his father-in-law, Louis VII. From Paris he made all manner of undutiful demands on his father.

Simultaneously with the flight of young Henry, his brothers, Richard and Geoffrey, decamped for Paris. Richard's grievance was, that his wife, the princess Alice of France, was withheld from him; while

4

Geoffrey insisted, as he had arrived at the mature age of sixteen, that the duchy of Bretagne, and his wife Constance, whose dower it was, should be given to his sole control.

Reports had been brought to Eleanora, that her husband meditated a divorce; for some lady had been installed, with almost regal honors, in her apartments at Woodstock. Court scandal pointed at her daughter-in-law, the princess Alice, whose youthful charms, it was said, had captivated her father-in-law, and for that reason the damsel was detained from her affianced lord, prince Richard. Enraged at these rumors, Eleanora resolved to seek the protection of the king of France; but as she was surrounded by Henry's Norman garrisons, she possessed so little power in her own domains as to be reduced to quit them in disguise. She assumed male attire, and had travelled part of her way in this dress, when Henry's Norman agents followed and seized her, before she could reach the territories of her divorced husband. They brought her back very rudely, in the disguise she had adopted, and kept her prisoner in Bourdeaux, till the arrival of her husband. Her sons pursued their flight safely, to the court of the king of France.

Now commenced that long, dolorous, and mysterious imprisonment, which may be considered the third era in the life of Eleanora of Aquitaine. But the imprisonment of queen Eleanora was not stationary; we trace her, carried with her royal husband, in a state of restraint, to Barfleur, where he embarked for England. He had another prisoner, in company with Eleanora; this was his daughter-in-law, the young Marguerite, who had contumaciously defied him, left the royal robes he had made for her coronation, unworn, upon his hands, and scorned the crown he had offered to place on her brow, if not consecrated by Becket. With these royal captives, Henry II. landed at Southampton, some time in July, 1173.

Then was queen Eleanora consigned to confinement, which lasted, with but short intervals, for sixteen years. Her prison was no worse place than her own royal palace at Winchester, where she was well guarded by her husband's great justiciary and general, Ranulph de Glanville, who likewise had the charge of the royal treasury, at the same place. That Glanville treated her with respect, is evident from some subsequent events.

Henry II. seems to have indulged his eldest and his youngest sons with the most ruinous fondness; he always kept them near him, if possible, while prince Richard and prince Geoffrey, equally beloved by their mother, were chiefly resident with her, on the continent.

The lengthened imprisonment of queen Eleanora infuriated her subjects in Aquitaine. The troubadours roused the national spirit in favor of their native princess, by such strains as these, which were the war-songs that animated the contest maintained by Richard in the name of his mother:

"Daughter of Aquitania, fair fruitful vine, thou hast been torn from thy country, and led into a strange land. Thy harp is changed into the voice of mourning, and thy songs into sounds of lamentation. Brought up in delicacy and abundance, thou enjoyedst a royal liberty, living in the bosom of wealth, delighting thyself with the sports of thy women, with their songs to the sound of the lute and tabor; and now thou mournest, thou weepest, thou consumest thyself with sorrow. Return, poor prisoner—return to thy cities if thou canst; and if thou canst not, weep and say, 'Alas, how long is my exile!' Weep, weep, and say 'My tears are my bread both day and night.'"

These expressions of tenderness for the daughter of the old national chiefs of Aquitaine, are followed by a cry of malediction against the towns which, either from force or necessity, still adhered to the king of the foreign race:

"Woe to the traitors which are in Aquitaine, for the day of their chastisement is at hand! La Rochelle dreads that day. She doubles her trenches, she girds herself all round with the sea, and the noise of her great works is heard beyond the mountains."

For nearly two years, the Angevin subjects of Henry II., and the Aquitanian subjects of his captive queen, gave battle to each other; and from Rochelle to Bayonne, the dominions of queen Eleanora were in a state of insurrection.

Prince Richard having got possession of the whole of Aquitaine, his father commanded him to surrender it to his mother, queen Eleanora, whom he had brought as far as Normandy, to claim her right. The moment the prince received this mandate, he gave up the territory, and hastened to Normandy to welcome the queen, and congratulate her on her restoration to freedom.

This release is recorded by the friend of the queen, abbot Benedict. From him we learn, that, during the year 1186, Eleanora exercised sovereign power at Bourdeaux, and then resigned it to her son Richard, who, in the mean time, had made his peace with his father.

Henry II. was with his queen during this period; for Benedict declares that, the following April, they sailed from Barfleur to England. Eleanora was again put under some restraint at Winchester Palace, which she quitted no more till the death of king Henry, three years afterwards.

King Henry, when he was carried forth to be buried, was first apparelled in his princely robes, having his crown on his head, gloves on his hands, and shoes on his feet, wrought with gold; spurs on his heels, a ring of gold on his finger, a sceptre in his hand, his sword by his side, and his face uncovered. But this regalia was of a strange nature; for the corpse of Henry, like that of the Conqueror, had been stripped and plundered; and when those who were charged with the funeral demanded the ornaments in which Henry was to lie in state, the treasurer, as a favor, sent a ring of little value, and an old sceptre. As for the crown with which the warlike brow of Henry was encircled, it was but the gold fringe from a lady's petticoat, torn off for the occasion; and in this odd attire, the greatest monarch in the world went down to his last abode.

The first step taken by Richard I., on his accession to the English crown, was to order his mother's release from her constrained retirement at Winchester Palace. From a captive, queen Eleanora in one moment became a sovereign; for the reins of the English government were placed in her hands, at the time of her release. She made a noble use of her authority, according to a manuscript cited by Tyrrell.

Eleanora departed for Aquitaine as soon as her son had settled her English dower, and Richard embarked at Dover, for Calais, to join the crusade, taking with him but ten ships from the English ports. His troops were disembarked, and he marched across France, to his mother's dominions, where he formally resigned to her the power he had exercised, during his father's lifetime, as her deputy.

We see Eleanora taken from captivity by her son Richard, and invested with the high authority of queen-regent: there is no reason to suppose that that authority was revoked; for, in every emergency during the king's absence, she appears as the guiding power. For this purpose she absented herself from Aquitaine, whose government she placed in the hands of a deputy, her grandson Otho, of Saxony; and at the end of the reign of Cœur de Lion, we find her, according to the words of Matthew Paris, "governing England with great wisdom and popularity."

Queen Eleanora, when thus arduously engaged in watching over the interests of her best beloved son, was approaching her seventieth year—an age when rest is imperiously demanded by the human frame. But years of toil still remained before her, ere death clossed her weary pilgrimage in 1204; and these years were laden with sorrows, which drew from her that pathetic alteration of the regal style, preserved in her letter to the pope, on occasion of the captivity of Cœur de Lion, where she declares herself—

"Eleanora, by the wrath of God, queen of England."

Eleanora of Aquitaine is among the very few women who have atoned for an ill-spent youth, by a wise and benevolent old age. As a sovereign, she ranks among the greatest of female rulers.

BERENGARIA OF NAVARRE,

QUEEN OF RICHARD I.

BERENGARIA, the beautiful daughter of Sancho the Wise, king of Navarre, was first seen by Richard Cœur de Lion, when count of Poitou, at a grand tournament given by her gallant brother at Pampeluna, her native city. Richard was then captivated by the beauty of Berengaria, but his engagement to the fair and frail Alice of France prevented him from offering her his hand.

No one can marvel that the love of the ardent Richard should be strengthened, when he met the beautiful, the cultivated, and virtuous Berengaria, in the familiar intercourse which sprung from his friendship with her gallant brother · but a long and secret engagement, replete with "hope deferred," was the fate of Richard the Lion-hearted and the fair flower of Navarre.

Soon after Richard ascended the English throne, he sent his mother, queen Eleanora, to the court of her friend, Sancho the Wise, to demand the princess Berengaria in marriage; "for," says Vinisauf, "he had long loved the elegant girl." Sancho the Wise not only received the proposition with joy, but intrusted Berengaria to the care of queen Eleanora. The royal ladies travelled from the court of Navarre together, across Italy, to Naples, where they found the ships belonging to Eleanora had arrived in the bay. But etiquette forbade Berengaria to approach her lover till he was free from the claims of Alice; therefore she sojourned with queen Eleanora, at Brindisi, in the spring of 1191, waiting the message from king Richard, announcing that he was free to receive the hand of the princess of Navarre.

It was at Messina that the question of the engagement between the princess Alice and the king of England was debated with Philip Augustus. her brother; and more than once, the potentates assembled for the crusade expected that the forces of France and England would be called into action, to decide the right of king Richard to give his hand to another lady than the sister of the king of France.

King Philip contended that Richard held in his hand his sister's dower, the good city of Gisors. Upon this, the king of England brought the matter to a conclusion, in these words :—

> "'Now,' said king Richard,
>   'That menace may not be,
> For thou shalt have ward
>   Of Gisors thy citée,
> And treasure ilk a deal,'
>   Richard yielded him his right,
> His treasure and his town,
>   Before witness at sight,
> (Of clerk and eke baron,)
>   His sister he might marry,
> Wherever God might like,
>   And, to make certainty,
> Richard a quittance took."

Richard then embarked in his favorite galley, named by him Trenc-the-mere. He had previously, in honor of his betrothment, instituted an order of twenty-four knights, who pledged themselves in a fraternity with the king, to scale the walls of Acre; and that they might be known in the storming of that city, the king appointed them to wear a blue band of leather on the left leg, from which they were called Knights of the Blue Thong.

The season of Lent prevented the immediate marriage of Richard and his betrothed; and, as etiquette did not permit the unwedded maiden, Berengaria, to embark in the Trenc-the-mere under the immediate protection of her lover, she sailed, in company with queen Joanna, in one of the strongest ships, under the care of a brave knight, called Stephen de Turnham.

After these arrangements, Richard led the van of the fleet, in Trenc-the-mere, bearing a huge lantern at her poop, to rally the fleet in the darkness of night. Thus, with a hundred and fifty ships and fifty galleys, and accompanied by his bride and his sister, did Lion-hearted Richard hoist sail for Palestine, where Philip Augustus had already indolently commenced the siege of Acre.

Preparations were made at Limoussa, for the nuptials and coronation of king Richard and Berengaria. We are able to describe the appearance made by these royal personages, at this high solemnity. King Richard's costume, we may suppose, varied little from that in which he gave audience to the despot Isaac, a day after the marriage had taken place.

"A satin tunic of rose-color was belted round his waist; his mantle was of striped silver tissue, brocaded with silver half-moons; his sword, of fine Damascus steel, had a hilt of gold, and a silver-scaled sheath: on his head he wore a scarlet bonnet, brocaded in gold, with figures of animals. He bore a truncheon in his hand. His Spanish steed was led before him, saddled and bitted with gold, and the saddle was inlaid with precious stones: two little golden lions were fixed on it, in the place of a crupper: they were figured with their paws raised, in act to strike each other." In this attire, Vinisauf adds, "that Richard, who had yellow curls, a bright complexion, and a figure like Mars himself, appeared a perfect model of military and manly grace."

The effigy of queen Berengaria, at Espan, certainly presents her as a bride—a circumstance which is ascertained by the flowing tresses, royal matrons always wearing their hair covered, or else closely braided.

Her hair is parted, à la vierge, on the brow; a transparent veil, open on each side, like the Spanish mantillas, hangs behind, and covers the rich tresses at their length; the veil is confined by a regal diadem, of peculiar splendor, studded with several bands of gems, and surmounted by *fleurs-de-lis*, to which so much foliage is added, as to give it the appearance of a double crown; perhaps because she was crowned queen of Cyprus as well as England. Our antiquaries affirm that the peculiar

5

character of Berengaria's elegant but singular style of beauty, brings
conviction to every one that looks on her effigy, that it is a carefully
finished portrait.

At his marriage, king Richard proclaimed a grand feast.

> " To Limoussa the lady was led,
> His feast the king did cry,
> Berengare will be wed,
> And sojourn thereby.
> The third day of the feast
> Bishop Bernard of Bayonne
> Newed oft the geste
> To the queen he gave the crown."

"And there in the joyous month of May, 1191," says an ancient
writer, "in the flourishing and spacious isle of Cyprus, celebrated as the
very abode of the goddess of love, did king Richard solemnly take to
wife his beloved lady Berengaria."

After the conclusion of the nuptials, and coronation of Berengaria,
her royal bridegroom once more hoisted his flag on his good galley
Trenc-the-mere, and set sail, in beautiful summer weather, for Palestine.
Berengaria and her sister-in-law again sailed, under the protection of sir
Stephen de Turnham; such being safer than companionship with the
warlike Richard. Their galley made the port of Acre before the Trenc-
the-mere.

There is not a more pleasant spot in history, than the tender friendship of Berengaria and Joanna, who formed an attachment, amidst the
perils and terrors of storm and siege, ending only with their lives. How
quaintly, yet expressively, is their gentle and feminine love for each
other marked, by the sweet simplicity of the words:

> " They held each other dear,
> And lived as doves in cage!"

noting, at the same time, the harem-like seclusion in which the royal
ladies dwelt, while sharing the crusade campaign.

The autumn of 1192 had commenced, when king Richard concluded his peace with Saladin, and prepared to return, covered with fruitless glory, to his native dominions. A mysterious estrangement had, at this time, taken place between him and Berengaria; yet the chroniclers do not mention that any rival had supplanted the queen, but merely that accidents of war had divided him from her company.

The king bade farewell to his queen and sister, and saw them embark, the very evening of his own departure. The queens were accompanied by the Cypriot princess, and sailed from Acre, under the care of Stephen de Turnham, September the 29th. Richard meant to return by a different route across Europe. He travelled in the disguise of a Templar, and embarked in a ship belonging to the master of the Temple. This vessel was wrecked off the coast of Istria, which forced Richard to proceed homewards through the domains of his enemy, Leopold of Austria. But to his ignorance of geography is attributed his near approach to Leopold's capital. After several narrow escapes a page sent by Richard, to purchase provisions at a village near Vienna, was recognized by an officer who had made the late crusade with Leopold. The boy was seized, and, after enduring cruel torments, he confessed where had left his master.

When Leopold received certain intelligence where Richard harbored, the inn was searched, but not a soul found there who bore any appearance of a king. "No," said the people, "there is no one here, without he be the Templar in the kitchen, now turning the fowls which are roasting for dinner." The officers of Leopold took the hint, and went into the kitchen, where, in fact, was seated a Templar, very busy turning the spit. The Austrian chevalier, who had served in the crusade, knew him, and said quickly, "There he is—seize him!"

Cœur de Lion started from the spit, and did battle for his liberty right valiantly, but was overcome by numbers.

The revengeful Leopold immediately imprisoned his gallant enemy, and immured him so closely in a Styrian castle, called Tenebreuse, that for months no one knew whether the lion-hearted king was alive or dead. Richard, whose heroic name was the theme of admiration in Europe, and the burden of every song, seemed vanished from the face of the earth.

Better fortune attended the vessel that bore the fair freight of the

three royal ladies. Stephen de Turnham's galley arrived, without accident, at Naples, where Berengaria, Joanna, and the Cypriot princess,
landed safely, and, under the care of Sir Stephen, journeyed to Rome.

The Provençal traditions declare, that here Berengaria first took
the alarm, that some disaster had happened to her lord, from seeing
a belt of jewels offered for sale, which she knew had been on his
person when she parted from him. At Rome she likewise heard
some vague reports of his shipwreck, and of the enmity of the emperor Henry VI.

Berengaria was detained at Rome, with her royal companions, by
her fear of the emperor, for upwards of half a year. At length the
pope, moved by her distress and earnest entreaties, sent them, under
the care of Messire Mellar, one of the cardinals, to Pisa, whence they
proceeded to Genoa, where they took shipping to Marseilles. At
Marseilles, Berengaria was met by her friend and kinsman, the king
of Arragon, who showed the royal ladies every mark of reverence,
gave them safe conduct through his Provençal dominions, and sent
them on, under the escort of the count de Sancto Egidio.

It was a long time before Richard's friends could with any certainty
make out his locality. He was utterly lost for some months. Blondel,
a troubadour knight and poet, who had been shipwrecked with him
on the coast of Istria, and who had sought him through the cities of
southern Germany, sang, beneath the tower Tenebreuse in which he
was confined, a *tenson* which Richard and he had composed together.
Scarcely had he finished the first stanza, when Richard replied with the
second. Blondel directly went to queen Eleanora, and gave her tidings
of the existence of her son, and she took measures for his release. Her
letters to the pope are written with a passionate eloquence, highly illustrative of that tradition of the south which names her among the poets
of her country.

After an absence of four years, three months, and nine days, king
Richard landed at Sandwich, in April, the Sunday after St. George's
day, in company with his royal mother, who had the pleasure of surrendering to him his dominions, both insular and continental, without
diminution.

After a second coronation, Richard went in progress throughout

England, with his royal mother, to sit in judgment on those castellans who had betrayed their fortresses to his brother John.

King Richard finished his progress by residing some months in his Angevin territories. Although he was in the vicinity of the loving and faithful Berengaria, he did not return to her society. The reason of this estrangement was, that the king had renewed his connection with a number of profligate and worthless associates, the companions of his long bachelorhood in his father's lifetime.

The final restoration of Berengaria to the affections of her royal husband, took place a few months after, when Richard proceeded to Poictiers, where he was reconciled to his queen, and kept Christmas, and the new year of 1196, in that city, with princely state and hospitality. It was a year of great scarcity and famine, and the beneficent queen exerted her restored influence over the heart of the king, by persuading him to give all his superfluous money in bountiful alms to the poor, and through her goodness many were kept from perishing. From that time queen Berengaria and king Richard were never parted. She found it best to accompany him in all his campaigns, and we find her with him at the hour of his death.

Higden, in the Polychronichon, gives this testimony to the love that Berengaria bore to Richard: "The king took home to him his queen Berengaria, whose society he had for a long time neglected, though she were a royal, eloquent, and beauteous lady, and for his love had ventured with him through the world."

Richard's death took place April 6th, 1199. His queen unquestionably was with him when he died. She corroborated the testimony that he left his dominions, and two-thirds of his treasures, to his brother John.

Queen Berengaria fixed her residence at Mans in the Orleannois, where she held a great part of her foreign dower. Here she founded the noble abbey of L'Espan.

Once queen Berengaria left her widowed retirement, when she met her brother-in-law, king John, and his fair young bride, at Chinon, her husband's treasure city. Here she compounded with the English monarch, for the dower she held in England, for two thousand marks per annum, to be paid half-yearly. After being entertained with royal mag-

nificence, and receiving every mark of respect from the English court,
the royal widow bade farewell to public splendor, and retired to conventual seclusion, and the practice of constant charity.

The date of Berengaria's death has generally been fixed about the
year 1230; but that was only the year of the completion of her abbey
of Espan, and of her final retirement from the world; as from that
time she took up her abode within its walls, and finished there her
blameless life, at an advanced age, some years afterwards.

From early youth to her grave, Berengaria manifested devoted love
for Richard; uncomplaining when deserted by him, forgiving when he
returned, and faithful to his memory unto death, the royal Berengaria,
queen *of* England, though never *in* England, little deserves to be forgotten, by any admirer of feminine and conjugal virtue.

ISABELLA OF ANGOULÊME,

No one would have imagined that Isabella of Angoulême was destined to become the future queen of England, when king John ascended the throne; for she was then not only the engaged wife of another, but, according to the custom of the times, had been actually consigned to her betrothed, for the purpose of education.

Isabella was the only child and heiress of Aymer or Americus, count of Angoulême, surnamed Taillefer. By maternal descent she shared the blood of the Capetian sovereigns, her mother, Alice de Courtenay, being the daughter of Peter de Courtenay, fifth son of Louis VI. king of France.

Isabella was actually abiding at one of the castles of her betrothed, when her parents sent for her to be present at a day of high ceremonial, on which they paid their homage to king John for the province of Angoumois. Indeed, it may be considered certain that the young lady herself, as their sole heir, was required to pay her personal homage to her lord paramount, as duke of Aquitaine.

It was at the high festival of king John's recognition in Angoulême, as sovereign of Aquitaine, that the English king first saw the beautiful fiancée of Lusignan. He was thirty-two; she had just entered her fifteenth year; notwithstanding which disparity, he became madly enamored of her. The parents of Isabella, when they perceived their sovereign thus captivated with her budding charms, dishonorably en-

couraged his passion, and by deceitful excuses to the count of Eu, prevented the return of Isabella to the castle of Valence; a proceeding the
more infamous, since subsequent events plainly showed that the heart of
the maiden secretly preferred her betrothed.

The lady Isabella, as much dazzled as her parents by the splendor of
the triple crowns of England, Normandy, and Aquitaine, would not
acknowledge that she had consented to any marriage contract with
count Hugh. As Isabella preferred being a queen to giving her hand to
the man she really loved, no one could right the wrongs of the ill-treated
Lusignan.

King John and Isabella were married at Bordeaux, some time in the
month of August, 1200. Their hands were united by the archbishop
of Bordeaux, who had previously held a synod, assisted by the bishop
of Poitou, and solemnly declared that no impediment existed to the
marriage.

This event threw count Hugh of Lusignan into despair; he did not,
however, quietly submit to the destruction of his hopes, but challenged
to mortal combat the royal interloper between him and his betrothed.
John received the cartel with remarkable coolness, saying, that if count
Hugh wished for combat, he would appoint a champion to fight with
him; but the count declared that John's champions were hired bravoes
and vile mercenaries, unfit for the encounter of a wronged lover and
true knight. Thus, unable to obtain satisfaction, the valiant Marcher
waited his hour of revenge; while king John sailed with his bride in
triumph to England, where he was anxious that she should be recognized as his wife, not only by the peers, but by the people.

Her coronation was appointed for the eighth of October, and there exists a charter in the Tower, expressing "that Isabella of Augoulême
was crowned queen by the common consent of the barons, clergy, and
people of England." She was crowned on that day by the archbishop
of Canterbury.

The whole of the intervening months, between October and Easter,
were spent by the king and queen, in a continual round of feasting and
voluptuousness. At the Easter festival of 1201, they were the guests
of archbishop Hubert, at Canterbury, where they were once more
crowned, or rather they wore their crowns, according to the ancient

English custom at this high festival; it being the office of the primate of England, always to place them on the heads of the king and queen on such occasions, when he was abiding in the vicinity of royalty.

King John, regardless of the tempest that muttered around him, established himself at Rouen, and gave way to a career of indolent voluptuousness, little in accordance with the restless activity of his warlike nobility. In that era, when five in the morning was the established breakfast-time, and half-past ten in the forenoon the orthodox dinner-hour, for all ranks and conditions of men, the court were scandalized at finding that king John never left his pillow before mid-day, at which time his barons saw him, with contempt, issuing from the chamber of the fair Isabella. This mode of life made him far more unpopular, in the thirteenth century, than the perpetration of a few more murders and abductions, like those with which his memory stands already charged. His young queen shared some of this blame, as the enchantress who kept him chained in her bowers of luxury. The royal pair paid, however, some attention to the fine arts, for the magnificent mosaic pavement of the palace of Rouen, was laid down while the queen kept her court there.

The passion of John for his queen, though it was sufficiently strong to embroil him in war, was not exclusive enough to secure conjugal fidelity; the king tormented her with jealousy, while on his part he was far from setting her a good example, for he often invaded the honor of the female nobility. The name of the lover of Isabella has never been ascertained, nor is it clear that she was ever guilty of any dereliction from rectitude. But John revenged the wrong that, perhaps, only existed in his malignant imagination, in a manner peculiar to himself. He made his mercenaries assassinate the person whom he suspected of supplanting him in his queen's affections, with two others supposed to be accomplices, and secretly hung the bodies over the bed of Isabella. Her surprise and terror when she discovered them may be imagined, though it is not described by the monastic writers who darkly allude to this dreadful scene.

After this awful tragedy, the queen was consigned to captivity, being conveyed to Gloucester abbey, under the ward of one of her husband's mercenary leaders.

6

The queen had brought John a lovely family, but the birth of his children failed to secure her against harsh treatment: she was at this time the mother of two sons and a daughter. Isabella inherited the province of the Angoumois in the year 1213, at which time it is probable that a reconciliation took place between the queen and her husband, since her mother, the countess of Angoulême, came to England, and put herself under the protection of John. Soon after he went to Angoulême, with Isabella.

To facilitate the restoration of the Poictevin provinces, again seized by Philip Augustus, John found it necessary to form an alliance with his former rival, count Hugh de Lusignan. That nobleman perversely chose to remain a bachelor, in order to remind all the world of the perfidy of that faithless beauty who had broken her betrothment for a crown. The only stipulation which could induce him to assist king John was, that he would give him the eldest daughter of Isabella, as a wife, in the place of the mother. In compliance with this singular request, the infant princess Joanna was betrothed to him immediately, and forthwith delivered to him, that she might be educated and brought up in one of his castles, as her mother had been before her. After this alliance, count Hugh effectually cleared the Poictevin borders of the French invaders; and king John, flushed with his temporary success, returned with his queen, to plague England with new acts of tyranny.

John consigned to the care of Isabella, at this time, his heir, prince Henry, with whom she retired to Gloucester, where the rest of the royal children were abiding. The queen had, in the year 1214, become the mother of a second daughter, and in the succeeding year she gave birth to the princess Isabella.

Scarcely had the queen retreated to the strong city of Gloucester, when that invasion by prince Louis of France took place, which is so well known in general history. The barons, driven to desperation by John's late outrages, offered the heir of France the crown, if he would aid them against their tormentor.

Hunted into an obscure corner of his kingdom, in the autumn of 1216, king John confided his person and regalia to the men of Lynn in Norfolk. But as his affairs summoned him northward, he crossed the

Wash to Swinshead Abbey, in Lincolnshire. The tide coming in unexpectedly, swept away part of his army and his baggage. His splendid
regalia was swallowed in the devouring waters, and John himself scarcely
escaped with life. The king arrived at Swinshead Abbey unwell and
dispirited, and, withal, in a malignant ill temper.

In all probability the king was seized with one of those severe typhus
fevers, often endemic, in the fenny countries, at the close of the year.
The symptoms of alternate cold and heat, detailed by the chroniclers,
approximate closely with that disease.

Whether by the visitation of God, or through the agency of man, the
fact is evident, that king John was stricken with a fatal illness at Swinshead; but, sick as he was, he ordered himself to be put in a litter, and
carried forward on his northern progress. At Newark, he could proceed
no further, but gave himself up to the fierce attacks of the malady. He
sent for the abbot and monks of Croxton, and made full confession of
all his sins; (no slight undertaking;) he then forgave his enemies, and
enjoined those about him to charge his son, Henry, to do the same; and,
after taking the eucharist, and making all his officers swear fealty to his
eldest son, he expired.

The queen and the royal children were at Gloucester, when the news
of the king's death arrived. Isabella and the earl of Pembroke immediately caused prince Henry to be proclaimed in the streets of that city.

Only nine days after the death of John, the queen caused her young
son to be crowned, in the cathedral of Gloucester. Although so recently
a widow, the extreme exigencies of the times forced Isabella to assist at
her child's coronation. The regal diadem belonging to his father being
lost in Lincoln Washes, and the crown of Edward the Confessor being
far distant in London, the little king was crowned with a gold throat
collar belonging to his mother. A very small part of England recognized the claims of Isabella's son; even Gloucester was divided, the citizens who adhered to the young king being known by the cross of Aquitaine, cut in white cloth on their breasts.

Before her year of widowhood had expired, Isabella retired to her
native city, Angoulême, July, 1217. The princess Joanna resided in
the vicinity of her mother's domains, being at Valence, the capital of the
count de la Marche. Nothing could be more singular than the situation

of queen Isabella, as mother to the promised bride of count Hugh, and
that bride but seven years old. The valiant Lusignan himself was absent
from his territories, venting his superfluous combativeness, and soothing
his crosses in love, by a crusade which he undertook in 1216. The
demise of his father obliged him to revisit Poitou in 1220, where he was
frequently in company with the queen of England, who was at the same
time his false love, and the mother of his little wife. Isabella, at the age
of thirty-four, still retained that marvellous beauty which had caused her
to be considered the Helen of the middle ages. It is therefore no great
wonder that she quickly regained her old place in the constant heart of
the valiant Marcher. Accordingly, we find this notation in Matthew of
Westminster, that in the year 1220, or " about that time, Isabella, queen-
dowager of England, having before crossed the seas, took to her husband
her former spouse, the count of Marche, in France, without leave of her
son, the king, or his council."

The king of France was liege lord of count de la Marche; but
the countess-queen was infuriated whenever she saw her husband arrayed
against the territories of her son, and her sole study was, how French
Poitou could be rendered independent of the king of France.

Several years of disastrous warfare ensued. The husband of Isabella
nearly lost his whole patrimony, while the district of the Angoumois
was overrun by the French.

In this dilemma, the countess-queen and her lord determined to send
their heir, the young Hugh de Lusignan, to see how king Louis seemed
disposed towards them. That amiable monarch received the son of his
enemies with such benevolence, that the count de la Marche, taking his
wife and the rest of the children with him, to the camp of St. Louis,
threw themselves at his feet, and were very kindly received, on no
worse conditions, than doing homage to prince Alphonso, for three
castles.

It might have been supposed that the restless spirit of Isabella was
tamed by these disasters; but soon after, 1244, the life of king Louis
was twice attempted : the last time the assassins were convicted, and
before their execution confessed that they had been suborned, by queen
Isabella, to poison the good king of France. Isabella gave color to the
accusation by flying for sanctuary to the abbey of Fontevraud, " where

the was hid in the secret chamber, and lived at her ease," says Matthew Paris; "though the Poictevins and French, considering her as the origin of the disastrous war with France, called her by no other name than Jezebel, instead of her rightful appellation of Isabel." Matthew says, the whole brunt of this disgraceful business fell upon her unfortunate husband and son. They were seized, and about to be tried on this accusation of poisoning, when count de la Marche made appeal to battle, and offered to prove in combat with his accuser Alphonso, brother to St. Louis, that his wife was belied. Alphonso, who appears to have had no great stomach to the fray, declined it, on the plea that count Hugh was so "treason-spotted," it would be pollution to fight with him. Then Isabella's young son Hugh dutifully offered to fight, in the place of his sire, and Alphonso actually appointed the day and place to meet him; nevertheless, he again withdrew, excusing himself on the plea of the infamy of the family. "This sad news," says old Matthew, "for evil tidings hasten fast, soon reached the ears of Isabella, in the secret chamber of Fontevraud."

The affront offered to her brave young son seems to have broken the heart of Isabella. She never came out of the secret chamber again, but, assuming the veil, died of a decay brought on by grief, in the year 1246.

As a penance for her sins, she desired to be buried humbly, in the common cemetery at Fontevraud. Some years afterwards her son, Henry III., visiting the tombs of his ancestors at Fontevraud, was shocked at being shown the lowly grave of his mother: he raised for her a stately tomb, with a fine enamelled statue, in the choir at Fontevraud, near Henry II. and Eleanora of Aquitaine, her mother-in-law.

ELEANOR OF PROVENCE,

SURNAMED LA BELLE,

QUEEN OF HENRY III.

ELEANOR of Provence was perhaps the most unpopular queen that ever presided over the court of England. She was unfortunately called to share the crown and royal dignity of a feeble-minded sovereign, at an earlier age than any of her predecessors; for, at the time of her marriage with king Henry, she had scarcely completed her fourteenth year, a period of life when her education was imperfect, her judgment unformed, and her character precisely that of a spoiled child, of precocious beauty and genius—perilous gifts! which in her case served but to foster vanity and self-sufficiency.

From her accomplished parents the youthful Eleanor inherited both a natural taste, and a practical talent for poetry, which the very air she breathed tended to foster and encourage. Almost before she entered her teens, she had composed an heroic poem in her native Provençal tongue.

This work is still in existence, and is to be found in MS., in the royal library at Turin. The composition of this romance was the primary cause, to which the princess, or (as she was then styled) the infanta of Provence, owed her elevation to the crown-matrimonial of England. Her father's major-domo and confidant, Romeo, was the person to whose able management count Berenger was indebted for his success in matching his portionless daughters, with the principal potentates of Europe. No doubt, to Romeo's sagacious advice the following steps taken by young Eleanor may be attributed.

She sent to Richard, earl of Cornwall, Henry the Third's brother, a fine Provençal romance of her own inditing, on the adventures of Blandin of Cornwall, and Guillaume of Miremas, his companion, who undertook great perils for the love of the princess Briende and her sister Irlonde (probably Britain and Ireland), dames of incomparable beauty.

Richard of Cornwall, to whom the young infanta sent, by way of a courtly compliment, a poem so appropriately furnished with a paladin of Cornwall for a hero, was then at Poitou, preparing for a crusade, in which he hoped to emulate his royal uncle and namesake, Richard I. He was highly flattered by the attention of the young princess, who was so celebrated for her personal charms that she was called Eleanor la Belle; but as it was out of his power to testify his grateful sense of the honor, by offering his hand and heart to the royal Provençal beauty in return for her romantic rhymes, he being already the husband of one good lady (the daughter of the great earl protector Pembroke) he obligingly recommended her to his brother Henry III. for a queen.

Henry discreetly made choice of three sober priests, for his procurators at the court of count Berenger. The bishops of Ely and Lincoln, and the prior of Hurle; to these were added the master of the Temple. Though Henry's age more than doubled that of the fair maid of Provence, of whose charms and accomplishments he had received such favorable reports, and he was aware that the poverty of the generous count her father was almost proverbial, yet the king's constitutional covetousness impelled him to demand the enormous portion of twenty thousand marks, with this fairest flower of the land of roses and sweet song.

Count Berenger, in reply, objected on the part of his daughter, to the very inadequate dower Henry would be able to settle upon her during the life of his mother queen Isabella. Henry, on this, proceeded to lower his demands from one sum to another, till finding that the impoverished but high-spirited Provençal count was inclined to resent his sordid manner of bargaining for the nuptial portion, and being seriously alarmed lest he should lose the lady, he in a great fright wrote to his ambassadors, "to conclude the marriage forthwith, either with money or without, but at all events to secure the lady for him, and conduct her safely to England without delay."

The contract was then joyfully signed by count Berenger, and the infanta Eleanor was delivered, with all due solemnity, to the ambassadors.

When the royal bride commenced her journey to England, she was attended on her progress by all the chivalry and beauty of the south of France, a stately train of nobles, ladies, minstrels, and jongleurs, with crows of humble followers. She embarked for England, landed at Dover, and, on the 4th of January, 1236, was married to King Henry III. at Canterbury, by the archbishop, St. Edmund of Canterbury.

The most sumptuous and splendid garments ever seen in England were worn at the coronation of the young queen of Henry III. The peaceful and vigorous administration of Pembroke and Hubert de Burgh had filled England with wealth and luxury, drawn from their commerce with the south of France. The citizens of London wore at this splendid ceremony garments called cyclades, a sort of upper robe, made not only of silk, but of velvet worked with gold. Henry III., who was, like his father, the greatest fop in his dominions, did not, like king John, confine the orders of his wardrobe rolls to the adornment of his own person; but liberally issued benefactions of satin, velvet, cloth of gold, and ermine, for the appareling of his royal ladies. No homely dress of green cloth was ordered for the attire of his lovely queen; but when a mantle lined with ermine was made by his tailors for himself, another as rich was given out for Eleanor.

The elegant fashion of chaplets of gold and jewels, worn over the hair, was adopted by this queen, whose jewelry was of a magnificent order, and is supposed to have cost her doting husband nearly £30,000; an enormous sum if reckoned according to the value of our money. Eleanor had no less than nine guirlands, or chaplets, for her hair, formed of gold filagree and clusters of colored precious stones. For state occasions she had a great crown, most glorious with gems, worth £150C

7

at that era; her girdles were worth 5000 marks; and the coronation present given by her sister, queen Marguerite of France, was a large silver peacock, whose train was set with sapphires and pearls, and other precious stones, wrought with silver. This elegant piece of jewelry was used as a reservoir for sweet waters, which were forced out of its beak, into a basin of silver chased.

Henry did not forget his own apparel, when he endowed his queen so richly with jewels; he was noted as the first prince who wore the costly material called baudekins, and, arrayed in a garment of this brilliant tissue of gold, he sat upon his throne, and "glittered very gloriously," when his young and lovely queen shared his third coronation.

The expenses of Eleanor's coronation were enormous. So great was the outlay beyond the king's resources, that Henry expended the portion of his sister Isabella, just married to the emperor of Germany, for the purpose of defraying them.

In the fourth year of her marriage Eleanor brought an heir to England. The young prince was born on the 16th of June, 1239, at Westminster, and received the popular name of Edward, in honor of Edward the Confessor; for whose memory Henry III. cherished the deepest veneration.

One great cause of the queen's unpopularity in London, originated from the unprincipled manner in which she exercised her influence to compel all vessels freighted with corn, wool, or any peculiarly valuable cargo, to unlade their cargoes at her hithe, or quay, called Queenhithe; because at that port (the dues of which formed a part of the revenues of the queen-consorts of England), the tolls were paid according to the value of the lading. This arbitrary mode of proceeding was without parallel on the part of her predecessors, and was considered as a serious grievance, by the masters of vessels, and merchants in general. At last Eleanor, for a certain sum of money, sold her rights in this quay to her brother-in-law, Richard, earl of Cornwall, who for a quit-rent of fifty pounds per annum, let it as a fee-farm to John Gisors, the mayor of London, for the sake of putting an end to the perpetual disputes, between the merchants of London and the queen.

Ladies' head-dresses were singularly elegant, in the youth and middle age of this beautiful queen. The hair was gathered up under a golden network, over which was thrown the veil, or coverchef. Those women who ventured to walk in the street with only the caul, garland, and bandeaus, without the sheltering veil or coverchef, were deemed improper characters, and liable to insult. The unmarried females wore their hair flowing in ringlets on the shoulders, or, if their tresses were very long and luxuriant, braided in two tails, and tied with ribbons, or a knot of gems, at the ends. The veil, surmounted with a bandeau, was assumed when they rode or walked in the open air. The queen is sometimes represented with the homely gorget or wimple, in illuminations of that time. The gorget fashion imitated, in cambric or lawn, the knight's helmet, with an aperture, cut like the vizor, for the face to peep through; and very lovely that face must have been which did not look ugly through so hideous an envelope.

When Henry III. appointed Eleanor regent of England, he left the great seal in her custody, but enclosed in its casket, sealed with the impression of his own privy seal, and with the signets of his brother, Richard earl of Cornwall, and others of his council. It was only to be opened on occasions of extreme urgency.

No sooner had queen Eleanor got the reins of empire in her own hands, unrestrained by the counterbalancing power of the great earl of Leicester, who had volunteered his services to king Henry against the insurgent Gascons, than she proceeded to play the sovereign in a more despotic manner, in one instance at least, than had ever been attempted by the mightiest monarch of the Norman line.

The arbitrary proceedings of the queen-regent were regarded with indignant astonishment by a city governed by laws peculiar to itself— London being, in fact, a republic within a monarchy, whose privileges had hitherto been respected by the most despotic sovereigns.

In the beginning of the year, Eleanor received instructions from the king to summon a parliament, for the purpose of demanding an aid for carrying on the war in Gascony. But finding it impossible to obtain this grant, queen Eleanor sent the king five hundred marks from her own private coffers, as a new year's gift, for the immediate relief of his more pressing exigences. Henry then directed his brother to extort from the luckless Jews the sum required, for the nuptial festivities of his heir.

The active part taken by queen Eleanor and her eldest son, in the mismanagement of the king's affairs at this critical period, is recorded by Matthew Paris, who is certainly a credible witness, and one who had every means of information on the subject, since, from the great respect in which his talents were held by king Henry, he was invited to dine at the royal table every day, and, as he himself states, frequently wrote in the presence, and from the dictation of the king.

In this year, notwithstanding the reluctance of the queen, king Henry was induced to sign an amicable arrangement with the barons, by which he bound himself to confirm the provisions of Oxford. This agreement, which might have averted the storm of civil strife, was regarded with fierce impatience by some of the destructives of the thirteenth century, who, eager for plunder and athirst for blood, finding they were likely to be disappointed in the object which had led them to rank themselves on the side of the reforming barons and their great dictator, Montfort, raised a dreadful uproar in London against the unhappy Jews, whose wealth excited their envy and cupidity.

T. Wikes, a contemporary chronicler, thus details the particulars of this tumult, which was the prelude to a personal attack upon the queen. At the sound of St. Paul's great bell, a numerous mob sallied forth, led on by Stephen Buckrell, the marshal of London, and John Fitz-John, a powerful baron. They killed and plundered many of these wretched people without mercy. The ferocious leader, John Fitz-John, ran through with his sword, in cold blood, Kokben Abraham, the wealthiest Hebrew resident in London. Besides plundering and killing five hundred of this devoted race, the mob turned the rest out of their beds, undressed as they were, keeping them so the whole night. The next morning they commenced the work of plunder with such outrageous yells, that the queen, who was then at the Tower, seized with mortal terror, got into her barge with many of her great ladies, the wives and daughters of the noblest, intending to escape by water to Windsor Castle. But the raging populace, to whom she had rendered herself most obnoxious, as soon as they observed the royal barge on the river, made a general rush to the bridge, crying—"Drown the witch!—drown the witch!" at the same time pelting the queen with mud, addressing the most abusive language to her, and endeavoring to sink the vessel by hurling down blocks of wood and

stone of an enormous weight, which they tore from the unfinished buildings of the bridge. The poor ladies were pelted with rotten eggs, and
sheep's bones, and every thing vile. If the queen had persisted in shooting the arch, the boat must have been swamped, or her vessel dashed to
pieces, by the formidable missiles that were aimed at her person. As it
was, she with difficulty escaped the fury of the assailants by returning
to the Tower. Not considering herself safe there, she took sanctuary at
night in the bishop of London's palace at St. Paul's, whence she was
privately removed to Windsor Castle, where prince Edward kept garrison with his troops. This high-spirited prince never forgave the Londoners for the insult they had offered to his mother.

Eleanor never forgot her terror at London bridge, which had the
effect of hurrying forward the civil war. At the time when the barons
had agreed to refer their grievances to the arbitration of St. Louis, the
brother-in-law of the queen, king Henry took Eleanor with him to
France, and left her there in October, 1264, with her children, at the
court of her sister Marguerite.

The decision of St. Louis, though really a rational one, did not satisfy
the barons, who protested against it on the grounds of family partiality,
and England was forthwith involved in the flames of civil war.

So well, indeed, had the royal cause prospered in the commencement
of the struggle, that when the rival armies were encamped within six
miles of each other, near Lewes, the barons sent word to the king, that
they would give him thirty thousand marks if he would consent to a
pacification. Prince Edward, who was burning to avenge the insults
which had been offered to the queen his mother, dissuaded Henry from
accepting these terms, and the battle of Lewes followed.

> "The king and his meinie were in the priorie,
> When Simon came to field and raised his bannere;
> He shewed forth his shield, his dragon full austere;
> The king said on high, 'Simon, je vous defie!'"

The battle of Lewes was lost through the reckless fury with which
the fiery heir of England pursued the flying Londoners, in order to
avenge their incivility in pelting his mother at their bridge. He followed

them with his cavalry, shouting the name of queen Eleanor, as far as
Croydon, where he made a merciless slaughter of the hapless citizens.
When he returned to the field of battle with his jaded cavalry, he found
his father, who had lost the support of all the horse, taken prisoner with
his uncle the king of the Romans, and Edward had no other resource
than surrendering himself to Leicester, who conveyed him, with king
Henry, as captive to the castle of Wallingford.

The remnant of the royal army retreated to Bristol Castle, under the
command of seven knights, who reared seven banners on the walls. The
queen was said by some to be safe in France, but old Robert of Gloucester asserts that she was espy in the land for the purpose of liberating
her brave son. Let this be as it may, she sent word to Sir Warren de
Basingbourne, her son's favorite knight, one of the gallant defenders of
Bristol, that Wallingford was but feebly guarded, and that her son
might be released, if he and the rest of the Bristol garrison would attack
it by surprise. Directly Sir Warren received the queen's message, he,
with three hundred horse, crossed the country, and arrived at Wallingford on a Friday, just as the sun rose, and, right against All Hallows
church, made the first fierce attack on the castle, and won the outermost
wall. The besieged defended themselves furiously, with cross-bows and
battle engines: at last they called out to Sir Warren, that "if they
wanted sire Edward, the prince, they should have him, but bound hand
and foot, and shot from the mangonol,"—a terrific war engine used for
casting stones. As soon as the prince heard of this murderous intention,
he demanded leave to speak with his friends, and coming on the wall,
assured them, "that if they persevered in his mother's intentions he
should be destroyed." Whereupon Sir Warren and his chevaliers
retired in great dejection.

The queen, thus disappointed in the liberation of her gallant heir,
soon after found a partisan, in a lady strongly attached to her. This
was lady Maud Mortimer. Lord Roger Mortimer had, much against
the wishes of his lady, given his powerful aid to Leicester; but having
received some affront since the victory of Lewes, he now turned a com-
placent ear to the loyal pleadings of lady Maud, in behalf of the queen
and her son. What all the valor of Sir Warren failed to accomplish,
the wit of woman effected. Lady Maud Mortimer having sent her in-

structions to prince Edward, he made his escape by riding races with his attendants till he had tired their horses, when he rode up to a thicket, where dame Maud had ambushed a swift steed. Mounting his gallant courser, Edward turned to his guard, and bade them "commend him to his sire the king, and tell him he would soon be at liberty," and he galloped off; while an armed party appeared on the opposite hill, a mile distant, and displayed the banner of Mortimer.

During the captivity of her husband and son, it is asserted that Eleanor of Provence made more than one private visit to England. Ostensibly, she resided in France, with her younger children, under the kind protection of her sister, queen Marguerite. Meantime, she had, directly after the disastrous field of Lewes, borrowed all the money she could raise on her jewels and credit, and proceeded to muster forces, and equip a fleet. Matthew of Westminster does full justice to the energetic efforts of "this noble virago," as he styles queen Eleanor, for the liberation of her husband. "She succeeded," he says, "in getting together a great army, commanded by so many dukes and earls as seemed incredible;" and those who knew the strength and power of that army affirmed, "that if they had once landed in England, they would presently have subdued the whole population of the country; but God in his mercy," continues the chronicler, "ordered it otherwise;" for while the queen and her foreign troops remained wind-bound on the other side of the water, the battle of Evesham was fought and won, by her valiant son, prince Edward.

The nuptials of queen Eleanor's second son, Edmund, earl of Lancaster and Derby, with the beautiful Aveline, heiress of William Fortibus, earl of Albemarle, had been celebrated on the 8th of April, 1270, before his departure for the Holy Land. The youthful bride died before his return, in the first year of her nuptials.

Her death was quickly followed by that of the king of the Romans; for grief of which, king Henry fell into the deepest dejection of mind, and, having been in person to quell a riot in Norwich, in which great part of the cathedral was burnt, he was attacked with a mortal sickness at Bury St. Edmunds: but his anxiety to settle the affairs of the kingdom caused him to insist on being carried on to London by short stages. When the dying monarch arrived in the metropolis, finding his dissolution at hand, he summoned Gilbert de Clare, earl of Gloucester, into his presence, and made him swear to preserve the peace of England, during the absence of prince Edward. He expired on the 16th of November, 1272, aged sixty-six, having reigned fifty-six years and twenty days.

It has been generally asserted that Eleanor of Provence retired to the nunnery of Ambresbury, soon after the coronation of her son Edward I.; but this does not appear to have been the case, for several of her precepts and letters are dated from Waltham, Guildford, Lutgershall, and other places. She retired to Ambresbury as a residence in 1280, but she did not take the veil till four years afterwards.

The four younger sons of queen Eleanor, Richard, John, William, and Henry, all died before the king their father; so that, of her nine children, two sons only were surviving at the time she retired to Ambresbury. In the year 1280, her son, king Edward, visited her there, when he was on his march to Wales.

Two years after this date, king Edward again visited his widowed mother in her monastic retreat. Her profession as a nun did not take place till the year 1284, when she was solemnly veiled, in the church of Ambresbury; and, according to the words of her contemporary Wikes, "she laid down the diadem from her head, and the precious purple from her shoulders, and with them all worldly ambition." She persuaded her young granddaughter, the princess Mary, the fifth daughter of Edward I. and his queen Eleanora of Castille, to take the vows at the same time, together with Eleanor, daughter to the deceased duchess of Bretagne.

She received the tenderest attention and respect from her son, king Edward, who regarded her with great affection; and once, when he was going to France to meet the king, his cousin, on a matter of the greatest importance, and had advanced as far as Canterbury on his journey, receiving intelligence of the sudden and alarming illness of his mother, he instantly gave up his French voyage and hastened to her.

Eleanor of Provence survived the king, her husband, nineteen years. She died at the nunnery of Ambresbury, June 24th, during the absence of her son in Scotland.

ELEANORA OF CASTILLE,

SURNAMED THE FAITHFUL,

FIRST QUEEN OF EDWARD I.

THE marriage of the Infanta Donna Eleanora of Castille with prince Edward, heir of England, happily terminated a war, which her brother, king Alphonso, surnamed the Astronomer, was waging with Henry III., on account of some obsolete claims the Castillian monarch laid to the province of Gascony.

Alphonso stipulated that the English prince should come to Burgos, to receive the hand of his bride, five weeks before Michaelmas day, 1254; otherwise the contract should be null and void.

When the preliminaries of the marriage were settled, the queen of England, Eleanor of Provence, set out for Bordeaux, with her son prince Edward, and from thence travelled across the Pyrenees with him to Burgos, where they arrived August 5th, 1254, within the time limited by the royal astronomer.

A stately festival was held in the capital of Castille, in honor of the nuptials of the young Infanta with the heir of England. At a tournament given by king Alphonso, the prince received knighthood from the sword of his brother-in-law. Edward was just fifteen, and the princess some years younger, at the time of their espousals.

8

After the chivalric festivities at Burgos had ceased, queen Eleanor re-crossed the Pyrenees, accompanied by her son and young daughter-in-law.

Prince Edward and his young bride passed over to Bordeaux in 1256; and while Eleanora was completing her education, the young prince led the wandering life of a knight-errant, "haunting tournaments," wherever they were given. He was at Paris, tilting at a very grand jousting match in 1260, when news was brought him of the violent dissensions between the English barons and his father, which led to the fearful civil war that convulsed England for more than three years. During the whole of that disastrous era, his young princess resided in France with the rest of the royal family, either with queen Marguerite of France, or with her own mother at Ponthieu.

After the heroic efforts of prince Edward had freed his father and restored him to his throne, and the country breathed in peace after the dreadful strife at Evesham, the royal ladies of England ventured to return. On the 29th of October, 1265, Eleanor of Provence, queen of England, with her daughter-in-law, Eleanora of Castille, landed at Dover, where they were received by Henry III. and prince Edward; from thence they were escorted to Canterbury, where the royal party was magnificently entertained by the archbishop.

Prince Edward had left his wife an uninformed girl; she was now a lovely young woman of twenty, to whose character the uncertainty of fortune had assuredly given a favorable bias. The prince conveyed his restored wife to St. John's Smithfield, after a magnificent welcome by the citizens.

This was the abode of Eleanora of Castille when she attended the court at Westminster, but her favorite residence was the castle of Windsor. Here her eldest child was born, the year after her return to England; he was named John, after his grandfather of evil memory. In the succeeding year, 1266, Eleanora gave birth, at Windsor, to a princess named Eleanora, and the year after to prince Henry. The beauty of these children, and their early promise, so much delighted their royal grandfather, that he greatly augmented the dower of the mother.

Prince Edward took up the cross in 1269, and his virtuous princess resolved to share the perils of his Syrian campaign.

In vain did the ladies of Eleanora represent to her the hardships and dangers, ever attendant on a crusade; for death on the Asiatic coast threatened in many forms besides the sword. The princess replied in words that deserve to be remembered and noted. "Nothing," said this admirable lady, "ought to part those whom God hath joined, and the way to heaven is as near, if not nearer, from Syria, as from England or my native Spain."

Edward sailed from Portsmouth, and met his consort at Bordeaux; they proceeded to Sicily, where they sojourned during the winter, with the expectation that St. Louis, the king of France, would unite in the crusade. Soon after their arrival, tidings were brought of the death of St. Louis, at Tunis, and the discomfiture of his army.

The army of the prince being reduced by sickness, want and desertion, he considered that it was useless to tarry longer in Syria. Leaving behind him a reputation not inferior to that of his great-uncle, Cœur de Lion, Edward turned his back most reluctantly on the Holy Land; and, with his princess and her infant daughter, arrived safely at Sicily, where heavy tidings awaited them.

The news first reached them that prince John, their lovely and promising heir, whose talents were unequalled for his years, had died August 1, 1272. Scarcely had the princess and her husband received this intelligence, when they heard of the death of their second son, Prince Henry; and a third messenger brought the news to Messina, that king Henry III. was dead, and that prince Edward was now Edward I. of England. The firmness and resignation, with which Eleanora and Edward bore the loss of their promising boys, surprised every one at the Sicilian court; but when the prince heard of the death of his royal sire, he gave way to a burst of anguish so bitter, that his uncle Charles of Anjou, king of Sicily, who was in company with him astonished at his manner of receiving intelligence that hailed him king, asked him "how it was that he bore the loss of both his sons with such quiet resignation, and abandoned himself to grief at the death of an aged man?" Edward made this memorable answer:—

"The loss of infants may be repaired by the same God that gave them; but when a man has lost a good father, it is not in the course of nature for God to send him another."

Edward, with his queen, made a progress homeward through all his French provinces, tilting at the tournaments as he went. Passing through Paris, he did homage to the king of France for Aquitaine and its dependencies, before he returned to assume the English crown. The king and queen landed at Dover, August 2, 1273.

At the coronation of Edward and Eleanora preparations were made for the exercise of the most profuse hospitality; the whole areas of the Palace Yards, old and new, were filled with wooden buildings, open at the top, to let out the smoke of cooking. Here, for a whole fortnight, were prepared successions of banquets, served up for the entertainment of all comers; where the independent franklin, the stout yeoman from the country, and the rich citizen and industrious artisan from the metropolis, alike found a welcome, and were entertained gratuitously. Good order was general, and every one delighted with this auspicious commencement of the new reign. Edward and Eleanora were crowned by the hands of Robert Kilwardly, archbishop of Canterbury. One of the most extraordinary features of this coronation is recorded in an old black-letter manuscript chronicle.

" King Edward was crowned and anointed as right heir of England, with much honor and worship, with his virtuous queen; and after mass the king went to his palace to hold a royal feast among all the peers that had done him honor and worship. And when he was set at his meat king Alexander of Scotland came to do him service, and to worship with a *quentyse*, and a hundred knights with him, horsed and arrayed. And when they were light off their horses, they let their horses go whither they would, and they that could catch them had them to their own behoof. And after that came sir Edmund, the king's brother, a courteous knight and a gentleman of renown, and the earl of Gloucester. And after them came the earl of Pembroke and the earl of Warren, and each of them led a horse by their hand, and a hundred of their knights did the same. And when they were alight off their horses they let them go wherever they would, and they that could take them had them still at their liking."

Early in spring, 1284, Edward carried his queen to his newly-built castle of Caernarvon, a stronghold he had just finished, to awe the insurgents of the principality. This truly royal fortress, according to the antiquary Pennant, appears at present, in its external state, precisely as when queen Eleanora first entered the stupendous gateway so many centuries ago.

To this mighty castle, Edward brought Eleanora, at a time when her situation promised an increase to the royal family.

The prince was born April 25th, when fires were not indispensable in a small, close chamber. As a soldier's wife, used to attend her lord in all campaigns, from Syria to Scotland, the queen had, in all probability, met with far worse accommodations, than in the forlorn chamber in the Eagle Tower. The queen certainly provided a Welsh nurse for her infant: she thus proved her usual good sense, by complying with the prejudices of the country.

Edward I. was at Rhuddlan castle, negotiating with the despairing magnates of Wales, when news was brought him by Griffith Lloyd, a Welsh gentleman, that the queen had made him father of a living son of surpassing beauty. The king was transported with joy; he knighted the Welshman on the spot, and made him a magnificent donation of lands.

The king hastened directly to Caernarvon, to see his Eleanora and her boy; and three days after, the castle was the rendezvous of all the chiefs of North Wales, who met to tender their final submission to Edward I., and to implore him, as their lord paramount, to appoint them a prince who was a native of their own country, and whose native tongue was neither French nor Saxon, which they assured him they could not understand.

Edward told them he would immediately appoint them a prince, who could speak neither English nor French. The Welsh magnates, expecting he was a kinsman of their own royal line, declared they would instantly accept him as their prince, if his character was void of reproach; whereupon the king ordered his infant son to be brought in and presented to them, assuring the assembly, "that he was just born a native of their country, that his character was unimpeached, that he could not speak a word of English or French, and that, if they pleased, the first words he uttered should be Welsh." The fierce mountaineers little expected such a ruler: they had, however, no alternative but submission, and, with as good a grace as they might, kissed the tiny hand which was to sway their sceptre, and vowed fealty to the babe of the faithful Eleanora.

The queen soon changed her residence to the magnificent palace of Conway Castle, where all the elegancies of an age further advanced in luxury than is generally supposed, were assembled round her.

The death of king Alexander of Scotland, in 1285, opened a new prospect for still further aggrandizing the progeny of queen Eleanora. The heiress of Scotland, the princess Margaret of Norway, great-niece to Edward I., was, by the consent of the nobles of Scotland, solemnly betrothed to Edward of Caernarvon, prince of Wales, and every prospect appeared that the island crowns would be happily united, in the persons of the infant son of Eleanora, and the little queen of Scotland. After this pacification of the whole island, the king and queen resided three years in Aquitaine. Eleanora then gave birth to her seventh and eighth daughters, the princesses Beatrice and Berengaria.

When the queen returned to England, she was urged to devote her fourth daughter, the princess Mary, to the cloister. Her reluctance to relinquish this child is noted by most chroniclers, and produced more than one pathetic epistle from dignitaries of the church, on the impropriety of withholding from heaven a chosen lamb, from her numerous flock. Among the other admirable qualities of Eleanora, we find freedom from the prejudices of her era. She kept a happy medium between the bold infidelity of her philosophic brother Alphonso, the mathematician, and the superfluous devotion of the middle ages. The princess Mary was, however, veiled, at the age of ten years, at Ambresbury, 1289. The year after her profession the queen added a ninth daughter, the princess Blanche, to her family.

Eleanora reared and educated her numerous train of beautiful princesses, in a retired angle of Westminster Palace, which was given, on account of their residence there, the appellation of the Maiden Hall.

The autumn of the year 1290 brought threatening clouds to the prosperity of the island kingdoms, and to the royal family of queen Eleanora. The little queen, Margaret of Scotland, was to be sent this year from Norway to Scotland, and thence, by agreement, to the court of England, that she might be educated under the care of the admirable queen of Edward I. The bishop of St. Andrews wrote to king Edward, that a report was spread of the young queen's death, on her homeward voyage. Edward, who had already sent the bishop of Durham and six regents, to take possession of Scotland, in the names of Edward of Caernarvon, and Margaret of Norway, was startled into prompt action at these alarming tidings. He took a hasty farewell of his beloved queen, and charged her to follow him with all convenient speed.

Edward had not reached the Scottish borders, when the fatal news reached him that Eleanora, the faithful companion of his life, in travelling through Lincolnshire, to join him, previously to his entering Scotland, had been seized with a dangerous autumnal fever, at Herdeby, near Grantham.

Ambition, at the strong call of conjugal love, for once released its grasp on the mighty heart of Edward. In comparison with Eleanora, dead or dying, the coveted crown of Scotland was nothing in his estimation. He turned southward instantly; but though he travelled with the utmost speed, he arrived too late to see her living once more. His admirable queen had expired, November 29th, at the house of a gentleman named Weston. She died, according to our calculation, in the forty-seventh year of her age.

The whole affairs of Scotland, however pressing they might be, were obliterated, for a time, from the mind of the great Edward by the acute sorrow he suffered for the death of Eleanora; nor, till he had paid the duties he considered due to her breathless clay, would he attend to the slightest temporal business. In the bitterest grief he followed her corpse in person during thirteen days, in the progress of the royal funeral, from Grantham to Westminster. At the end of every stage the royal bier rested, surrounded by its attendants, in some central part of a great town, till the neighboring ecclesiastics came to meet it in solemn procession, and placed it before the high altar of the principal church. At every one of these resting-places the royal mourner vowed to erect a cross in memory of the *chère reine*, as he passionately called his lost Eleanora. Thirteen of these splendid monuments of his affection once existed; those of Northampton and Waltham still remain models of architectural beauty. The principal citizens of London, with their magistrates, came several miles on the north road, clad in black hoods and mourning cloaks, to meet the royal corpse and join the solemn proces-

sion. The hearse rested, previously to its admission into Westminster
Abbey, at the spot now occupied by the statue of Charles I., which
commanded a grand view of the abbey, the hall, and palace of Westminster.

The queen of Edward I. must have been a model of feminine beauty.
No wonder that the united influence of loveliness, virtue, and sweet
temper, should have inspired in the heart of her renowned lord an attachment so deep and true.

Foreigner as she was, Eleanora of Castille entirely won the love and
good-will of her subjects. Walsingham thus sums up her character:
"To our nation she was a loving mother, the column and pillar of the
whole realm; therefore, to her glory, the king her husband caused all
those famous trophies to be erected, wherever her noble corse did rest;
for he loved her above all earthly creatures. She was a godly, modest,
and merciful princess; the English nation in her time was not harassed
by foreigners, nor the country people by the purveyors of the crown.
The sorrow-stricken she consoled as became her dignity, and she made
them friends that were at discord."

MARGUERITE OF FRANCE,

THE early death of the brave son and successor of St. Louis, king Philip le Hardi, left his youngest daughter, the princess Marguerite, fatherless at a very tender age. She was brought up under the guardianship of her brother, Philip le Bel, and carefully educated by her mother, queen Marie, a learned and virtuous princess, to whom Joinville dedicated his immortal memoirs. Marguerite early showed indications of the same piety and innate goodness of heart which, notwithstanding some superfluity of devotion, really distinguished the character of her grandfather.

If Marguerite of France possessed any comeliness of person, her claims to beauty were wholly overlooked by contemporaries, who surveyed with admiration the exquisite persons of her elder brother and sister, and surnamed them, by common consent, Philip le Bel and Blanche la Belle. The eldest princess of France was full six years older than Marguerite, and was withal the reigning beauty of Europe, when Edward I. was rendered the most disconsolate of widowers, by the death of Eleanora of Castille. If an historian may be believed, who is so completely a contemporary that he ceased to write before the second Edward ceased to reign, Marguerite was substituted in a marriage-treaty, commenced by Edward for the beautiful Blanche, by a diplomatic manœuvre, unequalled for craft since the days of Leah and Rachel.

It has been seen that grief in the energetic mind of Edward I.

assumed the character of intense activity; but after all was done that human ingenuity could contrive, or that the gorgeous ceremonials of the Roman church could devise, of Funeral honors to the memory of the *chère reine*, his beloved Eleanora, the warlike king of England sank into a morbid state of melancholy. His contemporary chronicler emphatically says—

> " His solace all was reft sith she was from him gone.
> On fell things he thought, and waxed heavy as lead,
> For sadness him o'ermastered since Eleanor was dead."

A more forlorn widowerhood no pen can portray than is thus described by the monk of Piers.

It is exceedingly curious to observe how anxious Edward was, to ascertain the qualifications of the princess Blanche. His ambassadors were commanded to give a minute description not only of her face and manners, but of the turn of her waist, the form of her foot and of her hand; likewise *sa façoun*, perhaps dress and demeanor.

The result of this inquisition was, that Blanche was perfectly lovely, for *ne plus bel creature nul trouve*. Moreover, sire Edward, at his mature age, became violently in love (from report) of the charms of Blanche la Belle. The royal pair began to correspond, and the damsel admonished him by letter, that he must in all things submit to her brother, king Philip. In truth, the extreme wish of king Edward to be again united in wedlock with a fair and loving queen, induced him to comply with conditions too hard, even for a young bride to exact, who had a hand, a waist, and a foot perfect as those of Blanche la Belle. Philip demanded that Gascony should be given up by Edward for ever, as a settlement on any posterity Edward might have by his beautiful sister. To this our king agreed; but when he surrendered the province, according to the feudal tenure, to his suzeraine, the treacherous Philip refused to give it up, or let him marry his beautiful sister; and just at this time the name of Marguerite, the youngest sister of Blanche, a child of little more than eleven years of age, is found in the marriage-treaty between England and France.

A fierce war immediately ensued, lasting from 1294 to 1298, during which time Edward, who at sixty had no time to lose, was left half married to Blanche; for, according to Piers of Langtoft, who seemed intimately acquainted with this curious piece of secret history, the Pope's dispensation had already been completed.

It was not till the year 1298 that any pacific arrangement took place, between Edward and the brother of Blanche. The treaty was then renewed for Marguerite, who had grown up in the mean time. The whole arrangement was referred to the arbitration of the Pope, who decreed " that Guienne was to be restored to the right owner; that Edward I. should marry Marguerite, and that she should be paid the portion of fifteen thousand pounds left her by king Philip le Hardi, her father." This sum, Piers verily believes, Philip le Bel meant to appropriate to his own use.

Piers does not say why the younger sister was substituted instead of Blanche, but he seems to insinuate in these lines that she was the better character:—

> Not dame Blanche the sweet,
> Of whom I now spake,
> But dame Marguerite
> *Good withouten lack.*

Marguerite was married to Edward, who met her at Canterbury, by Robert de Winchelsea, September 8th, 1299, when she was in her seventeenth year.

Marguerite of France is the first instance of a queen consort of England who ventured to stand between a mighty Plantagenet in his wrath and his intended victim. We learn, by the statement contained in an act of pardon by Edward I., that Godferey de Coigners "had committed the heavy transgression and malefaction of making the coronal of gold that crowned the king's rebel and enemy, Robert de Brus, in Scotland, and that he had secretly hidden and retained this coronal till a fitting occasion, but that these treasonable doings had since been discovered and convicted by the king's council." No doubt, Godferey the goldsmith would have been dealt with, according to the tender mercies shown to Wallace and Fraser, if he had not found a friend in queen

Marguerite; "for," says Edward I., "we pardon him solely at the intercession of our dearest consort, Marguerite queen of England."

The citizens of Winchester were likewise deeply indebted to queen
Marguerite, whose beneficent interference relieved them from the terrible consequences of king Edward's displeasure   To the mayor of Winchester had been confided the safe keeping of Bernard Pereres; a host-
age of some importance, whom the city of Bayonne had delivered to the
king, as a pledge of their somewhat doubtful loyalty. Bernard made
his escape. On which king Edward sternly commanded his sheriff of
Hampshire to seize upon the city of Winchester, and to declare its liberties void; thus reducing the free citizens to the state of feudal villeins.
The mayor he loaded with an enormous fine of 300 marks, and incarce-
rated him in the Marshalsea till it was paid. In despair the Winchester citizens appealed to the charity of queen Marguerite. She recollected that when she was first married she had been received at Winchester,
with the most affectionate demonstrations of loyalty; moreover, she
remembered that her husband had given her a charter, which entitled
her to all the fines levied from the men of Winchester. Armed with
this charter, she went to her loving lord, and claimed the hapless mayor
and his fine as her personal property. She then remitted half the fine;
took easy security for the remainder, and set the mayor at liberty; nor
did she cease pleading with her consort, till he had restored to Winchester the forfeited charters.

During her husband's absence in Scotland, queen Marguerite retired
for security to Winchester, where she was deservedly beloved; here she
gave birth to a princess—her third, but the king's sixteenth child. The
infant was called Eleanora, after Edward's first queen and his eldest
daughter, who was deceased at that time. She died in a few months.

Before king Edward reached the Scottish border he fell ill, at Burgh
on Sands. He survived a few days, till the prince of Wales came up
with the remaining forces, time enough to receive his last commands,
which breathed implacable fury against the Scots. The dying warrior,
moreover, commanded his son "to be kind to his little brothers Thomas
and Edward, and, above all, to treat with respect and tenderness his
mother, queen Marguerite."

The original MS. of the queen's chronicler, John o'London, is a great curiosity. It is written in Latin on vellum, very finely and legibly penned, and ornamented with initial letters, illuminated with gold and colors; the centres of the most of these are unfinished, and the manuscript itself is a fragment. The description of Edward's person is accompanied by an odd representation of his face, in the midst of an initial letter. The features bear the same cast as the portraits of the king; there is the small haughty mouth; the severe penetrating eyes, and the long straight nose; the king is meant to be shown in glory, but the head is surrounded with three tiers of most suspicious-looking flames. However, such as it is, it doubtless satisfied the royal widow, to whom the work was dedicated. "The noble and generous matron, Margareta, by the grace of God, queen of England, invites all men to hear these pages." The plan of the oration is to describe the doleful bewailings of all sorts and conditions of persons for the loss of the great Edward. Of course, the lamentation of the royal widow holds a distinguished place in the *commemoratio*. It commences thus: "The lamentable commendation of Margareta, the queen. Hear, ye isles, and attend my people, for is any sorrow like unto my sorrow? Though my head wears a crown, joy is distant from me, and I listen no more to the sound of my cithara and organs. I mourn incessantly, and am weary of my existence. Let all mankind hear the voice of my tribulation, for my desolation on our earth is complete." * * * The queen's chronicler proceeds to paraphrase the lament for Saul and Jonathan; at length he remembers the royal Marguerite by adding, "At the foot of Edward's monument, with my little sons, I weep and call upon him. When Edward died, all men died to me."

These lamentations for a husband more than seventy, from a widow twenty-six, seem a little exaggerated; yet the after-life of the royal Marguerite proved their sincerity.

Although queen Marguerite appeared in public earlier than was usual, for the etiquette of royal widowhood in the fourteenth century, it was in obedience to the dying commands of her royal lord, whose heart was set on a French alliance. Soon after her husband's death she went to Boulogne with her son-in-law, and assisted at his marriage with her niece Isabella.

After she returned to England she lived in retirement, spending her magnificent dower in acts of charity, and in the encouragement of historians and architects.

Queen Marguerite's principal residence was Marlborough Castle, on the borders of the forest of Savernake; it was there she died at the early age of thirty-six, on the 14th of February, 1317.

ISABELLA OF FRANCE,

SURNAMED THE FAIR,

QUEEN OF EDWARD II.

SINCE the days of the fair and false Elfrida, of Saxon celebrity, no queen of England has left so dark a stain on the annals of female royalty, as the consort of Edward II., Isabella of France. She was the eleventh queen of England from the Norman Conquest, and with the exception of Judith, the consort of Ethelwolph, a princess of higher rank than had ever éspoused a king of England. She was the offspring of a marriage between two sovereigns; Philip le Bel, king of France, and Jane, queen of Navarre.

Isabella was born in the year 1295, and when about four years old, her name was included in the twofold matrimonial treaty which Geoffrey de Joinville, as the envoy of Edward I., negotiated between that monarch and the princess Marguerite, sister of the king of France, and the prince of Wales, with the princess Isabella his daughter.

A solemn act of betrothment took place at Paris, in the year 1303, when the pope's dispensation for this union was published. The count of Savoy and the earl of Lincoln, as the procurators of Edward prince of Wales, affianced the young princess, on his part, in the presence of her illustrious parents, Philip IV. of France, and Jane, queen of France and Navarre.

After appointing his recalled favorite, Piers Gaveston, guardian of the realm, Edward sailed, early on Monday morning, January 22, 1308, accompanied by his mother-in-law, queen Marguerite, to meet his bride. He landed at Boulogne, where Isabella had already arrived with her royal parents. There king Edward performed homage for Guienne and Ponthieu, to king Philip.

The next day, being the festival of the conversion of St. Paul, the nuptials of Isabella and her royal bridegroom were celebrated, in the famous cathedral church of Boulogne, with peculiar magnificence.

The beauty of the royal pair excited the greatest admiration; for the bridegroom was the handsomest prince in Europe, and the precocious charms of the bride had already obtained for her the name of Isabella the Fair. Who of all the royal and gallant company, witnesses of these espousals, could have believed their fatal termination, or deemed that the epithet of She-Wolf of France could ever have been deserved by the bride?

The king and queen remained at Dover two days, where Piers Gaveston joined them. The moment the king saw him, he flew to him, fell on his neck, and called him "brother;" conduct which greatly displeased the queen and her uncles. From Dover the royal party proceeded to Eltham, where they remained till the preparations were completed for the coronation.

It is possible that if Isabella had been of an age more suitable to that of her husband, and of a less haughty temper, her beauty and talents might have created a counter-influence to that of the Gascon favorite, productive of beneficial effects; but, at the period of his marriage, Edward was in his three-and-twentieth year, and evidently considered a consort who was only entering her teens, as entitled to a very trifling degree of attention, either as a queen or a wife. Isabella was however, perfectly aware of the importance of her position in the English court; and even had she been as childish in mind as she was in age, she was too closely allied in blood to the great leaders of the disaffected peers of England, Thomas earl of Lancaster, and his brother Henry, earl of Derby, to remain quiescently in the background.

It was not, however, till the fifth year of Isabella's marriage with Edward II., that any well-grounded hope existed of her bringing an heir to England; and the period at which this joyful prospect first became apparent was amidst the horrors of civil war.

This auspicious event took place on the 13th day of November, in the year 1312, when Isabella, then in the eighteenth year of her age, and the fifth of her marriage, brought into the world the long desired heir of England, afterwards that most renowned of our monarchs, Edward III., surnamed of Windsor, from the place of his birth.

Isabella's influence, after this happy event, was very considerable with her royal husband, and at this period her conduct was all that was prudent, amiable, and feminine. It was through her mediation that a reconciliation was at length effected between king Edward and his barons, and tranquillity restored to the perturbed realm.

It was in 1321 that the storm gathered again among the lord marchers, which led to the barons' war, and brought Isabella and Roger Mortimer into acquaintance with each other.

We now come to that eventful period when Isabella exchanged the lovely character of a peace-maker for that of a vindictive political agitator, and finally branded her once-honored name with the foul stains of adultery, treason, and murder.

While king Edward was battling the rebellious barons, the queen, for greater security, took up her abode in the Tower. In this royal fortress she gave birth to her youngest child, the lady Joanna, who from that circumstance was called Joanna de la Tour.

Some time before the birth of the princess Joanna, the two Mortimers, uncle and nephew, having been taken in arms against the king, were brought to the Tower as state prisoners, under sentence of death and confiscation of their great estates. Roger Mortimer, lord of Chirk, the uncle, died of famine, through the neglect or cruelty of his jailers in failing to supply him with the necessaries of life, it has been said, soon after his capture. Roger Mortimer, the nephew, was in the pride and vigor of manhood, and possessed of strength of constitution, and energy of mind, to struggle with any hardship to which he might be exposed. The manner in which he contrived, while under sentence of death in one of the prison lodgings of the Tower of London, to create so powerful an interest in the heart of the beautiful consort of his offended sovereign, is not related by any of the chroniclers of that reign. It

10

is possible, however, that Isabella's disposition for intermeddling in poli
tical matters might have emboldened this handsome and audacious rebel
to obtain personal interviews with her, under the color of being willing
to communicate to her the secrets of his party. He was the husband of
a French lady, Jane de Joinville, the heiress of Sir Peter Joinville, and
was in all probability only two well acquainted with the language that
was most pleasing to the ear of the queen, and the manners and refinements of her native land, which in civilization was greatly in advance
of the bellicose realm of England. Be this as it may, Mortimer was
reprieved through the good offices of some powerful intercessor; and
the king commuted his sentence of death into perpetual imprisonment
in the Tower. This occasioned some astonishment, when it was remen-
bered that Mortimer was the first who had commenced the civil war by
his fierce attack on the lands of Hugh Despencer, who was his sworn
foe, and who at this very time had regained more than his former sway
in the council of king Edward; but at that time the influence of the
queen was paramount to any other, and it was probably on this account
that the deadly feud commenced between her and the two Despencers,
which ended so fatally to both.

In the succeeding year, 1323, we find the tameless border chief, from
his dungeon in the Tower, organizing a plan for the seizure, not only of
that royal fortress, but Windsor and Wallingford. Again was Mortimer
condemned to suffer death for high treason, but through the agency of
Adam Orleton, and Beck, bishop of Durham he obtained a respite. On
the 1st of August, the same year, Gerard Alspaye, the valet of Segrave,
the constable of the Tower, who was supposed to be in co-operation
with him, gave the men-at-arms a soporific portion in their drink provided by the queen; and while the guards were asleep, Mortimer passed
through a hole he had worked in his own prison into the kitchen of the
royal residence, ascended the chimney, got on the roof of the palace,
and from thence to the Thames side by a ladder of ropes. Segrave's
valet then took a sculler and rowed him over to the opposite bank of the
river, where they found a party of seven horsemen pertaining to Mortimer waiting to receive him. With this guard he made his way to the
coast of Hampshire; from thence, pretending to sail to the Isle of
Wight, the boat in reality conveyed the fugitives on board a large

ship, provided by Ralf Bottom, a London merchant, which was an-
chored off the Needles: this ship landed them safely in Normandy;
and from thence Mortimer got to Paris.

Edward was in Lancashire when he heard of the escape of Mortimer: he roused all England with a hue and cry after him, but
does not seem to have had the least idea of his destination, as he
sought him chiefly in the Mortimers' hereditary demesnes, the marches
of Wales.

Directly Mortimer was in safety, the queen commenced her deep-
laid schemes for the ruin of his powerful enemies, the Despencers,
whom she taught the people to regard as the cause of the sanguinary
executions of Lancaster and his adherents.

The Despencers had succeeded in obtaining the same sort of ascendency over the mind of the king that had been once enjoyed by
Gaveston; and the whole authority of his feeble despotism was committed to their administration. Their first act was to curtail the revenues
of the queen. This imprudent step afforded Isabella a plausible excuse for declaring open hostilities against them. No one had ever
offended her without paying a deadly penalty for their rashness.

She perceived that she had lost her influence with her royal husband, during his absence in the civil war in the north; and though
it is evident that an illicit passion on her part had preceded the
alienation of the king's regard for her, she did not complain the less
loudly of her wrongs on that account.

The feuds between the royal pair proceeded to such a height, that
Isabella denied her company to her lord, and he refused to come
where she was. The queen passionately charged this estrangement
on the Despencers, and reiterated her complaints to her brother.

King Charles testified his indignant sense of his sister's treatment,
by declaring his intention of seizing all the provinces held by king
Edward of the French crown, he having repeatedly summoned him
in vain to perform the accustomed homage for them. Edward was
not prepared to engage in a war for their defence, and neither he
nor his ministers liked the alternative of a personal visit to the court
of the incensed brother of queen Isabella, after the indignities that
had been offered to her.

In this dilemma, Isabella herself obligingly volunteered to act as a mediatrix between the two monarchs, provided she might be permitted to go to Paris to negotiate a pacification. Edward, who had so often been extricated from his political difficulties by the diplomatic talents of his fair consort, was only too happy to avail himself of her proposal.

A hollow reconciliation was effected between Isabella and the Despencers, who were delighted at the prospect of her departure from England; and the royal pair parted, apparently on terms of the most affectionate confidence and good will.

Isabella sailed for France in the beginning of May, attended only by the lord John Cromwell and four knights. She landed at Calais, and proceeded to Paris, where the first fruits of her mediation was a truce between her brother and the king, her husband. She then negotiated an amicable treaty, proposing the surrender of Guienne, already forfeited by the neglect of the feudal homage to the king of France, which was to be restored at her personal instances, by her brother, to the king of England, on condition of his performing the accustomed homage, and remunerating the king of France for the expenses of the war. This was to take place at a friendly interview between the two monarchs at Beau-vais.

The Despencers, anticipating with alarm the great probability of the queen regaining her wonted ascendency over the mind of her royal husband, dissuaded him from crossing to the shores of France, even when his preparations for the voyage were completed. Isabella, who was well informed of these demurs, and perfectly understood the vacillating character of her husband, proposed to him that he should invest their son, the prince of Wales, with the duchy of Guienne and the earldom of Ponthieu, and send him as his substitute to perform the homage for those countries to the king, her brother, king Charles having signified his assent to such an arrangement, in compliance with her solicitations.

Edward, far from suspecting the guileful intentions of his consort, eagerly complied with this proposal; and the Despencers, not being possessed of sufficient penetration to understand the motives which prompted the queen to get the heir of England into her own power, fell into the snare.

On the 12th of September, 1325, prince Edward, attended by the bishops of Oxford, Exeter, and a splendid train of nobles and knights, sailed from Dover, and landing at Boulogne, was joined by the queen his mother on the 14th, who accompanied him to Paris, where his first interview with the king his uncle took place in her presence, and he performed the act of feudal homage on the 21st, at the Bois de Vincennes.

The wording of the treaty negotiated between Isabella and her brother, the king of France, was couched in such ambiguous terms, as to leave considerable matter of dispute between king Edward and that monarch, even after the required homage had been performed by the heir of England, for the fiefs held of the French crown. This difference, which regarded the province of Agenois, had been contrived by Isabella, to afford a plausible pretext for prolonging her stay in Paris. She was there joined by her paramour, Mortimer, and all the banished English lords who had fled from the persecutions of the Spencers flocked round her. She held frequent councils and meetings with the declared enemies of king Edward's person and government, and she altogether avoided the commissioners, by whose advice the king had appointed her to be guided.

But Walter Stapleton, the loyal bishop of Exeter, whom she had endeavored to draw into her conspiracy, withdrew to England, informed the king of her proceedings, and urged him to command her immediate return, with the prince of Wales. King Edward vainly issued his private letters and royal summonses to his consort and son for that purpose: his most peremptory orders were disregarded by Isabella, who asserted "that it was the intention of the Despencers to cause her to be put to death if she returned to England:" on which the king of France, her brother, wrote to king Edward, "that he could not permit her to return to him, unless she were guaranteed from the evil that was meditated against her by her enemies the Despencers."

Her party in England had now, through the malignant activity of her special agent, Adam Orleton, bishop of Hereford, become so strong, that about this time she received a deputation from the confederate barons, assuring her "that if she could only raise a thousand men, and would come with the prince to England, at the head of that force, they would place him on the throne to govern by her guidance."

The queen had already been very active in securing the assistance of many enterprising young nobles, and soldiers of fortune, who were, by her persuasive words and fair promises, ready to attend her; but though she had conducted her preparations with great secrecy, the Despencers had information of her proceedings, and, if we may trust the assertions of Froissart, they circumvented her, by the skilful distribution of counter bribes among the ministers of the king of France; nay, he even goes so far as to say that the Despencers addressed their golden arguments to king Charles himself, so successfully, that he withdrew his countenance from his royal sister, and forbade any person, under pain of punishment, to aid or assist her in her projected invasion of England.

Queen Isabella arrived at Harwich on the 25th of September, 1326, on the domain of Thomas of Brotherton, the king's brother, who was the first that greeted her on her landing.

Her force consisted of two thousand seven hundred and fifty-seven soldiers well appointed, commanded by lord John of Hainault, brother to her ally, the sovereign of Hainault. Roger Mortimer commanded her English partisans.

The historian of Harwich declares that it was wonderful how the common people flocked to her. Every generous feeling in the English character had been worked upon by her emissaries, who had disseminated inflammatory tales of the persecutions she had endured from the king, her husband, and his barbarous ministers. It was asserted that she had been driven into a foreign land by plots against her life, and that she was the most oppressed of queens—the most injured of wives.

So blinding was the excitement which at this crisis, pervaded all classes of the people, that the glaring falsehood of her statements, as to the cause of her quitting England, was forgotten; the improprieties of her conduct, which had excited the disgust of her own countrymen, and caused the king, her brother, to expel her with contempt from his dominions, were regarded as the base calumnies of the Despencers. The facts that she came attended by her paramour, an outlawed traitor, and at the head of a band of foreign mercenaries, to raise the standard of revolt against her husband and sovereign, having abused her maternal influence over the mind of the youthful heir of England, to draw him

into a parricidal rebellion, excited no feeling of moral or religious repro-
bation in the nation.

When the alarming intelligence of the landing of the queen's armament reached the king, he was paralyzed, and, instead of taking measures for defence, he sat down to write pathetic letters to the pope and
the king of France, entreating their succor or interference.

"The queen and all her company," says Froissart, "the lords of
Hainault and their suite, took the shortest road for Bristol, and in every
town through which they passed were entertained with every mark of
distinction. Their forces augmented daily until they arrived at Bristol,
which they besieged. The king and the younger Hugh Despencer shut
themselves up in the castle; old sir Hugh and the earl of Arundel
remained in the town, but these the citizens delivered up soon after to
the queen, who entered Bristol, accompanied by sir John Hainault, with
all her barons, knights, and squires.

The king and the younger sir Hugh, endeavored to escape to the
Welsh shore in a boat which they had behind the castle; but after toss-
ing about some days, and striving in vain against the contrary winds,
which drove them repeatedly back within a mile of the castle, from
whence they were trying to escape, sir Hugh Beaumont, observing the
efforts of this unfortunate bark, rowed out with a strong force in his
barge, to see who was in it. The king's exhausted boatmen were soon
overtaken, and the consequence was, that the royal fugitive and his hapless favorite were brought back to Bristol, and delivered to the queen,
as her prisoners.

Now the evil nature of Isabella of France blazed out in full view.
Hitherto her beauty, her eloquence, and her complaints, had won all
hearts towards her cause; but the touchstone of prosperity showed her
natural character.

Previously to her quitting Bristol, the queen summoned a parliament, in the king's name, to meet at Westminster, Dec. 15th, "in which
Isabella, queen consort, and Edward, son of the king, the guardian of
the realm, and the lords, might treat together."

In this memorable parliament the misdemeanors of the absent sovereign were canvassed, his deposition was decreed, and his eldest son was

elected to his office, and immediately proclaimed king in Westminster Hall, by the style and title of Edward III.

When the decision of her own faction was made known to Isabella, she burst into a passion of weeping, and these counterfeit tears so wrought upon the generous unsuspicious nature of her son, that he made a solemn vow not to accept the offered crown of England, unless it was his royal father's pleasure voluntarily to resign it to him.

Isabella had overacted her part; and her party were a little disconcerted at the virtuous resolution of the princely boy, as they had never dreamed of making the consent of the king, to his own deposition, a preliminary to the inauguration of his successor; but they found nothing less would satisfy the young Edward, as to the lawfulness of his title to the throne.

The unhappy king had already been compelled to resign the great seal, to the delegates of his queen and parliament, at Monmouth Castle. Adam Orleton, the traitor bishop of Hereford, was the person employed by the queen to demand it: and as the king quiescently resigned it to him, he was deputed, with twelve other commissioners, to require the unfortunate monarch to abdicate his royal dignity, by delivering up his crown, sceptre, and the rest of the regalia, into their hands.

The commissioners proceeded on their ungracious errand to Kenil worth Castle, where the king was kept as a state prisoner, but with honorable treatment, by his noble captor, Henry of Lancaster. The pitiless traitor Orleton was the spokesman, and vented the insatiable malice of his heart, in a series of the bitterest insults against his fallen sovereign, under the pretence of demonstrating the propriety of depriving him of a dignity of which he had proved himself unworthy.

Edward listened to the mortifying detail of the errors of his life and government, with floods of tears; and when Orleton enlarged on the favor shown him, by the magnates of his kingdom, in choosing his son for his successor, instead of conferring the crown on a stranger, he meekly acknowledged it to be such, and withdrew to prepare himself for the resignation of the outward symbols of sovereignty.

De la Moor, the faithful servant of Edward II., gives a pathetic account of the scene in the presence-chamber at Kenilworth Castle, where the commissioners, in the presence of Henry Plantagenet, earl of

Leicester, the earl of Lancaster's eldest son, were drawn up, in formal array, by Orleton, to renounce their homage to king Edward, and to receive his personal abdication of the royal dignity. After a long pause, the unfortunate prince came forth from an inner apartment, clad in mourning weeds, or, as the chronicler expresses it, "gowned in black," the late struggle of his soul being sufficiently denoted by the sadness of his features; but on entering the presence of his obdurate subjects, he sank down in a deep swoon, and lay stretched upon the earth as one dead. The earl of Leicester and the bishop of Winchester immediately flew to his assistance, and, raising him in their arms, with some tenderness supported him. After much trouble, they succeeded in restoring their unhappy master to a consciousness of his misery. "As piteous and heavy as this sight was," continues the chronicler, "it failed to excite the compassion of any other of the queen's commissioners. Scarcely, indeed, had the king recovered from his indisposition, before the relentless Orleton, regardless of the agony he had inflicted, proceeded to a repetition of his cruel insults."

The king gave way to a fresh paroxysm of weeping; and being much pressed for his decision, he at length replied, that "he was aware that for his many sins he was thus punished, and therefore he besought those present to have compassion upon him in his adversity;" adding, "that much as he grieved for having incurred the hatred of his people, he was glad that his eldest son was so gracious in their sight, and gave them thanks for choosing him to be their king."

As soon as the commissioners returned to London with the regalia, and signified the abdication of the late sovereign to the queen and the parliament, the prince of Wales was publicly proclaimed king on the 20th of January, 1327, and Walter, archbishop of Canterbury, preached a sermon in Westminster Abbey, preparatory to the coronation, taking for his text, not any verse from Scripture, but the words, *Vox populi vox Dei.*

The most remarkable feature at this coronation was the hypocritical demeanor of the queen-mother Isabella, who, though she had been the principal cause of her husband's deposition, affected to weep during the whole of the ceremony.

The parliament, immediately after the coronation, appointed a coun-

11

cil of regency for the guardianship of the youthful sovereign and the realm, consisting of twelve bishops and peers.

The queen made no remonstrance against this arrangement, but, having military power in her own hands, she seized the government, and made Roger Mortimer (whom she had caused her son to create earl of March) her prime minister, and Adam Orleton her principal counsellor. This precious trio managed the affairs of the kingdom between them. After this arrangement, Isabella, hitherto the most accomplished of dissimulators, threw off the mask, and, with the sanction of a parliament made up of her partisans, appropriated to herself a dower exceeding two-thirds of the revenues of the kingdom.

Meantime, the deposed sovereign, Edward II., continued to write from his prison the most passionate letters of entreaty to Isabella to be permitted to see her and their son; he was encouraged, perhaps, by the presents which (according to Walsingham) she occasionally sent him, of fine apparel, linen, and other trifling articles, accompanied by deceitful messages, expressing solicitude for his health and comforts, and lamenting that she was not permitted by the parliament to visit him. Nothing was, however, further from the heart of Isabella than feelings of tenderness or compassion for her hapless lord. The moment she learned that her uncle, Henry of Lancaster, had relented from his long-cherished animosity against his fallen sovereign, and was beginning to treat him with kindness and respect, she removed him from Kenilworth, and gave him into the charge of the brutal ruffians, sir John Maltravers and sir Thomas Gurney, who had hearts to plan and hands to execute any crime for which their agency might be required.

By this pair the royal victim was conducted, under a strong guard, first to Corfe Castle, and then to Bristol, where public sympathy operated so far in his favor that a project was formed by the citizens for his deliverance. When this was discovered, the associate-traitors, Gurney and Maltravers, hurried him to Berkeley Castle, which was destined to be his last resting-place. On the road thither, he was treated in the most barbarous manner by his unfeeling guards, who took fiend-like delight in augmenting his misery, by depriving him of sleep, compelling him to ride in thin clothing in the chilly April nights, and crowning him with hay, in mockery.

According to De la Moor, the queen's mandate for the murder of her royal husband was conveyed in that memorable Latin distich from the subtle pen of Adam Orleton, the master-fiend of her cabinet; it is capable, by the alteration of a comma, of being read with two directly opposite meanings:

"Edwardum occidere nolite timere, bonum est.
Edwardum occidere nolite, timere bonum est.

"Edward to kill fear not, the deed is good.
Edward kill not, to fear the deed is good."

On the night of the 22d of September, 1327, exactly a twelvemonth after the return of the queen to England, the murder of her unfortunate husband was perpetrated, with circumstances of the greatest horror. No outward marks of violence were perceptible on his person, when the body was exposed to public view in Gloucester cathedral, but the rigid and distorted lines of the face bore evidence of the agonies he had undergone, and it is reported that his cries had been heard at a considerable distance from the castle, where this barbarous regicide was committed. "Many a one woke," adds the narrator, "and prayed to God for the harmless soul, which that night was departing in torture."

The public indignation, in that part of the country, was so greatly excited against the infamous instruments of the queen and Mortimer, that they were fain to make their escape beyond seas, to avoid the vengeance of the people.

The murdered king was interred, without funeral pomp, in Gloucester cathedral, and Isabella endeavored, by the marriage festivities of her son and his young queen, to dissipate the general gloom, which the suspicious circumstances attending the death of her unhappy consort had occasioned. But so universal was the feeling of disgust which the conduct of the queen and her favorite Mortimer excited, that nothing but the despotism she had succeeded in establishing, enabled her to keep possession of her usurped power.

The death of Charles le Bel, without male issue, having left Isabella the sole surviving child of Philip le Bel, her eldest son, Edward III., considered that he had the best claim to the sovereignty of France. But his mother not only prevented him from asserting his own claims, but compelled him, sorely against his will, to acknowledge those of his rival, by performing homage for the provinces held of the French crown.

Edward returned from his last conference with king Philip at Amiens, out of humor with himself, and still more so with his mother. The evil odor in which Isabella's reputation was generally held, both at home and abroad, though perhaps concealed from him in his own court (where he was as yet but a state puppet, surrounded by her creatures), was conveyed to him through a variety of channels, as soon as he was beyond the limits of her usurped authority. Edward was sensibly touched when informed of these things, and determined no longer to be a quiescent witness of his mother's dishonor.

The parliament was summoned to meet at Nottingham a fortnight after Michaelmas, and the youthful sovereign considered that it would be a favorable time for the arrest of his mother's paramour, when all the barons of England were assembled round him in support of his royal authority.

The particulars of this most interesting crisis are related in the words of the lively chronicler, from whom Stowe has taken his graphic narrative of the arrest of the queen and her lover.

Froissart, after relating the particulars of Mortimer's death, adds, " The king soon after, by the advice of his council, ordered his mother to be confined in a goodly castle, and gave her plenty of ladies to wait upon her, as well as knights and squires of honor. He made her a handsome allowance to keep and maintain the state to which she had been accustomed, but forbade her ever to go out or show herself abroad, except at certain times, and when any shows were exhibited in the court of the castle."

Castle Rising, in Norfolk, was the place where queen Isabella was destined to spend the long years of her widowhood.

In the thirty-first year of his reign king Edward granted safe-conduct to William de Leith, to wait on queen Isabella at her castle of Rising, he coming from Scotland, probably with news from her daughter,

queen Joanna, who was then very sick. This person was physician to
the queen of Scotland.

The next year Isabella died at Castle Rising, August 22d, 1358,
aged sixty-three. She chose the church of the Gray Friars, where the
mangled remains of her paramour Mortimer had been buried, eight-and-
twenty years previously, for the place of her interment; and, carrying
her characteristic hypocrisy even to the grave, she was buried with the
heart of her murdered husband on her breast.

PHILIPPA OF HAINAULT,

QUEEN OF EDWARD III.

THE happy union of the illustrious Philippa with her thrice renowned lord had been previously cemented by mutual perference, manifested in the first sweet springtime of existence, when prince Edward took refuge with his mother, queen Isabella, at the court of Hainault.

"Count William of Hainault had, at that time, four daughters," says Froissart; "these were Margaret, Philippa, Joanna, and Isabel. The young prince, during his mother's residence in Hainault, paid more court and attention to Philippa than to any of the others; the young lady also conversed with him more frequently, and sought his company oftener than any of her sisters." This was in 1326, when prince Edward was in his fifteenth year, and the lady Philippa a few months younger. She possessed some Flemish beauty, being tall in stature, and adorned with the brilliant complexion for which the women of that country are celebrated.

A poet of her time has commemorated "her roseate hue and beauty bright;" and we can well imagine, though Philippa's matron charms became a little too exuberant in after life, that, as a sweet tempered Flemish girl in her fifteenth year, her early bloom was very lovely.

Although a decided affection subsisted between young Edward and Philippa, it was not considered in accordance with the royal etiquette of that era, for the heir of England to acknowledge that he had disposed of his heart without the consent of his parliament and council.

Queen Isabella undertook the arrangement of this affair, and soon led the public authorities to the decision, that a daughter of the count of Hainault would be the most desirable alliance for her son.

Philippa was married at Valenciennes by procuration. She embarked for England at Wisan, landed at Dover with all her suite, and arrived in London, December 23, 1327, with a retinue and display of magnificence in accordance with the great wealth of her country. She was escorted by her uncle, John of Hainault, and not by her father, as was expected.

The hands of Edward and Philippa were united at York, January 24, 1328. The magnificence of the espousals was heightened by the grand entry of a hundred of the principal nobility of Scotland, who had arrived in order to conclude a lasting peace with England, cemented by the marriage of the king's little sister Joanna. The parliament and royal council were likewise convened at York, and the flower of the English nobility, then in arms, were assembled round the young king and his bride.

The royal pair kept Easter at York, and after the final peace with Scotland they returned southward from Lincoln to Northampton, and finally settled, in June, at the beautiful summer palace of Woodstock, which seems the principal abiding place of Philippa, while her young husband was yet under the tutelage of Mortimer and the queen mother.

While the young king was yet under the dominion of his unworthy mother, his consort, Philippa, gave birth to her first-born, afterwards the celebrated hero Edward, surnamed the Black Prince. He first saw the light at the palace of Woodstock, June 15, 1330. The great beauty of this infant, his size, and the firm texture of his limbs, filled every one with admiration who saw him. Like that renowned queen-regent of France, Blanche of Castille, mother of St. Louis, Philippa chose to nourish her babe at her own bosom. It is well known, that the portraits of the lovely young Philippa and her princely boy formed the favorite models, for the Virgin and Child, at that era.

In the decline of the year 1330, Edward III. shook off the restraints imposed upon him by his unworthy mother and her ferocious paramour. He executed justice on the great criminal Mortimer, in the summary and hasty way, in which he was always inclined to act, when under the impulse of passion, and at a distance from his queen. No one can wonder tnat he was impatient to destroy the murderer of his father and of his uncle. Still this eagerness to execute sudden vengeance under the influence of rage, whether justly or unjustly excited, is a trait in the character of this mighty sovereign which appears in his youth; and which it is necessary to point out in order to develope the beautiful and nearly perfect character of his queen.

Edward and Philippa were in England during the winter of 1334. At the palace of Woodstock, on February the 5th, the queen brought into the world Elizabeth (likewise called Isabella), the princess-royal. The queen undertook another campaign in the succeeding spring. That year her father sent king Edward a present of a rich helmet, made of gold and set with precious stones; with a remonstrance against wasting his strength in Scotland, where there was no plunder to be got, when the same expense would prosecute his claims on France.

About this time, the heart of the mighty Edward swerved for a while from its fidelity to Philippa; and had not the royal hero been enamored of a lady of exemplary virtue, the peace of the queen might have been for ever destroyed. Sir William Montacute had been rewarded for the good service he did the king, in the beginning of his reign, by the title of the earl of Salisbury. He had married the fair Catherine de Grason, and received the castellanship of Wark Castle, whither he had taken his countess, who lived in retirement away from the court. In the mean time, Salisbury had been captured in the French war. His castle in the north, which was defended by his countess and his nephew, was besieged in the second Scottish war, by king David. When in great danger, young Montacute, by a bold personal adventure, carried the news of the distress of the countess to king Edward, who was encamped near Berwick. At the approach of Edward, the king of Scots raised the siege of Wark. The royal hero's interview with Catherine the Fair follows, in the words of Froissart:

"The moment the countess heard of the king's approach, she ordered all the gates to be thrown open, and went to meet him most richly dressed; insomuch, that no one could look at her but with wonder and admiration at her noble deportment, great beauty, and affability of behavior. When she came near king Edward, she made her obeisance to the ground, and gave him thanks for coming to her assistance, and then

12

conducted him into the castle, to entertain and honor him, as she was very capable of doing.

"Every one was delighted with her; but the king could not take his eyes off from her, so that a *spark of fine love* struck upon his heart, which lasted a long time; for he did not believe that the whole world produced any other lady, so worthy of being beloved. Thus they entered the castle, hand in hand. The countess led him first to the hall, and then to the best chamber, which was very richly furnished, as belonging to so fine a lady. King Edward kept his eyes so fixed upon the countess, that the gentle dame was quite abashed. After he had sufficiently examined his apartment, he retired to a window, and, leaning on it, fell into a profound reverie.

"The countess left him to order dinner to be made ready, and the tables set, and the hall ornamented and set out; likewise to welcome the knights and lords who accompanied the king. When she had given all the orders to her servants she thought needful, she returned with a cheerful countenance to king Edward, and said—

" 'Dear sir, what are you musing on? Such meditation is not proper for you, saving your grace. You ought rather to be in high spirits, having freed England from her enemy without loss of blood.'

"The king replied—'Oh, dear lady, you must know that, since I have been in this castle, some thoughts have oppressed my mind that I was not before aware of; so that it behooves me to reflect. Being uncertain what may be the event, I cannot withdraw my attention.'

" 'Dear sir,' answered the lady, 'you ought to be of good cheer, and feast with your friends, to give them more pleasure, and leave off pondering; for God has been very bountiful to you in your undertakings, so that you are the most feared and renowned prince in Christendom. If the king of Scotland have vexed you by the mischiefs he hath done in your kingdom, you will speedily be able to make reprisal in his dominions. Therefore, come, if it please you, into the hall to your knights, for dinner will soon be served.'

" 'Oh, sweet lady," said king Edward, 'there be other things which touch my heart, and lie heavy there, than what you talk of. For, in good truth, your beauteous mien, and the perfections of your face and behavior, have wholly overcome me; and so deeply impress my heart, that my happiness wholly depends on meeting a return to my flame, which no denial from you cán ever extinguish.'

"'Oh, my dread lord,' replied the countess, 'do not amuse yourself by laughing at me with trying to tempt me, for I cannot believe you are in earnest as to what you have just said. Is it likely that so noble and gallant a prince as you are would ever think of dishonoring either me or my husband, a valiant knight, who has served you so faithfully, and who now lies in a doleful prison on your account? Certainly, sir, this would not redound to your glory; nor would you be the better for it, if you could have your wayward will."

"The virtuous lady then quitted the king, who was astonished at her words. She went into the hall to hasten dinner; afterwards she approached the king's chamber, attended by all the knights, and said to him—

"'My lord king, your knights are all waiting for you, to wash their hands; for they, as well as yourself, have fasted too long.'

"King Edward left his apartment, and came to the hall, where, after he had washed his hands, he seated himself, with his knights, at the dinner, as did the lady also; but the king ate very little, and was the whole time pensive, casting his eyes, whenever he had the opportunity, on the countess. Such behavior surprised his friends; for they were not accustomed to it, never having seen the like before in their king. They supposed it was his chagrin, at the departure of the Scots without a battle. The king remained at the castle the whole day, without knowing what to do with himself. Thus did he pass that day and a sleepless night, debating the matter with his own heart. At daybreak he rose, drew out his whole army, raised his camp, and made ready to follow the Scots. Upon taking leave of the countess, he said—

"'My dear lady, God preserve you safe till I return, and I pray that you will think well of what I have said, and have the goodness to give me a different answer.'

"'My gracious liege,' replied the countess, 'God of his infinite goodness preserve you, and drive from your noble heart such villanous thoughts; for I am, and ever shall be, ready to serve you, but only in what is consistent with my honor and with yours.'

" The king left her, quite astonished at her answers."

The love of king Edward wandered from queen Philippa, but for a short time; yet it was owing to the high principles of Catherine the Fair that he never swerved into the commission of evil.

In the first years of her marriage queen Philippa had been the constant attendant on her husband in his campaigns; the annals of the year 1346 display her character in a more brilliant light, as the sagacious ruler of his kingdom and the victorious leader of his army.

After the order of the Garter had been fully established, king Edward reminded his valiant knights and nobles, that, with him, they made a vow to assist distressed ladies; he then specified that the countess de Montfort particularly required the aid of his chivalry, for her lord was held in captivity by Philip de Valois, in the towers of the Louvre, while the countess was endeavoring to uphold the cause of her infant son, against the whole power of France. He signified his intention of giving his personal support to the heroic countess, and of leaving queen Philippa as regent of England during his absence.

The first English military despatch ever written was addressed to queen Philippa and her council, by Michael Northborough, king Edward's warlike chaplain: it contains a most original and graphic detail of the battle of Cressy. It is dated, at the siege, before the town of Calais; for the battle of Cressy was but an interlude of that famous siege.

It was now Philippa's turn to do battle-royal, with a king. As a diversion in favor of France, David of Scotland advanced into England, a fortnight after the battle of Cressy, and burned the suburbs of York. At this juncture Philippa herself hastened to the relief of her northern subjects. Froissart has detailed with great spirit the brilliant conduct of the queen at this crisis :—

" The queen of England, who was very anxious to defend her kingdom, in order to show she was in earnest about it, came herself to Newcastle-upon-Tyne. She took up her residence there to wait for her forces. On the morrow the king of Scots, with full forty thousand men, advanced within three short miles of the town of Newcastle; he sent to inform the queen that, if her men were willing to come forth from the town, he would wait and give them battle. Philippa answered, 'that she accepted his offer, and that her barons would risk their lives for the realm of their lord the king.'"

The queen's army drew up in order for battle at Neville's Cross. Philippa advanced among them mounted on a white charger, and entreated her men to do their duty well, in defending the honor of their lord the king, and urged them, "for the love of God to fight manfully." They promised her "that they would acquit themselves loyally to the utmost of their power, and perhaps better than if the king had been there in person." The queen then took her leave of them, and recommended them "to the protection of God and St. George."

There is no vulgar personal bravado of the fighting woman, in the character of Philippa. Her courage was wholly moral courage, and her feminine feelings of mercy and tenderness led her, when she had done all that a great queen could do, by encouraging her army, to withdraw from the work of carnage, and pray for her invaded kingdom while the battle joined.

The English archers gained the battle, which was fought on the lands of lord Neville. King David was taken prisoner, on his homeward retreat, but not without making the most gallant resistance.

"When the queen of England (who had tarried in Newcastle while the battle was fought) heard that her army had won the victory, she mounted, on her white palfrey, and went to the battle-field. She was informed on the way that the king of Scots was the prisoner of a squire named John Copeland, who had rode off with him, no one knew whither. The queen ordered him to be sought out, and told 'that he had done what was not agreeable to her, in carrying off her prisoner without leave.' All the rest of the day the queen and her army remained on the battle-field they had won, and then returned to Newcastle for the night."

Philippa lodged David, king of the Scots, in the Tower of London; he was conducted, by her orders, in grand procession, through the streets, mounted on a tall black war-horse, that every one might recognize his person, in case of escape. Next day she sailed for Calais, and landed three days before All Saints. The arrival of Philippa occasioned a stir of gladness in the besieging camp. Her royal lord held a grand court to welcome his victorious queen, and made a magnificent fête for her ladies. Philippa brought with her the flower of the female nobility of England, many ladies being anxious to accompany her to Calais, in order to see fathers, husbands, and brothers, all engaged in this famous siege.

Meantime, the brave defenders of Calais were so much reduced by famine as to be forced to capitulate. At first Edward resolved to put them all to the sword. By the persuasions of sir Walter Mauny, he somewhat relaxed from his bloody intentions. "He bade sir Walter," says Froissart, "return to Calais with the following terms:—'Tell the governor of Calais that the garrison and inhabitants shall be pardoned, excepting six of the principal citizens, who must surrender themselves to death, with ropes round their necks, bareheaded, and barefooted, bringing the keys of the town and castle in their hands.' Sir Walter returned to the brave governor of Calais, John de Vienne, who was waiting for him on the battlements, and told him all he had been able to gain from the king. The lord of Vienne went to the market-place, and caused the bell to be rung, upon which all the inhabitants assembled in the town hall. He then related to them what he had said, and the answers he had received, and that he could not obtain better conditions. Then they broke into lamentations of grief and despair, so that the hardest heart would have had compassion on them; and their valiant governor, lord de Vienne, wept bitterly. After a short pause, the most wealthy citizen of Calais, by name Eustace St. Pierre, rose up and said, 'Gentlemen, both high and low, it would be pity to suffer so many of our countrymen to die through famine; it would be highly meritorious in the eyes of our Saviour if such misery could be prevented. If I die to serve my dear townsmen, I trust I shall find grace before the tribunal of God. I name myself first of the six.'

"When Eustace had done speaking, his fellow-citizens all rose up and almost adored him, casting themselves on their knees, with tears and groans. Then another citizen rose up, and said he would be the second to Eustace; his name was John Daire: after him, James Wisant, who was very rich in money and lands, and kinsman to Eustace and John; his example was followed by Peter Wisant, his brother; two others then offered themselves, which completed the number demanded by king Edward. The governor mounted a small horse, for it was with difficulty he could walk, and conducted them through the gate to the barriers; he said to Sir Walter, who was there waiting for him—

" ' I deliver up to you, as governor of Calais, these six citizens, and swear to you they were, and are at this day, the most wealthy and respectable inhabitants of the town. I beg of you, gentle sir, that of your goodness you would beseech the king that they may not be put to death.' ' I cannot answer what the king will do with them,' replied sir Walter; ' but you may depend upon this, that I will do all I can to save them.' The barriers were then opened, and the six citizens were conducted to the pavilion of king Edward. When Sir Walter Mauny had presented these six citizens to the king, they fell upon their knees, and, with uplifted hands, said—

" ' Most gallant king, see before you six citizens of Calais, who have been capital merchants, and who bring you the keys of the town and castle. We surrender ourselves to your absolute will and pleasure, in order to save the remainder of our fellow-citizens and inhabitants of Calais, who have suffered great distress and misery. Condescend, then, out of your nobleness, to have compassion on us.'

" All the English barons, knights, and squires, that were assembled there in great numbers, wept at this sight; but king Edward eyed them with angry looks, for he hated much the people of Calais, because of the great losses he had suffered at sea by them. Forthwith he ordered the heads of the six citizens to be struck off. All present entreated the king to be more merciful, but he would not listen to them. Then sir Walter Mauny spoke:—' Ah, gentle king, I beseech you restrain your anger. Tarnish not your noble reputation by such an act as this! Truly the whole world will cry out on your cruelty, if you should put to death these six worthy persons.' For all this, the king gave a wink to his marshal, and said, ' I will have it so;' and ordered the headsman to be sent for, adding, ' the men of Calais had done him such damage, it was fit they suffered for it.'

" At this, the queen of England, who was very near her lying-in, fell on her knees before king Edward, and with tears said,—' Ah, gentle sir, since I have crossed the sea with great peril to see you, I have never asked you one favor; now, I most humbly ask as a gift, for the sake of the Son of the blessed Mary, and as a proof of your love to me, the lives of these six men.'

"King Edward looked at her for some time in silence, and then said, —'Ah, lady, I wish you had been any where else than here; you have entreated in such a manner that I cannot refuse you. I therefore give them you—do as you please with them.'

"The queen conducted the six citizens to her apartments, and had the halters taken from about their necks; after which she new clothed them, and served them with a plentiful dinner; she then presented each with six nobles, and had them escorted out of the camp in safety."

After the grand crisis of the capture of Calais, Philippa resided chiefly in England. Our country felt the advantage of the beneficent presence of its queen. Philippa had in her youth established the woollen manufactures: she now turned her sagacious intellect towards working the coal mines in Tynedale—a branch of national industry, whose inestimable benefits need not be dilated upon.

Notwithstanding their great strength and commanding stature, scarcely one of the sons of Philippa reached old age; even "John of Gaunt, time-honored Lancaster," was only fifty-nine at his demise: the premature introduction to the cares of state, the weight of plate armor, and the violent exercises in the tilt-yard—by way of relaxation from the severe toils of partisan warfare—seem to have brought early old age on this gallant brotherhood of princes. The queen had been the mother of twelve children; eight survived her.

Philippa had not the misery of living to see the change in the prosperity of her family; to witness the long pining decay of the heroic prince of Wales; the grievous change in his health and disposition; or the imbecility, that gradually took possession of the once mighty mind of her husband. Before these reverses took place, the queen was seized with a dropsical malady, under which she languished about two years. All her sons were absent, on the continent, when her death approached, excepting her youngest, Thomas of Woodstock.

On the return of Froissart, he found his royal mistress was dead, and he thus describes her deathbed, from the detail of those who were present and heard her last words. "I must now speak of the death of the most courteous, liberal, and noble lady that ever reigned in her time, the lady Philippa of Hainault, queen of England. While her son, the duke of Lancaster, was encamped in the valley of Tourneham, ready to give battle to the duke of Burgundy, this death happened in England, to the infinite misfortune of king Edward, his children, and the whole kingdom. That excellent lady the queen, who had done so much good, aiding all knights, ladies, and damsels, when distressed, who had applied to her, was at this time dangerously sick at Windsor Castle; and every day her disorder increased. When the good queen perceived that her end approached, she called to the king, and extending her right hand from under the bedclothes, put it into the right hand of king Edward, who was oppressed with sorrow, and thus spoke:

"'We have, my husband, enjoyed our long union in happiness, peace, and prosperity. But I entreat, before I depart, and we are for ever separated in this world, that you will grant me three requests.' King Edward, with sighs and tears, replied—'Lady, name them; whatever be your requests, they shall be granted.' 'My lord,' she said, 'I beg you will fulfil whatever engagements I have entered into with merchants for their wares, as well on this as the other side of the sea; I beseech you to fulfil whatever gifts or legacies I have made, or left to churches wherein I have paid my devotions, and to all my servants, whether male or female; and when it shall please God to call you hence, you will choose no other sepulchre than mine, and that you will lie by my side in the cloisters of Westminster Abbey.' The king in tears replied, 'Lady, all this shall be done.'

"Soon after, the good lady made the sign of the cross on her breast, and having recommended to the king her youngest son Thomas, who was present, praying to God, she gave up her spirit, which I firmly believe was caught by holy angels, and carried to the glory of heaven, for she had never done any thing by thought or deed to endanger her soul. Thus died this admirable queen of England, in the year of grace 1369, the vigil of the Assumption of the Virgin, the 14th of August.

13

A. Bouvier   W. J. Edwards

Anne of Bohemia,
Queen to Richard the 2nd

ANNE OF BOHEMIA,

SURNAMED THE GOOD,

FIRST QUEEN OF RICHARD II.

THE ancestors of the princess Anne of Bohemia originated from the same country as the Flemish Philippa; she was the nearest relative to that beloved queen whose hand was attainable; and by means of her uncle, duke Winceslaus of Brabant, she brought the same popular and profitable commercial alliance to England.

Anne of Bohemia was the eldest daughter of the Emperor Charles IV. by his fourth wife, Elizabeth of Pomerania; she was born about 1367, at Prague, in Bohemia. The regency who governed England during king Richard II.'s minority, demanded her hand for their young king, just before her father died, in the year 1380.

Richard II. was the sole surviving offspring of the gallant Black Prince and Joanna of Kent. Born in the luxurious south, the first accents of Richard of Bordeaux were formed in the poetical language of Provence, and his infant tastes linked to music and song—tastes which assimilated ill with the manners of his own court and people. His mother and half-brothers, after the death of his princely father, had brought up the future king of England with the most ruinous personal indulgence, and unconstitutional ideas of his own infallibility. He had inherited more of his mother's levity, than his father's strength of character; yet the domestic affections of Richard were of the most vivid and enduring nature, especially towards the females of his family; and the state of distress and terror to which he saw his mother reduced by the insolence of Wat Tyler's mob, was the chief stimulant of his gallant behavior when that rebel fell beneath the sword of Walworth.

When these troubles were suppressed, time had obviated the objection to the union of Richard and Anne. The young princess had attained her fifteenth year, and was considered capable of giving a rational consent to her own marriage; and after sending a letter to the council of England, saying, she became the wife of their king with full and free will, "she set out," says Froissart, "on her perilous journey, attended by the duke of Saxony and his duchess, who was her aunt, and with a suitable number of knights and damsels."

The English parliament was sitting, when intelligence came that the king's bride, after all the difficulties and dangers of her progress from Prague, had safely arrived at Dover, on which it was prorogued; but first, funds were appointed, that with all honor the bride might be presented to the young king.

Anne of Bohemia was married to Richard II. in the chapel-royal of the palace of Westminster, the newly erected structure of St. Stephen "On the wedding-day, which was the twentieth after Christmas, there were," says Froissart, "mighty feastings. That gallant and noble knight, sir Robert Namur, accompanied the queen, from the time when she quitted Prague, till she was married. The king at the end of the week carried his queen to Windsor, where he kept open and royal house. They were very happy together. She was accompanied by the king's mother, the princess of Wales, and her daughter, the duchess of Bretagne, half-sister to king Richard, who was then in England, soliciting for the restitution of the earldom of Richmond, which had been taken from her husband by the English regency, and settled in part of dower on queen Anne. Some days after the marriage of the royal pair, they returned to London, and the coronation of the queen was performed most magnificently. At the young queen's earnest request, a general pardon was granted by the king, at her consecration." The afflicted people stood in need of this respite, as the executions, since Tyler's insurrection, had been bloody and barbarous beyond all precedent. The land was reeking with the blood of the unhappy peasantry, when the humane intercession of the gentle Anne of Bohemia put a stop to the executions.

The mediation obtained for Richard's bride the title of "the good queen Anne;" and years, instead of impairing the popularity, usually so evanescent in England, only increased the esteem felt by her subjects for this beneficent princess.

Grand tournaments were held directly after the coronation. Many days were spent in these solemnities, wherein the German nobles, who had accompanied the queen to England, displayed their chivalry, to the great delight of the English. Our chroniclers call Anne of Bohemia, "the beauteous queen." At fifteen or sixteen, a blooming German girl is a very pleasing object; but her beauty must have been limited to stature and complexion, for the features of her statue are homely and undignified. A narrow, high-pointed forehead, a long upper lip, cheeks, whose fulness increased towards the lower part of the face, can scarcely entitle her to claim a reputation for beauty. But the head-dress she wore must have neutralized the effects of her face in some degree, by giving an appearance of breadth to her narrow forehead. This was the horned cap which constituted the head-gear of the ladies of Bohemia and Hungary; and in this "moony tire" did the bride of Richard present herself to the astonished eyes of her female subjects.

To Anne of Bohemia is attributed the honor of being the first, in that illustrious band of princesses, who were the nursing mothers of the Reformation. The Protestant church inscribes her name at the commencement of the illustrious list in which are seen those of Anne Boleyn, Katharine Parr, lady Jane Grey, and queen Elizabeth. Whether the young queen brought those principles with her, or imbibed them from her mother-in-law, the princess of Wales, it is not easy to ascertain. A passage quoted by Huss, the Bohemian reformer, leads to the inference that Anne was used to read the Scriptures in her native tongue. "It is possible," says Wickliffe, in his work called the 'Threefold Bond of Love,' "that our noble queen of England, sister of the Cæsar, may have the Gospel written in three languages, Bohemian, German, and Latin: now, to hereticate her (brand her with heresy) on that account, would be Luciferian folly." The influence of queen Anne over the mind of her young husband was certainly employed by Joanna, princess of

Wales, to aid her in saving the life of Wickliffe, when in great danger at the council of Lambeth, in 1382.

Anne of Bohemia, unlike Isabella of France, who was always at war with her husband's favorites and friends, made it a rule of life to love all that the king loved, and to consider a sedulous compliance with his will as her first duty. In one instance alone did this pliancy of temper lead her into the violation of justice; this was in the case of the repudiation of the countess of Oxford.

"There were great murmurings against the duke of Ireland," says Froissart; "but what injured him most was his conduct to his duchess, the lady Philippa, daughter of the lord de Courcy, a handsome and noble lady. For the duke was greatly enamored with one of the queen's damsels, called the landgravine. She was a tolerably handsome, pleasant lady, whom queen Anne had brought with her from Bohemia. The duke of Ireland loved her with such ardor, that he was desirous of making her, if possible, his duchess by marriage. All the good people of England were much shocked at this, for his lawful wife was granddaughter to the gallant king Edward and the excellent queen Philippa, being the daughter of the princess Isabella. Her uncles, the dukes of Gloucester and York, were very wroth at this insult."

The first and last error of Anne of Bohemia was the participation in this disgraceful transaction, by which she was degraded in the eyes of subjects who had warmly admired her meek virtues. The offensive part taken by the queen in this transaction was, that she actually wrote, with her own hand, an urgent letter to pope Urban, persuading him to sanction the divorce of the countess of Oxford, and to authorize the marriage of her faithless lord with the landgravine. Whether the maid of honor were a princess or a peasant, she had no right to appropriate another woman's husband. The queen was scarcely less culpable in aiding and abetting so nefarious a measure, to the infinite injury of herself, and of the consort she so tenderly loved.

The queen's good offices as a mediator were required in the year 1392, to compose a serious difference between Richard II. and the city of London. Richard had asked a loan of a thousand pounds from the citizens, which they peremptorily refused. An Italian merchant offered the king the sum required, upon which the citizens raised a tumult, and tore the unfortunate loan-lender to pieces. This outrage being followed by a riot, attended with bloodshed, Richard declared "that as the city did not keep his peace, he should resume her charters," and actually removed the courts of law to York. In distress, the city applied to queen Anne to mediate for them. Fortunately, Richard had no other favorite at that time than his peace-loving queen, "who was," say the ancient historians, "very precious to the nation, being continually doing some good to the people; and she deserved a much larger dower than the sum settled on her, which only amounted to four thousand five hundred pounds per annum."

The manner in which queen Anne pacified Richard, is preserved in a Latin chronicle poem, written by Richard Maydeston, an eye-witness of the scene; he was a priest attached to the court, and in favor with Richard and the queen.

Through the private intercession of the queen, the king consented to pass through the city, on his way from Shene to Westminster Palace, on the 29th of August.

"When they arrived at Southwark the queen assumed her crown; which she wore during the whole procession through London: it was blazing with various gems of the choicest kinds; her dress was likewise studded with precious stones, and she wore a rich carcanet about her neck; she appeared—according to the taste of Maydeston—'fairest among the fair,' and from the benign humility of her gracious countenance, the anxious citizens gathered hopes that she would succeed in pacifying the king. During the entry of the royal pair into the city, they rode at some distance from each other. At the first bridge-tower the king and queen were met by the lord mayor and other authorities, followed by a vast concourse of men, women, and children, every artificer bearing some symbol of his craft. Before the Southwark-bridge gate the king was presented with a pair of fair white steeds, trapped with gold cloth, figured with red and white, and hung full of silver bells. 'Steeds such as Cæsar might have been pleased to yoke to his car.'"

Queen Anne then arrived with her train, when the lord mayor Venner presented her with a small white palfrey, exquisitely trained, for her own riding. The lord mayor commenced a long speech with these words :

"O generous offspring of imperial blood, whom God hath destined worthily to sway the sceptre as consort of our king !"

He then proceeds to hint that mercy and not rigor best became the queenly station, and that gentle ladies had great influence with their loving lords; then entering into the merits of the palfrey, he commended its beauty, its docility, and the convenience of its ambling paces, and the magnificence of its purple housings. After the animal had been graciously accepted by the queen, she passed over the bridge and came to the bridge-portal on the city side : but some of her maids of honor, who were following her, in two wagons, or charrettes, were not quite so fortunate in their progress over the bridge.

Old London Bridge was, in the fourteenth century, and for some ages after, no such easy defile for a large influx of people to pass through : though not then encroached upon by houses and shops, it was encumbered by fortifications and barricades, which guarded the draw-bridge towers in the centre, and the bridge-gate towers at each end. In this instance the multitudes pouring out of the city, to get a view of the queen and her train, meeting the crowds following the royal procession, the throngs pressed on each other so tumultuously, that one of the charrettes containing the queen's ladies was overturned—lady rolled upon lady, all being sadly discomposed in the upset; and, what was worse, nothing could restrain the laughter of the rude plebeian artificers; at last the equipage was righted, the discomfited damsels replaced, and the charrette resumed its place in the procession. But such a reverse of horned caps did not happen without serious inconveniences to the wearers, as Maydeston very minutely particularizes.

As the king and queen passed through the city, the principal thoroughfares were hung with gold cloth and silver tissue, and tapestry of silk and gold. When they approached the conduit at Cheapside, red and white wine played from the spouts of a tower erected against it; the royal pair were served "with rosy wine smiling in golden cups," and an angel flew down in a cloud, and presented to the king, and then to the queen, rich gold circlets worth several hundred pounds. Another conduit of wine played at St. Paul's eastern gate, where was stationed a band of antique musical instruments, whose names alone will astound modern musical ears. There were persons playing on tympanies, monochords, cymbals, psalteries, and lyres; zambucas, citherns, situlas, horns, and viols. Our learned Latinist dwells with much unction on the symphonious chorus produced by these instruments, which, he says, "wrapt all hearers in a kind of stupor." No wonder!

At the monastery of St. Paul's the king and queen alighted from their steeds, and passed through the cathedral on foot, in order to pay their offerings at the holy sepulchre of St. Erkenwald. At the western gate they remounted their horses, and proceeded to the Ludgate. There, just above the river bridge,—which river, we beg to remind our readers, was that delicious stream, now called Fleet-ditch,—was perched "a celestial band of spirits, who saluted the royal personages, as they passed the Fleet-bridge, with enchanting singing, and sweet psalmody, making, withal, a pleasant fume by swinging incense-pots; they likewise scattered fragrant flowers on the king and queen as they severally passed the bridge."

At the Temple barrier, above the gate, was the representation of a desert, inhabited by all manner of animals, mixed with reptiles and monstrous worms, or, at least, by their resemblances; in the background was a forest; amidst the concourse of beasts, was seated the holy Baptist John, pointing with his finger to an Agnus Dei. After the king had halted to view this scene, his attention was struck by the figure of St. John, for whom he had a peculiar devotion, when an angel descended from above the wilderness, bearing in his hands a splendid gift, which was a tablet, studded with gems, "fit for any altar," with the crucifixion embossed thereon. The king took it in his hand and said, "Peace to this city; for the sake of Christ, his mother, and my patron St. John, I forgive every offence."

Then the king continued his progress towards his palace, and the queen arrived opposite to the desert and St. John, when lord mayor Venner presented her with another tablet, likewise representing the crucifixion. He commenced his speech with these words,—

"Illustrious daughter of imperial parents, Anne—a name in Hebrew

14

signifying grace, and which was borne by her who was the mother of
the mother of Christ,—mindful of your race and name, intercede for us
to the king; and as often as you see this tablet think of our city, and
speak in our favor."

Upon which the queen graciously accepted the dutiful offering of
the city, saying, with the emphatic brevity of a good wife, who knew
her influence, "Leave all to me."

By this time the king had arrived at his palace of Westminster, the
great hall of which was ornamented with hangings more splendid than
the pen can describe. Richard's throne was prepared upon the King's
Bench, which royal tribunal he ascended, sceptre in hand, and sat in
great majesty, when the queen and the rest of the procession entered
the hall.

The queen was followed by her maiden train. When she approached
the king, she knelt down at his feet, and so did all her ladies. The
king hastened to raise her, asking,

"What would Anna?—declare, and your request shall be granted."

The queen's answer is perhaps a fair specimen of the way in which
she obtained her empire over the weak but affectionate mind of Richard; more honeyed words than the following, female blandishment
could scarcely devise.

"Sweet," she replied, "my king, my spouse, my light, my life!
Sweet love, without whose life mine would be but death! Be pleased
to govern your citizens as a gracious lord. Consider, even to-day,
how munificent their treatment! What worship, what honor, what
splendid public duty, have they at a great cost paid to thee, revered
king! Like us, they are but mortal, and liable to frailty. Far from
thy memory, my king, my sweet love, be their offences, and for their
pardon I supplicate, kneeling thus lowly on the ground."

Then, after some mention of Brutus and Arthur, ancient kings of
Britain,—which no doubt are interpolated flourishes of good Master
Maydeston, the queen concludes her supplication, by requesting "that
the king would please to restore to these worthy and penitent plebeians
their ancient charters and liberties."

" Be satisfied, dearest wife," the king answered, "loth should we be
to deny thee any reasonable request of thine."

While Richard was preparing for a campaign in Ireland, which country had revolted from his authority, his departure was delayed by a terrible bereavement. This was the loss of his beloved partner. It is supposed she died of the pestilence that was then raging throughout Europe, as her decease was heralded by an illness of but a few hours. Froissart says, speaking of the occurrences in England, June, 1394— "At this period the lady Anne, queen of England, fell sick, to the infinite distress of king Richard and all her household. Her disorder increased so rapidly, that she departed this life at the feast of Whitsuntide, 1394. The king and all who loved her were greatly afflicted at her death. King Richard was inconsolable for her loss, as they mutually loved each other, having been married young. This queen left no issue, for she never bore a child."

ISABELLA OF VALOIS,

SURNAMED THE LITTLE QUEEN.

SECOND QUEEN OF RICHARD II.

THE union of Isabella of Valois with Richard II. presented an anomaly
to the people of England unprecedented in their annals.   They saw
with astonishment an infant, not nine summers old, sharing the throne
as the chosen queen-consort of a monarch who had reached his thirtieth
year.

Richard, whose principal error was attention to his own private feelings in preference to the public good, considered, that by the time this
little princess grew up, the lapse of years would have mellowed his grief
for the loved and lost Anne of Bohemia; he could not divorce his heart
from the memory of his late queen sufficiently to give her a successor
nearer his own age.

Isabella of Valois was the daughter of Charles VI. of France and
Isabeau of Bavaria, that queen of France afterwards so notorious for her
wickedness; but at the time of the marriage of Richard II. with her
little daughter, queen Isabeau was only distinguished for great beauty
and luxurious taste in dress and festivals.

The princess Isabella was precocious in intellect and stature, and
was every way worthy of fulfilling a queenly destiny.   Unlike her sisters, Michelle and Katherine, who were cruelly neglected in their infant
years, she was the darling of her parents and of the court of France.

Isabella is no mute on the biographical page; the words she uttered
have been chronicled; and though so young, both as the wife and
widow of an English king, research will show that her actions were of
some historical importance. She had been carefully educated, as she
proved when the English nobles waited upon her; for when the earl
marshal dropped upon his knee, saying,—

" 'Madam, if it please God, you shall be our lady and queen.'

" She replied instantly, and without any one prompting her, 'Sir, if
it please God and my lord and father, that I be queen of England, I
shall be well pleased thereat, for I have been told I shall then be a
great lady.'

" She made the earl marshal rise, and taking him by the hand, led
him to queen Isabeau, her mother, who was much pleased at her answer,
as were all who heard it. The appearance and manners of this young
princess were very agreeable to the English ambassadors, and they
thought among themselves she would be a lady of high honor and
worth."

About this time the king of France sent to England the count St.
Pol, who had married Richard's half-sister, Maud Holland, surnamed the
Fair. King Richard promised his brother-in-law that he would come to
Calais, and have an interview with the king of France, when his bride
was to be delivered to him; and if a peace could not be agreed upon, a
truce for thirty or forty years was to be established.

" At 11 o'clock of the Saturday morning, the feast of St. Simon and
St. Jude, the king of England, attended by his uncles and nobles, waited
on the king of France in his tent. Dinner-tables were laid out; that
for the kings was very handsome, and the sideboard was covered with
magnificent plate. The two kings were seated by themselves, the king
of France at the top of the table, and the king of England below him,
at a good distance from each other.

When dinner was over, which lasted not long, the cloth was removed,
the tables carried away, and wine and spices brought. After this the
young bride entered the tent, attended by a great number of ladies and
damsels. King Charles led her by the hand, and gave her to the king
of England, who immediately rose and took his leave. The little queen
was placed in a very rich litter, which had been prepared for her; but

of all the French ladies who were there, only the lady de Courcy went with her, for there were many of the principal ladies of England in presence.

On the Tuesday, which was All Saints' day, the king of England was married by the archbishop of Canterbury in the church of St. Nicholas, of Calais, to the lady Isabella of France. Great was the feasting on the occasion; and the heralds and minstrels were so liberally paid, that they were satisfied.

Several authors declare that young Isabella was crowned at Westminster with great magnificence, and there actually exist, in the Fœdera, a summons for her coronation on Epiphany Sunday, 1397.

Windsor was the chief residence of the royal child, who was caлed queen-consort of England. Here her education proceeded, under the superintendence of the second daughter of Ingelram de Courcy; and here the king, whose feminine beauty of features and complexion somewhat qualified the disparity of years between a man of thirty and a girl of ten, behaved to his young wife with such winning attention, that she retained a tender remembrance of him long after he was hurried to prison and the grave. His visits occasioned her a cessation from the routine of education; while his gay temper, his musical accomplishments, his splendor of dress, and softness of manner to females, made her royal husband exceedingly beloved by the young heart of Isabella.

While Richard's affairs remained in a feverish and unsettled state, the English court was thrown into consternation by the death of the heir-presumptive of the kingdom, Roger Mortimer, who was at that time lord-deputy of Ireland. There was a strong attachment between Richard and his chivalric heir; the king passionately bewailed him, and resolved he make an expedition to Ireland, to quell the rebellion that ensued on the death of his viceroy.

He tarried some hours at Windsor Castle, on his road to the western coast, in order to bid his young queen farewell before he departed for Ireland. Although only eleven years of age, Isabella had grown tall and very lovely; she was rapidly assuming a womanly appearance. The king seemed greatly struck with the improvement in her person, and the progress she had made in her education. He treated her with the utmost deference; and, if the chronicles of her country are to be believed, he entirely won her young heart at this interview.

The scene of Richard's parting from Isabella was Windsor church. He had previously assisted at a solemn mass, and indulged his musical tastes by chanting a collect; he likewise made a rich offering. On leaving the church, he partook of wine and comforts at the door, with his little consort, then lifting her up in his arms he kissed her repeatedly, saying, "Adieu, madame, adieu, till we meet again."

The king immediately commenced his march to Bristol, and embarked on his ill-timed expedition.

The landing of Henry of Bolingbroke at Ravenspur, during Richard's absence, had an immediate effect on the destination of the little queen Isabella; the regent York hurried her, from the castle of Windsor, to the still stronger fortress of Wallingford, where she remained while England was lost by her royal lord, and won by his rival, Henry of Bolingbroke.

The young queen found herself in the power of the usurper almost simultaneously with her unfortunate husband. Directly the news arrived that Richard had surrendered himself, the garrisons of the royal castles of Windsor and Wallingford yielded to Henry of Bolingbroke. Tradition declares, that the young Isabella met her luckless husband on the road, during his sad pilgrimage towards the metropolis, as a captive to Henry, and that their meeting and parting were tender and heartbreaking.

It is asserted by all authors of that day, that the heart of the young Isabella was devoted to Richard; the chroniclers of her own country especially declare, "that he had behaved so amiably to her that she loved him entirely." While, by a cruel policy, her youthful mind was torn with the pangs of suspense and the pain of parting from her native attendants, Richard was conveyed from Shene by night, and lodged secretly in the Tower, with such of his friends and ministers as were peculiarly obnoxious to the Londoners.

The young queen was removed to Sunning Hill; there she was kept a state prisoner, and sedulously misinformed regarding the events that had befallen her husband. The last hopes of king Richard ended in despair, when his cousin Aumerle had yielded the loyal city of Bristol, and his brother-in-law Huntingdon gave up Calais, and swore fealty to Henry IV.

Richard's doom was now sealed. He was hurried from the Tower to Pontefract Castle; meantime, the confederate lords flew to arms, and, dressing up king Richard's chaplain, Maudelain, in royal robes, proclaimed that the deposed king had escaped from his jailers.

Thus was queen Isabella left a widow in her thirteenth year; the death of her royal lord was concealed from her a considerable time; but she learned the murderous manner of it soon enough, to reject with horror all offers of union with the heir of Lancaster. Young as she was, Isabella gave proofs of a resolute and decisive character; traits of firm and faithful affection were shown by this youthful queen, which captivated the minds of the English, and caused her to be made the heroine of many an historical ballad,—a species of literature that the people of the land much delighted in at that time.

The young widow remained in a state of captivity at Havering Bower, while her royal father in France was laboring under a long and dolorous fit of insanity; brought on by anxiety for his daughter's fate. The French council of regency demanded the immediate restoration of the young queen, but Henry IV. would not hear of it, answering, "that she should reside in England like other queen-dowagers, in great honor, on her dower; and that if she had unluckily lost a husband, she should be provided with another forthwith, who would be young and handsome, and every way deserving of her love. Richard of Bordeaux was too old for her, but the person now offered was suitable in every respect; being no other than the prince of Wales."

It seems strange that Isabella, who had expressed such infant pride in being queen of England, should give up voluntarily all prospect of enjoying that station with a youthful hero, whose age was so suitable to her own; yet so it was. But she was inflexible in her rejection of the gallant Henry of Monmouth, and "mourned her murdered husband in a manner exceedingly touching, as all who approached her, French or English, bore witness." Her refusal would have been of little avail, if her family and country had not seen the matter in the same light. In

15

reply to Henry IV.'s proposition, the French regency declared "that during the grievous illness of their lord king Charles, they could not give away his eldest daughter without his consent." Therefore, months passed away, and the maiden queen-dowager still continued a mourning widow, in the bowers of Havering. It is recorded that king Henry and his gallant heir did, in that interval, all in their power to win her constant heart from the memory of Richard, but in vain. She was just of the age to captivate the fancy of an ardent young prince like Henry of Monmouth; nor can there exist a doubt, by the extreme pertinacity with which he wooed the widow of his cousin, that she was beloved by him.

When Charles VI. recovered his senses, he sent the .ount d'Albret to inquire into the situation of Isabella. King Henry and his council were at Eltham, where the French ambassador was splendidly entertained by him.

The council of Henry IV. meantime anxiously deliberated on the destination of the young queen. It came at last to the decision, that Isabella, being of tender age, had no right to claim revenue as queendowager of England; but that, as no accommodation could be effected by the marriage with the prince of Wales, she ought to be restored to her friends directly, with all the jewels and paraphernalia that she brought with her.

July was far advanced before the maiden widow of Richard II. was restored to her parents; during which time Henry IV. and his son tried every means in their power to shake her childish constancy to the memory of Richard. But her "steady aversion," as Monstrelet calls her refusal, remained the same; the situation of this child was extraordinary, and her virtuous firmness, more probable in a royal heroine of twenty-eight than in one who had seen little more than half as many summers. At last, the usurper resolved to restore the young widow to France, but refused to return her dowry, saying, that as a great favor he would agree to deduct its amount from the sum total that France still owed England, for the ransom of king John.

Leulinghen, a town between Boulogne and Calais, a sort of frontier ground of the English territory, was the spot appointed for the restoration of Isabella to her uncle of Burgundy. "It was on the 26th of July, 1402, when Sir Thomas Percy, with streaming tears, took the young queen by the arm, and delivered her with good grace into the hands of Waleran count St. Pol, surnamed the Righteous, and received certain letters of quittance for her from the French. In these the English commissioners declared, that the young queen was just as she had been received, and Percy offered to fight à l'outrance any one who should assert the contrary." To do the French justice, they could not have welcomed back their young princess royal with more enthusiasm and loyalty, if she had been dowered with all the wealth of England, instead of returning destitute, and plundered of all but her beauty and honor.

The betrothment of Isabella to her youthful cousin took place at Compiegne, where her mother, queen Isabeau, met the duke of Orleans and his son. Magnificent fêtes took place at the ceremony, consisting of "banquets, dancings, jousts, and other jollities." But the bride wept bitterly while her hand was pledged to a bridegroom so much younger than herself; the court charitably declared that her tears flowed on account of her losing the title of queen of England; but the heart of the fair young widow had been too severely schooled in adversity to mourn over a mere empty name. Her thoughts were on king Richard.

The husband of Isabella became duke of Orleans in 1407, when his father was atrociously murdered in the Rue Barbette, by his kinsman, the duke of Burgundy.

The following year Isabella was married to her cousin: the previous ceremony had been only betrothment. The elegant and precocious mind of this prince soon made the difference of a few years between his age and that of his bride forgotten. Isabella loved her husband entirely; he was the pride of his country, both in mind and person. He was that celebrated poet duke of Orleans, whose beautiful lyrics are still reckoned among the classics of France. Just as Isabella seemed to have attained the height of human felicity, adored by the most accomplished prince in Europe, beloved by his family, and with no present alloy in her cup of happiness, death claimed her as his prey in the bloom of her

life. She expired at the castle of Blois, in her twenty-second year, a
few hours after the birth of her infant child, Sept. 13th, 1410. Her
husband's grief amounted to frenzy; but after her infant was brought
to him by her attendants, he shed tears, and became calmer while
caressing it.

JOANNA OF NAVARRE,

QUEEN OF HENRY IV.

JOANNA was the second daughter of a prince of evil repute, Charles d'Albret, king of Navarre, surnamed the Bad, whose mother was the only child of Louis X. of France, by Clemence of Hungary; and, being barred by the Salique law from the throne of France, espoused the count of Evreux, and transmitted to her son the petty kingdom of Navarre. By this illustrious maternal descent, the father of Joanna was the representative of the elder line of St. Louis. Her mother was Jane, the daughter of the gallant and unfortunate John, king of France. Joanna was born about the year 1370.

In the year 1386, a marriage was negotiated between Joanna and John de Montfort, duke of Bretagne, surnamed the Valiant. This prince, who was in the decline of life, had already been twice married. On the death of his last duchess without surviving issue, the dukes of Berri and Burgundy, fearing the duke would contract another English alliance, proposed their niece, Joanna of Navarre, to him for a wife. The lady Jane of Navarre, Joanna's aunt, had married, seven years previously, the viscount de Rohan, a vassal and kinsman of the duke of Bretagne, and it was through the agency of this lady that the marriage between her new sovereign and her youthful niece was brought about.

That this political union was, notwithstanding the disparity of years and the violent temper of the duke, agreeable to the bride, there is full

evidence in the grateful remembrance which Joanna retained of the
good offices of her aunt on this occasion, long after the nuptial tie
between her and her mature lord had been dissolved by death, and
she had entered into matrimonial engagements with Henry IV. of
England.

In the year 1388, Joanna brought an heir to Bretagne, who was baptized Pierre, but the duke afterwards changed his name to John. This
much-desired event was soon followed by the birth of the princess Marie.
The duchess, whose children were born in very quick succession, was
on the eve of her third confinement, when her lord's secret treaties with
his old friend and brother-in-law, Richard II. of England, drew from the
regents of France very stern remonstrances. An embassy extraordinary, headed by no less a person than the duc de Berri, was sent by the
council to complain of his intelligence with the enemies of France, and
to require him to renew his oath of allegiance as a vassal peer of that
realm.

So far, however, was the duke of Bretagne from being impressed
with the high rank and importance of these envoys, that, suspecting
they intended to appeal to his nobles against his present line of conduct,
he determined, in violation of those considerations which in all ages
have rendered the persons of ambassadors sacred, to arrest them all, and
keep them as hostages till he had made his own terms with France. Le
Moine de St. Denis, a contemporary historian, declares, " he heard this
from the very lips of the ambassadors, who related to him the peril from
which they escaped, through the prudence of Joanna." Fortunately for
all parties, it happened that her young brother, Pierre of Navarre, was
at the court of Nantes, and, being apprised of the duke's design, hastened to Joanna, whom he found at her toilet, and confided to her the
alarming project then in agitation.

Joanna, who was then in hourly expectation of the birth of her
fourth child, immediately perceived the dreadful consequences that
would result from such an unheard-of outrage. She took her infants in
her arms, and flew to the duke's apartments, half-dressed as she was,
with her hair loose and dishevelled, and throwing herself at his feet,
bathed in tears, conjured him, " for the sake of those tender pledges of
their mutual love, to abandon the rash design that passion had inspired,

which, if persisted in, must involve himself and all belonging to him in utter ruin."

The duke, who had kept his design a secret from his wife, was surprised at the manner of her address. After an agitated pause, he said—"Lady, how you came by your information, I know not; but, rather than be the cause of such distress to you, I will revoke my order." Joanna then prevailed on him to meet the ambassadors in the cathedral the next day, and afterwards to accompany them to Tours, where the king of France gave him a gracious reception, and induced him to renew his homage, by promising to unite his second daughter Joanna of France with the heir of Bretagne.

The duke of Bretagne undertook a voyage to England, in 1398, to induce king Richard to restore to him the earldom of Richmond, which had been granted by Richard II. to his first queen, Anne of Bohemia, and, after her death, to Jane of Bretagne, the sister of the duke, who was married to Raoul Basset, an English knight.

It was in the following year that Joanna first became acquainted with her second husband, Henry of Bolingbroke, during the period of his banishment from his native land. Henry was not only one of the most accomplished warriors and statesmen of the age in which he lived, but remarkable for his fine person and graceful manners.

The assistance rendered by the duke of Bretagne to the future husband of his consort, was the last important action of his life. He was, at that time, in declining health, and had once more involved himself in disputes with Clisson and his party.

On the 1st of November, 1399, the duke breathed his last; and Joanna having been appointed by him as regent for their eldest son, the young duke, with the entire care of his person, assumed the reins of government in his name.

When Joanna had exercised the sovereign authority as regent for her son a year and a half, the young duke, accompanied by her, made his solemn entrance into Rennes, March 22, 1401, and took the oaths in the presence of his prelates and nobles, having entered his twelfth year.

Joanna put her son in possession of the duchy at so tender an age, as a preliminary to her union with Henry IV., who had been in a great measure indebted to the good offices of her late lord for his elevation to the throne of England. Henry had been for some years a widower; his first wife was Mary de Bohun, the co-heiress of the earl of Hereford, lord-constable of England.

Joanna, to whom the proposal of a union with this prince appears to have been peculiarly agreeable, being aware that a serious obstacle existed on the important subject of religion, kept the affair a profound secret, till she could obtain from the pope of Avignon a general dispensation to marry any one whom she pleased, within the fourth degree of consanguinity, without naming the person; Henry (who had been educated in Wickliffite principles) being at that time attached to the party of Boniface, the pope of Rome, or the anti-pope, as he was styled by those who denied his authority.

Joanna's agents negotiated this difficult arrangement so adroitly, that the bull was executed, according to her desire, March 20, 1402, without the slightest suspicion being entertained by the orthodox court of Avignon, that the schismatic king of England was the mysterious person, within the forbidden degrees of consanguinity, whom Benedict had so obligingly granted the duchess-dowager of Bretagne liberty to espouse.

When Joanna had thus outwitted her pope, she despatched a trusty squire of her household, named Antoine Riczi, to conclude her treaty of marriage with king Henry. After the articles of this matrimonial alliance were signed, Joanna and her royal bridegroom were espoused, by procuration, at the palace of Eltham, on the third day of April, 1402, Antoine Riczi acting as the proxy of the bride. What motive could have induced the lovely widow of John the Valiant of Bretagne to choose a male representative on this interesting occasion, it is difficult to say; but it is certain that Henry promised to take his august *fiancée* to wife in the person of the said Antoine Riczi, to whom he plighted his nuptial troth, and on his finger he placed the bridal ring. This act was performed with great solemnity in the presence of the archbishop of Canterbury, the king's half-brothers, the Beaufort princes, the earl of Worcester, lord-chamberlain of England, and other officers of state.

Great preparations were made by the citizens of London to meet and welcome the newly-married consort of the sovereign of their choice, on her approach to the metropolis.

There is an exquisite drawing in a contemporary manuscript, illustrative of Joanna's coronation, which took place, February 26th, 1403, not quite three weeks after her bridal. She is there represented as a very majestic and graceful woman, in the meridian glory of her days, with a form of the most symmetrical proportions, and a countenance of equal beauty. Her attitude is that of easy dignity. She is depicted in her coronation robes, which are of a peculiarly elegant form. Her dalmatica differs little in fashion from that worn by our sovereign lady queen Victoria, at her inauguration. It partially displays her throat and bust, and is closed at the breast with a rich cordon and tassels. The mantle has apertures through which the arms are seen; they are bare, and very finely moulded. She is enthroned, not by the side of her royal husband, but with the same ceremonial honors that are paid to a queen-regnant, in a chair of state placed singly under a rich canopy, emblazoned, and elevated on a very high platform, of an hexagonal shape, approached on every side by six steps. Two archbishops have just crowned her, and are still supporting the royal diadem on her head. Her hair falls in rich curls on her bosom. In her right hand she holds a sceptre, and in her left an orb surmounted by a cross—a very unusual attribute for a queen-consort, as it is a symbol of sovereignty, and could only have been allowed to queen Joanna as a very especial mark of her royal bridegroom's favor.

In this picture, a peeress in her coronet and robes of state, probably occupying the office of mistress-of-the-robes, stands next the person of the queen, on her right hand, and just behind her are seen a group of noble maidens wearing wreaths of roses, like the train-bearers of her majesty queen Victoria; affording a curious but probably forgotten historical testimony, that such was the costume prescribed anciently, by the sumptuary regulations for the courtly demoiselles, who were appointed to the honor of bearing a queen of England's train at her coronation.

Joanna of Navarre was the first widow, since the Norman conquest, who wore the crown-matrimonial of England. She was, as we have seen, the mother of a large family. Her age, at the period of her second nuptials, must have been about three-and-thirty; and if past the morning freshness of her charms, her personal attractions were still very con-

16

siderable. Her monumental effigy represents her as a model of feminine loveliness. Her exemplary conduct as the wife of the most irascible prince in Christendom, and the excellence of her government as regent for her eldest son, had afforded unquestionable evidence of the prudence and wisdom of this princess; and she was in possession of a very fine dower; yet the marriage was never popular in England.

The bridal festivities of Henry IV. and his new queen were soon interrupted, by the news of a descent of the French, on the Isle of Wight; but the inhabitants compelled the invaders to retire to their ships with dishonor.

Notwithstanding her unpopularity with the English, Joanna took infinite pains to promote a good understanding between her husband and the duke her son. Henry, in his letters to the duke of Bretagne, May 1407, addresses him as "his dearest son," and expresses "his earnest wish, on account of the close tie existing between them through his dearest consort, that peace and amity might be established to prevent the effusion of Christian blood." The duke in reply says, "As our dearest mother, the queen of England, has several times signified her wish that all good friendship should subsist between our very redoubted lord and father, Henry king of England, and lord of Ireland, her lord and spouse, on one part, and ourselves on the other, we desire to enter into an amicable treaty."

Accordingly, a truce between England and Bretagne was, through the mediation of Joanna, proclaimed on the 13th of September, 1407. The town of Hereford was added to the queen's dower by king Henry the same year; and she was, with his sons, the prince of Wales, Thomas, John, and Humphrey, recommended by him to the parliament for further pecuniary grants.

An interesting proof of Joanna's respect for the memory of her first lord, the husband of her youth and the father of her children, is to be found in one of the royal briefs in the Fœdera, dated February 24th, 1408, in which king Henry says, "At the request of our dearest consort, an alabaster tomb has been made for the defunct duke of Bretagne, formerly her husband, to be conveyed in the barge of St. Nicholas of Nantes to Bretagne, with three of our English lieges, the same who made the tomb—viz: Thomas Colyn, Thomas Holewell, and Thomas

Poppeham, to place the said tomb in the church of Nantes, John Guye harde, the master of the said barge, and ten mariners of Bretagne; and the said barge is to be considered by the English merchants under our especial protection."

Avarice was the besetting sin of Joanna of Navarre; and this sordid propensity probably originated from the pressure of pecuniary cares with which she had had to contend as princess of Navarre, as duchess of Bretagne, and during the first years of her marriage with king Henry. Her conduct as a step-mother appears to have been conciliating. Even when the wild and profligate conduct of the heir of England had estranged him from his father's councils and affections, such confidential feelings subsisted between young Henry and Joanna, that he employed her influence for the purpose of obtaining the king's consent to the marriage of the young earl of March, at that time ward to the prince.

Henry IV., at that time sinking under a complication of infirmities, was probably indebted to the cherishing care of his consort for all the comfort he was capable of enjoying in life; and Joanna, who had learned so well how to adapt herself, while in early youth, to the wayward humors of her first husband (the most quarrelsome prince in Europe), was doubtless an adept in the art of pleasing, and of governing without appearing to do so.

Henry expired on St. Cuthbert's day, March 19th, 1413. He was buried by the side of Edward the Black Prince, with great pomp and state, Henry V. and all his nobility being present, upon Trinity Sunday next following the day of his death.

In the first years of her widowhood, queen Joanna received every mark of attention and respect from the new king, Henry V., who was anxious to avail himself of her good offices with her son, the duke of Bretagne, in order to secure the alliance of that prince in his projected wars with France. Henry V., in his letters and treaties, always styles the duke of Bretagne his dearest brother, and the duke reciprocates the title when addressing him. Joanna certainly exerted her influence with her son, in order to induce him to enter into amicable arrangements with England.

According to some historians, Joanna was intrusted by her royal step-son with a share in the government, when he undertook his expedition against France.

The same day that Henry quitted the metropolis, June 18th, after having been in solemn procession to St. Paul's with the lord-mayor and corporation of the city of London, to offer his prayers and oblations for the success of his expedition, he returned to Westminster, for the purpose of taking a personal leave of queen Joanna.

Whosoever might exult in the national triumph of Agincourt, Joanna had little cause for joy. The husband of her eldest daughter, the gallant duke of Alençon, who clove king Henry's jewelled coronal with his battle-axe in the *mêlée*, was there slain. Her brother, Charles of Navarre, the constable of France, died of his wounds the following day; and Arthur, her young gallant son, was a captive. No trifling tax must the widowed queen have paid for greatness, when, instead of putting on her mourning weeds, and indulging in the natural grief of a fond mother's heart, for these family calamities, she was called upon to assume the glittering trappings of state, and to take the leading part in a public pageant of rejoicing. Till this latter duty was performed, as befitted the queen of England, she forbore to weep, and to make lamentation for the dead; or to bewail the captivity of him, who was held a prisoner in the train of the royal victor.

The trials of Joanna only commenced with the battle of Agincourt, for she had to endure much maternal anxiety as to the future position of her eldest son, the reigning duke of Bretagne, with whose temporizing conduct Henry V. was greatly exasperated; and she had to perform the hard task of welcoming, with deceitful smiles and congratulations, the haughty victor, who had wrought her house such woe, and who was the arbiter of her son Arthur's fate. Arthur of Bretagne, as earl of Richmond, was Henry's subject, and, by bearing arms against him at Agincourt, had violated his liegeman's oath, and stood in a very different position with his royal step-brother, from the other prisoners. Well was it for him, considering the vindictive temper of Henry V., that the queen had in former times laid that prince under obligations, by assisting him, in time of need, with pecuniary aid. The first interview between Joanna and her captive son is, perhaps one of the most touching passages in history. They had not seen each other since 1404, when

Arthur, as a boy, visited the court of England, to receive the investiture of the earldom of Richmond from his royal step-father, Henry IV., twelve years before. Joanna, anxious to ascertain whether he retained any remembrance of her person (which, perhaps, she felt was faded by years of anxious tendance on a dusband sick alike in body and mind), yet, fondly hoping that maternal instinct would lead him to his mother's arms, placed one of her ladies in her chair of state, and retired among her attendants, two of whom stood before her, while she watched what would follow. Arthur, as might be expected, took the queen's representative for his mother; she supported the character for some time, and desired him to pay his compliments to her ladies. When, in turn, he came to Joanna, her heart betrayed her, and she exclaimed, "Unhappy son, do you not know me?" The call of nature was felt; both mother and son burst into tears. They then embraced with great tenderness, and she gave him a thousand nobles, which the princely youth distributed among his fellow-prisoners, and his guards, together with some apparel. But, after this interview, Henry V. prevented all communication between the mother and her son.

Her favorite residence was the sylvan retreat of Havering Bower. She also kept her state sometimes at Langley, where her retirement was enlivened occasionally by shows, as the rude theatrical entertainments of the fifteenth century were designated. We learn, from a contemporary chronicle, that in the ninth year of Henry VI. a grievous and terrible fire took place, at the manor of the lady queen Joanna, at Langley, in which there was great destruction of the buildings, furniture, gold and silver plate, and household stuff. These disasters happened "through the want of care, and drowsiness, of a player, and the heedless keeping of a candle."

This fire is the last event of any importance that befell the royal widow. Joanna was treated with all proper consideration, by the grandson of her deceased consort, the young king Henry VI. While residing at her palace of Langley, 1437, she was honored with a new-year's gift, from this amiable prince, as a token of his respect. This was a tablet of gold, garnished with four balass rubies, eight pearls, and in the midst a great sapphire. The tablet had been formerly presented to the young king, by my lady of Gloucester; whether by Jacqueline or Eleanora Cobham, is left doubtful.

In the July following, Joanna died at Havering Bower. This event is thus quaintly noted by the chronicle of London, a contemporary record :—

"This same year, 9th of July, died queen Jane, king Henry IV.'s wife. Also the same year died all the lions in the Tower, the which was nought seen in no man's time before out of mind."

KATHERINE OF VALOIS,

SURNAMED THE FAIR,

CONSORT OF HENRY V.

KATHERINE OF VALOIS was a babe in the cradle when Henry V., as prince of Wales, became an unsuccessful suitor for the hand of her eldest sister Isabella, the young widow of Richard II.

Katherine was the youngest child of Charles VI., king of France, and his queen, Isabeau of Bavaria; she was born at a period when her father's health and her mother's reputation were both in evil plight. She first saw the light, Oct. 27, 1401, at the Hôtel de St. Paul, in Paris, a palace which was used during the reign of Charles VI. as a residence of retirement for the royal family, when health required them to lead a life of more domestic privacy than was possible at the king's royal court of the Louvre. The young princess was reared at the Hôtel de St. Paul, and there did her unfortunate sire, Charles VI., spend the long agonizing intervals of his aberrations from reason, during which the infancy of his little daughter was exposed to hardships such as seldom fall to the lot of the poorest cottager.

Queen Isabeau joined with the king's brother, the duke of Orleans, in pilfering the revenues of the royal household, and to such a degree did this wicked woman carry her rapacity, as to leave her little children without the means of supporting life. These royal infants were shut up in the Hôtel de St. Paul, wholly neglected by their vile mother; the

princess Michelle being then only five years old, and the princess Katherine little more than three. The poor children, says their contemporary
chroniclers, were in a piteous state, nearly starved and loathsome with
dirt, having no change of clothes, or even of linen. The whole sustenance they had was from the inferior attendants who had not deserted
the place, all the servants of the royal family being left by the profli
gate and reckless Isabeau without food or wages.

The state of Katherine's hapless father, who occupied a part of the
palace of St. Paul, was still more deplorable; but he was unconscious
of his misery, till one day he suddenly regained his senses, and observed
the disarray and neglect around him. The instant Charles VI. recovered
from his attack of delirium, he appears to have resumed his royal func-
tions, without any intermediate time of convalescence. The consequence
was, that directly the news was brought to the queen that her husband
spoke and looked composedly, a sense of her guilt caused her to de-
camp with Louis of Orleans to Milan.

After the duke of Burgundy had caused the assassination of Orleans
in the streets of Paris, the conduct of queen Isabeau became so infamous that she was imprisoned at Tours; and her daughter Katherine (the
only one of the princesses who was not betrothed or consecrated) was
taken from her. There is reason to believe that Katherine was brought
up in the convent of Poissy, where her sister Marie took the veil.

From time to time Henry IV. made attempts to obtain a wife for his
heir. At last, both the prince and his father seemed to have determined on
obtaining the hand of the fair Katherine, the youngest of the princesses
of France, and a private mission was confided to Edward, duke of
York, to demand her in marriage for the prince of Wales. York was
absent, on this errand, at the time of the death of Henry IV.

After the death of his royal sire, Henry V. did not establish himself
in the sovereignty without a short but fierce civil war, which partly assumed a religious character, and partly was founded on the report that
king Richard II. was alive, and ready to claim his own.

When these agitations had subsided, Henry V. renewed his application for the hand of the princess Katherine. At the same time he demanded with her an enormous dowry.

Charles VI. would have given Katherine to Henry with a dowry of

450,000 crowns. This the English hero refused with disdain. Henry desired no better than a feasible excuse to invade France; he therefore resolved to win Katherine the Fair at the point of the sword, together with all the gold and provinces he demanded with her hand.

Henry's first care was to sell or pawn all the valuables he possessed, in order to raise funds for the French expedition, on which he had set his ambitious mind. Extended empire, rich plunder, and the hand of the beautiful young Katherine of Valois, were the attainments on which all the energies of his ardent character were centred.

From Southampton, Henry V. sent Antelope, his poursuivant-of-arms, with a letter to Katherine's father, dated from that port, to show the reality of his intentions of invasion. He demanded the English provinces and the hand of Katherine, otherwise he would take them by force. The king of France replied, "If that was his mind, he would do his best to receive him; but as to the marriage, he thought it would be a strange way of wooing Katherine, covered with the blood of her countrymen."

Henry landed at the mouth of the Seine, three miles from Harfleur, and, after tremendous slaughter on both sides, took that strong fort of the Seine by storm, in the beginning of October. Notwithstanding this success, disease and early winter brought Henry into a dangerous predicament, till the English Lion turned at bay at Agincourt, and finished the brief and late campaign with one of those victories which shed an everlasting glory on the annals of England—

> "So glared he when, at Agincourt, in wrath he turned at bay,
> And crushed and torn beneath his paws the princely hunters lay."
>
> MACAULAY.

The dreadful panic into which this victory threw France, and the numbers of her nobles and princes slain and taken prisoners, were the chief advantages Henry gained by it.

Meantime Katherine and her family were thrown into the utmost consternation by the victories of this lion-like wooer. Queen Isabeau, taking advantage of all this confusion, escaped from her palace-restraint at Tours; and, joining with the duke of Burgundy, not only gained

17

great power, as regent for her distracted consort, but obtained the control of her beautiful daughter.

However the queen might have neglected Katherine when an infant,
she was no sooner restored to her as a lovely young woman than she
obtained prodigious influence over her. The maternal feelings of Isabeau seemed centred on Katherine alone, to the unjust exclusion of her
other children. Katherine had very early set her mind on being queen
of England, and it will soon be shown how completely Isabeau entered
into all her daughter's wishes.

In order to fulfil this object, when it was found that Rouen could no
longer sustain its long dolorous siege, Isabeau sent ambassadors with
Katherine's picture, to ask Henry "whether so beautiful a princess required such a great dowry as he demanded with her?" The ambassadors declared they found Henry at Rouen, "proud as a lion;" that he
gazed long and earnestly on the portrait of Katherine, acknowledged
that it was surpassingly fair, but refused to abate a particle of his exorbitant demands.

The close of the year 1418 saw the fall of the wretched city of Rouen,
and increased the despair of Katherine's country and family. Queen
Isabeau resolved that, as the picture of the princess had not succeeded
in mollifying the proud heart of the conqueror, she would try what the
personal charms of her Katherine could effect. A truce was obtained
with Henry V., who had now pushed his conquests as far as Melun.
The poor distracted king of France, with the queen Isabeau and her
beautiful daughter Katherine, in a richly ornamented barge, came to
Pontoise, in hopes of effecting an amicable arrangement with the conqueror. At Pontoise a large inclosure was made with planks, within
which the conferences were to be carried on ; it was also surrounded by
a deep ditch, having on one side the bank of the Seine. There were
several entrances well secured by three barriers, and tents and pavilions,
made of blue and green velvet, worked with gold, were pitched for
repose and refreshment.

Notwithstanding the king of France was very much indisposed, he
and queen Isabeau, the princess, the duke of Burgundy, and his council,
escorted by a thousand combatants, went to the place of conference near
Melun, and entered the tents without the inclosure.

Then the king of England arrived, attended by his brothers, the dukes of Clarence and Gloucester, and a thousand men-at-arms. He entered the tent pitched for him, and when they were about to commence the conference, the queen on the right hand, followed by the lady Katherine, entered the inclosure. At the same time the king of England, with his brothers and council, arrived on this neutral ground by another barrier, and with a most respectful obeisance met and saluted queen Isabeau; and then king Henry not only kissed her, but the lady Katherine.

They entered the tent pitched for the conference, king Henry leading queen Isabeau. Henry seated himself opposite to Katherine, and gazed at her most intently, while the earl of Warwick was making a long harangue in French, which he spoke very well. After they had remained some long time in conference, they separated, taking the most respectful leave of each other.

This barrier scene is evidently meant to be depicted by the celebrated ancient painting once in the possession of Horace Walpole. Henry VII. had this picture painted for his chapel at Shene, and, as the well-known likeness of Henry V. is striking, there is reason to believe the same care was taken in portraying the features of Katherine of Valois. The oval shape of her face, her clear ivory complexion, and large dark eyes, coincide with the descriptions of the old French chroniclers. Katherine's chin is too short, or the face would be perfect; the expression is inane and passionless. She wears an arched crown, and a species of veil, trimmed at each side with ermine, and reaching to the shoulders. Her mantle, of the regal form, is worn over a close gown, tight to the throat; a strap of ermine passes down the front, and is studded with jewels.

Three weeks afterwards, all the royal personages, with the exception of the lady Katherine, met for another conference, at the barrier-ground of Pontoise. As the view of Katherine's beauty had not induced Henry to lower his demands, queen Isabeau resolved that the English conqueror should see her no more. Henry was exceedingly discontented at this arrangement. "For," says Monstrelet, "the princess was very handsome, and had most engaging manners, and it was plainly to be seen that king Henry was desperately in love with her." Yet the second conference ended, without the least abatement in his exorbitant requisitions.

After the English hero had waited unavailingly a few days, in hopes of being courted by the family of his beloved, he impatiently demanded a third interview, meaning to modify his demands;—when lo! to his infinite displeasure, when he arrived at Pontoise, he found the tents struck, the barriers pulled down, and the pales that marked out the neutral ground taken away—every thing showing that the marriage-treaty was supposed to be ended.   Henry V. was infuriated at the sight, and in his transports betrayed how much he had become enamored of Katherine.   He turned angrily to the duke of Burgundy, who was the only person belonging to the royal family of France attending the conference, and said abruptly—

" ' Fair cousin, we wish you to know that we *will* have the daughter of your king, or we will drive him and you out of his kingdom.'   The duke replied, 'Sire, you are pleased to say so; but, before you have succeeded in driving my lord and me out of this kingdom, I make no doubt that you will be heartily tired.'   Many hard words passed, too tedious to report, and, taking leave of each other, they separated, and each went his way."

Before two years had elapsed, the family of Katherine were forced by dire distress to sue for the renewal of the marriage-treaty.   Henry's career of conquest proceeded with terrific rapidity; he made himself master of most of the towns between Normandy and the French capital, while his brother, the duke of Clarence, and his friend, the earl of March, had already thundered at the gates of Paris.   Henry was requested to name his own terms of pacification.   He haughtily replied, "that he had been deceived and baffled so many times, that he would treat with no one but the princess Katherine herself, whose innocency, he was sure, would not try to deceive him."

Notice of this speech being immediately conveyed to queen Isabeau, she made the bishop of Arras return instantly, to tell king Henry "that if he would come to Troyes, Katherine should espouse him there; and that as her inheritance he should have the crown of France after the death of king Charles;" and to gain the more credit, the bishop of Arras secretly delivered to the king a love-letter, written by the fair hand of Katherine herself, so full of sweetness, that Henry V. considered his happiness as certain.

As soon as these terms were agreed upon, Henry, accompanied by his brothers, Clarence and Gloucester, with sixteen hundred combatants, mostly archers, advanced to Troyes, where he arrived on the 20th of May, 1420. The new duke of Burgundy, clothed in the deepest mourning for his murdered sire, met Henry at a little distance from Troyes, and conducted him in great pomp to the Hôtel de Ville, where lodgings were prepared for him. When Henry was presented the next day to Katherine, who was with her mother, enthroned in the church of Notre Dame, he was attired in a magnificent suit of burnished armor; but, instead of a plume, he wore in his helmet a fox's tail ornamented with precious stones.

The betrothment of Henry and Katherine instantly followed; and, when the English monarch received Katherine's promise, he placed on her finger a ring of inestimable value, supposed to be the same worn by our English queen-consorts at their coronation. After the conclusion of the ceremony, Henry presented to his betrothed bride his favorite knight, sir Louis de Robsart, to whom he committed the defence of her person, and the office of guarding her while in France. The real meaning of which ceremony was, that Henry V. took the princess into his own custody after betrothment, and would have retained her by force, if her family had changed their minds regarding his marriage. Katherine was now *his* property; and it was the duty of sir Louis de Robsart to guard the safekeeping of that property.

"On Trinity Sunday, June 3," says Monstrelet, "the king of England wedded the lady Katherine, at Troyes, in the parish church near which he lodged. Great pomp and magnificence were displayed by him and his princes, as if he had been king of the whole world."

The archbishop of Sens went in state to bless the bed of the queen, and during the night a grand procession came to the bedside of the royal pair, bringing them wine and soup, because Henry chose in all things to comply with the ancient customs of France; and it appears this strange ceremonial was one of the usages of the royal family. The next day, after a splendid feast, where the knights of the English court proposed a succession of tournaments, he let them know "that playing at fighting was not to be the amusement of his wedding, but the actual siege of Sens, where they might tilt and tourney as much as they chose."

Thus was the honeymoon of Katherine the fair passed at sieges and leaguers; her bridal music was the groans of France. Horror, unutterable horror, was the attendant on these nuptials. But not a word, not a sign of objection to the cruelties and slaughter that followed her marriage, is recorded; nor did the royal beauty ever intercede for her wretched country with her newly-wedded lord.

The royal pair spent their Christmas at Paris; but, at the end of the festival, Henry thought it best to pay some attention to the prayer of his faithful commons, who had lately begged that he, with his gracious queen, would please to return to England, to comfort, support, and refresh them by their presence. Accordingly, Henry set out with his queen on a winter journey through France, escorted by the duke of Bedford, at the head of six thousand men. Queen Katherine arrived at Amiens on St. Vincent's day, and was lodged in the hotel of maitre Robert le Jeune, bailiff of Amiens, and many costly presents were made to her by that magistrate.

The royal pair embarked at Calais, and landed at Dover, February 1st, "where," observes Monstrelet, "Katherine was received as if she had been an angel of God."

The magnificent coronation of the queen took place as early after her landing as the 24th of February. She was led on foot from Westminster Palace to the abbey, between two bishops, and was crowned by the hands of archbishop Chichely, on the 24th of February, 1421. It is expressly mentioned that Katherine sat on the King's Bench at Westminster Hall, by Henry's side, at the coronation feast.

Soon after, the disastrous news arrived of the defeat and death, at the fatal field of Baugy, of that stainless knight, the king's best-beloved brother, Thomas, duke of Clarence. Henry had not intended to leave England till after the birth of the heir, which the situation of his young queen led him to expect; but now, burning to avenge Clarence, he hurried to France, June 10, leaving his Katherine in the care of the duke of Bedford. He had laid especial command on his wife at his parting, which was, not to let his heir be born at Windsor.

It is certain, however, that Katherine disobeyed her royal lord, either from want of belief in astrology, or because she chose that her child should first see the light in that stately fortress, where his great and fortunate ancestor, Edward III., was born.

On the 6th of December, 1421, the son of Katherine came into a world which assuredly proved most disastrous to him. When the news was brought to Henry the V. that Katherine had brought him an heir, he was prosecuting the siege of Meaux. He eagerly inquired "where the boy was born?" and being answered "at Windsor," the king repeated with a sigh to his chamberlain, lord Fitzhugh, the following oracular stave, which certainly does little honor to his talents as an impromptu versifier:—

> "I, Henry, born at Monmouth,
> Shall small time reign and much get;
> But Henry of Windsor shall long reign and lose all.
> But as God will, so be it."

Early in the same spring Katherine wrote her warlike lord a most loving letter, declaring that she earnestly longed to behold him once more. This epistle was answered by a permission to join him in France.

Queen Katherine crossed the sea, and landed at Harfleur, on the 21st of May, 1422, escorted by the duke of Bedford, and an army of twenty thousand men, destined to complete the conquest of her unhappy country. At the head of this mighty reinforcement she traversed France, in royal state.

The last year's harassing warfare had greatly injured the constitution of Henry V. He was ill when his queen arrived, but he paid no regard to his failing health—he scarcely allowed himself a day's repose.

In the castle of Vincennes, near Paris, which has often been the theatre of the destinies of France, Katherine and her mother attended the last hours of Henry V.

He made a very penitential end, but was so little conscious of his blood-guiltiness, that when his confessor was reading the seven Psalms in the service for the dying, he stopped him when he came to the verse, "Build thou the walls of Jerusalem," with an earnest protestation, "that

when he had completed his conquests in Europe, he always intended to
undertake a crusade." When he had arranged his affairs, he asked his
physicians " how long he had to live?" One of them replied, on his
knees, " that, without a miracle, he could not survive two hours at the
most."

" Comfort my dear wife," he said to the duke of Bedford, "the most
afflicted creature living." In a will he made on his death-bed, he
leaves Katherine a gold sceptre. He expired on the 31st of August,
1422.

At the time of Henry's death, his fair widow had not attained her
twenty-first year. Her affection was, as the dying hero observed to his
brother, most violent, but it certainly proved in the end rather evanescent.

Our warlike barons were not a little embarrassed by the mutations
of this world, which had snatched from them a leader of singular energies, both as monarch and warrior, and, placing a little babe at their
head, made them directors of a nursery. The chivalric earl of Warwick had the guardianship of the king's person at a very early age; a
fact illustrated by a beautiful contemporary drawing in the pictorial history of the earl. He is represented holding the king, a most lovely
infant of fourteen months old, in his arms, while he is showing him to
the peers in parliament. One of the lords is presenting the infant monarch with the orb. The royal babe is curiously surveying it, and, with
an arch look, gently placing one dimpled hand upon the symbol of sovereignty, seems doubtful whether it is to be treated with reverence or
chucked, like a cannon ball, into the midst of the august assembly.
Another representation of the earl of Warwick gives us an idea of the
costume of royal infants in the middle ages; for the limners of that age
drew what they saw before them, and invented nothing. Warwick is
delineated in the Rous Roll, holding his royal charge in his arms. The
babe is about eighteen months old; he is attired in a little crimson
velvet gown; and has on his head a velvet cap, turned up with a miniature crown; moreover he holds a toy sceptre in his baby hand, which
he looks much inclined to whisk about the head of the stout earl, who
is so amiably performing the office of a nursery-maid. It is to be pre-
sumed that the earl carried the little king on all state occasions, while

his governess, dame Alice Boteler, and his nurse, Joan Astley, had possession of him in his hours of retirement.

After these arrangements were effected, Katherine the Fair retires behind a cloud so mysterious, that for thirteen years of her life we have no public document which tells of her actions; and the biographer is forced to wander in search of particulars into the pleasant, but uncertain regions of tradition and private anecdote.

Deep obscurity hangs over the birth and origin of Katherine's second husband, Owen Tudor. Some historians declare that the father of Owen was a brewer at Beaumaris. Nevertheless, he drew his line from a prince of North Wales, called Theodore; which, pronounced according to the Saxon tongue, was corrupted into Tudor, and even to the meaner sound of Tidder.

The next fact regarding Owen is, that he certainly belonged to the brave Welsh band with whom Henry V. most prudently entered into amicable terms, on the death of the warlike Glendower. These hardy warriors, it is well known, under the command of Davy the One-eyed, did good service at Agincourt.

In this station Owen Tudor is next found keeping guard on the infant king and his mother, at Windsor Castle, and very soon after the death of Henry V. it appears the handsome Welsh soldier attracted the attention of the royal widow of England.

While Owen was on guard at Windsor, on some festival, he was required to dance before the queen; and, making too elaborate a pirouette, he was not able to recover his balance, but fell into the queen's lap, as she sat upon a low seat, with all her ladies about her. The queen's manner of excusing this awkwardness gave her ladies the first suspicion that she was not entirely insensible to the attractions of the brave Welshman. As her passion increased, and she indulged herself in greater intimacy with the object of it, those of her ladies, who could take the liberty, remonstrated with the queen, and represented "how much she lowered herself by paying any attention to a person, who, though possessing some personal accomplishments and advantages, had no princely nor even gentle alliances, but belonged to a barbarous clan of savages, reckoned inferior to the lowest English yeomen." Upon which the queen declared, "that being a Frenchwoman, she had

18

not been aware that there was any difference of race in the British island."

The precise time when Katherine's love led her to espouse the Welsh soldier, it is impossible to ascertain; what priest married them, and in what holy place their hands were united, no document exists to prove; and strange it is, that Henry VII., with all his elaborate boast of royal descent, should not have left some intimation of the time and place of the marriage of Katherine and Owen.

Katherine's life of retirement enabled her to conceal her marriage for many years, and to give birth, without any very notorious scandal, to three sons successively. The eldest was born at the royal manor-house of Hadham; from the place of his birth he is called Edmund of Had-ham. The second was Jasper of Hatfield, from another of the royal residences. The third, Owen, first saw the light at some inconvenient season, when Katherine was forced to appear at the royal palace of Westminster. The babe was carried at once into the monastery, where he was reared, and afterwards professed a monk.

While Katherine was devoting herself to conjugal affection and maternal duties, performed by stealth, her royal son was crowned, in his eighth year, king of England, at Westminster, with great pomp, in which his mother took no share.

A strong suspicion of the queen's connection with Tudor seems to have been first excited in the minds of Henry VI.'s guardians, towards the end of the summer of 1436; at which time Katherine either took refuge in the abbey of Bermondsey, or was sent there under some restraint.

The children, to whom queen Katherine had previously given birth in secret, were torn from her by the orders of the council, and consigned to the keeping of a sister of the earl of Suffolk. This cruelty perhaps hastened the death of the unfortunate queen. The pitying nuns who attended her declared she was a sincere penitent, and among all other small sins she expressed the deepest contrition for having disobeyed her royal husband Henry V., and perversely chosen the forbidden castle of Windsor as the birthplace of the heir of England.

To use the poor queen's own pathetic words, " the silent and fearful conclusion of her long, grievous malady " took place on the 3d of January, 1437.

Katherine was buried with all the pomp usual to her high station. Her body was removed to the church of her patroness, St. Katherine, by the Tower, where it laid in state, February 18th, 1437 : it then rested at St. Paul's, and was finally honorably buried in Our Lady's Chapel, at Westminster Abbey.

MARGARET OF ANJOU,

QUEEN OF HENRY VI.

THE history of Margaret of Anjou, from the cradle to the tomb, is a
tissue of the most striking vicissitudes, and replete with events of
more powerful interest than are to be found in the imaginary career of
any heroine of romance; for the creations of fiction, however forcibly
they may appeal to our imaginations, fade into insignificance before the
simple majesty of truth.

René of Anjou, the father of Margaret, was the second son of Louis
II., king of Sicily and Jerusalem, duke of Calabria and Anjou, and
count of Provence by Yolante of Arragon. In 1420 René was, in his
thirteenth year, espoused to Isabella, the heiress of Lorraine, who was
only ten years old at the period of her nuptials. This lady, who was
the direct descendant of Charlemagne, in addition to her princely patrimony, brought the beauty, the high spirit, and the imperial blood of that
illustrious line, into the family of Anjou. Her youngest daughter, Margaret, was in all respects a genuine scion of the Carlovingian race; she
also inherited her father's love of learning, and his taste for poetry and
the arts.

Scarcely had Margaret of Anjou entered her teens, when her precocious charms and talents created the most lively sensations at the court
of her aunt, the queen of France.

"The report of these charms," according to a learned, but somewhat
imaginative French author, "first reached Henry VI., the young bach-

sior king of England, through the medium of a gentleman of Anjou,
named Champchevrier, a prisoner at large (belonging to sir John Fal-
stoff), with whom king Henry was accustomed to converse occasionally;
and he gave so eloquent a description of the rare endowments which
nature had bestowed on the portionless daughter of the impoverished
king of the Two Sicilies, that Henry despatched him to the court of
Lorraine, to procure a portrait of the young princess."

Champchevrier obtained a portrait of Margaret, painted by one of
the first artists in France, who was employed by the earl of Suffolk.
This is not unlikely, for Suffolk was the ostensible instrument in this
marriage; but the real person with whom the project for the union
between Henry VI. and Margaret of Anjou originated, appears to have
been no other than cardinal Beaufort, the great-uncle of the king. The
education of Henry having been superintended by the cardinal, he
was fully aware of the want of energy and decision in his character,
which rendered it desirable to provide him with a consort whose intel-
lectual powers would be likely to supply his constitutional defects, and
whose acquirements might render her a suitable companion for so learned and refined a prince.

In Margaret of Anjou all these requisites were united with beauty,
eloquence, and every feminine charm calculated to win unbounded influence over the plastic mind of the youthful sovereign.   She was, moreover, at that tender and unreflective age, at which she might be rendered
a powerful auxiliary in the cardinal's political views.   Under these circumstances, there can be little doubt that Champchevrier had received
his cue from the cardinal, when he described to Henry, in such glowing
colors, the charms and mental graces of the very princess to whom he
had determined to unite him, both for the reasons we have before stated,
and as a means of concluding a peace with France.

Henry VI. was then in his four-and-twentieth year, beautiful in person, of a highly cultivated and refined mind, wholly pure in thought
and deed.

When the proposal was made in form, to the father of the young
Margaret, he replied, in the spirit of a knight-errant, " That it would be
inconsistent with his honor to bestow his daughter in marriage on the
usurper of his hereditary dominions, Anjou and Maine;". and he de-

manded the restoration of these provinces, as an indispensable condition
in the marriage-articles. This demand was backed by the king of
France, and, after a little hesitation, ceded by king Henry and his
council.

As soon as the conditions of the marriage were settled, Suffolk returned to bring the subject into parliament, where he had to encounter
a stormy opposition from the duke of Gloucester and his party. Suffolk,
however, only acted as the agent of cardinal Beaufort, who possessed an
ascendency, not only in the council, but with the parliament; and
above all, the inclinations of the royal bachelor being entirely on his
side, his triumph over Gloucester was complete. Suffolk was dignified
with the title of marquess, and invested with full power to espouse the
lady Margaret of Anjou, as the proxy of his sovereign.

The bridal festivities lasted eight days, and the spot where the tournament was held, is still called, in memory of that circumstance, the
Place de Carrière.

At the conclusion of the eight day's fête, Margaret was solemnly delivered to the marquess and marchioness of Suffolk, and took a mournful farewell of her weeping kindred and friends. "Never," say the
chroniclers of her native land, "was a young princess more deeply
loved in the bosom of her own family." Charles VII. of France, who
was tenderly attached to the accomplished niece of his queen, accompanied her two leagues from Nanci, clasped her at parting many times in
his arms, and said, with his eyes full of tears,—

"I seem to have done nothing for you, my niece, in placing you on
one of the greatest thrones in Europe; for it is scarcely worthy of possessing you." Sobs stifled his voice; the young queen could only
reply with a torrent of tears; they parted, and saw each other no
more. Charles returned to Nanci, with his eyes swollen with weeping.
A harder parting took place with her father, who went with her as far
as Bar; there he commended her to God, but neither the father nor the
daughter could speak to each other, but turned away with full hearts
without uttering a single word.

These regrets,—in which persons who were, by the etiquettes and
restraints of royalty, taught to conceal every emotion of the heart, so
passionately indulged on this occasion,—are sufficient evidence of the

amiable and endearing qualities of the youthful Margaret, or her loss
would not have been so deeply lamented, when she was departing from
a precarious and a care-clouded home, to fulfil a destiny, whose perspec-
tive was, at that time, brilliant.

For the first two years of Margaret of Anjou's union with Henry
VI., cardinal Beaufort was the supreme director of the power of the
crown. King Henry, new to the delights of female society, was intoxi-
cated with the charms, the wit, and graceful manners of his youthful
bride, of whom an elegant French historian thus speaks,—"England
had never seen a queen more worthy of a throne than Margaret of
Anjou. No woman surpassed her in beauty, and few men equalled her
in courage. It seemed as if she had been formed by Heaven to supply
to her royal husband the qualities which he required, in order to become a great king." Another chronicler, quoted by Stowe, says—
" This woman excelled all others, as well in beauty and favor as in art
and policy, and was in courage inferior to none."

These brilliant characteristics were yet in the germ, when Margaret
of Anjou was unfortunately called to share the throne of England at a
period of life when her judgment was immature, and the perilous endowments of wit, genius, and lively perceptiveness, were more likely to
create enemies than to secure friends.

That enlightened statesman-historian, Philip de Comines, who was
well acquainted with queen Margaret, attributes all the misfortunes that
afterwards befell her, and the overthrow of the house of Lancaster, to
her rash interposition in the feud between Somerset and Warwick, in
which she indicated her preference for the former, in a way that never
was forgiven by Warwick." "The queen had acted much more prudently," says Comines, "in endeavoring to have adjusted the dispute
between them, than to have said, 'I am of this party, and I will maintain it.'" And so it prove by the event.

It is probable that the red rose was originally worn by Margaret as a
compliment to Somerset, in token that she espoused his cause, and that
his great political opponent, the duke of York, assumed the white, as a
symbol of hostility to him and his adherents.

Rosettes of white and crimson ribbon or even of paper among the
common soldiers, were worn as the substitutes of these ill-omened

flowers, by the partisans of the royal claimants of the throne, during the struggle between the houses of York and Lancaster, poetically called, from these badges, the " War of the Roses."

It was at this period, when the ill-success that attended the arms of England abroad increased the clamors of the enemies of the government at home, that queen Margaret, for the first time, afforded a prospect of bringing an heir to the throne. About six months before the birth of her child, Margaret had to mourn over the death of her beloved mother, the high-minded and heroic Isabella of Lorraine, who died, February 28, 1453, aged only forty-three. Margaret's mourning weeds were blue, probably of that deep, dark, melancholy tint which has recently been called French black.

The loss of a mother—of such a mother, too, as Isabella of Lorraine—could not have been otherwise than keenly felt by Margaret, who had, in childhood and early youth, shared and solaced so many of her trying adversities. But a heavier calamity than even the death of that dearly beloved parent oppressed the royal matron, as the dreaded hour of peril and anguish drew near, from which the consorts of monarchs are no more exempted than the wives of peasants.

King Henry was seized with one of those alarming attacks of malady, to which his grandfather, Charles VI. of France, was subject. The agitating character of public events, and the difficulties with which the court had had to contend, for the last four years, had been too much for a prince of acute sensibility, and who had, moreover, hereditary tendency to inflammation of the brain. For a time both mind and body sank under the accumulated pressure, and he remained in a state that left little hope for his life and none for his reason.

King Henry was at Clarendon when he was first seized with this dangerous malady ; but after a few days he was by slow degrees conveyed to his palace at Westminster, where queen Margaret, on the 13th of October, 1453, gave birth to a prince, the unfortunate Edward of Lancaster, whom Speed pathetically calls " the child of sorrow and infelicity."

Henry remained vibrating between life and death, and perfectly unconscious of an event the anticipation of which had, a few months earlier, been hailed by him with transports of joy.

19

Queen Margaret had not completed her twenty-fourth year, and the king was just thirty-three, when they became the parents of this their only son, whose birth, so far from being of the slightest political advantage to them, had the worst possible influence on their fortunes, by determining the duke of York to contest the crown of England with Henry, at swords' points, instead of waiting for its natural reversion to him, at the death of his royal kinsman.

Queen Margaret, at this period, exercised the royal power, in the name of the king, assisted by the duke of Somerset, and cardinal Kemp, archbishop of Canterbury and chancellor of England.

When the situation of the king was made known to his peers of parliament, they, on the 27th of March, appointed the duke of York protector and defender of the king, during the king's pleasure, or till such time as Edward the prince should come to age of discretion. The parliament thus evidently acted under the impression, that the king's indisposition was a mental aberration, that would last as long as he lived, and at the same time they showed a desire of preserving the rights of the reigning family, by reserving this office for an infant not six months old.

Henry VI. began to amend in November; by the ensuing Christmas he was so much recovered, that on St. John's day he sent his almoner to Canterbury, with his offering, and his secretary to make his oblation at the shrine of St. Edward. From the testimony of a contemporary witness, who describes the state of the king at this period, Henry appears to have been like a person just awakened from a long dream, when reason and convalescence returned. The touching particulars of the infant prince's recognition by his royal father, are thus quaintly narrated, in the letter to which we have just alluded:

"On Monday at noon the queen came to him and brought my lord prince with her, and then he asked, 'what the prince's name was?' and the queen told him, 'Edward;' and then he held up his hands, and thanked God thereof. And he said he never knew him till that time nor wist what was said to him, nor wist where he had been, whilst he had been sick, till now; and he asked who were the godfathers, and the queen told him, and he was well apaid (content). And she told him the cardinal was dead, and he said he never knew of it till this time; then he said one of the wisest lords in this land was dead. And my lord of Winchester (bishop), and my lord of St. John of Jerusalem, were with him the morrow after Twelfth day, and he did speak to them as well as ever he did, and when they came out they wept for joy. And he saith he is in charity with all the world, and so he would all the lords were. And now he saith matins of Our Lady, and evensong, and heareth his mass devoutly."

Margaret immediately took prompt measures for Henry's restoration to the sovereign authority, by causing him to be conveyed, though still very weak, to the House of Lords, where he dissolved the parliament, and the duke of Somerset was immediately released and reinstated in his former post.

The triumph of the royal cause was brief; Calais and the naval power of England were at the command of Margaret's determined adversary, Warwick; and from that quarter the portentous storm-clouds began once more to threaten.

The band of veterans which Warwick brought from Calais swelled into a puissance, whose numbers have been variously reported by historians, from twenty-five thousand to forty thousand men. With this force he and his military *élève*, Edward, earl of March, triumphantly entered London, July 2d, 1460, the citizens throwing open their gates for their admittance. On the ninth of the same month, they measured swords with the royal army at Northampton.

Queen Margaret was not herself in the battle, but, with her boy, the infant hope of Lancaster, was posted at a short distance from the scene of action, on a spot whence she could command a prospect of the field, and communicate with her generals. When, however, she witnessed the treachery of lord Grey, and the headlong rush of her disordered troops, to repass the river they had crossed that morning so full of hope and ardor, the pride and courage of the heroine yielded to maternal terror; and, forgetful of every other consideration but the preservation of her boy, she fled precipitately, with him and a few faithful followers, towards the bishopric of Durham. But Durham was no place of refuge for the queen, who had previously incurred the ill-will of the citizens, by some arbitrary measure or imprudent burst of temper.

On the road she was joined by the duke of Somerset, and, after a

thousand perils, succeeded in reaching Harlech Castle, an almost im-
pregnable fortress in North Wales, where she was honorably received
and manfully protected, by Dafyd ap Jeuan ap Einion, a Welsh chief
tain, who, in stature and courage resembled one of the doughty Cam
brian giants of metrical romance.

In this rocky fastness, which appeared as if formed by nature for
the shelter of the royal fugitives, they remained safe from the vindictive
pursuit of their foes, while the unfortunate king was conducted to
London, by those whom the fortunes of war had rendered the arbiters
of his fate.

Henry was compelled, by those who had the custody of his person, to give the regal sanction to a peremptory mandate, for the return of his consort and son to the metropolis, attaching no milder
term than that of high treason to a wilful disobedience of this in-
junction.

Margaret was a fugitive, without an army, without allies, kindred, or
money, when she received this summons, together with the intelligence,
that the rights of her boy had been passively surrendered, by his unfortunate sire, to the hostile princes of the line of York. Tidings that
would have overwhelmed any other female with despair had the effect
of rousing all the energies of her nature into that resistless determination of purpose, which for a time redeemed the cause of Lancaster
from ruin.

The king of Scotland was the son of a Lancastrian princess; his
sister Margaret, the late dauphiness of France, had been closely connected with Margaret of Anjou, both by marriage and friendship; and
she resolved on trying the efficacy of a personal application to that
monarch, for assistance in this emergency.

Her negotiations at the court of Scotland were prosperous, and her
measures so vigorous, that, in less than eight days after she had received
the order, in king Henry's name, for her immediate return to London,
she was at the head of an army, had crossed the Scottish border, un-
furled the banner of the red Rose, and, strengthened by all the chivalry
of Northumberland, Cumberland, Lancashire, and Westmoreland, presented herself at the gates of York, before the leaders of the white Rose
party were fully aware that she was in England.

The duke of York, who had by no means anticipated this prompt and bold response to the proclamation he had enforced his royal captive to send to the fugitive queen, left London with the earl of Salisbury, at the head of such forces as could be hastily collected, to check the fierce career of the lioness whom they had rashly roused from her slumberous stupor of despair.

Margaret had drawn up her puissance in three bodies. The central force was commanded by Somerset, under her directions, it is said: but it is by no means certain that she played the Amazon, by fighting in , person on this, or any other occasion. The other two squadrons were ambushed to the right and left, under the orders of the earl of Wiltshire and lord Clifford; and as soon as York had entered the plain, and was engaged by the van-guard, they closed him in on either side, "like," says Hall, "a fish in a net, or a deer in a buck-stall, so that in less than half-an-hour he, manfully fighting, was slain, and his army discomfited." Two thousand of the Yorkists lay dead on the field, and the ruthless Clifford, on his return from the pursuit, in which he had slain the young earl of Rutland, in cold blood, on Wakefield bridge, severed the head of the duke of York from his lifeless body, crowned it with paper, and presented it to queen Margaret on the point of a lance, with these words: "Madame, your war is done; here is your king's ransom."

Margaret pushed on, with resistless impetuosity, to the metropolis, with the intention of rescuing her captive lord from the thraldom in which he had been held, ever since the battle of Northampton.

While Margaret was thus providing as far as possible for the safety of her consort, Warwick, leading his royal prisoner in his train, intercepted her army at the head of his forces. The earl took possession of St. Albans, and filled the streets with archers to oppose her passage. Here a furious conflict took place almost hand to hand, neither party giving quarter.

On the approach of night, the Yorkists dispersed and fled, leaving their royal prisoner, king Henry, nearly alone in a tent, with Lord Montague, his chamberlain, and two or three attendants.

The queen was not herself aware of the proximity of her captive lord to the scene of her triumph, till his faithful servant, Howe, ran to lord Clifford's quarters, to announce the fact. Attended by Clifford, she flew to greet him, and they embraced with the most passionate tokens of joy.

Margaret exultingly presented the young prince of Wales, who had been her companion during the perils of that stormy day, to his enfranchised sire and sovereign, and requested Henry to bestow knighthood on the gallant child, and thirty more of their adherents, who had particularly distinguished themselves in the fight.

The victorious queen, with the king, the prince of Wales, and the northern lords, went immediately to return thanks to God in the abbey-church of St. Albans, for the deliverance of the king. They were received by the abbot and monks, with hymns of triumph, at the church-door.

The danger that threatened their lives and properties, and the disgust created by the rash and vindictive conduct of the queen, decided all London and its vicinity to raise the white Rose banner on the approach of the heir of York, with Warwick, at the head of forty thousand men; and the firm refusal of the Londoners to admit the queen, and her ill-disciplined and lawless troops, within their walls, compelled Margaret, with her forces, to fall back towards the northern counties. She carried with her king Henry and their son, the prince of Wales. The next day Edward entered London in triumph; he was received by the citizens as their deliverer; and on the 4th of March he was proclaimed king, with universal acclamations, by the style and title of Edward IV.

The recognition of Edward IV. by the Londoners, though generally considered as the death-blow to the cause of Lancaster, only served to rouse the queen to greater energy of action. She was the heroine of the northern aristocracy and the midland counties, who, though they had suffered so severely for their devotion to her cause, were still ready to rally, at her need, round the banner of the red Rose. An army of sixty thousand men was, in the course of a few days, at her command; but her generals, Somerset and Clifford, prevailed on Margaret to remain with the king and the young prince of Wales, at York, while they engaged the rival sovereign of England.

The result of this dreadful battle, where the strength and flower of the Lancastrians perished, is best described in the immortal verse of laureate Southey:—

" Witness Aire's unhappy water,
Where the ruthless Clifford fell ;
And where Wharfe ran red with slaughter
On the day of Towcester's field,
Gathering in its guilty flood
The carnage and the ill-spilt blood
That forty thousand lives could yield.
Cressy was to this but sport,
Poictiers but a pageant vain,
And the work of Agincourt
Only like a tournament."

Margaret fled, with her consort and her son, to Newcastle, and from thence to Alnwick Castle.

From Alnwick, Margaret proceeded to Berwick, with her husband, her son, and a few faithful ladies and followers, who attended the perilous wanderings of the Lancastrian court. While there, the desperation of her husband's cause betrayed the distressed queen into the unpopular measure of surrendering Berwick to the Scotch.

While Margaret of Anjou, with the formidable activity of a chessqueen, was attempting, from her safe refuge in Scotland, to check her adversary's game, she was, with the king her husband, and her little son, proscribed and attainted by the parliament of the rival sovereign of England, and it was forbidden to all their former subjects to hold any sort of communication with them, on pain of death. The whole of England was now subjected to the authority of Edward IV.; yet their was still an undying interest pervading the great body of the people in favor of the blameless monarch, to whom their oaths of allegiance had been, in the first instance, plighted.

And many were the faithful hearts ready to sacrifice fortune and life at the call of the royal heroine of the red Rose, who, at the age of thirty-two, was still in the meridian splendor of her beauty, and the full power of her genius.

It was to exert her personal influence with Louis, and to implore his succor in the cause of her unfortunate husband, that Margaret undertook her first voyage to the continent. Leaving king Henry at the court of

Scotland, she, with her young son, the prince of Wales, sailed from Kirk-cudbright, and landed in Bretagne, April 8th, 1462.

According to one of her French biographers, "Margaret, being entirely destitute of money, was indebted for the means of performing this voyage to the gratitude of a French merchant, to whom, in her early days, she had rendered an important service at her father's court at Nanci.

Queen Margaret of England and Louis XI of France were the children of a tenderly attached brother and sister, René and Mary of Anjou, and they had been companions in childhood; but the ties of kindred and affection were little regarded by the cold and selfish son of Charles VII. When the distressed queen, with her disinherited son, threw herself at his feet, and, with floods of tears, implored his assistance in behalf of her dethroned consort, she found him callous to her impassioned eloquence, and not only indifferent to her grief, but eager to proffit by the adverse circumstances which had brought her as a suppliant to the foot of his throne.

It was fruitless for Margaret to look for succor from her own family. King René and his son were engaged in a desperate and ruinous contest with Alphonso, king of Arragon, which the resources of Anjou and Provence were overtaxed to support. Kindred and countrymen had failed her in her sore adversity, but her appeal to all true knights to aid her in her attempts to redress the wrongs of her royal spouse, and vindicate the rights of her son, met with a response which proved that the days of chivalry were not ended. "If we are to believe the French historians," says Guthrie, "Pierre Brezé, the seneschal of Normandy, impelled by a more tender motive than that of compassion or ambition, entered as a volunteer, with two thousand men, into her service."

Margaret sailed for England in October, after an absence of five months, and, eluding the vigilance of Edward's fleet, which had been long in waiting to intercept her, she made the coast of Northumberland. She attempted to land at Tynemouth, but the garrison pointed their cannon against her. According to some accounts, she resolutely effected her purpose, but had scarcely set her foot on shore, when the foreign levy, understanding that Warwick was in the field at the head of forty thousand men, fled to their ships in a panic, leaving queen Margaret, her son, and Brezé, almost alone.

Hope must have been an undying faculty of Margaret's nature, and at this crisis it animated her to exertions almost beyond the powers of woman. The winter was unusually severe, and she, the native of a southern clime, exposed herself unshrinkingly to every sort of hardship. Once more she sought and obtained assistance from the Scotch, and placed her devoted champion, Brezé, at the head of the forces with which she was supplied. She then brought king Henry into the field, who had previously been hidden in her safe refuge at Harlech Castle.

In the spring of 1463, Percy was defeated and slain at Hedgely Moor, by Montague, and a few days later "England was again set on a field" at the fatal battle of Hexham. "King Henry," says Hall, "was the best horseman of his company that day, for he fled so fast, no one could overtake him; yet he was so closely pursued, that three of his horsemen, or body-guard, with their horses, trapped in blue velvet, were taken—one of them wearing the unfortunate monarch's cap of state, called a bicocket, embroidered with two crowns of gold, and ornamented with pearls.

When the victorious Yorkists broke into the camp at Levels, Margaret seized with mortal terror for the life of her boy, fled with him on foot into an adjacent forest, guarded only by de Brezé. Here, in momentary dread of being overtaken by the foe, she pursued her doubtful way by the most unfrequented paths; before long she unfortunately fell in with a gang of robbers, who, attracted by the richness of her dress and that of the young prince, surrounded and despoiled them of their jewels and costly robes of state. While they were quarrelling about the division of the plunder, Margaret, whose intrepidity and presence of mind had been the means of extricating her from a similar peril when captured by lord Stanley's followers, after the battle of Northampton, snatched her son up in her arms, and fled to a distant thicket, unobserved by the pitiless ruffians, who were deciding their dispute at swords' points.

When the shades of evening closed round, the fugitive queen and her son crept fearfully from their retreat, and, uncertain whither to turn for refuge, began to thread the tangled mazes of the forest, dreading,

20

above every other peril, the misfortune of falling into the hands of king Edward's partisans. It was possible that one random turn might lead them into this very danger.   While Margaret, bewildered with doubt and alarm, was considering what course to pursue, she perceived, by the light of the moon, another robber, of gigantic stature, advancing towards her with a drawn sword. Gathering courage from the desperation of her situation, Margaret took her son by the hand, and presenting him to the freebooter, with the dignity of look and bearing that were natural to her, she said, " Here, my friend, save the son of your king."

Struck with astonishment at the majestic beauty of the mother, and the touching loveliness of the boy, the robber dropped his weapon at the feet of the royal suppliants, and offered to conduct them to a place of safety. A few words explained to the queen that this outlaw was a Lancastrian gentleman, who had been ruined in king Henry's service, and she frankly committed herself and her son to his care. Taking the prince in his arms, he led the queen to his own retreat, a cave in Hexham Forest, where the royal fugitives were refreshed, and received such attention as his wife was able to afford.

Such was the retreat in which the queen and prince remained *perdu*, for two days of agonizing suspense. On the third morning their host encountered sir Pierre de Brezé, who, with his squire Barville, and an English gentleman, having escaped the robbers at Hexham, had been making anxious search for her and the prince.

From these devoted friends Margaret learned the escape of her royal husband, and the terrible vengeance that had been executed on Somerset, and her faithful adherents, the lords Hungerford and Roos. Margaret is said to have received these tidings with floods of tears, the first she had shed since the overthrow of the despairing hopes of Lancaster on the red field of Hexham.

. A few hours later, the English gentleman by whom Brezé was accompanied, having gone into the neighboring villages to gather tidings of public events, encountered the duke of Exeter, and Edmund Beaufort, the brother and successor of the unfortunate Henry duke of Somerset. He conducted them to the retreat of the proscribed queen and the youthful hope of Lancaster.

Margaret's spirits revived at the sight of these princes, whom she had numbered with the slain of Hexham, and she determined to send them to their powerful kinsman, the duke of Burgundy, to solicit an asylum, at the court of Dijon, for herself and the prince of Wales; while she once more proceeded to the court of Scotland, where she imagined king Henry had found refuge. On quitting the dwelling of the generous outlaw, from whom she had received such providential succor in her dire distress, she accorded all she had to bestow—her grateful thanks; but the dukes of Somerset and Exeter offered a portion of their scanty supply of money, as a reward to his wife for the services she had rendered to the queen; but, with a nobility of soul worthy of a loftier station, she refused to receive any portion of that which might be so precious to them at a time of need.

"Of all I have lost," exclaimed the queen, "I regret nothing so much as the power of recompensing such virtue."

Accompanied by Brezé and his squire, and attended by the outlaw of Hexham in the capacity of a guide, Margaret and the young prince her son took the road to Carlisle, where a passage to Scotland had been previously engaged for them, by the care of the gentleman who had accompanied Brezé; and they safely landed at Kirkcudbright. The treaty which had been concluded between king Edward and the Scottish regency rendered it necessary for Margaret to maintain a strict incognito.

The tidings were such as to convince her that she must hoard her energies for better days; and though she privately visited Edinburgh, to try the effect of her personal eloquence once more, she only found that her presence caused great uneasiness to the government. All the favor she could obtain was assistance for returning to her friends in Northumberland, who still continued with determined valor to hold out the fortress of Bamborough. From this place, Margaret, with a heavy heart, embarked for Flanders, with her son and some of her ladies, who had taken refuge there, after the disappearance of their royal mistress. Sir John Fortescue—who had abandoned his office as lord-chief-justice of England, to follow the fortunes of the proscribed queen and his princely pupil,—Dr. Morton, afterwards the famous cardinal archbishop of York, and about two hundred of the ruined adherents of Lancaster, shared her flight.

The distracted state of king René's affairs in his own dominions, utterly precluded him from exerting himself in his daughter's service, though not unfrequently solicited to draw his knightly sword in her cause.   The Provençal bards took the heroism and misfortunes of their hapless princess for their theme, and Réne's own minstrel and name-sake was accustomed to assail his royal ear, in his festal halls, with these strains :—

"Arouse thee, arouse thee, king Réne,
Nor let sorrow thy spirit beguile!
Thy daughter, the spouse of king Henry,
Now weeps, now implores with a smile."

René, however, was compelled to remain a passive sympathizer in Margaret's affliction.   All he could do for her was to afford her an asylum in her adversity.   Here Margaret, bereaved of all the attributes of royalty, save those that were beyond the power of adverse fortune to alienate, dwelt with the remnant of her ruined friends, and occupied herself in superintending the education of the last tender bud of the red Rose of Lancaster, whom she yet fondly hoped to see restored to his country, and his former lofty expectations.

A deeper shade of gloom pervaded the exiled court of Margaret, when the tidings reached her, through her secret adherents in England, that her unfortunate consort had at length fallen into the hands of his successful rival.

When king Henry fled from the lost battle of Hexham, he gained an asylum among his loyal subjects of Westmoreland and Lancashire, where he was many months concealed, sometimes in the house of John Machell, at Crackenthorp, sometimes like a hermit in a cave.

King Henry's retreat in Lancashire was betrayed by a monk of Abingdon, and he was taken by the servants of sir John Harrington as he sat at dinner at Waddington Hall.   He was conducted to London in the most ignominious manner, with his legs fastened to the stirrups of the sorry nag on which he was mounted, and an insulting placard affixed to his shoulders.   At Islington he was met by the earl of Warwick, who issued a proclamation forbidding any one to treat him with respect, and

afforded an example of wanton brutality to the mob, by leading the
royal captive thrice round the pillory, as if he had been a common felon,
crying aloud, "Treason, treason, and behold the traitor!"

Henry endured these outrages with the firmness of a hero, and the
meekness of a saint. "Forsooth, and forsooth, ye do foully to smite the
Lord's anointed," was his mild rebuke to a ruffian who was base enough
to strike him in that hour of misery. The following touching lines,
which have been attributed to Henry VI., were probably written during
his long imprisonment in the Tower:—

> "Kingdoms are but cares,
>   State is devoid of stay,
> Riches are ready snares,
>   And hasten to decay.
>
> "Who meaneth to remove the rocke
>   Out of his slimy mud,
> Shall mire himself, and hardly 'scape
>   The swelling of the flood."

An emissary of Margaret, who was taken in a stronghold of her outlawed adherents (which had so long held out in defiance of Edward and
all his puissance) accused the earl of Warwick of having, in his late
mission to the continent, spoken favorably of the exiled queen in his
conference with Louis XI., at Rouen. Warwick refused to leave his
castle to be confronted with his accuser. Two years afterwards he was
in arms with the avowed intention of hurling Edward IV. from the
throne, but was forced to retreat to France, where king Louis received
him.

Queen Margaret, in the December of 1469, left her lonely castle in
Verdun, with prince Edward, to meet Louis XI., her father, her brother, her sister Yolante, and Ferry count of Vaudemonte, who had all
assembled there, to hold a council on the best means of improving the
momentous crisis for the cause of Lancaster.

Maître Nicolle Giles, in his history, says—"The streets of Paris
were gayly dressed to welcome them, and they were lodged in the
palace, where they received the news of the landing of the earl of War-

wick, and that king Henry was freed, and in possession of his kingdom; upon which queen Margaret with all her company resolved to return to England."

On the 24th of March she put to sea, and on Easter-eve her fleet made the port of Weymouth. They went immediately to the abbey of Cearne, a small religious house close by, to refresh themselves after the fatigues of the voyage.

When the dreadful news of the death of Warwick and the recapture of king Henry, was brought to Margaret on the following day, she fell to the ground in a deep swoon, and for a long time remained in a speechless stupor of despair, as if her faculties had been overpowered by the greatness of this unexpected blow. When she revived to consciousness, it was only to bewail the evil destiny of her luckless consort. " In her agony, she reviled the calamitous temper of the times in which she lived, and reproached herself," says Hall, " for all her painful labors, now turned to her own misery, and declared ' she desired rather to die than live longer in this state of infelicity,'" as if she foresaw the dark adversities that were yet in store for her.

Queen Margaret's retreat was made known to king Edward, as he was on his way to Worcester, and he was assured that she should be at his command. She was brought to him at Coventry, May 11th, by her old enemy, sir William Stanley, by whom, it is said, the first news of the massacre of her beloved son was revealed to the bereaved mother, in a manner, that was calculated to aggravate the bitterness of this dreadful blow.

Margaret, in the first transports of maternal agony, invoked the most terrible maledictions on the head of the ruthless Edward and his posterity, which Stanley was inhuman enough to repeat to his royal master, together with all the frantic expressions she had used against him during their journey. Edward was at first so much exasperated, that he thought of putting her to death; but no Plantagenet ever shed the blood of a woman, and he contented himself by forcing her to grace his triumphant progress towards the metropolis.

The same night that Margaret of Anjou was brought as a captive to the Tower of London, she was made a widow. " That night, between eleven and twelve of the clock," writes the chronicler in Leland, " was king Henry, being prisoner in the Tower, put to death, the duke of Gloucester and divers of his men being in the Tower, that night." "May God give him time for repentance, whoever he was, who laid his sacrilegious hands on the Lord's anointed," adds the continuator of the Chronicles of Croyland.

Tradition points out an octagonal room in the Wakefield tower as the scene of the midnight murder of Henry VI. It was here that he had, for five years, eaten the bread of affliction during his lonely captivity from 1465. A few learned manuscripts, and devotional books, a bird that was the companion of his solitude, his relics, and the occasional visits of one or two learned monks, who were permitted to administer to his spiritual wants, were all the solaces he received in his captivity.

The imprisonment of queen Margaret was at first very rigorous, but it was, after a time, ameliorated through the compassionate influence of Edward's queen, Elizabeth Woodville, who probably retained a grateful remembrance of the benefits she had formerly received from her royal mistress.

Five marks a week were allotted by Edward IV. for the maintenance of the unfortunate Margaret during her imprisonment in Wallingford Castle. Her tender-hearted father, king René, was unwearied in his exertions for her emancipation, which was at length accomplished, at the sacrifice of his inheritance of Provence, which he ceded to Louis XI. at Lyons, in 1475, for half its value, that he might deliver his beloved child from captivity. The agreement between Edward IV. and Louis XI., for the ransom of Margaret of Anjou, was finally settled, August 29th, 1475, while Edward was in France. Louis undertook to pay fifty thousand crowns for her liberation, at five instalments. The first instalment of her ransom was paid to Edward's treasurer, lord John Howard, November 3d, the same year, and the bereaved and heart-broken widow of the holy Henry, after five years' captivity, was conducted from her prison at Wallingford Castle to Sandwich. Her retinue, when she landed in France, according to Prevost, consisted of three ladies and seven gentlemen; but these must have been sent by the king of France, since the miserable sum allotted to Haute for her travelling expenses allows for little attendance. The feelings may be imagined with which she took a last farewell of the English shores, where, thirty years before, she had landed in the pride and flush of youthful beauty, as its monarch's bride, and all the chivalry of the land thronged to meet and do her honor. Now it was treason even to shed a tear of pity for her sore afflictions, or to speak a word of comfort to her. Truly might she have said, "See if any sorrow be like unto my sorrow!"

She safely arrived at Dieppe, in the beginning of January, 1476. It was requisite, for the validity of the deeds of renunciation she had to sign, that she should be at liberty. Therefore, sir Thomas Montgomery took her to Rouen, and on the 22d resigned her to the French ambassadors; and on the 29th of January, she signed a formal renunciation of all rights her marriage in England had given her.

There is something touching in the very simplicity of the Latin sentence with which the deed begins, that was wrung from the broken-hearted heroine, who had, through so many storms of adversity, defended the rights of her royal consort and son. While they remained in life, she would have died a thousand deaths, rather than relinquish even the most shadowy of her claims; but the dear ones were no more, now—

> " Ambition, pride, the rival names
> Of York and Lancaster,
> With all their long contested claims,
> What were they then to her."

We now come to that era of Margaret's life in which a noble author of our time, lord Morpeth, in one exquisite line, describes her as,

> " Anjou's lone matron in her father's hall."

Like Naomi, Margaret returned empty and desolate to her native land, but not like her, attended by a fond and faithful daughter-in-law, for the unhappy widow of her son had been compelled to wed king Edward's brother, Richard of Gloucester.

The home to which her father welcomed Margaret was at that time at Reculée about a league from Angers, on the river Mayence, where he had a castle that commanded a view of the town, with a beautiful garden, and a gallery of painting and sculpture, which he took delight in adorning with his own paintings, and ornamented the walls of his garden with heraldic designs carved in marble. It was in such pursuits as these that René like a true Provençal sovereign, sought forgetfulness of his afflictions. But Margaret's temperament was of too stormy a nature to admit of the slightest alleviation to her grief. Her whole time was spent in painfully retracing the direful scenes of her past life, and in passionate regrets for the bereavements she had undergone. The canker-worm that was perpetually busy within, at length made its ravages outwardly visible on her person, and effected a fearful change in her appearance. The agonies and agitation she had undergone, turned the whole mass of her blood; her eyes, once so brilliant and expressive, became hollow, dim, and perpetually inflamed, from excessive weeping; and her skin was disfigured with a dry, scaly leprosy, which transformed this princess, who had been celebrated as the most beautiful in the world, into a spectacle of horror.

The last tie that bound Margaret to the world was severed by the death of her father, and she wished to end her days in profound retirement. Her efforts to obtain the bodies of her murdered husband and son were ineffectual; but, till the last day of her life, she employed some faithful ecclesiastics in England to perform, at the humble graves of her loved and lost ones, those offices deemed needful for the repose of their souls.

On her death-bed she divided among her faithful attendants the few valuables that remained from the wreck of her fortunes; and, worn out with the pressure of her sore afflictions of mind and body, she closed her troublous pilgrimage at the chateau of Damprièrre, August 25th, in the fifty-first year of her age.

ELIZABETH WOODVILLE.

THE fifteenth century is, above all other eras, remarkable for unequal marriages made by persons of royal station. Then, for the first time since the reigns of our Plantagenets commenced, was broken that high and stately etiquette of the middle ages, which forbade king or kaiser to mate with partners below the rank of princesses. In that century, the marriage of the handsome Edward IV. with an English gentlewoman caused as much astonishment at the wondrous archery of Dan Cupid, as was fabled of old—

> " When he shot so true
> That king Cophetua wed the beggar maid."

But the mother of Elizabeth Woodville had occasioned scarcely less wonder in her day, when, following the example of her sister-in-law, queen Katherine, she, a princess of Luxemburgh by birth, and, as the widow of the warlike duke of Bedford, the third lady of the realm, chose for her second helpmate, another squire of Henry V., Richard Woodville, who was considered the handsomest man in England.

The duchess's dower was forfeited in consequence of her marriage with Woodville, but restored on her humble supplication to parliament, through the influence of her husband's patron, cardinal Beaufort. Grafton Castle was the principal residence of the duchess. Probably Eliza-

beth Woodville was born there, about 1431, some years before the discovery of her parent's marriage. Her father, sir Richard Woodville,
was one of the English commanders at Rouen, under the duke of York,
during that prince's regency.

After the death of the unfortunate queen-mother Katherine, and that
of the queen dowager Joanna, the duchess of Bedford became for some
time, in rank, the first lady in England, and always possessed a certain
degree of influence in consequence. Her husband was in the retinue
sent to escort Margaret of Anjou to England; he was afterwards rapidly
advanced at court, made baron, and finally earl of Rivers; and the
duchess of Bedford became a great favorite of the young queen. The
duchess was still second lady in England, yet her rank was many degrees more exalted than her fortune; therefore, as her children grew
up, she was glad to provide for them at the court of her friend, queen
Margaret. Her eldest daughter, the beautiful Elizabeth Woodville, was
appointed maid of honor to that queen, little deeming that she was one
day to fill her place on the English throne. While yet in attendance
on her royal mistress, she captured the heart of a brave knight, sir
Hugh Johns, a great favorite of Richard duke of York. Sir Hugh had
nothing in the world wherewithal to endow the fair Woodville but a
sword, whose temper had been proved in many a battle in France: he
was, moreover, a timid wooer, and very impolitically, deputed others to
make to the beautiful maid of honor the declaration of love which he
wanted courage to speak himself.

Richard duke of York was protector of England when he thus, in
regal style, recommended his landless vassal to the love of her who was
one day to share the diadem of his heir.

Even if Elizabeth's heart had responded to this earnest appeal of her
lover's princely master, yet she was too slenderly gifted by fortune to
venture on a mere love-match. She probably demurred on this point,
and avoided returning a decisive answer.

The time is not distinctly specified of the marriage of Elizabeth
Woodville with John Gray; it probably took place soon after her rejection of the Yorkist champion. This wedlock was certainly a great
match for the penniless maid of honor; for it was equal to several of
the alliances of the Plantagenet princesses.

Tradition declares this was a most happy marriage, although Elizabeth and Gray must have been frequently separated by the ferocious contest between York and Lancaster, which commmenced directly after their union.

Elizabeth's husband, Gray, lord Ferrers, commanded the cavalry of queen Margaret, during that furious charge which won the day for Lancaster, at the second battle of St Albans. The red Rose was for a brief space triumphant, but the young victorious leader died of his wounds the 28th of February, 1461, and his beautiful Elizabeth was left desolate. Fortunately, her mother was near the army, if not with queen Margaret.

The mother of Elizabeth was a *diplomatiste* of most consummate ability; insomuch that the common people attributed her influence over the minds of men to sorcery. The manner in which she reconciled herself to young Edward, when she had so lately been aiding and abetting queen Margaret, after the stormy scene that had occured between that prince and her lord and son at Calais, and after her son-in-law had, by his valor, almost turned the scale of victory against the house of York, is really unaccountable; but the effect of her influence remains, in no equivocal terms, on the Issue Rolls of Edward's exchequer.

Is it possible that the fair widow of sir John Gray first became acquainted with the victor, in the depths of her distress for the loss of her husband, and that Edward's sudden passion for her induced his extraordinary profession of affection for her mother and father, who were, till the death of sir John Gray, such stanch Lancastrians? If this singular entry in the Issue Rolls may be permitted to support this surmise, then did the acquaintance of Elizabeth and Edward commence two or three years earlier than all former histories have given reason to suppose. Whatever be the date of this celebrated triumph of love over sovereignty, tradition paints out precisely the scene of the first interview between the lovely widow and the youthful king. Elizabeth waylaid Edward IV. in the forest of Whittlebury, a royal chase, when he was hunting in the neighborhood of her mother's dower-castle, at Grafton. There she waited for him, under a noble tree, still known in the local traditions of Northamptonshire by the name of the Queen's Oak. Under the shelter of its branches the fair widow addressed the young

monarch, holding her fatherless boys by the hands; and when Edward
paused to listen to her, she threw herself at his feet, and pleaded earnestly for the restoration of Bradgate, the inheritance of her children.
Her downcast looks and mournful beauty not only gained her suit, but
the heart of the conqueror.

The Queen's Oak, which was the scene of more than one interview
between the beautiful Elizabeth and the enamored Edward, stands in
the direct track of communication between Grafton Castle and Whittlebury Forest; it now rears its hollow trunk, a venerable witness of one
of the most romantic facts that history records.

Edward tried every art, to induce Elizabeth to become his own
on other terms than as the sharer of his regal dignity; the beautiful
widow made this memorable reply: "My liege, I know I am not good
enough to be your queen, but I am far too good to become your
mistress."

She then left him to settle the question in his own breast; for she
knew he had betrayed others, whose hearts had deceived them into al-
lowing him undue liberties. Her affections, in all probability, still clave
to the memory of the husband of her youth, and her indifference increased the love of the young king. The struggle ended in his offering
her marriage. The duchess of Bedford, when she found matters had
proceeded to this climax, took the management of the affair, and, pretending to conceal the whole from the knowledge of her husband,
arranged the private espousals of her daughter and the king. In the
quaint words of Fabyan, the marriage is thus described:—"In most
secret manner, upon the 1st of May, 1464, king Edward spoused Elizabeth,' late being wife of sir John Gray. Which spousals were solemnized early in the morning at the town called Grafton, near to Stoney
Stratford."

Of all persons, the marriage of Elizabeth gave the most offence to
the mother of Edward IV. This lady, who had assumed all the state of
a queen, before the fall of her husband, Richard, duke of York, at
Wakefield, was infuriated at having to give place to the daughter
of a man who commenced his career as a poor squire, of ordinary
lineage. Among other arguments against her son's wedlock was,
that the fact of Elizabeth being a widow ought to prevent her mar-

riage with a king, since the sovereignty would be dishonored by such
bigamy.

This is the version king Edward's courtiers chose to give of the
conversation; but there is little doubt the duchess of York reproached
her son with the breach of his marriage-contract with Elizabeth Lucy,
the predecessor of Elizabeth Woodville in the affections of Edward.

It was at the ancient palace of Reading, on Michaelmas Day, 1464,
that Edward IV. finally declared Elizabeth to be his wedded wife. A
council of the peers was convoked there, when the king took Elizabeth
by the hand, and presented her to them as his rightful queen. She was
then led by the young duke of Clarence, in solemn pomp, to the stately
abbey-church of Reading, where she was publicly declared queen, and,
having made her offering, received the congratulations of all the nobility assembled there, among whom, some authorities declare, was the
earl of Warwick.

The coronation of Elizabeth was appointed at Westminster Abbey,
Whitsunday, the 26th of May. She was carried through the city to
her palace of Westminster, in a litter borne on long poles, like a sedan
chair, supported by stately pacing steeds. The new-made knights all
rode, on this occasion, in solemn procession before the queen's litter.
She was crowned next day, with great solemnity, in Westminster Abbey, the young duke of Clarence officiating as high steward. After the
coronation, the queen sat in state at a grand banquet in Westminster
Hall, where the bishop of Rochester, who sang the mass at her consecration, took his place at the king's right hand, and the duke of Buckingham (now the king's brother-in-law, by reason of his wedlock with
Katharine Woodville) sat at his left.

The enmity between Elizabeth and Warwick had not at this time
amounted to any thing serious, since he stood as godfather to her eldest
daughter, born at Westminster Palace, 1466. The baptism of this
princess for a while conciliated her two grandmothers, Cicely, duchess
of York, and Jaquetta, duchess of Bedford, who were likewise her
sponsors. The christening was performed with royal pomp, and the
babe received her mother's name of Elizabeth,—a proof that Edward
was more inclined to pay a compliment to his wife than to his haughty
mother

Some months after the queen had brought an heiress to the throne, she ventured on another affront to the all-powerful minister, general, and relative of her royal lord. Warwick had set his mind on marrying Anne, the heiress of the duke of Exeter, to his nephew, George Neville. Meantime the queen slily bought the consent of the rapacious duchess of Exeter, for four thousand marks, and married the young bride to her eldest son by sir John Gray, at Greenwich Palace, October 1466. The queen's eagerness for wealthy alliances was punished by the loss of her purchase-money, for the heiress of Exeter died in her minority.

Elizabeth's court is described in a lively manner, by an eye-witness, who was her guest, both at Windsor and Westminster, in 1472. This person was Louis of Bruges, lord of Grauthuse, governor of Holland, who had hospitably received Edward, when he fled, in the preceding year, from England, and landed with a few friends at Sluys, "the most distressed company of creatures," as Comines affirms, "that ever was seen;" for Edward had pawned his military cloak, lined with martin fur, to pay the master of his ship, and was put on shore in his waistcoat. The lord of Grauthuse received him, and fed and clothed him. This Fleming had previously performed a mighty service for Edward, when, as ambassador from Philip of Burgundy, he had visited Scotland, and broken the contract between the daughter of the Scots queen-regent, and the son of Margaret of Anjou.

Finally, Grauthuse lent Edward IV. money and ships, without which he would never have been restored to his country and queen. After his restoration, Edward invited his benefactor to England, in order to testify his gratitude, and introduce him to his queen. A journal, written either by this nobleman or his secretary, has been lately brought to light, containing the following curious passages:—" When the lord of Grauthuse came to Windsor, my lord Hastings received him, and led him to the far side of the quadrant (the quadrangle of Windsor Castle), to three chambers, where the king was then with the queen. These apartments were very richly hung with cloth of gold arras; and when he had spoken with the king, who presented him to the queen's grace, they then ordered the lord chamberlain Hastings to conduct him to his chamber, where supper was ready for him."

After his refreshment the king had him brought immediately to the queen's own withdrawing-room, where she and her ladies were playing at the marteaux; and some of her ladies were playing at closheys of ivory, and some at divers other games, the which sight was full pleasant. Also king Edward danced with my lady Elizabeth, his eldest daughter. "In the morning, when matins were done, the king heard in his own chapel (that of St. George, at Windsor Castle), Our Lady mass, which was most melodiously sung. When the mass was done, king Edward gave his guest a cup of gold, garnished with pearl. In the midst of the cup was a great piece of unicorn's horn, to *my* estimation seven inches in compass; and on the cover of the cup a great sapphire. Then the king came into the quadrant. My lord prince, also, borne by his chamberlain, called master Vaughan, bade the lord Grauthuse welcome." (The innocent little prince was then only eighteen months old.) "Then the king took his guest into the little park, where they had great sport, and there the king made him ride on his own horse, a right fair hobby, the which the king gave him. The king's dinner was ordained (ordered) in the lodge of Windsor Park. After dinner, the king showed his guest his garden and vineyard of pleasure. Then the queen did ordain a great banquet in her own apartments, at which king Edward, her eldest daughter, the duchess of Exeter, the lady Rivers, and the lord of Grauthuse, all sat with her at one mess; and at another table, sat the duke of Buckingham, my lady, his wife, my lord Hastings, chamberlain to the king, my lord Berners, chamberlain to the queen, the son of lord Grauthuse, and master George Barthe, secretary to the duke of Burgundy. There was a side table, at which sat a great *view* of ladies, all on one side of the room. Also on one side of the outer chamber sat the queen's gentlewoman. And when they had supped, my lady Elizabeth, the king's eldest daughter, danced with the duke of Buckingham, her aunt's husband."

It appears to have been the etiquette of this court, that this young princess, then but six years old, should only dance with her father or uncles.

"Then about nine of the clock, the king and the queen, with her ladies and gentlewomen, brought the lord of Grauthuse to three chambers of pleasaunce, all hanged with white silk and linen cloth, and all

22

the floors covered with carpets. There was ordained a bed for himself, of as good down as could be gotten. The sheets of Rennes cloth; also fine festoons; the counterpane cloth of gold, furred with ermines. The tester and *ceiler* also shining cloth of gold; the curtains of white sarcenet; as for his head-suit and pillows, they were of the queen's own ordering. In the second chamber was likewise another state-bed, all white. Also in the chamber was made a couch with feather-beds, and hanged above like a tent, knit like a net, and there was a cupboard. In the third chamber was ordained a bayne (bath) or two, which were covered with tents of white cloth.''

Could the present age offer a more luxurious or elegant arrangement in a suit of sleeping-rooms, than in those provided by Elizabeth for her husband's friend?

The queen presided over the espousals of her second son, Richard, duke of York, with Anne Mowbray, the infant heiress of the duchy of Norfolk. St. Stephen's chapel, where the ceremony was performed, January, 1477, was splendidly hung with arras of gold on this occasion. The king, the young prince of Wales, the three princesses, Elizabeth, Mary, and Cicely, were present; the queen led the little bridegroom, who was not five, and her brother, earl Rivers, led the baby bride, scarcely three years old. They afterwards all partook of a rich banquet, laid out in the painted chamber. The innocent and ill-fated infants then married, verified the old English proverb, which says.

> " Early wed, early dead.''

The death of Edward IV. is said to have been hurried by the pain of mind he felt at the conduct of Louis XI., who broke the engagement he had made to marry the dauphin to the princess Elizabeth of York; but intermittent fever was the immediate cause of his death. When expiring he made his favorites, Stanley and Hastings, vow reconciliation with the queen and her family; and, propped with pillows, the dying monarch exhorted them to protect his young sons. He died with great professions of penitence.

Edward expired at Westminster, April 9th, 1483. On the day of his death, his body, with the face, arms, and breast uncovered, was laid out on a board for nine hours, and all the nobility, and the lord-mayor and aldermen of London, sent for to recognize it, and testify that he was really dead.

Elizabeth was left, in reality, far more desolate and unprotected in her second than in her first widowhood. The young king was pursuing his studies at Ludlow Castle, and presiding over his principality of Wales, under the care of his accomplished uncle, Rivers, and the guardianship of his faithful chamberlain, Vaughan, the same person who carried him in his arms, after the queen and his royal father, on all public occasions, when the little prince was a lovely babe of eighteen months old.

Elizabeth sat at the first council after the death of her husband, and proposed that the young king should be escorted to London with a powerful army. Fatally for himself and his royal master's children, jealousy of the Woodvilles prompted Hastings to contradict this prudent measure. He asked her insolently, "Against whom the young sovereign was to be defended? Who were his foes? Not his valiant uncle Gloucester? Not Stanley, or himself? Was not this proposed force rather destined to confirm the power of her kindred, and enable them to violate the oaths of amity they had so lately sworn by the death-bed of their royal master?" He finished by vowing, "that he would retire from court, if the young king was brought to London surrounded by soldiers."

Thus taunted, the hapless Elizabeth gave up, with tears, the precautionary measures her maternal instinct had dictated; the necessity for which not a soul in that infatuated council foreboded but herself, and even *she* was not aware of her real enemy. The turbulent and powerful aristocracy, at the head of whom was Hastings, and who had ever opposed her family, were the persons she evidently dreaded. The duke of Gloucester had been very little at court since the restoration, and never yet had entered into angry collision with the Woodvilles. He was now absent, at his government of the Scottish borders. When he heard of the death of the king, he immediately caused Edward V. to be proclaimed at York, and wrote a letter of condolence to the queen, so full of deference, kindness, and submission, that Elizabeth thought she should have a most complying friend in the first prince of the blood.

The council commanded earl Rivers to bring up the young king, unattended by the militia of the Welsh border,—those hardy soldiers, who had more than once turned the scale of conquest in favor of York; if they had now been headed by the gallant Rivers, they would have insured the safety of Edward V.

The astounding tidings, that the duke of Gloucester, abetted by the duke of Buckingham, had intercepted the young king, with an armed force, on his progress to London, had seized his person, and arrested earl Rivers and lord Richard Gray, on the 29th of April, were brought to the queen, at midnight, on the 3d of May. Elizabeth then bitterly bewailed the time that she was persuaded from calling out the militia. In that moment of agony she, however, remembered, that while she could keep her second son in safety, the life of the young king was secure. "Therefore," says Hall, "she took her young son, the duke of York, and her daughters, and went out of the palace of Westminster into the sanctuary, and there lodged in the abbot's place, and she, and all her children and company, were registered as sanctuary persons." Dorset, the queen's eldest son, directly he heard of the arrest of his brother, weakly forsook his important trust, as constable of the Tower, and came into Sanctuary to his mother. "Before day broke, the lord-chancellor, then the archbishop of Rotherham, who lived in York Place, beside Westminster Abbey, having received the news of the duke of Gloucester's proceedings, called up his servants, and took with him the great seal, and went to the queen, about whom he found much heaviness, rumble, haste, and business, with conveyance of her (household) stuff into sanctuary." The queen sat alone below on the rushes, in a state of desolation. Another chronicler adds to this picturesque description, "that her long fair hair, so renowned for its beauty, escaped from its confinement, and, streaming over her person, swept on the ground:" —a strange contrast with the rigid etiquette of royal widows' costume, which commanded not only that such profusion of glittering tresses should be hid under hood and veil, but that even the queen's forehead should be covered with a white frontlet, and her chin, to the upper lip, with a piece of lawn called a barb. The faithful archbishop acquainted the sorrowing queen with a cheering message, "sent him by lord Hastings in the night."

"'Ah, woe worth him!' replied Elizabeth, 'for it is he that goeth about to destroy me and my blood.'"

The queen took with her into sanctuary Elizabeth, seventeen years old at this time, afterwards married to Henry VII. The next princess, Mary, had died at Greenwich, a twelvemonth before this calamitous period. Cicely, whom Hall calls "less fortunate than fair," was in her fifteenth year; she afterwards married lord Wells. These three princesses had been the companions of their mother in 1470, when she had formerly sought sanctuary. Richard, duke of York, born at Shrewsbury in 1472, was at this time eleven years old. Anne, born in 1474, after the date of her father's will (in which only the eldest daughters are named), was about eight years old. Katherine, born at Eltham, about August, 1479, then between three and four years old; she afterwards married the heir of Devonshire. Bridget, born at Eltham, 1480, Nov. 20th, then only in her third year; she was devoted to the convent from her birth, and was afterwards professed a nun at Dartford.

The queen had, in council, appointed May 4th for her son's coronation; his false uncle, however, did not bring him to London till that day Edward V. then entered the city, surrounded by officers of the duke of Gloucester's retinue, who were all in deep mourning for the death of the late monarch. At the head of this posse rode Gloucester himself, habited in black, with his cap in his hand, oft-times bowing low, and pointing out his nephew (who wore the royal mantle of purple velvet) to the homage of the citizens. Edward V. was at first lodged at the bishop of Ely's palace; but as the good bishop (in common with all the high clergy) was faithful to the heirs of Edward IV., the young king was soon transferred to the regal apartments in the Tower, under pretence of awaiting his coronation. Gloucester's next object was to get possession of prince Richard, then safe with the queen. After a long and stormy debate, between the ecclesiastical peers and the temporal peers, at a council held in the Star Chamber (close to Elizabeth's retreat), it was decided "that there might be sanctuary men and women, but as children could commit no crime for which an asylum was needed, the privileges of sanctuary could not extend to them ; therefore the duke of Gloucester, who was now recognized as lord-protecter, could possess himself of his nephew by force, if he pleased." The archbishop of Canterbury was unwilling that force should be used, and he went with a deputation of the temporal peers, to persuade Elizabeth to surrender her son. When they arrived at the Jerusalem Chamber, the archbishop urged "that the young king required the company of his brother, being melancholy without a playfellow." To this Elizabeth replied,—

"Troweth the protector (ah, pray God he may prove a protector!) that the king doth lack a playfellow ? Can none be found to play with the king, but only his brother, which hath no wish to play because of sickness? as though princes, so young as they be, could not play without their peers—or children could not play without their kindred, with whom (for the most part) they agree worse than with strangers!"

At last she said, "My lord, and all my lords now present, I will not be so suspicious as to mistrust your truths." Then, taking young Richard by the hand, she continued, "Lo, here is this gentleman, whom I doubt not would be safely kept by me, if I were permitted; and well do I know there be some such deadly enemies to my blood, that, if they wist where any lay in their own bodies, they would let it out if they could. The desire of a kingdom knoweth no kindred; brothers have been brothers' bane, and may the nephews be sure of the uncle? Each of these children are safe while they be asunder. Notwithstanding, I here deliver him, and his brother's life with him, into your hands, and of you shall I require them before God and man. Faithful be ye I wot well, and power ye have, if ye list, to keep them safe; but if ye think I fear too much, yet beware ye fear not too little!" And therewithal, continued she, to the child, "Farewell, mine own sweet son! God send you good keeping! Let me kiss you once ere you go, for God knoweth when we shall kiss together again!"

And therewith she kissed and blessed him, and turned her back and wept, leaving the poor innocent child weeping as fast as herself.

When the archbishop and the deputation of lords had received the young duke, they brought him into the Star Chamber, where the lord protector took him in his arms, with these words, "Now, welcome, my lord, with all my very heart!" He then brought him to the bishop's palace at St. Paul's, and from thence honorably through the city to the young king at the Tower, out of which they were never seen abroad.

Soon afterwards, the faction of the duke of Gloucester presented a petition, to prevent the crown from falling to the issue of "the pretended marriage between king Edward and Elizabeth Gray, made without the assent of the lords of the land, and by the sorcery of the said Elizabeth and her mother Jaquetta (as the public voice is through the land), priv- ily and secretly, in a chamber, without proclamation by banns, according to the laudable custom of the church of England; the said king Edward being married and troth-plight a long time before to one Eleanor Butler, daughter to the old earl of Shrewsbury." A forced recognition of Richard as king, in the hall of Crosby House, his town residence, fol- lowed the presentation of this petition, and from that day, June 26th, the son of Elizabeth was considered deposed. The coronation of Rich- ard III. took place ten days after.

Among the gloomy range of fortresses belonging to the Tower, tra- dition has pointed out the Portcullis Tower as the scene of the murder of the young princes. The royal children were probably removed to this building when their uncle came to take possession of the regal apart- ments in the Tower, on the 4th of July. "Forthwith the two young princes were both shut up, and all their people removed, but only one, called Black Will, or Will Slaughter, who was set to serve them, and four keepers to guard them. The young king was heard to say, sigh- ingly, 'I would mine uncle would let me have my life, though he taketh my crown.' After which time the prince never tied his points, nor any thing attended to himself, but with that young babe, his brother, linger- ed in thought and heaviness till the traitorous deed delivered them from wretchedness."

"But when," continues sir Thomas More, "the news was first brought to the unfortunate mother, yet being in sanctuary, that her two sons were murdered, it struck to her heart like the sharp dart of death; she was so suddenly amazed that she swooned and fell to the ground, and there lay in great agony, like to a dead corpse. And after she was revived and came to her memory again, she wept and sobbed, and with pitiful screeches filled the whole mansion. Her breast she beat, her fair hair she tared and pulled in pieces, and calling by name her sweet babes, accounted herself mad when she delivered her younger son out of sanctuary, for his uncle to put him to death. After long lamentations, she kneeled down and cried to God to take vengeance, 'who,' she said, 'she nothing doubted would remember it;' and when in a few months Richard unexpectedly lost his only son, the child for whose advancement he had steeped his soul in crime, Englishmen declared that the imprecations of the agonized mother had been heard."

The wretched queen's health sank under the load of intense anguish inflicted by these murders, which had been preceded by the illegal execution of her son, lord Richard Gray, and of her noble-minded brother at Pontefract.

After the utter failure of Buckingham's insurrections, Elizabeth was reduced to despair, and finally was forced to leave sanctuary, and surrender herself and daughters into the hands of the usurper, March, 1484. For this step she has been blamed severely, by those who have not taken a clear and close view of the difficulties of her situation. She had probably, in the course of ten months, exhausted her own means, and tried the hospitality of the monks at Westminster. Moreover, though the king could not lawfully infringe the liberties of sanctuary, he could cut off supplies of food, and starve out the inmates, and he kept a guard of soldiers round the abbey, commanded by John Nesfield, who watched all comers and goers. Elizabeth, however, would not leave her retreat, without exacting a solemn oath, guaranteeing the safety of her children from Richard; which the usurper took in the presence of the lord-mayor and aldermen, as well as the lords of the council. The terms of Elizabeth's surrender are peculiarly bitter; for it is evident that she and her daughters not only descended into the rank of mere private gentlewomen, but she herself was held in personal restraint.

The successful termination of the expedition undertaken by the earl of Richmond, to obtain his promised bride, and the crown of England, at once avenged the widowed queen and her family on the usurper, and restored her to liberty. Instead of being under the despotic control of the royal hunchback's men-at-arms, the queen made joyful preparation to receive her eldest daughter, who was brought to her at Westminster, from Sheriff Hutton, with honor, attended by a great company of noble ladies.

Queen Elizabeth had the care of her daughter till the January following the battle of Bosworth, when she saw her united in marriage to Henry of Richmond, the acknowledged king of England.

One of Henry VII.'s first acts was to invest the mother of his queen with the privileges and state befitting her rank, as the widow of an English sovereign. She had never been recognized as queen-dowager excepting in the few wrangling privy councils that intervened, between the death of her husband, and her retreat into the abbey of Westminster; and even during these, her advice had been disregarded, and her orders defied; therefore to Henry VII., her son-in-law, she owed the first regular recognition of her rights, as widow of an English sovereign.

This queen had passed through a series of calamities, sufficient to wean the most frivolous person from pleasure and pageantry; she had to mourn the untimely deaths of three murdered sons, and she had four daughters wholly destitute, and dependent on her for their support; it can therefore scarcely be matter of surprise, that in the decline of life she seldom shared in the gayeties of her daughter's court.

Soon afterwards, Henry VII. sought to strengthen his interest in Scotland, by negotiating a marriage between James III. and his mother-in-law, a husband certainly young enough to be her son; yet his violent death alone prevented her from wearing the crown matrimonial of Scotland,—when she would have been placed in a situation to injure her son-in-law, if such had been her wish.

The daughter of Elizabeth attended her death-bed, and paid her affectionate attention; the queen alone was prevented, having taken to her chamber, preparatory to the birth of the princess Margaret. Elizabeth died the Friday before Whitsuntide, and as she expressed an earnest wish for speedy and private burial, her funeral took place on Whitsunday, 1492.

In 1810, when the place of sepulture for the family of George III. was in course of preparation, at the east end of St. George's chapel, an excavation was formed in the solid bed of chalk of the full size of the

23

edifice above, when two stone coffins, containing the bodies of queen Elizabeth Woodville and her son prince George, were discovered, fifteen feet below the surface: thus realizing the emphatic words of Southey—

> "Thou, Elizabeth, art here:
>   Thou to whom all griefs were known;
> Who wert placed upon a bier
>   In happier hour than on a throne."

ANNE OF WARWICK,

QUEEN OF RICHARD III.

ANNE OF WARWICK, the last of our Plantagenet queens, and the first who had previously borne the title of princess of Wales, was born at Warwick Castle, in the year 1454. On each side of the faded, melancholy portrait of this unfortunate lady, in the pictorial history of her maternal ancestry, called the Rous Roll, two mysterious hands are introduced, offering to her the rival crowns of York and Lancaster; while the white bear, the cognizance assumed by her mighty sire, Warwick the king-maker, lies muzzled at her feet, as if the royal lions of Plantagenet had quelled the pride of that hitherto tameless bear, on the blood-stained heath of Barnet.

Passing over events that led to the deposition of Henry VI., positive proof may be found, that Anne of Warwick and Richard of Gloucester were companions, when he was about fourteen, and she twelve years old. After Richard had been created duke of Gloucester, at his brother's coronation, it is highly probable he was consigned to the guardianship of the earl of Warwick, at Middleham Castle; for, at the grand enthronization of George Neville, the uncle of Anne, as archbishop of York, Richard was a guest at York Palace, seated in the place of honor, in the chief banquetting-room, upon the dais, under a cloth of estate or canopy, with the countess of Westmoreland on his left hand; his sister, the duchess of Suffolk, on his right; and the noble maidens his cousins, the lady Anne and the lady Isabel, seated opposite to him. These ladies must have been placed there expressly to please the prince, by affording him companions of his own age, since the countess of Warwick, their mother, sat at the second table, in a place much lower in dignity. Richard being the son of lady Anne's great aunt, an intimacy naturally subsisted between such near relatives. Majerres, a Flemish annalist, affirms that Richard had formed a very strong affection for his cousin Anne; but succeeding events proved, that the lady did not bestow the same regard on him which her sister Isabel did on his brother Clarence, nor was it to be expected, considering his disagreeable person and temper. As lady Anne did not smile on her crook-backed cousin, there was no inducement for him to forsake the cause of his brother, king Edward.

After Margaret was taken away to the Tower of London, Clarence privately abducted his sister-in-law, under the pretence of protecting her. As he was her sister's husband, he was exceedingly unwilling to divide the united inheritance of Warwick and Salisbury, which he knew must be done, if his brother Gloucester carried into execution his avowed intention of marrying Anne. But very different was the conduct of the young widow of the prince of Wales from that described by Shakspeare. Instead of acting as chief mourner to the hearse of her husband's murdered father, she was sedulously concealing herself from her abhorred cousin; enduring every privation to avoid his notice, and concurring with all the schemes of her self-interested brother-in-law, Clarence, so completely, as to descend from the rank of princess of Wales, to the disguise of a servant, in a mean house in London, in the hope of eluding the search of Gloucester; incidents too romantic to be believed without the testimony of a Latin chronicler of the highest authority, who affirms it in the following words:—"Richard duke of Gloucester wished to discover Anne, the youngest daughter of the earl of Warwick, in order to marry her; this was much disapproved by his brother, the duke of Clarence, who did not wish to divide his wife's inheritance. He, therefore, hid the young lady. But the cunning of the duke of Gloucester discovered her, in the disguise of a cook-maid in the city of London, and he immediately transferred her to the sanctuary of St. Martin's le Grand." She needed this asylum, because she was under the attainder in which her hapless mother and queen Margaret were included.

The unfortunate widow of prince Edward was, after this, removed to the protection of her uncle George, the archbishop of York, and was even permitted to visit and comfort her mother-in-law, queen Margaret, at the Tower; but as she still resisted marrying Richard, she was deprived of her uncle's protection, her last refuge against her hated cousin.

The marriage of the lady Anne and Richard duke of Gloucester took place at Westminster, 1473, probably a few days before the date of Paston's letter. Prevost affirms she was compelled by violence to marry Richard. Some illegalities were connected with this ceremony, assuredly arising from the reluctance of the bride, since the Parliamentary Rolls of the next year contain a curious act, empowering the duke of Gloucester "to continue the full possession and enjoyment of Anne's property, even if she were to *divorce him*, provided he did his best to be reconciled and re-married to her:"—ominous clauses relating to a wedlock of a few months!—but which prove that Anne meditated availing herself of some informality in her abhorred marriage; but if she had done so, her husband would have remained in possession of her property. The birth of her son Edward at Middleham Castle, 1474, probably reconciled the unhappy duchess of Gloucester to her miserable fate; but that her marriage was never legalized, may be guessed by the rumors of a subsequent period, when the venomous hunchback, her cousin-husband, meditated in his turn divorcing *her*.

Richard and Anne lived chiefly at Middleham Castle, in Yorkshire, an abode convenient for the office borne by the duke, as governor of the northern marches. As a very active war was proceeding with Scotland, in the course of which Richard won several battles, and captured Edinburgh, his reluctant wife was not troubled much with his company, but devoted herself to her boy, in whom all her affections were centred, and the very springs of her life wound up in his welfare.

The death of Edward IV. caused a great change in the life of Anne. The duke of Gloucester, who had very recently returned from Scotland, left Anne and his boy at Middleham, when he departed, with a troop of horse, to intercept his young nephew, Edward V., on pro-

... Anne a succession of astounding crimes, Richard ... the ... of his nephew's throne, and Anne of Warwick was ... to the ... of consort to an English monarch. She ... to London with her ... in time to share her husband's corona... ... and her arrival was but just before that event, as ... the ... of her ... it was only bought two days preceding the ... . There ... Three liveries to deliver for the use ... of ... and parts of gold, a cloth of gold, upon ... Some time had the tirewomen of Anne of War... ... in the dining of her regal robes, since this ... was ... in the 5th of the same month. Sunday, July ... Richard ... and previously been proclaimed king, conducted his ... in great state, by water from Baynard's Castle to ... where his hapless little prisoners were made to vacate the ... and were consigned to a tower near the Water Gate, ... the Bloody Tower. The same day Anne's only child, ... was created prince of Wales. The grand procession of the ... and their young heir, through the city, took place on ... when they were attended from the Tower by four thousand ... persons whom the king and queen called "gentlemen of the ... who were regarded by the citizens as an ungentle and sus... ...working pack of vagabonds. The next day, July 5th, the coro... ... Richard and his queen took place, with an unusual display of ... part of which had been prepared for the coronation of ... Edward V.

After the ceremony was over, queen Anne went to Windsor Castle, with the ... her son. There Richard left her, while he undertook a ... progress ending at Tewksbury. The queen and prince then ... their ... progress in which they were attended by many ... flowers and the Spanish ambassador, who had come to pro... ... a ... between the eldest daughter of his sovereigns, Ferdi... ... and Isabella, and the son of Richard III. The queen took up her ... at Warwick Castle, the place of her birth, and the grand feudal ... which belonged to the young earl of Warwick (the ... ... and the duke of Clarence) and it is especially ... it brought him with her. Richard III. joined his

queen at Warwick Castle, where they kept court with great magnificence for a week. It must have been at this visit that the portraits of
queen Anne, of Richard III., and their son, were added to the Rous Roll.
The popular opinion concerning Richard's deformity is verified by the
portrait; for his figure, if not crooked, is decidedly hunchy; nor must
this appearance be attributed to the artist's lack of skill in delineating
the human form, for the neighboring portrait, by the same hand, representing Anne's father, the great earl of Warwick, is as finely proportioned as if meant for a model of St. George. Richard, on the contrary,
has high thick shoulders, and no neck. Surely, if the king's ungainly
figure had not been matter of great notoriety, an artist capable of making such a noble sketch as that of the earl, would not have brought the
king's ears and shoulders in quite such close contact. Warwick was
dead, Richard was alive, when this series of portraits closes; therefore,
if any pictorial flattery exists, in all probability Richard had the advantage of it.

It is a doubtful point whether Anne approved of the crimes which
advanced her son. Tradition declares she abhorred them, but parliamentary documents prove she shared with sir James Tyrrel the plunder
of Richard's opponents, after the rebellion of Buckingham was crushed.
She received one hundred marks, the king seven hundred marks, and
sir James Tyrrel two manors from sir William Knyvet, being the purchase-money for his life. Anne's share of this plunder amounts to considerable more than her proportion of queen-gold.

If Anne had even passively consented to the unrighteous advancement of her family, punishment quickly followed; for her son, on the
last day of March, 1484, died at Middleham Castle "an unhappy death."
This expression, used by Rous, his family chronicler, leads his readers
to imagine that this boy, so deeply idolized by his guilty father, came
by his end in some sudden and awful manner. His parents were not
with him, but were as near as Nottingham Castle, when he expired.
The loss of this child, in whom all Anne's hopes and happiness were
garnered struck to her heart, and she never again knew a moment's
health or comfort; she seemed even to court death eagerly. Nor was
this dreadful loss her only calamity. Richard had no other child; his
declining and miserable consort was not likely to bring another; and if

he did not consider her in the way, his guilty and ruffianly satellites certainly did; for they began to whisper dark things concerning the illegality of the king's marriage, and the possibility of its being set aside. As Edward IV.'s parliament considered that it was possible for Anne to divorce Richard in 1474, it cannot be doubted that Richard could have resorted to the same manner in getting rid of her, when queen.

Her evident decline, however, prevented Richard from giving himself any trouble regarding a divorce; yet it did not restrain him from uttering peevish complaints to Rotherham, archbishop of York, regarding his wife's sickliness and disagreeable qualities.

Within the year that deprived Anne of her only son, maternal sorrow put an end to her existence, by a decline, slow enough to acquit her husband of poisoning her; a crime of which he is acused by most writers. She died at Westminster Palace, on March 16th, 1485, in the midst of the greatest eclipse of the sun that had happened for many years. Her funeral was most pompous and magnificent. Her husband was present, and was observed to shed tears, deemed hypocritical by the bystanders, but those who knew that he had been brought up with Anne, might suppose that he felt some instinctive yearnings of long companionship, when he saw her laid in that grave where his ambitious interests had caused him to wish her to be. Human nature, with all its conflicting passions and instincts, abounds with such inconsistencies, which are often startingly apparent in the hardest characters.

ELIZABETH OF YORK,

SURNAMED THE GOOD,

QUEEN OF HENRY VII.

THE princess Elizabeth was born at the palace of Westminster, February 11th, 1466. She was baptized in Westminster Abbey, with as much pomp as if she had been the heir apparent of England; indeed, the attention Edward IV. bestowed upon her in her infancy was extraordinary. He was actuated by a strong presentiment that this beautiful and gracious child would ultimately prove the representative of his line.

The fortunes of the young Elizabeth suffered the most signal reverse, directly she lost her royal sire and only efficient protector. From Westminster palace she was, with her second brother and younger sisters, hurried, by the queen her mother, into the sanctuary of Westminster, which had formerly sheltered her in childhood. But Elizabeth of York was no longer an unconscious child, who sported as gayly with her little sisters in the abbot of Westminster's garden as she did in the flowery meads of Shene. She had grown up into the beauties of early womanhood, and was the sharer of her royal mother's woes.

The treaty of betrothment, privately negotiated between Elizabeth of York and Henry of Richmond, by their respective mothers, was the first gleam of comfort that broke on the royal prisoners in sanctuary after the murder of the innocent princes in the Tower. The young princess promised to hold faith with her betrothed; in case of her

24

death before her contract was fulfilled, her next sister Cicely was to take her place.

The princess, according to Brereton, having accidentally met lord Stanley at a time and place convenient for conference, urged him passionately, by the name of "Father Stanley," and with many reminiscences of all he owed to her father, to assist her in the restoration of her rights. At first lord Stanley repulsed her, declaring he could not break the oath he had sworn to king Richard, observing, moreover, that women were proverbially "unstable of council." Elizabeth renewed her importunities, but when he seemed quite inflexible—

> "Her color changed as pale as lead,
> Her *face* that shone as golden wire,
> She tare it off beside her head."

After this agony she sunk into a swoon, and remained some time speechless. Lord Stanley was overcome by the earnestness of her anguish.

"Stand up, lady Bessy," he said, "now I see you do not feign, I will tell you that I have long thought of the matter as you do, but it is difficult to trust the secrecy of women, and many a man is brought to great woe by making them his confidents." He then added "that his adherents would rise at his bidding, if he could go to the northwest in person; but that he durst not trust a scribe to indite his intentions in letters." This difficulty the princess obviated by declaring that she could "indite and write as well as the scrivener who taught her." Then lord Stanley agreed she should write the letters without delay.

After the princess had written the dispatches, and lord Stanley had *sealed* them with his *seal*, they agreed that Humphrey Brereton, who had always been true to king Edward IV., should set out with the letters to the northwest of England. Lord Stanley and his man slept that night in Elizabeth's suite of apartments, but she watched till dawning of the day.

> " And Bessy waked all that night,
> There came no sleep within her eye,

"Soon in the morn, as the day-spring,
Up riseth the young Bessye,
And maketh haste in her dressing,
To Humphrey Brereton gone is she.
And when she came to Humphrey's bower,
With a small voice called she;
Humphrey answered that lady bright
Saying,—' Who calleth here so early?'
' I am king Edward's daughter right,
The countess Clere, young Bessey;
In all haste, with means and might,
Thou must come to Lord Stanley!' "

The lady "fair and sweet " guided Humphrey to the bedside of his master, who gave him directions for the safe delivery of six letters.

When Brereton returned from his expedition he found lord Stanley walking with king Richard in the palace garden; Stanley gave him a sign of secrecy, and Humphrey declared before the king, that he had been taking a vacation of recreation among his friends in Cheshire. After a coaxing and hypocritical speech of Richard, regarding his affection for the "poor commonality," he went to his own apartments in the palace. Brereton then obtained an interview of the princess, to whom he detailed the success of his expedition. Elizabeth received the intelligence with extraordinary gratitude, and agreed to meet her confederates in secret council when they arrived from the north.

The place of meeting was an old inn in the London suburbs, between Holborn and Islington; an eagle's foot was chalked on the door as the token of the place of meeting for the disguised gentlemen who came from Cheshire and Lancashire. Thither, according to our poet, the princess and Stanley repaired secretly by night, After Elizabeth had conferred with her allies, and satisfied herself that they would not murder Richmond, out of their Yorkist prejudices, if he trusted himself among the Stanley powers, she agreed to send him a ring of betrothal, with a letter, informing him of the strength of the party propitious to the union of York and Lancaster. Humphrey Brereton undertook the dangerous task of carrying the dispatches. He embarked at Liverpool, a port then little known to the rest of England; but the shipping, and all other matters there, were at the command of the house of Stanley.

Henry received Brereton civilly, he kissed the ring of rich stones that Elizabeth had sent him, but, with the characteristic caution which ever distinguished him, remained three weeks before he gave him an answer.

On the 1st of August, Henry sailed with the united fleets of France and Bretagne from Harfleur, on his chivalric enterprise to win a wife and crown.

On the evening of the 21st, the two rival armies encamped on the appropriately named heath of Redmore, near Bosworth. Richard went out at twilight to reconnoitre. He found a sentinel fast asleep at the outposts. The prompt tyrant stabbed him to the heart, with these stern soldierly words: "I found him asleep, and I leave him so."

Notwithstanding his ill rest, Richard was the next morning energetically active, reckoning on overwhelming Richmond at once by a tremendous charge of cavalry. Richmond must have possessed great moral courage to risk a battle, for his father-in-law was till the moment of onset dubious in his indications. At last lord Stanley and his brother sir William joined Richmond's forces, and the odds were turned against the usurper. Yet the battle raged on Redmore Heath for more than two hours. King Richard made in person three furious charges, the last being the most desperate, after his friend the duke of Norfolk was slain; when Richard, overthrowing all opposers, made his way to where Richmond's standard flew, in hopes of a personal encounter with his rival, he was borne down by numbers at the foot of the hill near Amyon-lays. His blood tinged the pretty brooklet which issues from the hill; it literally ran red that day, and to this hour the common people refuse to drink of its waters.

While these events were transacting, the royal maiden who was to prove the prize of the victor remained in the lonely halls of the Yorkshire castle of Sheriff Hutton, with no companion but its young and imbecile owner, her cousin Warwick. A sudden outburst of joy throughout the country, and the thronging of the population of the district

about the gates of her prison, told Elizabeth that her cause had prospered, and that Richard was overthrown. Soon after came sir Robert
Willoughby, sent by the new king, Henry VII., from Bosworth, with
orders to bring the princess Elizabeth and her cousin to London with all
convenient speed.

Henry VII., in the mean time, set out from Leicester, and by easy
journeys arrived in the metropolis. The lord mayor and citizens met
him at Shoreditch, and recognized him as king of England.

Elizabeth and Henry were within the prohibited degrees: to obtain
a special dispensation was the work of time; but, in order to indulge
the wishes of the nation for their immediate union, an ordinary dispensation was procured from the pope's resident legate, and the royal pair
united at Westminster, January 18, 1486. Their wedding-day was, in
the words of Bernard Andreas, "celebrated with all religious and glorious magnificence at court, and by their people with bonfires, dancing,
songs, and banquets, throughout all London."

Cardinal Bouchier, a prelate who was at the same time a descendant of the royal house of Plantagenet, and a prince of the church,
was the officiating prelate at the marriage. "His hand," according to the
quaint phraseology of Fuller, who records the circumstance, "held that
sweet posie, wherein the white and red roses were first tied together."

The queen had fixed her residence at Winchester by her husband's
express desire, as he wished her to give birth to his expected heir in the
castle of that city, because tradition declared it was built by king Arthur, his ancestor.

The queen gave all her family a surprise by producing her infant a
month sooner than was expected, yet the child was healthy, and very
lively. He was born September 20, 1486, at Winchester Castle. The
health of the queen, it appears, was always delicate, and she suffered
much from an ague at this time. Her mother-in-law, lady Margaret,
busied herself much at this time, for, besides regulating the etiquette of
the royal lying-in chamber, she likewise arranged the pageantry of the
young prince's baptism, and set forth the length and breadth of his
cradle, "fair adorned with painters' craft." Elizabeth of York had the
satisfaction of seeing her mother distinguished by the honor of standing
godmother for this precious heir.

The queen's ague continued, and it was long before she recovered her health; when it was restored, she founded a Lady Chapel at Winchester cathedral, as a testimony of gratitude for the birth of her heir.

She preceded the king to London; and, on the 3d of November, 1487, she sat in a window at St. Mary's hospital, Bishopgate Street, in order to have a view of the king's triumphant entry of the metropolis, in honor of the victory of Stoke. The queen then went with Henry to their palace at Greenwich.

And the next day, Saturday, after dinner, she set forth on her procession through the city to Westminster Palace. The crowd was immense, it being Elizabeth's first public appearance in the metropolis as queen since her marriage, and all the Londoners were anxious to behold her in her royal apparel. She must have been well worth seeing—she had not completed her twenty-second year, her figure was, like that of her majestic father, tall and elegant, her complexion brilliantly fair, and her serene eyes and perfect features were now lighted up with the lovely expression maternity ever gives to a young woman whose disposition is truly estimable. The royal apparel in which her loving subjects were so anxious to see her arrayed consisted of a kirtle of white cloth of gold, damasked, and a mantle of the same furred with ermine fastened on the breast with a great lace, or cordon, curiously wrought of gold and silk, finished with rich knobs of gold and tassels. " On her fair yellow hair, hanging at length down her back, she wore a caul of pipes (a piped network), and a circle of gold, richly adorned with gems." Thus attired, she quitted her chamber of state in the Tower, her train borne by her sister Cicely, who was still fairer than herself. She was preceded by four baronesses, riding gray palfreys, and by her husband's uncle Jasper, as grand steward. Her old friend, lord Stanley (now earl of Derby), was high constable, and the Earl of Oxford, lord chamberlain. Thus attended, she entered a rich open litter, whose canopy was borne over her head by four of the new knights of the Bath. She was followed by her sister Cicely and the duchess of Bedford, her mother's sister, in one car, and her father's sister, the duchess of Suffolk, mother to the unfortunate earl of Lincoln, lately slain fighting against Henry VII. at the battle of Stoke. The duchess of Norfolk rode in another car, and six baronesses on palfreys brought up the noble procession.   The citizens hung velvets and cloth of gold from the windows of Chepe, and stationed children, dressed like angels, to sing praises to the queen as she passed on to Westminster Palace.

The next morning she was attired in a kirtle of purple velvet furred with ermine bands in front.   On her hair she wore a circlet of gold, set with large pearls and colored gems.   She entered Westminster Hall with her attendants, and waited under a canopy of state till she proceeded to the abbey.   The way thither was carpeted with striped cloth, which sort of covering had been, from time immemorial, the perquisite of the common people.   But the multitude in this case crowded so eagerly to cut off pieces of the cloth, ere the queen had well passed, that before she entered the abbey several of them were trampled to death, and the procession of the queen's ladies "broken and disturbed."

The princess Cicely was the queen's trainbearer; the duke of Suffolk, her aunt's husband, carried the sceptre; and the king's uncle, Jasper duke of Bedford, carried the crown.   The king resolved that Elizabeth should possess the public attention solely that day; he therefore ensconced himself in a closely latticed box, erected between the altar and the pulpit in Westminster Abbey, where he remained with his mother, *perdue*, during the whole ceremony.   The queen's mother was not present, but her son Dorset, who had undergone imprisonment in the Tower on suspicion, during the earl of Lincoln's revolt, was liberated, and permitted to assist at his sister's coronation.

A stately banquet was prepared in Westminster Hall, solely for the queen and those who had assisted at her coronation.   The king, and the countess Margaret, his mother, were again present as unseen spectators, occupying a latticed seat erected in the recess of a window on the left of the hall.

Elizabeth's infants were reared and educated at Croydon.   Erasmus visited the princely children there when he was the guest of lord Mountjoy; the family picture he draws is a charming one; and oh! how its interest is augmented when it is considered that sir Thomas More and himself filled up the grouping!

He thus describes the queen's children: "Thomas More paid me a visit when I was Mountjoy's guest, and took me for recreation a walk to a neighboring country-palace where the royal infants were abiding prince Arthur excepted, who had completed his education. The prince-ly children were assembled in the hall, and were surrounded by their household, to whom Mountjoy's servants added themselves. In the mid-dle of the circle stood prince Henry, then only nine years old; he bore in his countenance a look of high rank, and an expression of royalty, yet open and courteous. On his right hand stood the princess Margaret, a child of eleven years, afterwards queen of Scotland. On the other side was the princess Mary, a little one of four years of age, engaged in her sports, whilst Edmund, an infant, was held in his nurse's arms." There is a group of portraits at Hampton Court representing three of these children; they have earnest eyes and great gravity of expression, but the childish features of the princess Margaret, who was then about six years of age, looked oddly out of the hood-coif, the fashionable head-dress of the era; even the babies in arms wore the same head-dress."

Much has been said regarding the coldness and unkindness of Henry VII. to his gentle partner; but if he indulged in some public jealousy of her superior title to the crown of England, and permitted her not to govern the kingdom whose title she secured to him, at least he gave her no rival in her court or home. The nearer the private life of this pair is examined, the more does it seem replete with proofs of greater do-mestic happiness than usually falls to the lot of royal personages. Hen-ry and Elizabeth were seldom apart, and many little traits may be quoted which evince unity of purpose, when they were together. Among others there is a pleasing union of their names in a valuable missal, once belonging to a lady of the queen, for this line is written in the hand of king Henry:—

"Madam I pray you remember me your loving maister Henry R."

Directly underneath is added, in the queen's hand:—

"Madam I pray you forget not me. Pray to God [in order] that I may have part of your prayers. Elysabeth the Quene."

The conjugal affection between the king and queen was now to be tried by an affliction they had little anticipated. This was the death of their promising son, Arthur prince of Wales, who died on the 2d of April, within five months of his marriage. Henry and Elizabeth were at Greenwich Palace when the news arrived of their heavy loss. The king's confessor, a friar Observant, was deputed by the privy council to break the sad news to him. Somewhat before the usual time the confessor knocked at the king's chamber door, and, when admitted, he requested all present to quit the room, and approached, saying, in Latin, "If we receive good from the hand of God, shall we not patiently sustain the ill he sends us?" "He then showed his grace that his dearest son was departed to God. When the king understood those sorrowful heavy tidings, he sent for the queen, saying, 'that he and his wife would take their painful sorrow together.'

"After she was come, and saw the king her lord in that natural and painful sorrow, as I have heard say, she, with full great, and constant, comfortable words, besought him that he would, after God, consider the weal of his own noble person, of his realm, and of her. 'And,' added the queen, 'remember that my lady, your mother, had never no more children but you only, yet God, by his grace, has ever preserved you, and brought you where you are now. Over and above God has left you yet a fair prince and two fair princesses; and God is still where he was, and we are both young enough. As your grace's wisdom is renowned all over Christendom, you must now give proof of it by the manner of taking this misfortune.'

"Then the king thanked her for her good comfort. But when the queen returned to her own chamber, the natural remembrance of her great loss smote so sorrowfully on her maternal heart, that her people were forced to send for the king to comfort her. Then his grace in great haste came, and with true gentle and faithful love soothed her trouble, telling her what wise counsel she had given him before, and 'that, if she would thank God for her dead son, he would do so likewise.'"

On Candlemas-day (February 2), the queen's accouchement took place: she brought into the world a living princess, who was named Katharine, after lady Courtenay. The fatal symptoms which threatened Elizabeth's life did not appear till a week afterwards, and must have been wholly unexpected, since the physician on whom the king depended for her restoration to health was absent at his dwelling-house beyond Gravesend. The king sent for this person, but it was in vain that Dr.

25

Hallyswurth travelled through the night, with guides and torches, to the royal patient in the Tower; the fiat had gone forth; and the gentle, the pious, the lovely Elizabeth expired on her own birthday, February 11, 1503, the day that she completed her thirty-seventh year.

KATHARINE OF ARRAGON.

FIRST QUEEN OF HENRY VIII.

AT a time when joy and prosperity were swelling in a flood-tide for her
native Spain, Katharine of Arragon first saw the light; for her renowned parents, king Ferdinand of Arragon, and donna Isabel, queen of
Castille, had made every city possessed by the Moors bow beneath their
victorious arms, with the exception of Granada and Malaga, which
alone bore the yoke of the infidel.

The early infancy of Katharine of Arragon was passed amidst the
storms of battle and siege; for queen Isabel of Castille herself, with her
young family, lodged in the magnificent camp with which her armies
for years beleaguered Granada. Nor was this residence unattended with
danger; once in particular, in a desperate sally of the besieged Moors,
the queen's pavilion was set on fire, and the young infantas rescued with
great difficulty from the flames.

The little Katharine, a few months after, accompanied her parents
in their grand entry, when the seat of Moorish empire succumbed to
their arms, and from that moment Granada was her home. At this time
she was four years old. In Granada the early education of the young
Katharine commenced. The first objects which greeted her awakening
intellect were the wonders of the Alhambra, and the exquisite bowers
of the Generaliffe; for in those royal seats of the Moorish dynasty was
Katharine of Arragon reared.

"Donna Catalina," says the manuscript of Bernaldes, "being at

Granada with the king and queen in the year 1501, there came ambas
sadors from the king of England to demand her for the prince of England, his son, called Arthur.   The union was agreed upon, and she set
off from Granada to England, parting from the Alhambra on the 21st of
May, in the year 1501.   Contrary winds forced her vessel back on the
coast of Old Castille, which occasioned great illness to donna Catalina.
After she was convalescent, she embarked more prosperously, on the
26th of September, in the best ship they had, of 300 tons, and after a
good voyage landed at a port called *Salamonte*, on the 2d of October,
where the senora donna Catalina was grandly received, with much feasting and rejoicing."

This was while she staid at Plymouth, where the nobility and gentry
of the neighboring counties crowded to do honor to their future queen,
and entertained her from the time of her arrival with west-country
sports and pastimes.   The steward of the royal palace, lord Brook, was
sent forward by Henry VII. directly the news was known of the
infanta's arrival, in order "to purvey and provide" for her.   The
duchess of Norfolk and the earl of Surrey likewise came to attend her.
The duchess was immediately admitted into her presence, and remained
with her as her companion.

On the day of St. Erkenwald, November the 14th, the young duke
of York (afterwards her second husband) led the infanta to St. Paul's.
"Strange diversity of apparel of the country of Hispania is to be
descriven," says the herald, "for the bride wore at the time of her marriage upon her head a coif of white silk, with a scarf bordered with
gold and pearl, and precious stones, five inches and a half broad, which
veiled great part of her visage, and her person."   This was the Spanish
mantilla.   Her gown was very large, both the sleeves and also the body,
with many plaits; and beneath the waist, certain round hoops bearing
out their gowns from their body after their country manner."   Such was
the first advent of the famous hoop or fardingale in England.

Great misrepresentation has taken place regarding the age of Katharine, at the time of her first marriage; one historian even affirming she
was nineteen; but as her birthday was at the close of the year 1485, it
stands to reason that when she wedded Arthur, November 1501, she had
not completed her sixteenth year, while prince Arthur, who was born

September 20, 1486, had just completed his fifteenth year. Katharine, therefore, instead of four years, was but ten months older than her husband.

Before Shrovetide, Katharine and her husband departed for Ludlow Castle, in Shropshire, where they were to govern the principality of Wales, holding a miniature court, modelled like that at Westminster.

Katharine performed the journey to Ludlow on horseback, riding on a pillion behind her master of horse, while eleven ladies followed her on palfreys. When she was tired, she rested in a litter borne between two horses. Such was the mode of travelling before turnpike roads had made the country traversable by wheel-carriages; for the horses which bore the litter made good their footing in paths where a wheel-carriage could not be kept upright.

The prince and princess of Wales were deservedly popular at Ludlow, but their residence there was of short continuance; for the prince, whose learning and good qualities made him the hope of England, was suddenly taken ill, and expired April 2, 1502. Some historians declare he died of a decline, others affirm that he was very stout and robust.

Queen Elizabeth, the mother-in-law of Katharine, though overwhelmed with grief for the sudden loss of her eldest born and best-beloved child, had sympathy for the young widow, thus left desolate in a strange land, whose tongue could scarcely have become familiar to her ear. The good queen sent for Katharine directly to London, and took the trouble of having a vehicle prepared for her accommodation.

Katharine was settled at the country palace of Croydon by queen Elizabeth, and this residence seems to have been her home. An ancient turreted house, still called Arragon House, opposite Twickenham church, is likewise pointed out as one of her dwellings during her widowhood. She received all maternal kindness from her mother-in-law, while that amiable queen lived.

The marriage-portion of Katharine consisted of 200,000 crowns. Half of that sum had been paid down with her. Her widow's dower consisted of one-third of the prince of Wales's revenue, but she was

expected to expend that income in England. Her father and mother
demurred on paying the remainder of her dowry, and expressed a wish
to have their daughter and her portion returned to them. Henry
VII. had an extreme desire to touch the rest of his daughter-in-law's
portion ; he, therefore, proposed a marriage between her and his surviving son, Henry. The sovereigns of Spain, her parents, accepted this
offer ; and it was finally agreed, that, on obtaining a dispensation from
the pope, Katharine should be married to her young brother-in-law,
prince Henry.

Katharine herself seems to have been very unhappy at this time.
She wrote to her father, "that she had no inclination for a second
marriage in England; still she begged him not to consider her tastes
or inconvenience, but in all things to act as suited him best." It is
here evident, that Katharine, a sensible young woman of eighteen,
felt a natural aversion to vow obedience to a boy more than five
years younger than herself; yet she does not plead as an excuse for
not fulfilling so disagreeable an engagement, that she considered it
repugnant to the laws of God or man. Surely, as she mentions
in her home letters that her will was averse to the second English
marriage, she would have likewise urged, that her conscience would
be outraged, could she have done so with truth; but distaste and
inconvenience are the strongest terms she uses. She was, notwithstanding these remonstrances, betrothed to Henry prince of Wales,
on the 25th of June, 1503, at the house of the bishop of Salisbury, in
Fleet Street.

Immediately after the accession of Henry VIII., he assured the
Spanish ambassador, Fuensalida, of his attachment to Katharine, and
was heard to declare that he loved her beyond all other women.

A most uncandid mystery is made of the time and place of this marriage by the earlier historians. Both, however, we have satisfactorily
discovered in the pages of Katharine's native chroniclers.

"Donna Catalina," says Bernaldes, "wedded the brother of her first
lord, who was called Enrico, in a place they call Granuche [Greenwich],
on the day of St. Bernabo [June 11], and was crowned afterwards, on
the day of St. John, with all the rejoicings in the world."

King Henry and queen Katharine came to the Tower from Greenwich, attended by many of the nobility, June 21. After creating twenty-four knights, Henry, accompanied by Katharine, on the 23d of June, proceeded in state through the streets of London, which were hung for the occasion with tapestry. The inhabitants of Cornhill, as the richest citizens, displayed cloth of gold. From Cornhill and the Old Change, the way was lined with young maidens, dressed in virgin white, bearing palms of white wax in their hands; these damsels were marshalled and attended by priests in their richest robes, who censed the queen's procession from silver censers as it passed.

Of all the pageants ever devised for royalty, this was the most ideal and beautiful. At that time Katharine was pleasing in person. "There were few women," says lord Herbert, "who could compete with queen Katharine when in her prime." She had been married but a few days, and was attired as a bride in white embroidered satin; her hair, which was black and very beautiful, hung at length down her back, almost to her feet; she wore on her head a coronal set with many rich orient stones. The queen, thus attired as a royal bride, was seated in a litter of white cloth of gold, borne by two white horses. She was followed by the female nobility of England, drawn in whirlicotes, a species of car that preceded the use of coaches. Thus she proceeded to the palace of Westminster, where diligent preparation was making for the coronation next day.

It was at the Christmas festivals at Richmond, the same year, that Henry VIII. stole from the side of the queen during the jousts, and returned in the disguise of a strange knight, astonishing all the company with the grace and vigor of his tilting; at first the king appeared ashamed of taking a public part in these gladiatorial exercises, but the applause he received on all sides soon induced him openly to appear on every occasion in the tilt-yard. Katharine kindly humored the childish taste of her husband for disguisings and maskings by pretending great surprise when he presented himself before her in some assumed character. On one occasion, he came unexpectedly into her chamber with his cousin, Bourchier, earl of Essex, and other nobles, in the disguise of Robin Hood and his men; "whereat," says Hollingshed, "the queen and her ladies were greatly amazed, as well for the strange sight as for their sudden appearance.

On an evening when the queen was set in glorious state in the white-hall at Westminster, a nobleman entered to inform her, "how that in a garden of pleasure was an arbor of gold, full of ladies, who were very desirous of showing pastime for the queen's diversion."

Katharine answered very graciously, "that both she and her ladies would be happy to behold them and their pastime."

Then a great curtain of arras was withdrawn, and the pageant moved forward. It was an arbor made with posts and pillars, covered with gold, about which were twined branches of hawthorn, roses, and eglantines, all made of satin and silk, according to the natural colors of the flowers. In the arbor were six fair ladies in gowns of white and green satin, their gowns covered with letters of gold, being H and K, knit together with gold lacing. Near the bower stood the king himself, and five lords, dressed in purple satin, likewise covered with gold letters,—H and K; and every one had his name in letters of bullion gold. The king's name was Cour-Loyal, and all the rest bore some such appellations. Then the king and his company danced before Katharine's throne. But while this fine fancy-ball was performing, a very different scene was transacting at the lower end of the white-hall. The golden arbor, which was intended to receive again the illustrious performers, had been rolled back to the end of the hall, where stood a vast crowd of the London populace, who were the constant witnesses of the grand doings of the English court in the middle ages, and, indeed, on some occasions, seem to have assimilated with the chorus of the Greek drama. Their proceedings this evening were, however, not quite so dignified; the arbor of gold having been rolled incautiously within reach of their acquisitive fingers, the foremost began to pluck and pull at its fine ornaments; at last they made a regular inbreak, and completely stripped the pageant of all its ornaments; nor could the lord steward of the palace repel these intruders, without having recourse to a degree of violence which must have disturbed the royal ballet. Meantime, the king and his band having finished their stately pavons and "corontos high" with the utmost success, his majesty, in high good humor, bade the ladies come forward and pluck the golden letters and devices from his dress and that of his company. Little did the young king imagine what pickers and stealers were within hearing; for scarcely had he given leave for this courtly scramble, when forward rushed the plebeian intruders, and seizing not only on him, but his noble guests, plucked them bare of every glittering thing on their dresses with inconceivable celerity; what was worse, the poor ladies were despoiled of their jewels, and the king was stripped to his doublet and drawers. As for the unfortunate sir Thomas Knevet, who climbed on a high place, and fought for his finery, the mob carried off all his clothes. At last the guards succeeded in clearing the hall without bloodshed. The king, laughing heartily, handed the queen to the banquet in his own chamber, where the court sat down in their tattered condition, treating the whole scramble as a frolic; the king declaring that they must consider their losses as *largess* to the commonalty.

This strange scene throws light on the state of society at that time; for the outrage was not committed by a *posse* of London thieves, but by people in respectable stations of middle life; since Hall says "one shipmaster of the port of London gat for his share in the scramble some letters of beaten gold, which he afterwards sold for 3*l.* 18*s.* 8*d.*"

The succeeding year, when Henry VIII. invaded France in person, he intrusted his queen with the highest powers that had ever yet been bestowed on a female regent in England, for he not only placed the reins of government in her hands, but made her captain of all his forces, with the assistance of five of his nobles. She was, likewise, empowered to raise loans for the defence of the kingdom.

The situation of queen Katharine during her husband's absence was exactly similar to that of queen Philippa when left regent by Edward III. Like Philippa, Katharine had to repel a Scottish invasion; and it is no little honor to female government that the two greatest victories won against the Scots, those of Neville's Cross and Flodden Field, were gained during the administration of queens.

The French war concluded with a marriage between Louis XII. and the king's beautiful young sister Mary, whose heart was devoted to Charles Brandon, duke of Suffolk. Katharine accompanied the royal bride to Dover, October 1814, and bade her an affectionate and tearful farewell: with Mary went as attendant Anne Boleyn, then a girl.

26

The November following the queen became the mother of a living prince, but the infant died in a few days, to her infinite sorrow.

The king on new-year's night performed a ballet with the duke of Suffolk and two noblemen, and four ladies, all dressed in cloth of silver and blue velvet, after the mode of Savoy, the young and blooming duchess of Savoy being supposed to be in love with Suffolk.

On the very day this ballet was danced, the king of France died, and his lovely bride was left a widow, after eighty-two days' marriage. In a very short time she stole a match with the duke of Suffolk at Paris, who had been sent by the king to take care of her and her property.

The May-day after this royal love-match was distinguished by a most picturesque and poetical festival, such as never more was witnessed in England.

Katharine and the royal bride rode "a-maying" with the king from the palace of Greenwich to Shooter's Hill. Here the archers of the king's guard met them, dressed like Robin Hood and his outlaws, and begged that the royal party "would enter the good green wood, and see how outlaws lived."

On this, Henry, turning to the queen, asked her "if she and her damsels would venture in a thicket with so many outlaws?"

Katharine replied, "that where he went she was content to go."

The king then handed her to a sylvan bower, formed of hawthorn-boughs, spring flowers, and moss, with apartments adjoining, where was laid out a breakfast of venison. The queen partook of the feast, and was greatly delighted with this lodge in the wilderness. When she returned towards Greenwich with the king, they met on the road a flowery car, drawn by five horses; each was ridden by a fair damsel. The ladies and their steeds personated the attributes of the spring. The horses had their names lettered on their head-gear, and the damsels had theirs on their dresses. The first steed was Caude, or heat, on him sat the lady Humid; the second was Memeon, on which rode the lady Vert, or verdure; on the third, called Phaeton, was the lady Vegetive; on the steed Rimphon sat the lady Plesaunce; on the fifth, Lampace, sat the lady Sweet Odor. In the car was the lady May, attended by Flora. All these damsels burst into a sweet song when they met the queen at the foot of Shooter's Hill, and preceded the royal party carolling hymns to the May, till they reached Greenwich Palace.

The amusements of the day concluded with the king and his brother-in-law, the duke of Suffolk, riding races on great coursers, which were like the Flemish breed of dray-horses. Strange races these must have been, but this is the first mention of horse-racing made in English history.

Katharine again became a mother, and this time her hopes were not blighted. She brought into the world a girl, February 18, 1516, who was likely to· live. This infant was baptized Mary, after her aunt, the queen of France.

Nothing can show the disposition of Katharine in its truly beautiful character more than the motives which led to her intimacy with the daughter of Clarence. When Ferdinand of Castille demurred on the marriage of his daughter Katharine to prince Arthur, his excuse was, that while a male heir bearing the name of Plantagenet existed, the crown of England was not secure in the Tudor family. Whereupon Henry VII. had the innocent Edward Plantagenet, earl of Warwick, led out to execution, without a shadow of justice. The conscience of the excellent Katharine was infinitely grieved at this murder, of which she considered herself the cause, though innocently so.

As far as was in her power she made every reparation to the relatives of the unfortunate son of Clarence. She cultivated the friendship of his sister, Margaret countess of Salisbury, who was in her household at Ludlow. She gave her infant Mary to be suckled by Katharine Pole, the relative of the countess; she treated her son Reginald Pole as if he had been her own, and it is said, that she wished this gentleman to become her son-in-law. The great talents of Reginald, his beauty and noble courage, distinguished him from all his brothers. He was, however, brought up to the church.

Before the sad record of Katherine's sufferings is unrolled, let us present to the reader a description of her husband, ere his evil passions had marred his constitutional good humor, and even his animal comeliness. It is drawn by Sebastiano Giustiniani, the Venetian resident in England in 1519:—

"His majesty is about twenty-nine years of age, as handsome as

nature could form him, above any other Christian prince; handsomer
by far than the king of France. He is exceedingly fair, and as well-
proportioned as possible. When he learned that the king of France
wore a beard, he allowed his also to grow; which, being somewhat red,
has at present the appearance of being of gold. He is an excellent musician and composer, an admirable horseman, and wrestler. He possesses
a good knowledge of the French, Latin, and Spanish languages, and is
very devout. On the days on which he goes to the chase he hears mass
three times, but on the other days as often as five times. He has every
day service in the queen's chamber at vespers and complin. He is un-
commonly fond of the chase, and never indulges in this diversion without tiring eight or ten horses. These are stationed at the different places
where he proposes to stop. When one is fatigued he mounts another,
and by the time he returns home they have all been used. He takes
great delight in bowling, and it is the pleasantest sight in the world to
see him engaged in this exercise, with his fair skin covered with a beautifully fine shirt."

Katharine was at this time about thirty-four. The difference of
years is scarcely perceptible between a pleasing woman of that age and
a robust and burly man of twenty-nine. Her portrait represents her as
a very noble-looking lady of thirty; the face oval, the features very
regular, with a sweet calm look, but somewhat heavy, the forehead of
the most extraordinary height,—phrenologists would say with benevolence greatly developed. The oil-painting at Versailles has large dark
eyes and a bright brunette complexion. The hood cap of five corners
is bordered with rich gems, the black mantilla veil depends from the
back of the cap on each side, for she never gave up wholly the costume
of her beloved Spain; clusters of rubies are linked with strings of pearl
round her throat and waist, and a cordelière belt of the same jewels
hangs to her feet. Her robe is dark blue velvet, with a graceful train
bordered with sable fur; her sleeves are strait with ruffles, and slashed
at the wrists. Over them are great hanging sleeves of sable fur, of the
shape called *rebras*. She draws up her gown with her right hand; the
petticoat is gold-colored satin, barred with gold. Her figure is stately,
but somewhat column-like and solid. It realized very well the description of an Italian contemporary, who said that her form was *massive*.

Among the Strawberry Hill miniatures, that which represents Katharine of Arragon in her prime is the same, but much handsomer. It gives the idea of a most noble-looking woman.

It may be observed in Katharine's whole line of conduct, that she identified herself with the interests of England in all things, as if she had been a native-born queen. But she did not comply (and who can blame her?) with the customs of English women, who at that era scrupled not to accompany their husbands and brothers to cruel field-sports.

The great Erasmus, in some emphatic words addressed to Henry VIII., to whom he dedicated his Exposition of St. Luke, bears witness that the queen did not suffer these vain pursuits to divert her mind from duties: "Your noble wife," says he, "spends that time in reading the sacred volume which other princesses occupy in cards and dice."

The queen had expressed a wish to become the pupil of Erasmus in the Latin language, if he would have resided in England; he dedicated to her his treatise entitled "Christian Matrimony," and always cited her as an example to her sex. He gives a brilliant list of the great and virtuous men, who were patronized at the English court when Katharine presided as queen of Henry VIII., declaring the residence of the royal couple "ought rather to be called a seat of the muses than a palace."

For the first time in her life Katharine had, after her return from France, manifested some symptoms of jealousy, which was excited by Henry's admiration for Mary Boleyn. She reasoned with the young lady, and brought her to confession that she had been in fault—court scandals declare she acknowledged her guilt to the queen, but this is scarcely consistent with the disinterested love Mary then cherished for an honorable gentleman at court, whom she directly after married.

Queen Katharine and cardinal Wolsey had lived in the greatest harmony till this time, when his increasing personal pride urged him to conduct which wholly deprived him of the queen's esteem. One day, the duke of Buckingham was holding the basin for the king to wash, when it pleased the cardinal to put in his hands. The royal blood of

the duke rose in indignation, and he flung the water into Wolsey's
shoes, who, with a revengeful scowl, promised Buckingham "that he
would sit on his skirts." The duke treated the threat as a joke, for he
came to court in a jerkin, and, being asked by the king the reason of
this odd costume, he replied, that "it was to prevent the cardinal from
executing his threat, for if he wore no skirts they could not be sat upon."

As Wolsey could find no crime to lay to the charge of Buckingham,
he had recourse to the example of the preceding century, and got up
among other charges an accusation of treasonable sorcery against the
high-spirited noble, which speedily brought his head to the block.
Buckingham was one of Katharine's earliest friends in England.
The just and generous queen, after uselessly pleading for him
with the king, did not conceal her opinion of Wolsey's conduct in
the business.

The war with France, which followed the emperor's visit to England,
occasioned the return of Anne Boleyn to her native country, when she
received the appointment of maid of honor to queen Katharine, of whose
court she became the star.

The recent passion of Henry for Mary Boleyn probably blinded
the queen to the fact that he had transferred his love, with increased
vehemence, to her more fascinating and accomplished sister. His love
for Anne Boleyn was nevertheless concealed even from its object, till his
jealousy of young Percy caused it to be suspected by the world. Meantime, the queen's health became delicate, and her spirits lost their buoy-
ancy. Her existence was in a very precarious state from 1523 to 1526.
Probably the expectation of the queen's speedy demise prevented the
king from taking immediate steps for a divorce, after he had separated
Anne Boleyn and young Percy.

The first indications of the king's intentions were his frequent lamentations to his confessor, Dr. Langford, that his conscience was grieved by
his marriage with his brother's widow, mixed with regrets for the failure
of male offspring, and of the queen's hopeless state of ill health. Wolsey's enmity to the queen and her nephew caused him to be an ardent
inciter of the divorce; he had always, for the promotion of his power,
kept a circle of court spies about Katharine, and all his insidious arts
were redoubled at this juncture.

On Sunday afternoon, the 8th of November, 1528, the king convoked all his nobility, judges, and council, in the great room of his palace at Bridewell, and made a speech, which Hall declares he heard and recorded as much "as his wit would bear away." "If it be adjudged," said Henry, "that the queen is my lawful wife, nothing will be more pleasant or more acceptable to me, both for the clearing of my conscience, and also for the good qualities and conditions I know to be in her. For I assure you all, that besides her noble parentage she is a woman of most gentleness, humility, and buxomness, yea, and of all good qualities pertaining to nobility she is without comparison. So that if I were to marry again I would choose her above all women."

"Alas! my lords," answered the queen, "is it now a question whether I be the king's lawful wife or no, when I have been married to him almost twenty years and no objection made before? Divers prelates and lords, privy councillors of the king, are yet alive who then adjudged our marriage good and lawful; and now to say it is detestable is a great marvel to me. But of this trouble," she continued, turning to cardinal Wolsey, "I may only thank you, my lord of York, because, I ever wondered at your pride and vain glory, and abhorred your voluptuous life, and little cared for your presumption and tyranny, therefore of malice have you kindled this fire."

Wolsey denied these charges, but the queen gave no credit to his protestations.

It was not till the 28th of May, 1529, that a court summoned the royal parties. The king answered by two proctors; the queen entered, attended by four bishops and a great train of ladies, and, making an obeisance with much reverence to the legates, appealed from them, as prejudiced and incompetent judges, to the court of Rome; she then departed. The court sat every week, and heard arguments on both sides, but seemed as far off as ever in coming to any decision. At last the king and queen were cited by Dr. Sampson to attend the court in person, on the 18th of June. When the crier called, "Henry, king of England, come into court," he answered, "Here," in a loud voice from under his canopy, and proceeded to make an oration on the excellence of his wife, and his extreme unwillingness to part from her, excepting to soothe the pains and pangs inflicted on him by his conscience. Then "Katha-

rine, queen of England," was cited into court. The queen was already
present, seated in her chair of gold tissue; she answered, by protesting
against the legality of the court, on the grounds, that all her judges held
benefices presented by her opponent. The cardinals denied the justice
of her appeal to Rome on these grounds. Her name was again called.
She rose a second time; she took no notice of the legates, but crossed
herself with much fervor, and, attended by her ladies, made the circuit
of the court to where the king sat, and knelt down before him, saying,
in her broken English:

"Sir, I beseech you, for all the loves there hath been between
us, and for the love of God, let me have some right and justice.
Take of me some pity and compassion, for I am a poor stranger
born out of your dominions; I have here no unprejudiced counsellor, and I flee to you, as to the head of justice within your realm.
Alas! alas! wherein have I offended you? I take God and all
the world to witness, that I have been to you a true, humble, and
obedient wife, ever conformable to your will and pleasure. Therefore, most humbly do I require you, in the way of charity, and
for the love of God, who is the just Judge of all, to spare me the
sentence of this new court, until I be advertised what way my
friends in Spain may advise me to take; and if ye will not extend
to me this favor, your pleasure be fulfilled, and to God do I commit
my cause."

The queen rose up in tears; and, instead of returning to her seat,
made a low obeisance to the king, and walked out of court. "Madam,"
said Griffith, her receiver-general, on whose arm she leant, "you are
called back;" for the crier made the hall ring with the summons,
"Katharine, queen of England, come again into court." The queen
replied to Griffith, "I hear it well enough; but on—on—go you on,
for this is no court wherein I can have justice; proceed, therefore."

Sanders asserts, that she added, "I never before disputed the will
of my husband, and I shall take the first opportunity to ask pardon
for my disobedience." But, in truth, the spirit of just indignation,
which supported her through the above scene, is little consistent with
such superfluous dutifulness to a husband, who was in the act of re-
nouncing her.

Katharine was again summoned before the court, June 25th; and on refusing to appear was declared contumacious. An appeal to the pope, signed in every page with her own hand, was, however, given in, and read on her part. She likewise wrote to her nephew, declaring she would suffer death rather than compromise the legitimacy of her child.

The perplexed legates now paused in their proceedings: they declared that courts never sat in Rome from July to October, and that they must follow the example of their head.

At this delay Anne Boleyn so worked upon the feelings of her lover that he was in an agony of impatience. He sent for Wolsey to consult with him on the best means of bringing the queen to comply with the divorce. Wolsey remained an hour with the king, hearing him storm in all the fury of unbridled passion. At last Wolsey returned to his barge; the bishop of Carlisle, who was waiting in it at Blackfriars Stairs, observed, "that it was warm weather." "Yea, my lord," said Wolsey, "and if you had been chafed as I have been, you would say it was *hot.*"

At this juncture, pope Clement addressed a private letter of exhortation to Henry, advising him to take home queen Katharine and put away "one Anna," whom he kept about him. A public instrument from Rome soon followed this exordium, which confirmed the legality of Henry and Katharine's marriage, and pronounced their offspring legitimate. At first the king was staggered, and resolved to suspend his efforts to obtain the divorce. Cromwell offered his advice at that critical moment to separate the English church from the supremacy of Rome, and at the same time to enrich the king's exhausted finances by the seizure of church property. The consequences of this stupendous step fill many vast folios, devoted to the mighty questions of contending creeds and differing interests; the object of these unambitious pages is but to trace its effects on one faithful feminine heart, wrung with all the woes that pertain to a forsaken wife and bereaved mother.

The first step Cranmer took as archbishop of Canterbury was, to address a letter to the king, requesting permission to settle the question of the divorce. An archiepiscopal court was, accordingly, held at Dun-

27

stable, six miles from the queen's residence.   Here Katharine was repeatedly cited to appear, but she carefully avoided giving the least sign of recognition that such tribunal existed.   Finally, she was declared contumacious; and the sentence that her marriage was null and void, and never had been good, was read before two notaries in the Lady Chapel of Dunstable Priory.   Leave was given both to Katharine and the king to marry elsewhere if they chose.   On the day after Ascension day, May 23, 1533, this important decision was pronounced.

Sorrow had made cruel havoc in the health of the hapless queen, while these slow drops of bitterness were distilling,   When lord Montjoy, her former page, was deputed to inform her that she was degraded from the rank of queen of England to that of dowager princess of Wales, she was on a sick bed.

The same summer her residence was transferred to Bugden, (now called Buckden,) a palace belonging to the bishop of Lincoln, four miles from Huntingdon; her routine of life is most interestingly described in a curious manuscript of Dr. Nicholas Harpsfield, a contemporary, whose testimony is well worth attention, because it shows that the great and excellent Katharine continued to view her rival, Anne Boleyn, in the same Christian light as before, even in the last consummation of her bitterest trials considering her as an object of deep pity rather than resentment.   Katharine thus displays the highest power of talent bestowed on the human species, an exquisite and accurate judgment of character. Most correctly did she appreciate both Henry and his giddy partner. "I have credibly heard," says Dr. Harpsfield, "that, at a time of her sorest troubles, one of her gentlewomen began to curse Anne Boleyn. The queen dried her streaming eyes, and said earnestly, 'Hold your peace! curse not—curse her not, but rather pray for her, for even now is the time fast coming, when you shall have reason to pity her, and lament her case.'   And so it chanced indeed."   "At Bugden," pursues Harpsfield, "queen Katharine spent her solitary life in much prayer, great alms, and abstinence; and when she was not this way occupied, then was she and her gentlewomen, working with their own hands, something wrought in needlework, costly and artificially, which she intended to the honor of God, to bestow on some of the churches.

The queen regained in some degree her cheerfulness and peace of

mind at Bugden, where the country people began to love her exceedingly. They visited her frequently out of pure respect, and she received
the tokens of regard they daily showed her most sweetly and graciously.

The close of this sad year left the queen on her death-bed. As she
held no correspondence with the court, the king received the first intimation of her danger from Eustachio Chapuys, doctor of laws and di-
vinity, and Spanish ambassador.

When Katharine found the welcome hand of death was on her, she
sent to the king a pathetic entreaty to indulge her in a last interview
with her child, imploring him not to withhold Mary from receiving her
last blessing. This request was denied.

Katharine expired in the presence of Eustachio and lady Willoughby, with the utmost calmness. In the words of Dr. Harpsfield, " she
changed this woeful, troublesome existence for the serenity of the celestial life, and her terrestrial ingrate husband for that heavenly spouse
who will never divorce her, and with whom she will reign in glory for
ever."

ANNE BOLEYN,

SECOND QUEEN OF HENRY VIII.

THERE is no name in the annals of female royalty over which the enchantments of poetry and romance have cast such bewildering spells as that of Anne Boleyn. Her wit, her beauty, and the striking vicissitudes of her fate, combined with the peculiar mobility of her character, have invested her with an interest, not commonly excited by a woman, in whom vanity and ambition were the leading traits. Tacitus said of the empress Poppea, "that with her love was not an affair of the heart, but a matter of diplomacy; and this observation appears no less applicable to Anne Boleyn, affording, withal, a convincing reason that she never incurred the crimes for which she was brought to the block.

Sir Thomas Boleyn obtained for his wife the lady Elizabeth Howard, the daughter of the renowned earl of Surrey, afterwards duke of Norfolk, by his first wife Margaret Tylney. This noble alliance brought sir Thomas Boleyn into close connection with royalty, by the marriage of his wife's brother, the lord Thomas Howard, with the lady Anne Plantagenet, sister to Henry VII.'s queen.

No fairer spot than Blickling is to be seen in the county of Norfolk. Those magnificent arcaded avenues of stately oaks and giant chestnut-trees, whose majestic vistas stretch across the velvet verdure of the widely extended park, reminding us, as we walk beneath their solemn shades, of green cathedral aisles, were in their meridian glory three hun-

Jred and forty years ago, when Anne Boleyn first saw the light in the adjacent mansion.

The first years of Anne Boleyn's life were spent at Blickling with her sister Mary and her brother George, afterwards the unfortunate viscount Rochford.

After the death of lady Boleyn, Anne resided at Hever Castle, under the superintendence of a French governess, called Simonette, and other instructors, by whom she was very carefully educated, and acquired an early proficiency in music, needlework, and many other accomplish. ments. While her father was at court or elsewhere, Anne constantly corresponded with him. Her letters were fairly written by her own hand, both in her own language and in French.

These acquirements, which were rare indeed among ladies, in the early part of Henry VIIL's reign, rendered Anne a desirable *suivante* to the princess Mary Tudor, Henry's youngest sister, when she was affi-anced to Louis XII. of France, in September 1514.

We give the sketch of Anne, transcribed from the then unpublished manuscripts of George Cavendish, gentleman-usher to cardinal Wolsey :—

" This gentlewoman being descended on the father's side from one of the heirs of the earl of Ormond, and on the mother's from the house of Norfolk, was from her childhood of that singular beauty and toward-ness that her parents took all possible care for her good education. Therefore, besides all the usual branches of virtuous instruction, they gave her teachers in playing on musical instruments, singing, and dan-cing, insomuch that, when she composed her hands to play and her voice to sing, it was joined with that sweetness of countenance that three harmonies concurred ; likewise, when she danced, her rare proportions varied themselves into all the graces that belong either to rest or motion. Briefly, it seems that the most attractive perfections were evident in her. Yet did not our king love her at first sight, nor before she had lived some time in France, whither, in the train of the queen of France, and in company of a sister of the marquis of Dorset, she went A. D. 1514. After the death of Louis XII. she did not return with the dowager, but was received into a place of much honor with the other queen, and then with the duchess of Alençon, where she staid till some difference grew betwixt our king and Francis; therefore, as saith Du Tillet, and our records, 'about the time when our students at Paris were remanded, she, likewise, left Paris, her parents not thinking it fit for her to stay any longer.'"

With so many graces of person and manners as were possessed by the lovely Boleyn, it is remarkable that she had not previously disposed of both hand and heart to some noble cavalier in the gay and gallant court of France; but she appears to have been free from every sort of engagement when she returned to England. She was then, lord Herbert tells us, about twenty years of age, but according to the French historians, Rastal, a contemporary, and Leti (who all affirm that she was fifteen when she entered the service of Mary Tudor queen of France), she must have been two years older. The first time Henry saw her after her return to England was in her father's garden at Hever, where it is said he encountered her by accident, and admiring her beauty and graceful demeanor, he entered into conversation with her, when he was so much charmed with her sprightly wit, that on his return to Westminster he told Wolsey, "that he had been discoursing with a young lady who had the wit of an angel, and was worthy of a crown." "It is sufficient if your majesty finds her worthy of your love," was the shrewd rejoinder. Henry said, "that he feared she would never condescend in that way." "Great princes," observed Wolsey, "if they choose to play the lover, have that in their power which would mollify a heart of steel."

"Anne Boleyn was in stature rather tall and slender, with an oval face, black hair, and a complexion inclining to sallow; one of her upper teeth projected a little. She appeared at times to suffer from asthma. On her left hand a sixth finger might be perceived. On her throat there was a protuberance, which Chateaubriant describes as a disagreeably large mole, resembling a strawberry; this she carefully covered with an ornamented collar-band, a fashion which was blindly imitated by the rest of the maids of honor, though they had never before thought of wearing any thing of the kind. Her face and figure were in other respects symmetrical," continues Sanders; "beauty and sprightliness·sat on her lips; in readiness of repartee, skill in the dance, and in playing on the lute, she was unsurpassed."

As for the fair Boleyn herself, at the very time when most surrounded with admirers, she appears to have been least sensible to the pride of conquest, having engaged herself in a romantic love affair with Henry lord Percy, the eldest son of the earl of Northumberland, regardless of the family arrangement by which she was pledged to become the wife of the heir of sir Piers Butler.

Percy, like a true lover, gloried in his passion, and made no secret of his engagement, which was at length whispered to the king by some envious busybody, who had, probably, observed that Henry was not insensible to the charms of Anne Boleyn. The pangs of jealousy occasioned by this intelligence, it is said, first awakened the monarch to the state of his own feelings towards his fair subject, in whose conversation he had always taken the liveliest pleasure, without being himself aware that he regarded her with emotions inconsistent with his duty as a married man.

As for the young lady herself, she appears to have been wholly unconscious of the impression she had made on her sovereign's heart. In fact, as her whole thoughts were employed in securing a far more desirable object, namely, her marriage with the heir of the illustrious and wealthy house of Percy, it is scarcely probable that she would incur the risk of alarming her honorable lover by coquetries with the king. Under these circumstances, we think Anne Boleyn must be acquitted of having purposely attracted the attention of Henry in the first instance. On the contrary, she must, at this peculiar crisis, have regarded his passion as the greatest misfortune that could have befallen her, as it was the means of preventing her marriage with the only man whom we have the slightest reason to believe she ever loved.

If Anne, however, regarded the king with indifference, his feelings towards her were such that he could not brook the thought of seeing her the wife of another, though aware that it was not in his power to marry her himself. With the characteristic selfishness of his nature, he determined to separate the lovers.

Percy was banished the court, and not only commanded to avoid mistress Anne's company, but compelled to fulfil in all haste the hitherto unratified contract, which his father had made for him in his boyhood with lady Mary Talbot, one of the earl of Shrewsbury's daughters.

Anne Boleyn, whom Henry chose to punish for the preference she had manifested for young Percy, was discharged from queen Katharine's service, and dismissed to her father's house. "Whereat," says Cavendish, "mistress Anne was greatly displeased, promising that if ever it lay in her power she would be revenged on the cardinal, and yet he was not altogether to be blamed, as he acted by the king's command."

After a period sufficient to allow for the subsiding of ordinary feelings of displeasure had elapsed, the king paid an unexpected visit to Hever Castle. But Anne was either too indignant to offer her homage to the tyrant, whose royal caprice had deprived her of her affianced husband, or her father, having already felt the evil of having the reputation of one lovely daughter blighted by the attentions of the king, would not suffer her to appear, for she took to her chamber, under pretence of disposition, on Henry's arrival at the castle, and never left it till after his departure.

There is not any trace of Anne Boleyn's appearance at court till the year 1527. Having been injuriously dismissed from the service of the queen, she appears to have manifested a persevering resentment, for the affront she had received, by refusing to return when she had reason to believe her presence was desired by the jealous tyrant who had prevented her marriage with Percy.

It is scarcely probable that Anne continued unconscious of the king's passion, when he followed up all the favors conferred on her family by presenting a costly offering of jewels to herself. But when Henry proceeded to avow his love, she recoiled from his lawless addresses with the natural abhorrence of a virtuous woman, and falling on her knees she made this reply:—

"I think, most noble and worthy king, your majesty speaks these words in mirth, to prove me, without intent of degrading your princely self. Therefore, to ease you of the labor of asking me any such question hereafter, I beseech your highness, most earnestly, to desist and take this my answer (which I speak from the depth of my soul), in good part. Most noble king, I will rather lose my life than my virtue, which

28

will be the greatest and best part of the dowry I shall bring my husband."

The manner in which she repelled the sovereign's addresses only added fuel to his flame, and next he assailed the reluctant beauty with a series of love-letters of the most passionate character. The originals of these letters are still preserved in the Vatican, having been stolen from the royal cabinet and conveyed thither.

After an absence of four years, Anne Boleyn resumed her place in the palace of queen Katharine, in compliance, it is supposed, with her father's commands, and received the homage of her enamored sovereign in a less repulsive manner than she had done while her heart was freshly bleeding for the loss of the man whom she had passionately desired to marry. If her regrets were softened by the influence of time and absence, it is certain that her resentment continued in full force against Wolsey, for his conduct with regard to Percy.

Soon after the passion of Henry became obvious even to the queen, and occasioned her to upbraid him with his perfidy; but it does not appear that she condescended to discuss the matter with Anne.

Ambition had now entered her head; she saw that the admiration of the sovereign had rendered her the centre of attraction to all who sought his favor; and she felt the fatal charms of power—not merely the power which beauty, wit, and fascination, had given her, but that of political influence. In a word she swayed the will of the arbiter of Europe, and she had determined to share his throne as soon as her royal mistress could be dispossessed.

It must have been nearly at this crisis that the king was induced to declare to Anne Boleyn and her father, that it was his intention to make her his consort whenever he should be released from his present marriage. After this intimation he became a frequent visitor at Hever Castle. He used to ride thither privately from Eltham or Greenwich.

If Wyatt's enthusiastic encomiums may be credited, she still demurred on account of her respect and affection to the queen; her subsequent persecution of Katharine's virtuous friends, Fisher and More, is scarcely consistent with such delicacy of feeling; but the heart of Anne Boleyn, like other hearts, did not improve after a long course of flattery and prosperity.

Anne, however, had her anxieties at this crisis, for the opinion of all Christendom was so much against the divorce that Henry was disposed to waver. Luther himself declared, "that he would rather allow the king to take two wives than dissolve his present marriage; and the pope had already caused a secret suggestion of the same kind to be made to Cassalis, but it went no farther, such an arrangement not being very likely to please either of the ladies. At last Cromwell's bold expedient of separating England from the papal see smoothed Anne Boleyn's path to the queenly chair; her royal mistress was expelled from Windsor, and she became the king's constant companion; she rode with him on all his progresses, and, with glaring disregard to propriety, occupied apartments contiguous to his own. The dazzling prospect of a crown had rendered Anne forgetful of that delicacy of feeling which should have taught her to regard a stain as a wound.

Anne was now fast approaching to the lofty mark at which she had been aiming for the last five years. On the 1st of September the same year, as a preparatory step for her elevation to a still higher rank, Henry created Anne Boleyn marchioness of Pembroke, a royal title which had last been borne by his uncle, Jasper Tudor. The king rendered the honor conferred on his betrothed the more marked, because it identified her with his own family.

The time and place of Anne Boleyn's marriage with Henry VIII. are disputed points in history. Some authors have affirmed that she was privately united to the king at Dover the same day they returned from France, being the festival of St. Erkenwald. According to others, the nuptials were secretly performed in the presence of the earl and countess of Wiltshire, and the duke and duchess of Norfolk, in the chapel of Sopewell Nunnery.

Anne remained in great retirement, as the nature of the case required, for her royal consort was still, in the opinion of a majority of his sub-jects, the husband of another lady. It was, however, found impossible to conceal the marriage, without affecting the legitimacy of the expected heir to the crown. For this cause, therefore, on Easter eve, which this year was April 12th, the king openly solemnized again his marriage with Anne Boleyn, and she went in state as his queen.

The broad bosom of the Thames was the theatre of this commencing

scene of Anne Boleyn's triumph.   In obedience to the royal order, the
lord mayor and his civic train embarked at New Stairs at one o'clock,
May 19th.   In the city state barge was stationed a band playing on instruments called shalms and shag-bushes; but, notwithstanding these
uncivilized names, we are informed "they made goodly harmony."

When the queen entered her barge, those of the citizens moved for-
wards.   She was immediately preceded by the lord mayor, while the
bachelors' barge claimed their privilege of rowing on the right of the
royal barge, sounding points of triumph with trumpets and wind-instru-
ments, in which the queen took particular delight.   The barge of her
father, the earl of Wiltshire, that of the duke of Suffolk, and many of
the nobility, followed that of the queen.   Thus was she attended up the
Thames till she came opposite the Tower, when a marvellous peal of
guns was shot off.

Henry was then in the ominous fortress awaiting the arrival of her
who was still the desire of his heart and the delight of his eyes.   At
her landing the lord chamberlain and the heralds were ready to receive
her, and brought her to the king, who, with loving countenance, welcomed her at the postern by the water-side.   As soon as he met her, he
kissed her, and she turned about and thanked the lord mayor very
gracefully before he returned to his barge.

The whole of that evening, after she had entered the Tower, "the
barges hovered before it, making the goodliest melody."   The city
poured forth its humbler population in crowds on the neighboring
wharfs.   The adjacent bridge, then crested with fortified turrets and
embattled gateways, swarmed with human life.   It was a scene peculiar
to its era, which can never occur again, for modern times have neither
the power nor material to emulate it.   In the midst of that picturesque
splendor, who could have anticipated what was in store for Anne Boleyn
on the second anniversary of that gay and glorious day, and what was
to be transacted within the gloomy circle of that royal fortress of
which she then took such proud possession, when May 19th had twice
returned again?

The queen sojourned with her husband at the Tower some days,
during which time seventeen young noblemen and gentlemen were made
knights of the Bath, as attendants on her coronation.   The royal prog-

ress through the city, which was usual to all the queens her predecessors on the eve of their coronations, was appointed for Anne Boleyn on the last day of May, and never was this ceremony performed with more pomp.

The bright morrow was that coronation day, the grand ultimatum on which the heart and wishes of Anne Boleyn had been for so many years steadfastly fixed. It was, at the same time, Whitsunday, and the 1st of June, of all days the most lovely in England, when the fresh smile of spring still blends with early summer. That morning of high festival saw the queen early at her toilet, for she entered Westminster Hall, with her ladies, a little after eight, and stood under her canopy of state, in her surcoat and mantle of purple velvet, lined with ermine, and the circlet of rubies she wore the preceding day.

The king took no part in all this grand ceremonial, but remained in the cloister of St. Stephen's, where was made a little closet, in which he stood privately with several ambassadors, beholding all the service it was his pleasure should be offered to his new queen.

Notwithstanding the occasional mortifications which annoyed Anne on her first recognition as queen of England, she enjoyed all that grandeur and power could bestow. Henry, withal, in order to exalt her to the utmost in her queenly dignity, caused her initial A to be crowned and associated with his own regal H on the gold and silver coins that were struck after their marriage. Henry, who fully persuaded himself that the infant of which Anne expected soon to be the mother would prove a son, invited king Francis to become his sponsor. Francis obligingly signified his consent to the duke of Norfolk, and it was agreed that the anticipated boy should be named either Henry or Edward ; but, to the great disappointment of king Henry, on the 7th of September, 1533, queen Anne, after very dangerous travail, gave birth, between three and four o'clock in the afternoon to a daughter, afterwards the renowned queen Elizabeth. This event, so auspicious to England, took place in the old palace at Greenwich, of which not a vestige now remains.

Anne was now at the summit of human greatness. She had won the great political game for which she had, in the bitterness of disappointed love, vindictively entered the lists with the veteran statesman who had separated her from the man of her heart. She had had the vengeance she had vowed for the loss of Percy, and laid the pride and power of Wolsey in the dust. She had wrested the crown matrimonial from the brow of the royal Katharine. The laws of primogeniture had been reversed, that the succession to the throne might be vested in her issue, and the two men who were the most deservedly venerated by the king and the people of England, More and Fisher, had been sacrificed to her displeasure. But in all these triumphs there was little to satisfy the mind of a woman whose natural impulses were those of virtue, but who had violated the most sacred ties for the gratification of the evil passions of pride, vanity, and revenge. Anne Boleyn was a reader of the Scriptures, and must have felt the awful force of that text, which says, "What shall it profit a man if he gain the whole world and lose his own soul?" Conscious of her own responsibility, and finding far more thorns than roses in the tangled weary labyrinth of greatness, Anne directed her thoughts to the only true source of happiness, religion, which had hitherto been practised by her rather as a matter of state policy than as the emanation from a vital principle in the soul.

But, however powerful Anne's religious impressions might be, it is impossible that a real change of heart had taken place, while she continued to incite the king to harass and persecute his forsaken queen, Katharine, by depriving her of the solace of her daughter's company, and exacting from the disinherited princess submissions from which conscience and nature alike revolted. There were moments when Anne felt the insecurity of her position in a political point of view; and well must she have known how little reliance was to be placed on the stability of the regard of the man whose caprice had placed the queenly diadem on her brow At the best, she was only the queen of a party, for the generous and independent portion of the nobles and people of England still regarded Katharine as the lawful possessor of the title and place which Henry had bestowed on her.

When the long expected tidings of Katharine's death arrived, Anne, in the blindness of her exultation, exclaimed, "Now I am, indeed, a queen!"

The season was now at hand when Anne was, in her turn, to experience some of the bitter pangs she had inflicted on her royal mistress.

Her agonies were not the less poignant, because conscience must have told her that it was retributive justice which returned the poisoned chalice to her own lips, when she, in like manner, found herself rivalled and supplanted by one of her female attendants, the beautiful Jane Seymour. Jane must have been a person of consummate art; for she was on terms of great familiarity with the king before Anne entertained the slightest suspicion of their proceedings. Entering the room unexpectedly one day, the queen surprised Jane, seated on Henry's knee, receiving his caresses with every appearance of complacency. Struck, as with a mortal blow, at this sight, Anne gave way to a transport of mingled grief and indignation. Henry, dreading his consort's agitation might prove fatal to his hopes of an heir, endeavored to soothe and reassure her, saying, " Be at peace, sweetheart, and all shall go well for thee." But the cruel shock Anne had sustained brought on the pangs of premature travail; and after some hours of protracted agony, during which her life was in imminent peril, she brought forth a dead son, January 29th.

When the king was informed of this misfortune, instead of expressing the slightest sympathy for the sufferings of his luckless consort, he burst into her apartment, and furiously upbraided her " with the loss of his boy."

Anne, with more spirit than prudence, passionately retorted, " that he had no one to blame but himself for this disappointment, which had been caused by her distress of mind about that wench, Jane Seymour."

These scenes, which occurred in January, 1536, may surely be regarded as the first act of the royal matrimonial tragedy, which four months later was consummated on Tower Hill.

Anne slowly regained her health, but not her spirits. She knew the king's temper too well not to be aware that her influence was at an end for ever, and that she must prepare to resign, not only her place in his affections, but also in his state, to the new star by whom she had been eclipsed. When she found that she had no power to obtain the dismissal of her rival from the royal household, she became very melancholy, and withdrew herself from the gayeties of the court, passing all her time in the most secluded spots of Greenwich Park.

The inconsistency of Anne Boleyn's manners was, doubtless, the principal cause of her calamities. The lively, coquettish maid of honor could not forget her old habits, after her elevation to a throne; and the familiarity of her deportment to those with whom she had formerly been on terms of equality in the court of queen Katherine, encouraged her officers of state to address her with undue freedom. Such was her unbounded thirst for admiration, that even the low-born musician Mark Smeaton dared to insinuate his passion to her. These things were, of course, reported to her disadvantage by the household foes by whom she was surrounded. The king's impatience to rid himself of the matrimonial fetters which precluded him from sharing his throne with the object of his new passion would not brook delays, and, in the absence of any proof of the queen's disloyalty to himself, he resolved to proceed against her on the evidence of the invidious gossips' tales that had been whispered to him by persons who knew that he was seeking an occasion to destroy her.

The secret plot against the queen must have been organized by the first week in April, 1536; for on the 4th of that month the parliament was dissolved, as if for the purpose of depriving her of any chance of interference from that body in her behalf. The writs for the new parliament, which was to assemble on the 8th of June, after her death, were issued even before she was arrested, April 27th. Three days before that date, a secret committee was appointed of the privy council to inquire into the charges against her.

If the queen remained in ignorance of what was going on in the palace as most authors affirm, her powers of observation must have been very limited, and she could have had no faithful friend or counsellor immediately about her.

The public arrest of her brother and his luckless friends struck a chill to her heart, but of the nature of their offence, and that she was herself to be involved in the horrible charges against them, she remained in perfect unconsciousness till the following day. She sat down to dinner at the usual hour, but the meal passed over with uneasiness, for she took the alarm when she found that the king's waiter came not with his majesty's wonted compliment of "much good may it do you." Instead of this greeting, she observed a portentous silence among her ladies, and that her servants stood about, with their eyes glazed with tears and

downcast looks, which inspired her with dismay and strange apprehensions. Scarcely was the *surnap* removed, when the duke of Norfolk,
with Audley, Cromwell, and others of the lords of the council, entered.
At first, Anne thought they came from the king to comfort her for her
brother's arrest, but when she noticed the austerity of their countenances,
and the ominous presence of sir William Kingston, the lieutenant of
the Tower, behind them, she started up in terror, and demanded " why
they came." They replied, with stern brevity, " that they came by the
king's command to conduct her to the Tower, there to abide during his
highness's pleasure."

"If it be his majesty's pleasure," replied the queen, regaining
her firmness, " I am ready to obey;" and so, pursues our authority,
" Without change of habit, or any thing necessary for her removal,
she committed herself to them, and was by them conducted to her
barge."

It was on the 2d of May that Anne was brought as a woful prisoner
to her former royal residence—the Tower. Before she passed beneath
its fatal arch she sank upon her knees, as she had previously done in
the barge, and exclaimed, " Oh Lord, help me, as I am guiltless of
that whereof I am accused !" Then perceiving the lieutenant of the
Tower, she said, " Mr. Kingston, do I go into a dungeon ?" " No,
madam," said he, " to your own lodging, where you lay at your
coronation."

The recollections associated with that event overpowered her, and,
bursting into a passion of tears, she exclaimed, " It is too good for
me. Jesus, have mercy on me !" She knelt again, weeping apace,
" and, in the same sorrow, fell into a great laughter,"—laughter
more sad than tears. After the hysterical paroxysm had had its
sway, she looked wildly about her, and cried, " Wherefore am I here,
Mr. Kingston ?"

The clock was just on the stroke of five when Anne entered the
Tower. The lords, with the lieutenant, brought her to her chamber,
where she again protested her innocence : then, turning to the lords, she
said, " I entreat you to beseech the king in my behalf, that he will be
good lord unto me ;" as soon as she had uttered these words they departed.

29

There were times when Anne would not believe that Henry intended to harm her, and, after complaining that she was cruelly handled, she added, " But I think the king does it to prove me ;" and then she laughed, and affected to be very merry. Merriment more sad than tears, reminding us of

> " Moody madness, aughing wild
> Amidst severest woe."

Reason must have indeed tottered, when she predicted that there would be no rain in England till she was released from her unmerited thraldom. To this wild speech Kingston familiarly rejoined, " I pray then it be shortly, because of the dry weather, you know what I mean." " If she had her bishops they would plead for her," she said.

On the 16th of May, queen Anne and her brother, lord Rochford, were brought to trial in a temporary building which had been hastily erected for that purpose within the great hall of the Tower. There were then fifty-three peers of England, but from this body a selected moiety of twenty-six were named by the king as " lords triers," under the direction of the duke of Norfolk, who was created lord high steward for the occasion, and sat under the cloth of state.

She appeared immediately in answer to the summons, attended by her ladies and lady Kingston, and was led to the bar by the lieutenant and the constable of the Tower. The royal prisoner had neither counsel nor adviser of any kind, but she had rallied all the energies of her mind to meet the awful crisis ; neither female terror nor hysterical agitation were perceptible in that hour. The lord of Milherve tells us, " that she presented herself at the bar, with the true dignity of a queen, and curt-sied to her judges, looking round upon them all without any sign of fear." Of what nature the evidence was, no one can now form an opinion, for the records of the trial have been carefully destroyed.

After the verdict was declared, the queen was required to lay aside her crown and other insignia of royalty, which she did without offering an objection, save that she protested her innocence of having offended against the king.

This ceremony was preparatory to her sentence, which was pro-nounced by her uncle, the duke of Norfolk, as lord high steward of

England and president of tho court commissioned for her trial. She
was condemned to be burnt or beheaded at the king's pleasure. Anne
Boleyn heard this dreadful doom without changing color or betraying
the slightest symptom of terror, but when her stern kinsman and judge
had ended, she clasped her hands, and, raising her eyes to heaven, made
her appeal to a higher tribunal, in these words: "Oh Father! Oh Creator! Thou who art the way, the life and the truth, knowest whether I
have deserved this death." Then, turning to her earthly judges, she said,
"My lords, I will not say your sentence is unjust, nor presume that my
reasons can prevail against your convictions. I am willing to believe
that you have sufficient reasons for what you have done, but then they
must be other than those which have been produced in court, for I am
clear of all the offences which you then laid to my charge." Then, with
a composed air, she rose up, made a parting salutation to her judges,
and left the court as she had entered it.

On the 16th of May the king signed the death-warrant of his once
passionately loved consort, and sent Cranmer to receive her last confession.

She had drunk of the last drop of bitterness that mingled malice and
injustice could infuse into her cup of misery; and when she received
the awful intimation that she must prepare herself for death, she met
the fiat like one who was weary of a troublesome pilgrimage, and anxious to be released from its sufferings.

The time appointed by Henry for the execution of his unhappy consort was twelve o'clock at noon. This was kept a profound mystery
from the people till the time was at hand. A few minutes before that
hour, the fatal portals through which the royal victim was to pass for
the last time were thrown open, and she appeared dressed in a robe of
black damask, with a deep white cape falling over it on her neck. She
wore the pointed black velvet hood, which is familiar to us in her portraits; or, as some have said, a small hat with ornamented coifs under
it; perhaps the picturesque bangled hat which forms part of the costume
of her statue at Blickling Hall. The feverish state of excited feeling in
which she had passed the morning vigil, had probably recalled the
brightness to her eye, and a flush to her cheek, which supplied the loss
of her faded bloom; for she is said to have come forth in fearful beauty,

indeed, one writer says, "Never had the queen looked so beautiful before." She was led by the lieutenant of the Tower, and attended by the four maids of honor who had waited upon her in prison. She was conducted by sir William Kingston to the scaffold, which was erected on the green before the church of St. Peter ad Vincula. Having been assisted by sir William to ascend the steps of the platform, she there saw assembled the lord mayor, and some of the civic dignitaries.

When she had looked round her she turned to Kingston, and entreated him "not to hasten the signal for her death till she had spoken that which was on her mind to say;" to which he consented, and she then spoke: "Good Christian people, I am come hither to die, according to law, for by the law I am judged to die, and therefore I will speak nothing against it. I am come hither to accuse no man, nor to speak any thing of that whereof I am accused, as I know full well that aught that I could say in my defence doth not appertain unto you, and that I could draw no hope of life from the same."

She then with her own hands removed the hat and collar, which might impede the action of the sword, and taking the coifs from her head delivered them to one of her ladies. Then covering her hair with a little linen cap (for it seems as if her ladies were too much overpowered with grief and terror to assist her, and that she was the only person who retained her composure), she said, "Alas! poor head, in a very brief space thou wilt roll in the dust on the scaffold; and as in life thou didst not merit to wear the crown of a queen, so in death thou deservest not better doom than this."

The account given by the Portuguese spectator of this mournful scene is as follows:—

"And being minded to say no more, she knelt down upon both knees, and one of her ladies covered her eyes with a bandage, and then they withdrew themselves some little space, and knelt down over against the scaffold, bewailing bitterly and shedding many tears. And thus, and without more to say or do, was her head struck off; she making no confession of her fault, but saying, 'O Lord God have pity on my soul.'"

JANE SEYMOUR.

THIRD QUEEN OF HENRY VIII.

JANE was the eldest of the eight children of sir John Seymour, of Wolf
Hall, Wiltshire, and Margaret Wentworth, daughter of sir John Wentworth, of Nettlestead, in Suffolk. The Seymours were a family of
country gentry, who, like most holders of manorial rights, traced their
ancestry to a Norman origin. One or two had been knighted in the wars
of France, but their names had never merged from the herald's visitation rolls into historical celebrity. They increased their boundaries by
fortunate alliances with heiresses; but till the head of the family mar-
. ried into a collateral branch of the lordly line of Beaucamp, they scarcely took rank as second-rate gentry.

Jane's childhood and early youth are involved in great obscurity;
but there is reason to suppose that, like Anne Boleyn, her education
was finished and her manners formed at the court of France. Her portrait in the Louvre as a French maid of honor has given rise to this
idea. It is probable that she entered the service of Mary Tudor, where
her brother certainly was, for in a list of the persons forming the bridal
retinue of that queen, signed by the hand of Louis XII., we observe
among the *enfans d'oneur le fils de Mess. Seymour.* This must have been
Jane's brother Edward, afterwards so celebrated as the Protector Somerset. He was younger, however, than Jane, and it is very possible that
she had an appointment also, though not of such importance as Anne

Boleyn, who was granddaughter to the duke of Norfolk, and was associated with two of the sovereign's kinswomen, the ladies Gray, as maids
of honor to Mary, queen of France. Jane could boast of no such high
connections as these, and perhaps, from her comparatively inferior birth,
did not excite the jealousy of the French monarch like the ladies of
maturer years.

Henry's growing passion for Jane must have attracted the observation
and excited the jealousy of queen Anne, some time before she received
the fatal conviction that she was supplanted in his fickle regard by her
treacherous handmaid. It is said, that the queen's attention was one
day attracted by a jewel, which Jane Seymour wore about her neck, and
she expressed a wish to look at it. Jane faltered and drew back, and
the queen, noticing her hesitation, snatched it violently from her, and
found that it contained the portrait of the king, which, as she most truly
guessed, had been presented by himself to her fair rival. Jane Seymour
had far advanced in the same serpentine path which conducted Anne
herself to a throne, ere she had ventured to accept the picture of her
enamored sovereign, and well assured must she have been of success in
her ambitious views, before she presumed to wear such a love-token in
the presence of the queen.

Anne Boleyn was not of a temper to bear her wrongs patiently;
but Jane Seymour's star was in the ascendant, hers in the decline;
her anger was unavailing. Jane maintained her ground triumphantly.

While the last act of that diabolical drama was played out, which
consummated the destruction of poor Anne, it appears that her rival
had the discretion to retreat to her paternal mansion, Wolf Hall, in
Wiltshire. There the preparations for her marriage with Henry VIII.
were proceeding with sufficient activity to allow her royal wedlock to
take place the day after the axe had rendered the king a widower.
Henry himself remained in the vicinity of the metropolis, awaiting the
accomplishment of that event. The traditions of Richmond Park and
Epping Forest quote each place as the locale of the following scene.
On the morning of the 19th of May, Henry VIII., attired for the
chase, with his huntsmen and hounds around him, was standing
under a spreading oak breathlessly awaiting the signal gun from the
Tower, which was to announce that the axe had fallen on the neck

of his once "entirely beloved Anne Boleyn." At last, when the bright summer sun rode high towards its meridian, the sullen sound of the death-gun boomed along the windings of the Thames. Henry started with ferocious joy. "Ha, ha!" he cried with satisfaction, "the deed is done! Uncouple the hounds and away." The chase that day bent towards the west, whether the stag led it in that direction or not. At nightfall the king was at Wolf Hall, in Wilts, telling the news to his elected bride.

The next morning the king married the beautiful Seymour. It is commonly asserted that he wore white for mourning the day after Anne Boleyn's execution; he certainly wore white, not as mourning, but because he on that day wedded her rival.

From Marwell the king and his bride went to Winchester, where they sojourned a few days, and from thence returned to London, in time to hold a great court on the 29th of May. Here the bride was publicly introduced as queen, and her marriage festivities were blended with the celebration of Whitsuntide. The king paid the citizens the compliment of bringing his fair queen to Mercer's Hall, and she stood in one of the windows to view the annual ceremony of setting the city watch on St. Peter's eve, June 29th.

The lord chancellor Audley, when parliament met a few days after, introduced the subject of the king's new marriage, in a speech so tedious in length, that the clerks who wrote the parliamentary journals gave up its transcription in despair.

The speaker they chose was the notorious Richard Rich, who had sworn away the life of sir Thomas More. This worthy outdid the chancellor in his fulsome praises of the king, thinking proper to load his speech with personal flattery, "comparing him, for strength and fortitude, to Samson, for justice and prudence to Solomon, and for beauty and comeliness to Absalom."

Thus did the English senate condescend to encourage Henry in his vices, calling his self-indulgence self-denial, and all his evil good; inflating his wicked wilfulness with eulogy, till he actually forgot, according to Wolsey's solemn warning, "that there was both heaven and hell." While the biographer is appalled as the domestic features of this moral monster are unveiled, surely some abhorrence is due to the unison of atrocity that met in the hearts and heads of his advisers and flatterers.

The terror of the axe seems to have kept even this favored queen in the most humiliating state of submission during the brief term of her sceptred slavery.

Jane Seymour supported her unwonted burden of dignity as queen with silent placidity. Whether from instinctive prudence or natural taciturnity, she certainly exemplified the wise proverb "that the least said is the soonest mended;" for she passed eighteen months of regal life without uttering a sentence significant enough to bare preservation. Thus she avoided making enemies by sallies of wit and repartee, in which her incautious predecessors so often indulged. Indeed, it was generally considered that queen Jane purposely steered her course of royalty so that her manners appeared diametrically opposite to those of queen Anne. As for her actions, they were utterly passive, and dependent on the will of the king.

Jane's coronation, after being delayed by the pestilence, was still further procrastinated by her hopeful condition, which promised the long-desired heir to the throne.

When the hour came in which the heir of England was expected to see the light, it was by no means "the good hour" so emphatically prayed for in the ceremonial of her retirement. After a martyrdom of suffering, the queen's attendants put to Henry the really cruel question of "whether he would wish his wife or infant to be saved." It is affirmed, and it must be owned the speech is too characteristic of Henry to be doubted, that he replied, "The child by all means, for other wives could be easily found."

Another authority affirms that the queen entreated her assistants to take care of her infant in preference to herself. After all it is expressly declared by a circular notification, that the queen was happily delivered of a prince on Friday, October 12th, being the vigil of St. Edward's day; and had she been kept in a state of rational quiet, it is probable she might have recovered. But the intoxication of joy into which the king and the court were plunged at the appearance of the long-desired heir of England, seemed to deprive them of all consideration of consequences, or they would have kept the bustle attendant on the ceremonial of his christening far enough from her.

When all the circumstances of this elaborate ceremony are reviewed, no doubt can exist that it was the ultimate cause of queen Jane's death; it took place on the Monday night after the birth of the prince.

The arrangement of the procession, which commenced in her very chamber, was not injurious enough for the sick queen, but regal etiquette imperiously demanded that she should play her part in the scene; nor was it likely that a private gentlewoman raised to the queenly state, would seek to excuse herself from any thing pertaining to her dignity, however inconvenient. It was the rule for a queen of England, when her infant was christened, to be removed from her bed to a state pallet, which seems anciently to have fulfilled the uses of a sofa. This was decorated at the back with the crown and arms of England, wrought in gold thread; it was furnished with two long pillows, and two square ones, a coverture of white lawn five yards square, a counterpane of scarlet cloth lined with ermine, while propped with four cushions of crimson damask with gold reclined the queen, wrapped about with a round mantle of crimson velvet furred with ermine.

The baptism of the prince took place at midnight, in the chapel of Hampton Court, where the future defender of the reformed religion was presented at the font by his sister and catholic successor, the princess Mary. There, too, unconscious of the awful event that had changed her fortunes in the dawn of her existence, after she had been proclaimed heiress of the realm, came the young motherless Elizabeth, who had been roused from her sweet slumbers of infant innocence, and arrayed in robes of state, to perform the part assigned to her in the ceremony. In this procession Elizabeth, borne in the arms of the aspiring Seymour (brother to the queen), with playful smiles, carried the crysom for the son of her for whose sake her mother's blood had been shed on the scaffold, and herself branded with the reproach of illegitimacy. And there the earl of Wiltshire, the father of the murdered Anne Boleyn, and grandfather of the disinherited Elizabeth, made himself an object of contemptuous pity to every eye, by assisting at this rite, bearing a taper of virgin wax, with a towel about his neck.

How strangely associated seem the other personages who met in this

30

historical scene; how passing strange, in the eyes of those before whom
the scroll of their after life has been unrolled, it is to contemplate the
princess Mary joining Cranmer, afterwards sent to the stake in her reign,
who was associated with his enemy, the duke of Norfolk, as sponsors in
this baptismal rite!

The heir of England was borne back in solemn state, with trumpets
sounding before him, to his mother's chamber, there to receive her blessing. King Henry had remained seated by her pallet during the whole
of the baptismal rite, which, with all its tedious parade, took up two or
three hours, not being over till midnight. What with the presence of
king Henry—rather a boisterous inmate for a sick chamber—what with
the procession setting out from the chamber, and the braying of the
trumpets at her door when it returned (the herald especially notes the
goodly noise they made there), and, in conclusion, the exciting ceremonial of bestowing her maternal benediction on her newly baptized babe,
the poor queen had been kept in a complete hurry of spirits for many
hours. The natural consequence of such imprudence was, that on the
day after she was indisposed, and on the Wednesday so desperately ill,
that all the rites of the ancient catholic church were administered to her;
the official statements are still extant, and prove how completely mistaken those writers are who consider Jane Seymour as a protestant;
equally mistaken are those who affirm that she died, either directly after
the birth of Edward VI., or even two days afterwards; the fact is, she
lived nearly a fortnight.

In a circular, which is the first instance of a royal bulletin, minute
accounts are given of the queen's health; to which is added, " Her confessor hath been with her grace this morning, and hath done that which
to his office appertaineth, and even now is about to administer to her
grace the sacrament of unction. At Hampton Court this Wednesday
morning, eight o'clock."

Nevertheless, the queen was thought to be recovering on the 24th
of October. She did not, however, live over the night.

" The departure of queen Jane was as heavy to the king as ever was
heard tell of. Directly she expired, the king withdrew himself, as not
to be spoken to by any one. He left Hampton Court for Windsor, part
of his council remaining to order her funeral."

In a dispatch from the council to the ambassador of France, the death of the queen is clearly attributed to having been suffered to take cold, and eat improper food.

Two queens of Henry had been previously consigned to their last repose. Katharine of Arragon was buried as his brother's widow, and not as his wife. As to Anne Boleyn, her poor mangled corpse was not vouchsafed, as far as her unloving spouse was aware, the religious rites bestowed on the remains of the most wretched mendicant, who expires on the highway of our Christian land. Jane Seymour was the first spouse, out of three, whom he owned at her death as his wedded wife.

Jane Seymour was undeniably the first woman espoused by Henry VIII., whose title, both as wife and queen, was neither disputed by himself or his subjects. Whilst Katharine of Arragon lived, a great part of the people considered Anne Boleyn but as the shadow of a queen. Both Katharine and Anne were removed by death from rivalry. No doubts were ever raised to the legal rights of Jane as queen of England.

It was owing to this circumstance, as well as the dignity she derived from being the sultana-mother of his heir, that Henry, in his last will, commanded that the bones of his "loving queen Jane" were to be placed in his tomb. He likewise left directions for a magnificent monument to their mutual memories, which he intended should be erected in the Windsor Chapel. Both their statues were to be placed on the tomb; the effigy of Jane was to recline, not as in death, but as one sweetly sleeping; children were to sit at the corners of the tomb, having baskets of roses, white and red, made of fine oriental stones, jasper, cornelian, and agate, "which they shall *show* to take in their hands, and cast them down, on, and over the tomb, and down on the pavement, and the roses they cast over the tomb shall be enamelled and gilt, and the roses they cast on the steps and pavement shall be formed of the said fine oriental stones, and some shall be inlaid on the pavement."

KATHARINE PARR.

KATHARINE PARR was the first Protestant queen of England.' She was the only one among the consorts of Henry VIII. who, in the sincerity of an honest heart, embraced the doctrine of the Reformation, and imperilled her crown and life in support of her principles.

Katharine Parr was not only queen of England, but an English queen. Although of ancient and even royal descent, she claimed, by birth, no other rank than that of a private gentlewoman. Like Anne Boleyn and Jane Seymour, Katharine Parr was only the daughter of a knight; but her father, sir Thomas Parr, was of a more distinguished ancestry than either sir Thomas Boleyn or sir John Seymour.

The date generally assigned for the birth of Katharine Parr is 1510; but the correspondence between her mother and lord Dacre, in the fifteenth year of Henry VIII., in which her age is specified to be *under* twelve, will prove that she could not have been born till 1513. Her father, sir Thomas Parr, at that time held high offices at court, being master of the wards and comptroller of the household of Henry VIII.

It has been generally said that Katharine Parr received a learned education from her father; but as she was only in her fifth year when he died, it must have been to the maternal wisdom of lady Parr that she was indebted, for those mental acquirements which so eminently fitted her to adorn the exalted station to which she was afterwards raised.

Katharine was gifted by nature with fine talents, and these were im·
proved by the advantages of careful cultivation. She both read and
wrote Latin with facility, possessed some knowledge of Greek, and was
well versed in modern languages. How perfect a mistress she was of
her own, the elegance and beauty of her devotional writings are a stand·
ing monument.

Though dame Maud Parr had scarcely completed her twenty-second
year at the time of her husband's death, she never entered into a second
marriage, but devoted herself entirely to the superintendence of her
children's education.

Katharine must have been still in very tender age, when she was
given in marriage to her first husband, Edward, lord Borough of Gainsborough, a mature widower, with children who had arrived at man's
estate. Henry, the second of these sons, after his father's marriage with
Katharine Parr, espoused his friend and kinswoman, Katharine Neville,
the widow of sir Walter Strickland, of Sizergh ; and this lady, though
only twenty-nine at the time of her union, was fourteen years older than
her husband's stepmother.

In Gainsborough church, on the tomb of the first lord Borough,
father to Katharine Parr's husband, the arms of Borough were quartered
with Tallebois, Marmion, and Fitzhugh, which afford sufficient proof of
the ancestral connection of this nobleman with the Parrs. He appears
to have been related to Katharine somewhere about the fourth degree.
He died in 1528–9. Katharine, therefore, could not have exceeded her
fifteenth year at the period of her first widowhood.

Both the brother and the uncle of Katharine were now attached
to the royal household ; but many reasons lead us to suppose that Katha·
rine became an inmate of Sizergh Castle about this period. She was a
lovely, noble, and wealthy widow, in her sixteenth year, when deprived
of the protection of her last surviving parent.

At no other period of her life than the interval between her mother's
death and her own marriage with Neville, lord Latimer, could Katharine
Parr have found leisure to embroider the magnificent counterpane and
toilet-cover, which are proudly exhibited at Sizergh Castle, as trophies
of her industry, having been worked by her own hands, during a visit
to her kinsfolk there.

As the ornamental labors of the needle have become once more a source of domestic enjoyment to the ladies of England, and even the lords of the creation appear to derive some pleasure as lookers-on, in tracing the progress of their fair friends at the embroidering-frame, a brief description of these beautiful and well-preserved specimens of Katharine Parr's proficiency in that accomplishment may not be displeasing.

The material on which both counterpane and toilet-cover are worked is the richest white satin, of a fabric with which the production of no modern loom can vie. The centre of the pattern is a medallion, surrounded with a wreath of natural flowers, wrought in twisted silks and bullion. A spread eagle, in bold relief, gorged with the imperial crown, forms the middle. At each corner is a lively heraldic monster, of the dragon class, glowing with purple, crimson, and gold. The field is gayly beset with large flowers, in gorgeous colors, highly embossed and enriched with threads of gold.

The toilette is *en suite*, but of a smaller pattern. The lapse of three centuries has scarcely diminished the brilliancy of the colors, or tarnished the bullion; nor is the purity of the satin sullied, though both these queenly relics have been used, on state occasions, by the family in whose possession they have remained, as precious heirlooms and memorials of their ancestral connection with queen Katharine Parr.

How long Katharine continued the widow of lord Borough is uncertain; but she was probably under twenty years of age when she became, for the second time, the wife of a mature widower, and again undertook the office of a step-mother. It is not unlikely that her residence at Sizergh Castle might lead to her marriage with John Neville, lord Latimer, as lady Strickland was a Neville, of Thornton Briggs, and would naturally afford her kinsman every facility for his courtship to their fair cousin. Lord Latimer was related to Katharine in about the same degree as her first husband, lord Borough.

After Katharine became the wife of lord Latimer, she chiefly resided with him and his family, at his stately mansion of Snape Hall, in Yorkshire, which is thus described by Leland: "Snape, a goodly castle in a valley belonging to the lord Latimer, with two or three good parks well wooded about it."

That Katharine Parr was not only acquainted with Henry VIII., but possessed considerable influence over his mind, some years before there was the slightest probability of her ever becoming the sharer of his throne, is certified by the history of the Throckmorton family, to which we are principally indebted for the details.

The execution of the unfortunate queen, Katharine Howard, in February 1542, preceded the death of Katharine Parr's second husband, lord Latimer, about twelve months. The will of lord Latimer is dated September 12, 1542, but as it was not proved till the 11th of the following March, it is probable that he died early in 1543.

Katharine was not only pious, learned, and passing fair, but possessed of great wealth as the mistress of two ample jointures, both unencumbered. With these advantages, and connected as she was, either by descent or marriage, with some of the noblest families in England, even with royalty itself in no very remote degree, it is not to be supposed that she was left unwooed.

The circumstances that led to Henry's marriage with Katharine Parr are quaintly glanced at by her poet cousin, sir Thomas Throckmorton, who dates the advancement of his family from that event:—

> "But when the king's fifth wife had lost her head,
> Yet he mislikes the life to live alone,
> And once resolved the sixth time for to wed,
> He sought outright to make his choice of one—
> That choice was chance, right happy for us all,
> It brewed our bliss, and rid us quite from thrall."
>
> Throckmorton MS.

When Henry first made known to lady Latimer that she was the lady whom he intended to honor with the sixth reversion of his hand, she was struck with dismay, and in the terror with which his cruel treatment of his matrimonial victims inspired her, she actually told him "that it was better to be his mistress than his wife." A few months after marriage, such a sarcasm on his conduct as a husband might have cost Henry's best-loved queen her head. As it was, this cutting observation, from the lips of a matron of Katharine's well-known virtue, though it must have afforded him a mortifying idea of the estimation in which the dignity of queen-consort was regarded by the ladies of his court, had no other effect than to increase the eagerness of his suit to the reluctant widow.

Fear was not, however, her only objection to become the wife of Henry; love was for a while victorious over ambition, in the heart of Katharine. Her affection for Seymour rendered her very listless about the royal match, at first; but her favored lover presumed not to contest the prize, with his all-powerful brother-in-law and sovereign. A rival, of Henry's temper, who held the heads of wives, kinsmen, and favorites, as cheaply as tennis-balls, was not to be withstood. The Adonis of the court vanished from the scene, and the bride-elect, accommodating her mind, as she best might, to the change of bridegroom, prepared to assume, with a good grace, the glittering fetters of a queenly slave. The arrangements for the royal nuptials were made with a celerity truly astonishing; barely three months intervened between the proving of lord Latimer's will, and the day on which Cranmer grants a license "for the marriage of his sovereign lord, king Henry, with Katharine Latymer, late the wife of the lord de Latymer, deceased."

Two days afterwards, Katharine exchanged her briefly worn weeds of widowhood, for the bridal robes of a queen of England—robes that had proved fatal trappings to four of her five predecessors in the perilous dignity to which it was the pleasure of her enamored sovereign to advance her. The nuptials of Henry VIII. and Katharine Parr, instead of being hurried over secretly, in some obscure corner, like some unhallowed mystery (as was the case in his previous marriages with Anne Boleyn and Katharine Howard), were solemnized much in the same way as royal marriages are in the present times, without pageantry, but with all suitable observances.

It is scarcely possible but the cheek of Katharine must have blanched when the nuptial ring was placed on her finger, by the ruthless hand that had signed the death-warrant of two of his consorts within the last seven years. If a parallel might be permitted, between the grave facts of history, and the creations of romance, we should say that the situation of Henry VIII.'s queen greatly resembled that of the fair Scheherazade in the Arabian Nights' Entertainments, who voluntarily contracted matrimony with sultan Schriar, though

31

aware that it was his custom to marry a fresh wife every day, and cut off her head the next morning.

The sound principles, excellent judgment, and endearing qualities of Katharine Parr, and, above all, her superlative skill as a nurse, by rendering her necessary to the comfort of the selfish and irritable tyrant who had chosen her as a help meet for him in the season of premature old age and increasing disease, afforded her best security from the fate of her predecessors.

Katharine had now for the third time undertaken the office of a stepmother—an office at all times of much difficulty and responsibility, but peculiarly so with regard to the children of Henry VIII., who were the offspring of queens so fatally opposed as Katharine of Arragon, Anne Boleyn, and Jane Seymour, had successively been. How well the sound sense and endearing manners of Katharine Parr fitted her to reconcile the rival interests, and to render herself a bond of union between the disjointed links of the royal family, is proved by the affection and respect of her grateful step-children, and also by their letters after king Henry's death. Whether a man who had so glaringly violated the duties of a father to his daughters, as Henry had done, deserves any credit for paternal care in his choice of his sixth queen, it would be difficult to say ; but it was scarcely possible for him to have selected a lady better qualified to conduce to the happiness of his children, to improve their minds, and to fit them, by the inculcation of virtuous and noble sentiments, to adorn the high station to which they were born.

The dignity of the scholar and the queen are beautifully blended with the tenderness of the woman and the devotedness of the Christian, in the line of conduct adopted by Katharine Parr, after her elevation to a throne. Her situation at this period is not unlike that of Esther in the house of Ahasuerus. Her attachment to the doctrines of the Reformation naturally rendered her an object of jealous ill-will to Gardiner, bishop of Winchester, the leader of the anti-papal Catholic party ; and as early as the second week after her marriage, this daring ecclesiastic ventured to measure his power against that of the royal bride, by an attack on an humble society of reformers at Windsor.

One of the first fruits of queen Katharine's virtuous influence over the mind of the king, was the restoration of his daughters, the persecuted Mary and the young neglected Elizabeth, to their proper rank in the court, and recognition in the order of succession to the crown.

Notwithstanding the great difference in their religious tenets, a firm friendship ever subsisted between Katharine Parr and Mary. They were near enough in age to have been sisters, they excelled in the same accomplishments, and the great learning and studious pursuits of these royal ladies rendered them suitable companions for each other. The more brilliant talents of the young Elizabeth were drawn forth and fostered, under the auspices of her highly gifted stepmother. Katharine Parr took also an active part in directing the studies of the heir of England, and her approbation appears to have been the greatest encouragement the prince could receive.

The beauty, the talents, and rare acquirements of Katharine Parr, together with the delicate tact which taught her how to make the most of these advantages, enabled her to retain her empire over the fickle heart of Henry for a longer period than the fairest and most brilliant of her predecessors. But these charms were not the most powerful talismans with which the queen won her influence. It was her domestic virtues, her patience, her endearing manners, that rendered her indispensable to the irritable and diseased voluptuary, who was now paying the severe penalty of bodily tortures and mental disquiet, for the excesses of his former life. Henry had grown so corpulent and unwieldy in person, that he was incapable of taking the slightest exercise, much less of recreating himself with the invigorating field-sports, and boisterous pastimes, in which he had formerly delighted. The days had come unexpectedly upon him, in which he had no pleasure. His body was so swollen and enfeebled by dropsy, that he could not be moved to an upper chamber, without the aid of machinery. Hitherto, the excitement of playing the leading part in the public drama of royal pomp and pageantry, had been, with sensual indulgences, the principal objects of his life. Deprived of these, and with the records of an evil conscience to dwell upon in the weary hours of pain, his irascibility and impatience would have goaded him to frenzy, but for the soothing gentleness and tender attentions of his amiable consort. Katharine was the most skilful and patient of nurses, and shrunk not from any office, however humble, whereby she could afford mitigation to the sufferings of her royal husband. It is recorded of her, that she would remain for hours on her knees beside him, applying fomentations and other palliatives to his ulcerated leg, which he would not permit any one to dress but her.

Henry's anger was always the most deadly and dangerous, when he brooded over an offence in silence. Queen Katharine had been accustomed, in their hours of domestic privacy, to converse with him on theological subjects, in which he took great delight. The points of difference in their opinions, and the ready wit and eloquence with which the queen maintained her side of the question, gave piquancy to these discussions.

Henry was at first amused and interested, but controversies between husband and wife are dangerous pastimes to the weaker vessel, especially if she chance to have the best of the argument. On subjects of less importance to his eternal welfare, Katharine might possibly have had tact enough to leave the victory to her lord; but, laboring as she saw him under a complication of incurable maladies, and loaded with a yet more fearful weight of unrepented crimes, she must have been anxious to awaken him to a sense of his accountability to that Almighty Judge, at whose tribunal it was evident he must soon appear.

Henry, who was neither Catholic nor Protestant, had a "*sumpsimus*" of his own, which he wished to render the national rule of faith, and was, at last, exceedingly displeased that his queen should presume to doubt the infallibility of his opinions. One day she ventured, in the presence of Gardiner, to remonstrate with him on the proclamation he had recently put forth, forbidding the use of a translation of the Scriptures, which he had previously licensed. This was at a time when his constitutional irascibility was aggravated by a painful inflammation of his ulcerated leg, which confined him to his chamber. Perhaps Katharine, in her zeal for the diffusion of the truths of holy writ, pressed the matter too closely, for the king showed tokens of mislike, and cut the matter short. The queen made a few pleasant observations on other subjects, and withdrew. Henry's suppressed choler broke out as soon as she had left the room. "A good hearing it is," said he, "when women become such clerks; and much to my comfort, to come, in mine old age, to be taught by my wife!"

Gardiner, who was present, availed himself of this scornful sally to insinuate things against her majesty, which a few days before he durst not, for his life, have breathed to the king. But now that an offence had been given to the royal egotist's self-idolatry, he was ready to listen to any thing that could be said, in disparagement of his dutiful and conscientious wife. Her tender nursing, her unremitting attentions to his comfort, together with her amiable and affectionate conduct to his children, were all forgotten. Gardiner flattered him, to the top of his bent, on his theological knowledge and judgment. In short, " he crept so far into the king at that time," says Fox, " and he, and his fellows, so filled Henry's mistrustful mind with fears, that he gave them warrant to consult together about drawing of articles against the queen, wherein her life might be touched. This purpose was so finely handled, that it grew within a few days of the time appointed, and the poor queen suspected nothing, but, after her accustomed manner, visited the king, still to deal with him touching religion, as before." At this momentous crisis, when the life of the queen might be said to hang on a balance so fearfully poised that the descent of a feather would have given it a fatal turn, the bill of articles that had been framed against her, together with mandate for her arrest, were dropped by Wriothesley from his bosom, in the gallery at Whitehall, after the royal signature of the king had been affixed. Fortunately, it happened that it was picked up by one of the attendants of the queen, and instantly conveyed to her majesty, whose sweetness of temper and gracious demeanor had endeared her to all her household.

When Katharine Parr became aware from the perusal of the paper, so providentially brought to her, that a bill for her attainder was prepared, and saw that the king had treacherously given his sanction to the machinations of her foes, than she concluded that she was to be added to the list of his conjugal decapitations, and fell into an hysterical agony. She occupied an apartment contiguous to that of the sick and froward monarch; and as she fell from one fit into another, her shrieks and cries reached his ears. Finding they continued for many hours, either moved with pity, or, as Dr. Lingard shrewdly suggests, "incommoded by the noise," he sent to inquire what was the matter. Katharine's physician, Dr. Wendy, having penetrated the cause of her majesty's indisposition, informed the royal messenger "that the queen was dangerously ill, and

that it appeared that her sickness was caused by distress of mind."
When the king heard this, he was either moved with unwonted feelings
of compassion for the sufferings of his consort, or reminded, by his own
increasing infirmities, which had confined him, for the last two days, to
his bed, of her unrivalled skill as a nurse; and feeling, perhaps, for the
first time, how much he should miss her in that capacity if death
deprived him of her services, he determined to pay her a visit. This
act of royal condescension was the more remarkable, because it was
attended with great personal inconvenience to himself, for he was carried
in a chair into queen Katharine's apartment, being at that time unable
to walk. He found her heavy and melancholy, and apparently at the
point of death, at which he evinced much sympathy, as if really alarmed
at the idea of losing her. Perhaps he had not, till then, discovered that
she was dearer to him than her fairer and more passionately, but briefly
loved, predecessors, Anne Boleyn, and Katharine Howard. On this
occasion she testified a proper degree of gratitude for the honor of his
visit, "which," she assured him, "had greatly revived and rejoiced
her." She also adroitly offered an opening for an explanation of the
cause of Henry's displeasure, by expressing herself much distressed at
having seen so little of his majesty of late, adding, that her uneasiness
at this was increased by her apprehensions of having been so unhappy
as to have given him some unintentional offence. Henry replied only
with gracious and encouraging expressions of his good-will. During
the rest of this critical interview, Katharine behaved in so humble and
endearing a manner, and so completely adapted herself to the humor of
her imperious lord, that, in the excitement caused by the reaction of his
feelings, Henry betrayed to her physician the secret of the plot against
her life. The physician, being both a good and a prudent person, acted
as a mediator with his sovereign, in the first instance, and is said to
have suggested to the queen the proper means of securing a reconciliation with Henry.

The next evening the queen found herself well enough to return the
king's visit in his bedchamber. She came attended by her sister, lady
Herbert, and the king's young niece, lady Jane Gray, who carried the
candles before her majesty. Henry welcomed her very courteously,
and appeared to take her attention in good part, but presently turned

the conversation to the old subject of controversy, for the purpose of beguiling her into an argument. Katharine adroitly avoided the snare by observing, "that she was but a woman, accompanied with all the imperfections natural to the weakness of her sex; therfore, in all mat-ters of doubt and difficulty, she must refer herself to his majesty's better judgment, as to her lord and head; for so God hath appointed you," continues she, "as the supreme head of us all, and of you, next unto God, will I ever learn."

"Not so, by St. Mary," said the king; "ye are become a doctor, Kate, to instruct us, and not to be instructed of us, as oftentimes we have seen." "Indeed," replied the queen, "if your majesty have so conceived, my meaning has been mistaken, for I have always held it preposterous for a woman to instruct her lord; and if I have ever pre-sumed to differ with your highness on religion, it was partly to obtain information for my own comfort, regarding certain nice points on which I stood in doubt, and sometimes because I perceived that, in talking, you were better able to pass away the pain and weariness of your present infirmity, which encouraged me to this boldness, in the hope of profiting withal by your majesty's learned discourse." "And is it so, sweetheart?" replied the king; "then are we perfect friends." He then kissed her with much tenderness, and gave her leave to depart.

On the day appointed for her arrest, the king, being convalescent, sent for the queen to take the air with him in the garden. Katharine came, attended, as before, by her sister, lady Jane Gray, and lady Tyr-whit. Presently, the lord-chancellor Wriothesley, with forty of the guard, entered the garden, with the expectation of carrying off the queen to the Tower, for he had not received the slightest intimation of the change in the royal caprice. The king received him with a burst of indignation, and saluted him with the unexpected address of "Beast, fool, and knave," and, sternly withdrawing him from the vicinity of the queen he bade him "avaunt from his presence." Katharine, when she saw the king so greatly incensed with the chancellor, had the magna-nimity to intercede for her foe, saying, "she would become a humble suitor for him, as she deemed his fault was occasioned by mistake."

"Ah! poor soul," said the king, "thou little knowest, Kate, how

evil he deserveth this grace at thy hands. On my word, sweetheart, he
hath been to thee a very knave."

Katharine Parr treated the authors of the cruel conspiracy against
her life, with the magnanimity of a great mind, and the forbearance of
a true Christian. She sought no vengeance, although the reaction of
the king's anxious fondness would undoubtedly have given her the
power of destroying them, if she had been of a vindictive temper. But
though Henry was induced through the intercession of Katharine, to
overlook the offence of Wriothesley, he never forgave Gardiner the part
he had taken in this affair, which proved no less a political blunder, than
a moral crime.

Henry is said to have exhibited many public marks of coarse, but
confiding fondness for queen Katharine Parr, in his latter days. He
was accustomed to call her "sweetheart," and to lay his sore leg on her
lap before the lords and ladies-in-waiting; and sometimes, it is said, he so
far forgot the restraint of royalty, as to do so in the presence of the
whole court. The queen, who was still a very pretty little woman, and
quite young enough to have been his daughter, was careful to receive
these rude endearments, as flattering marks of the favor of her royal
lord. Yet, after the fearful warning she had received of the capricious
nature of his love, and the treachery of his disposition, she must have
regarded herself as a "poor pensioner on the bounties of an hour."
How indeed could the sixth wife of Henry pillow her head on his cruel
bosom, without dreaming of axes and flames, or fearing to see the curtains withdrawn by the pale spectres of his former matrimonial victims?

The unmerited fate of the gallant and accomplished Surrey has been
ever considered as one of the darkest blots of the crime-stained annals of
Henry VIII. It is somewhat remarkable that this monarch, who had
received a learned education, made pretensions to authorship, and affected to. be a patron of the belles-lettres, sent the three most distinguished literary characters of his court—sir Thomas More, lord Rochford, and Surrey—to the block, from feelings of private and personal
malice, and in so illegal a manner, that the executions of all three deserve no gentler name than murder. Surrey was beheaded on the 19th
of January, 1547. Henry then lay on his death-bed, and his swollen
and feeble hands having been long unequal to the task of guiding a pen,

a stamp with the fac-simile of the initials "H. R.," was affixed to the death-warrant in his presence.

When the physician announced to those in attendance on the sove-reign that the hour of his departure was at hand, they shrunk from the peril of incurring the last ebullition of his vindictive temper by warn-ing him of the awful change that awaited him. The queen, worn out with days and nights of fatiguing personal attendance on her wayward lord during the burning fever which had preyed upon him for more than two months, was in all probability unequal to the trial of witness-ing the last fearful scene; for she is not mentioned as having been pres-ent on that occasion. Sir Anthony Denny was the only person who had the courage to inform the king of his real state. He approached the bed, and, leaning over it, told him "that all human aid was now vain, and that it was meet for him to review his past life, and seek for God's mercy through Christ." Henry, who was uttering loud cries of pain and impatience, regarded him with a stern look, and asked, "What judge had sent him to pass this sentence upon him?" Denny replied, "Your physicians." When these physicians next approached the royal patient to offer him medicine, he repelled them in these words: "After the judges have once passed sentence on a criminal, they have no more to do with him; therefore begone!" It was then suggested that he should confer with some of his divines. "I will see no one but Cranmer," replied the king; "and not him as yet. Let me repose a little, and as I find myself so shall I determine." After an hour's sleep he awoke, and, becoming faint, commanded that Cranmer, who had withdrawn to Croydon, should be sent for with all haste. But the precious interval had been wasted; and before the archbishop entered, Henry was speech-less. Cranmer besought him to testify by some sign his hope in the saving mercy of Christ. The king regarded him steadily for a moment, wrung his hand and expired.

Henry VIII. expired at two o'clock in the morning of January 28th, 1547, at his royal palace at Westminster, in the thirty-eighth year of his reign, and the fifty-sixth of his age.

During the brief period of her royal widowhood, Katharine Parr, now queen-dowager, resided at her fine jointure-house at Chelsea, on the banks of the Thames, which, with its beautiful and extensive gardens,

occupied the pleasant spot now called Cheyne Pier. Some of the noble
trees in Mr. Druce's gardens appear coeval with that epoch, and are perhaps the same, under whose budding verdure queen Katharine was
accustomed to hold her secret meetings with her adventurous lover sir
Thomas Seymour, ere royal etiquette would allow her to give public
encouragement to his suit. Seymour renewed his addresses to Katharine so immediately after King Henry's death, that she was wooed and
won, almost before she had assumed the widow's hood and barb and
sweeping sable pall, which marked the relict of the departed majesty of
England. Katharine, after having been the wife of three mature widowers in succession, to the last of whom that joyless bauble, a crown, had
tricked her into three years, six months, and fourteen days of worse than
Egyptian bondage, found herself, in her thirty-fifth year, still handsome,
and apparently more passionately beloved than ever by the man of her
heart. Womanlike, she gave him full credit for constancy and disinterested love, and found it difficult to withstand his ardent pleadings to
reward his tried affection, by resigning to him the hand which had
been plighted to him, before her marriage with the king.

Although the precise date of Katharine Parr's fourth nuptials is uncertain, it is evident that the admiral's eloquence prevailed over her
punctilio, at a very early period of her widowhood, by persuading her
to consent to a private marriage. Leti affirms, that exactly thirty-four
days after king Henry's death, a written contract of marriage, and rings
of betrothal were exchanged between Katharine and sir Thomas Seymour, but the marriage was not celebrated till some months later.

After queen Katharine had been the wife of her beloved Seymour
some months, there was a prospect of her becoming a mother. Her
raptures at the anticipation of a blessing which had been denied to all
her other marriages, carried her beyond the bounds of discretion, and
her husband was no less transported than herself; the feelings of paternity with them amounted to passion.

On the 30th of August, 1548, Katharine Parr gave birth, at Sudley
Castle, to the infant whose appearance had been so fondly anticipated
both by Seymour and herself. It was a girl; and, though both parents
had confidently expected a boy, no disappointment was expressed.

It is difficult to imagine that the admiral, however faulty his *morale* might be on some points, could cherish evil intentions against her who had just caused his heart to overflow for the first time with the ineffable raptures of paternity. The charge of his having caused the death of queen Katharine by poison can only be regarded as a fabrication of his enemies; neither is there the slightest reason to believe that the un-favorable symptoms which appeared on the third day after her delivery, were either caused or aggravated by his unkindness. On the contrary, his manner towards her, when she was evidently suffering under the grievous irritability of mind and body incidental to puerperal fever, appears from the deposition of Lady Tyrwhit.

Katharine Parr expired on the second day after the date of her will, being the seventh after the birth of her child. She was only in the thirty-sixth year of her age, having survived her royal husband, Henry VIII., but one year, six months, and eight days.

MARY,

MARY, our first queen-regnant, was the only child of Henry VIII. and Katharine of Arragon who reached maturity; she first saw the light on the banks of the Thames, at Greenwich Palace, on Monday, at four in the morning, February 18, 1516. As she was a healthy babe, her birth consoled her parents for the loss of the two heirs male, who had preceded her, nor in her childhood was her father ever heard to regret her sex.

Mary was reared, till she was weaned, in the apartments of the queen her mother, and the first rudiments of her education were commenced by that tender parent as soon as she could speak.

It was the wish of queen Katharine that the Emperor Charles V., her nephew, might become her son-in-law, and all the political arrangements between her and her husband seemed to favor that wish.

By a solemn matrimonial treaty, signed at Windsor, the emperor engaged to marry the princess Mary when she attained her twelfth year; he was in the mean time exceedingly desirous that she should be sent to Spain, that she might be educated as his wife. But the doting affection of her parents could not endure the separation. The care of Mary's excellent mother was now sedulously directed to give her child an education that would render her a fitting companion to the greatest sovereign of modern history, not only in regard to extent of dominions, but in character and attainments.

The young princess was certainly educated according to the rigorous directions of Vives, and she is an historical example of the noxious effect that over-education has at a very tender age. Her precocious studies probably laid the foundation for her melancholy temperament and delicate health.

In the course of the summer of 1525, rumors reached the court of England that the emperor meant to forsake the princess Mary, and was privately engaged to Isabel of Portugal. This was probably the first sorrow experienced by Mary, who was observed to grow pale, with apprehension and jealousy, when the change of the emperor's intentions was discussed. The little creature had been persuaded by her maids that she was in love with Charles V., for about this time she sent a pretty message to him, through her father's ambassadors resident in Spain.

Mary, if not actually declared princess of Wales, as some authors have affirmed, assuredly received honors and distinctions which have never, either before or since, been offered to any one but the heir-apparent of England. A court was formed for her at Ludlow Castle, on a grander scale than those established either for her uncle Arthur, or Edward of York, both acknowledged princes of Wales, and heirs-apparent of England.

Mary took leave of her parents at the palace of Langley, in Hertfordshire, in September, 1525, previously to her departure for Ludlow Castle. Dr. Sampson gives a pleasing description of her person and qualities at this epoch. "My lady princess," he says in a letter to Wolsey, "came hither on Saturday; surely, sir, of her age, as goodly a child as ever I have seen, and of as good gesture and countenance. Few persons o her age blend sweetness better with seriousness, or quickness with deference; she is at the same time joyous and decorous in manners." In fact, contemporaries and all portraiture represent Mary at this period of her life as a lovely child. But if human ingenuity had been taxed to the utmost in order to contrive the most cruel contrast between her present and future prospects, it could not have been more thoroughly effected, than by first placing her in vice-regal pomp and state, as princess of Wales, at Ludlow Castle, and then afterwards blighting her young mind by hurling her undeservedly into poverty and contempt.

It was in her court, at Ludlow Castle, that Mary first practised to play the part of queen, a lesson she was soon compelled to unlearn, with the bitterest insults. Her education at the same time went steadily on with great assiduity. Fresh instructions were given to her council regarding her tuition when she parted from her royal parents; they emanated from the maternal tenderness and good sense of queen Katharine, whose earnest wish was evidently to render her daughter healthy and cheerful, as well as learned and accomplished.

The residence of Mary at Ludlow lasted about eighteen months, varied with occasional visits to Tickenhill, and to the magnificent unfinished palace of the unfortunate duke of Buckingham at Thornbury, lately seized by the king; her education meantime proceeded rapidly

Henry VIII., during the protracted discussion of the divorce, was at times extremely embarrassed by his affection for Mary, and her claims on his paternity. Sometimes he bestowed profuse caresses on her in public; and, at the first movement of the divorce, gave out that the inquiry was made only to settle her claims permanently to the succession. The princess, meantime, remained near her parents, in possession of the same state and distinction she had enjoyed since her birth.

An utter silence is maintained, alike in public history, and state documents, regarding that agonizing moment when the princess Mary was reft from the arms of her unfortunate mother, to behold her no more. No witness has told the parting, no pen has described it; but sad and dolorous it certainly was to the hapless girl, even to the destruction of health.

The succeeding year brought many trials to the unfortunate mother and daughter, who were still cruelly kept from the society of each other. The king proclaimed his marriage with Anne Boleyn. Cranmer pronounced the marriage of queen Katharine invalid.

The situation of Mary, when called to court at such a crisis, must have been trying in the extreme; nor could the most sedulous caution have guided her through the difficulties which beset her path, without incurring blame from one party or the other. There is, however, whatever the court gossips might say, the witness of her own letter, that she never denied the name of sister to the new-born infant; for when she was required to give up the title of princess, and call Elizabeth by no other appellation, "Sister," she said, "she would call the babe, but nothing more."

Her father threatened her—his threats were useless; and he proceeded to aggravate the case by declaring Mary's new-born rival his heiress (in default of male issue), a dignity till then enjoyed by Mary, who had lately, as such, exercised authority in the principality of Wales.

But neither threats nor deprivations had the least effect in bending the resolution of Mary. That her resistance did not spring from an exclusive devotion to her own interest, her subsequent concession proved; but her love for her injured mother was an absorbing feeling paramount to every other consideration, and, while Katharine of Arragon lived, Mary of England would have suffered martyrdom, rather than make a concession against the interest and dignity of that adored parent.

The death of Mary's tender and devoted mother opened the year 1536 with a dismal aggravation of her bitter lot. The sad satisfaction, of a last adieu between the dying queen and her only child, was cruelly forbidden. Mary was informed of the tidings of her mother's expected dissolution, and with agonizing tears and plaints implored permission to receive her last blessing; yet in vain, for Katharine of Arragon expired without seeing her daughter.

At the very time when all Europe anticipated the destruction of the princess Mary, a change took place in the current of events that influenced her fortunes. Her step-mother, queen Anne Boleyn, lost the male heir, who was expected wholly to deprive Mary of all claims to primogeniture, even in the eyes of her most affectionate partisans. Scarcely had queen Anne uttered the well-known exclamation of triumph on the death of Katharine of Arragon, before indications were perceptible that she had herself lost Henry's capricious favor; her fall and condemnation followed with rapidity.

In the midst of all her degradations, Mary was regarded with the utmost sympathy by her country; poets offered her their homage, and celebrated the beauty of her person at a time when no possible benefit could accrue to any one by flattering her.

The situation in which Mary was placed at court, on the occasional visits, was a very trying one. She was a young woman, whose person

was much admired, surrounded by parties, hostile to her both on a religious and political account, and she was wholly bereft of female protection. Her tender mother, and her venerable relative (lady Salisbury),
had both been torn from her—and who could supply their places in her
esteem and veneration? A perplexed and thorny path laid before her,
yet, at a time of life when temptation most abounds, she trod it free
from the reproach of her most inveterate political adversaries. The
writings of her contemporaries abound with praises of her virtuous conduct. "She was," says the Italian history of Pollino, " distinguished,
when a young virgin, for the purity of her life, and her spotless manners; when she came to her father's court, she gave surprise to all
those who composed it, so completely was decorum out of fashion there.
As to the king, he affected to disbelieve in the reality of female virtue,
and therefore laid a plot to prove his daughter. This scheme he carried
into effect, but remained astonished at the strength and stability of her
principles." Such an assertion, it is very hard to credit: it may be possible to find husbands willing to be as cruel as Henry if they had the
power; but, thanks be to God, who has planted so holy and blessed a
love as that of a father for his daughter in the heart of man, it is not
possible to find a parallel case in the annals of the present or the past.
And if a father could be believed capable of contriving a snare for the
honor of his daughter, it ought to be remembered that family honor is
especially compromised by the misconduct of the females who belong
to it; and Henry VIII. has never been represented as deficient in pride.
This singular assertion being, nevertheless, related by a contemporary,
it became the duty of a biographer to translate it.

More than one treaty of marriage had been negotiated by Henry,
for his daughter, since the disinheriting act of parliament had passed;
he always setting forth, that by the same act, it remained in his power
to restore her to her place in the succession, if agreeable to his will.
He had been so long used to amuse himself with these negotiations, that
they evidently formed part of his pastime. Yet Mary's early desire of
leading a single life was seldom threatened with contradiction, by any
prospect of these marriage-treaties being brought to a successful conclusion. Thus passed away the suit of the prince of Portugal, made the
same year.

33

An auspicious change took place in the situation of Mary, a few months after the sixth marriage of her father. Although the restoration to her natural place in the succession was not complete, yet the crown was entailed on her after prince Edward, or any son or daughter which Henry might have by his wife Katharine Parr, or any succeeding wives, by act of parliament, passed Feb. 7th, 1544.

The princess was invited to court, by an affectionate letter from the young king her brother, who was, before religious controversy occasioned variance, exceedingly fond of her. The royal family passed the Christmas, succeeding their father's death, in each other's society, on the most affectionate terms. From that time, however, the visits of Mary to court were few; as she could not agree with the tenets of the Protestants, she held herself as much in retirement as possible.

Mary's health was so very infirm in the spring of 1550, that her death was generally expected; she herself felt convinced that her end was near. Had she died at this time, how deeply venerated would her name have been to all posterity—how fondly would her learning, her charities, her spotless purity of life, her inflexible honesty of word and deed, and her fidelity to her friends, have been quoted and remembered by her country! Even her constancy to the ancient church would have been forgiven, as she was as yet innocent of the greatest offence a human being can commit against God and man—persecution for religion's sake. If she had never reigned, the envenomed hatred between Protestants and Catholics would have been less, and many horrid years of persecution and counter-persecution would have been spared.

As the young king's health declined, the homage offered to the princess Mary increased; and when she paid one of her state visits to him at Westminster, on occasion of the new year of 1553, her cortege was crowded with the principal nobility.

King Edward expired at Greenwich Palace, little more than a month afterwards. He disinherited, by an illegal will, not only the sister whose religion he hated, but his Protestant sister, Elizabeth, in order to bestow the crown on lady Jane Gray. It is a point that will admit strong historical controversy, whether, in this transaction, Edward was Northumberland's dupe or his victim.

When king Edward expired, sir Nicholas Throckmorton, who was present at his death, came in great grief to Throckmorton House, in the city, where his three brothers were assembled, to whom he revealed the king's death, and the intended proclamation of Northumberland's daughter-in-law as queen. The brothers, agreeing in a strong detestation of the house of Dudley, resolved that timely notice should be given to the princess Mary, and, therefore, called into consultation her goldsmith, who undertook to carry the important message; he set out accordingly to meet her, and was undoubtedly the man who intercepted her at Hoddesden, and revealed the real state of affairs. This information threw Mary into the greatest perplexity. She asked her goldsmith, "How he knew for a certainty the king was dead?' He answered, "Sir Nicholas knew it verily." This authority was exceedingly mistrusted by Mary, for, as sir Nicholas Throckmorton had assumed the phraseology of the most violent Calvinists at the court of Edward VI., she could not believe that his intentions were friendly to her cause.

She would not, however, despise the warning, though she did not fully confide in it, but diverged from the London road, towards Suffolk, with all her train. These events must have occurred on the afternoon of the 7th of July.

The fugitive heiress of England bent her flight in the direction of Cambridgeshire, as the nearest way to her seat of Kenninghall, through Bury St. Edmunds. As the soft shades of a July night fell round her hasty course over those desolate plains, which are intersected by the eastern road—once so familiar to the pilgrims bound to the Lady shrine of Walsingham, and since as much traversed by the frequenters of New-Market—the ladies and cavaliers of her faithful retinue began to discuss the recent death of the young king. They were all Catholics of the ancient ritual, and, of course, viewed the changes of the eventful times wholly according to their prejudices.

The same night Mary crossed the river, which separates Suffolk from its sister county, and arrived safely at her seat of Kenninghall, in Norfolk. Their was little rest for her, either in mind or body. By that time the news of the death of the king, her brother, was generally known, and it was necessary for her to take immediate steps for the assertion of her title to the throne.

Mary immediately took prompt measures for maintaining her right;

and certainly displayed in the course she pursued, an admirable union
of courage and prudence. She had neither money, soldiers, nor advisers;
sir Thomas Wharton the steward of her household, and her ladies, were
her only assistants in the first bold step she took. Had she been surrounded by the experienced veterans in arms and council that rallied
round her sister Elizabeth at Tilbury, more sagacious measures could
scarcely have been adopted; and had Elizabeth been the heroine of the
enterprise, instead of Mary, it would have been lauded to the skies as
one of the grandest efforts of female courage and ability the world had
ever known. And so it was; whether it be praised or not.

Sir Henry Jerningham and sir Henry Bedingfield brought their Norfolk tenantry to her aid before she left Kenninghall, which she did on
the representation that the country was too open, and the house not
strong enough to stand a siege. She resolved to fix her head-quarters
within an easy ride of the eastern coast, whence she could, on emergency, embark for the opposite shores of Holland, and seek the protection
of her kinsman, the emperor Charles V.

With this intention she left Kenninghall, July 11th, mounted on
horseback, and attended by her faithful knights, and ladies, she never
drew bridle till she reached the town of Framlingham, which is deep
embosomed in the Suffolk woodlands, and situated about twenty miles,
from Kenninghall. The treble circle of moats which girdle the hill-side,
town, and fortress of Framlingham, were then full and efficient, and the
whole defences in complete repair. Mary arrived there after nightfall
at the head of a little cavalry force, destined to form the nucleus of a
mighty army. The picturesque train of knights, in warlike harness, and
their men-at-arms, guarding equestrian maids of honor, with the heiress
of the English crown at their head, wended their way, by torchlight,
up the woodland eminence on which the Saxon town of Framlingham
is built. Thus they passed the beautiful church, where the bones of
the noble poet Surrey have since found rest, and ascended the mighty
causeway, over two deep moats, and paused at length beneath the embattled gateway, surmounted then, as now, by the arms of Howard.

Directly Mary stood within the magnificent area formed by the cir-
cling towers of Framlingham Castle, she felt herself a sovereign; she
immediately defied her enemies, by displaying her standard over the

gate-tower, and assumed the title of queen-regnant of England and Ireland.

The royal standard of England had not floated many hours over the towers of Framlingham Castle, before the chivalry of Suffolk mustered gallantly round queen Mary. Sir John Sulyard, the knight of Wetherden, was the first who arrived to her assistance, and to him was given the honorable post of guarding her person. Sir Henry Bedingfield's Suffolk tenants came in, completely armed, to the amount of 140 men; and Mary appointed their zealous master knight-marshal of her hourly increasing host. The young grandson of the imprisoned duke of Norfolk, lord Thomas Howard, then seventeen, appeared as one of the queen's defenders, and there is no question, but that the adherents of his house crowded round the banner of the disinherited heir of the murdered Surrey. Meantime, Sir Henry Jerningham undertook a most dangerous commission at Yarmouth, the success of which finally turned the scale in Mary's favor.

Sir William Drury, knight of the shire of Suffolk, and sir Thomas Cornwallis, high sheriff, soon joined the queen's muster at Framlingham, likewise sir John Shelton and sir John Tyrrel, both very zealous Catholics ; according to Fox, they were afterwards bitter persecutors of the Protestants. An extraordinary misapprehension exists, that Mary's recognition as queen was chiefly enforced by the Protestants of Suffolk, yet the leaders of her Framlingham force were not only Catholics, but most of their descendants are so to this day. Her army soon amounted to 13,000 men, all voluntarily serving without pay, though the queen prudently directed " that if any soldier seemed in need of aught, his captain was to supply his wants as if by way of gift, and charge the expense to her." In an incredibly short time a populous camp rose around the ancient walls of the castle, within whose mighty circle the queen herself sojourned.

The camp broke up at Framlingham the last day of July, when queen Mary commenced her triumphant march to the metropolis, from whence her sister Elizabeth set out, the same day, to meet her, at the head of a numerous cavalcade of nobility and gentry, amounting to a thousand persons. Among these were, in all probability, the privy council, who, it appears met their sovereign at Ingatestone. The queen's approach to her capital was gradual, and in the manner of a peaceful royal progress, receiving the homage of her faithful or penitent subjects at her various resting-places on the road.

The queen proceeded to the seat of sir William Petre, at Ingatestone, where the council, who had lately defied and denied her, were presented to her, for the purpose of kissing her hand.

The queen arrived at her seat of Wanstead, on the 3d of August, where she disbanded her army, excepting a body of horse—a bold measure, considering all that had recently been transacted in the metropolis; nevertheless, it was only a proper observance of the ancient laws and privileges of London.

The ladies who had accompanied the princess Elizabeth from London were introduced formally to queen Mary, at Wanstead, who kissed every one of them. Such is the tradition in a family whose ancestress attended that antique royal drawing room.

The queen was, on the 3d of August, escorted from Wanstead by great numbers of nobles and ladies, who came to grace her entrance into her capital. A foreigner who was an eye-witness, thus describes her appearance on this triumphant occasion : " Then came the ladies, married and single, in the midst of whom rode madame Mary, queen of England, mounted on a small white ambling nag, the housings of which were fringed with gold. The queen was dressed in violet velvet; she seemed about forty years of age, and was rather fresh-colored."

The old city portal of Aldgate, at which the queen made her entrance into the metropolis, was hung with gay streamers from top to bottom; over the gateway was a stage with seats, on which were placed the charity-children of the Spital, singing sweet chorusses of welcome to the victorious queen ; the street of Leadenhall, and all down to the Tower, through the Minories, was clean swept, and spread with gravel, and was lined with all the crafts in London, in their proper dresses, holding banners and streamers. The lord-mayor, with the mace, was ready to welcome her; and the earl of Arundel, with the sword of state. A thousand gentlemen, in velvet coats and richly embroidered cloaks, preceded queen Mary.

Next the queen rode her sister Elizabeth ; then the duchess of Norfolk and the marchioness of Exeter followed, and other noble dames,

according to their connection with the crown, and precedence. The
aldermen brought up the rear, and the city guard, with bows and jave-
lins. The guard which accompanied Mary—being 3000 horsemen, in
uniforms of green and white, red and white, and blue and white—were
dismissed by the queen with thanks, and all departed before she passed
the city-gate. Mary acted according to the intrepidity of her character,
in trusting her person wholly to the care of the civic guard; thus im-
plicitly relying on the fidelity of a city were a rival had reigned but a
few hours before.

She bent her way direct to the Tower, then under the care of sir
Thomas Cheyney, warden of the Cinque Ports. Here she meant to sojourn, according to the ancient custom of her predecessors, till the funeral
of the late sovereign.

When Mary entered the precincts of the Tower, a touching sight
presented itself to her. Kneeling on the green, before St. Peter's Church,
were the state-prisoners,—male and female, Catholic and Protestant,—
who had been detained lawlessly in the fortress during the reigns of
Henry VIII. and Edward VI.

There was Edward Courtenay, the heir to the earl of Devonshire,
now in the pride of manly beauty, who had grown up a prisoner from
his tenth year without education; there was another early friend of the
queen, the wretched duchess of Somerset; there was the aged duke of
Norfolk, still under sentence of death; there were the deprived bishops
of Durham and Winchester, the mild Cuthbert Tunstal, and the haughty
Stephen Gardiner, which last addressed a congratulation and supplication to the queen, in the name of all. Mary burst into tears as she
recognized them, and extending her hands to them, she exclaimed,
" Ye are my prisoners!" She raised them one by one, kissed them, and
gave them all their liberty.

The queen remained in privacy, sojourning at the royal apartments
of the Tower, till after the funeral of her brother, which was performed
with great magnificence.

Mary remained at the Tower till after the 12th of August. This is
apperant from the following minute from the privy council book:—

"The council delivered to the lord-mayor and recorder these words,
from the queen's own mouth, yesterday at the Tower, being the 12th of

August, on the occasion of a riot at St. Paul's Cross, about preaching:—
'Albeit her grace's conscience is *staid* (fixed) in matters of religion, yet
she meaneth graciously, not to compel and constrain other men's con-
sciences, otherwise than God shall (as she trusteth) put into their hearts
a persuasion of the *truth that she is in*, through the opening of his word
by godly, virtuous, and learned preachers; and she forbade the lord-
mayor to suffer, in any ward, open reading of the Scriptures in the
churches, or preaching by the curates, unless licensed by her.' "

Such was the first blow aimed at the Protestant church of England.
Mary was empowered to inflict it, as head of the very church whose
ministers she silenced by force of her supremacy. It is an instance of
the manner in which that tremendous power worked, and explains the
mystery why the great body of the English nation,—albeit not composed
of the most flexible of elements,—changed their ritual with magic
celerity, according to the differing opinions of four successive sovereigns,
but the truth was, in that evil century each sovereign was empowered
unfettered by parliament or convocation to change the entire ministra-
tion of the clergy throughout the realm, by the simple act of private
will. Thus the religious tuition of the parish churches in London, the
Sunday before the 12th of August, was according to the Protestant
church established by Edward VI., and the next Sunday according to
the anti-papal Catholic church of Henry the VIII. While queen Mary
continued head of the Church in England, a reconciliation with the see
of Rome was an impossibility.

The accession of queen Mary had not altered her affection for the
princess Elizabeth; whatever were their after jealousies, their first
difference had yet to take place, for, at the present time, wherever Mary
went, she led her sister by the hand, and never dined in public without
her.

Dramatic representations were among the entertainments at Mary's
coronation festival; these were superintended by Heywood, the comic
dramatist, whose attachment to the royal rital had caused him to take
refuge in France. By an odd coincidence, he returned to his native
country on the very same day that Bale, the sarcastic poet of the Reformers retreated to Geneva. If we may be permitted to judge by the
tone of their writings, pure Christianity and moral truth lost little by

the absence of either ribald railer; for they were nearer allied in spirit than their polemic hatred would allow. There is something irresistibly ridiculous in the change of places of these persons, resembling the egress and regress of the figures in a toy barometer, on the sudden alterations of weather, to which our island is subject.

The comedian Heywood, it has been shown, had served queen Mary from her childhood, beginning his theatrical career, as manager to one of those dramatic companies of infant performers, which vexed the spirit of Shakspeare into much indignation, and caused him to compare them to "little eyasses."

When Heywood, on his return from banishment, presented himself before his royal mistress,—

"What wind has blown you hither?" asked queen Mary.

"Two special ones," replied the comedian; "one of them, to see your majesty."

"We thank you for that," said Mary; "but, I pray, for what purpose was the other?"

"That your majesty might see *me.*"

A first-rate repartee for a player and a dramatist, and her majesty named an early day for beholding him in his vocation. He was appointed manager of the performances of her theatrical servants; and she often sent for him, to stand at the sideboard at supper, and amuse her with his jests; in which, it is said, the Protestant Reformation was not spared, though (according to Camden) the arrows of the wit glanced occasionally at his own church, even in these interviews with majesty.

Four days after her coronation, queen Mary performed the important office of opening her first parliament.

The first act of legislation was to restore the English laws, regarding life and property, to the state in which they stood, in the twenty-fifth year of Edward III. Since the accession of the Tudor line, a hideous change had taken place.

Early in January, count Egmont landed in Kent, as ambassador from Spain, to conclude the marriage-treaty between Mary and Philip. The first symptoms of a political storm, about to burst, were then perceptible, for the men of Kent rose partially in revolt, and Egmont was in some

34

danger of being torn to pieces by the common people for the queen's bridegroom. However, he arrived safely at Westminster, and, in a set speech, opened his mission to the queen. Her reply had some spice of prudery in its composition. She said, "It became not a female to speak in public on so delicate a subject as her own marriage; the ambassador might confer with her ministers, who would utter her intentions; but," she continued, casting down her eyes on her coronation-ring, which she always wore on her finger, "they must remember her realm was her first husband, and no consideration should make her violate the faith she pledged to her people at her inauguration."

On the 14th of January, the articles of the queen's marriage were communicated to the lord-mayor and the city of London. According to this document, Mary and Philip were to bestow on each other the titular dignities of their several kingdoms; the dominions of each were to be governed separately, according to their ancient laws and privileges.

Mary and her council, meantime, retired to Richmond Palace, and sat in earnest debate regarding the reception of don Philip, and the station he was to occupy in England. Unfortunately, Mary had no precedent to guide her in distinguishing between her duties as queen-regnant, and the submission and obedience the marriage-vow enforced from her as a wife. It is very evident that queen Mary considered that her duty, both as a married woman and a sedulous observer of the established customs of her country, was, as far as possible, to yield implicit obedience to her spouse. All the crimes, all the detestation with which the memory of this unfortunate lady has been loaded, certainly arose, not from intentional wickedness, but from this notion.

The queen was at Windsor Castle when the tidings arrived, that don Philip, and the combined fleets of England and Spain, amounting to one hundred and sixty sail, had made the port of Southampton, Friday, July 20th, after a favorable voyage from Corunna of but seven days.

Don Philip landed on the 20th of July. He was rowed on shore in a magnificent state barge, manned by twenty men, dressed in the queen's liveries of green and white. The barge was lined with rich tapestry, and a seat was provided for the prince, covered with gold brocade.

The queen's first interview with her affianced husband took place that evening, about ten o'clock, when don Philip was conducted privately to the bishop's palace. Mary received him "right lovingly," and convers- ed with him familiarly in Spanish, for about half an hour, when he went back to the deanery. The queen held a grand court, at three o'clock the next afternoon, when she gave don Philip a public audience. He came on foot from the deanery, attended by the lord high steward, the earl of Derby, the earl of Pembroke; likewise by some of his Spanish grandees, and their wives. He was dressed in black and silver, and adorned with the insignia of the Garter. The royal minstrels met him, and played before him; and the people shouted, "God save your grace!" He was thus conducted in great state to the hall of the bishop's palace, where the queen advanced, as far as the entrance, to receive him, and kissed him in the presence of the whole multitude. She led him to the pre- sence-chamber, where they both stood under the canopy of state, and conversed together before all the courtiers. At even-song he withdrew from the presence-chamber, and attended service at the cathedral, from whence he was conducted, by torch-light, to his residence at the deanery.

The marriage, which was both in Latin and English, proceeded, till it came to the part of the ceremony where the bride is given. The question was then asked, "Who was to give her?" and it seems to have been a puzzling one, not provided for; when the marquis of Winches- ter, the earls of Derby, Bedford, and Pembroke, came forward, and gave her in the name of the whole realm. Upon which the people gave a great shout, and prayed God to send them joy. The wedding-ring was laid on the book, to be hallowed. Some discusison had previously taken place in council, regarding this ring, which the queen decided, by declaring she would not have it adorned with gems, "for she chose to be wedded with a plain hoop of gold, like any other maiden," King Philip laid on the book three handfuls of fine gold coins, and some sil- ver ones. When the lady Margaret Douglas saw this, she opened the queen's purse, and her majesty was observed to smile on her, as she put the bridal gold within it.

The queen was dressed at her marriage in the French style, in a robe richly brocaded on a gold ground, with a long train splendidly bordered with pearls and diamonds of great size. The large re-bras sleeves were turned up with clusters of gold set with pearls and diamonds. Her chaperon or coif was boarded with two rows of large diamonds. The close gown, or kirtle, worn beneath the robe, was of white satin, wrought with silver. On her breast the queen wore that remarkable diamond of inestimable value, sent to her as a gift from king Philip, whilst he was still in Spain, by the marquis de Los Naves. So far, the dress was in good taste, but the addition of scarlet shoes and brodequins, and a black velvet scarf, added to this costume by the royal bride, can scarcely be considered improvements. The chair on which queen Mary sat is still shown at Winchester Cathedral; report says, it was a present from Rome, and was blessed by the pope.

Queen Mary's court, at this season, was the resort of men, whose undying names fill the history of that stirring century, whose renown, either for good or evil, is familiar in memory as household words.

All this splendor soon closed in the darkest gloom. The queen's health had been sinking since November set in; yet, inspired by her illusive hopes of offspring, she kept up her spirits with more than usual energy.

Her hope of bringing offspring was utterly delusive; the increase of her figure was but symptomatic of dropsy, attended by a complication of the most dreadful disorders, which can afflict the female frame; under which every faculty of her mind and body sunk, for many months. At this time commenced that horrible persecution of the Protestants, which has stained her name to all futurity. But if eternal obloquy was incurred by the half-dead queen, what is the due of the parliaments which legalized the acts of cruelty committed in her name?

For a few afternoons, the queen struggled to pay the attention to business she had formerly done, but her health gave way again in the attempt and she was seen no more at council. With her married life the independence of her reign ceased; from whatever cause, whether owing to her desperate state of health, or from her idea of wifely duty, Philip, whether absent or present, guided the English government.

"In the time of queen Mary," says a minute of council, quoted by Strype, "after the king of Spain was her husband, nothing was done in England but with the privity and directions of the said king's ministers."

Sir Thomas Smith, in an oration recommending single life to princes (by which word he means queen-regnants), traces all the cruelty of Mary's reign to her marriage.

Mary once more appeared in public at the commencement of the year 1556, pale as a corpse, and looking ten years older than when she was last seen. She reviewed her band of gentlemen-pensioners, in Greenwich Park; after which a tumbler came forth from the crowd, and volunteered so many droll antics for the royal diversion, that he elicited a hearty laugh and a reward from the sick queen. A deep obscurity remains on her locality throughout the chief part of this year, which was marked with persecution, insurrection, and famine; and the dreadful martyrdom of Cranmer took place in the spring.

Her death was near at hand; she had resided at Richmond in the spring, where she caught a bad intermittent fever, induced by the series of wet, ungenial seasons, prevalent throughout her reign. Finding she grew worse, she removed from thence to St. James's which had the most marshy site that London could offer. Here, however, the fever somewhat abated; but her spirits were oppressed with extreme melancholy, at the tidings of the death of her kinsman Charles V., which occurred in September, 1558.

The whole court had deserted Mary's palace, since her recognition of Elizabeth as her successor, and were seen passing and repassing on the road to Hatfield. Of this desertion the queen never complained; perhaps she thought it natural, and she had devoted friends around her, who paid her requisite attention; but Elizabeth often recalled it with horror, when pressed to name a successor.

The hand of death was on the queen throughout the 16th of November, but her previous sufferings had blunted the usual agonies of dissolution, for she was composed and even cheerful; between four and five in the morning of November 17th, after receiving extreme unction, at her desire, mass was celebrated in her chamber. At the elevation of the host, she raised her eyes to heaven, and at the benediction bowed her head, and expired. These particulars of the last moments of queen Mary were given by an eye-witness, White, bishop of Winchester, in her funeral sermon.

ELIZABETH.

SECOND QUEEN-REGNANT OF ENGLAND AND IRELAND.

QUEEN ELIZABETH first saw the light at Greenwich Palace, the favorite abode of her royal parents, Henry Eighth and Anne Boleyn. Her birth is thus quaintly but prettily recorded by the contemporary historian, Hall: "On the 7th day of September, being Sunday, between three and four o'clock in the afternoon, the queen was delivered of a fine lady, on which day the duke of Norfolk came home to the christening."

The queen was desirous of nourishing her infant daughter from her own bosom, but Henry, with his characteristic selfishness, forbade it, lest the frequent presence of the little princess in the chamber of her royal mother should be attended with inconvenience to himself.

Much of the future greatness of Elizabeth may reasonably be attributed to the judicious training of her sensible and conscientious governess, combined with the salutary adversity, which deprived her of the pernicious pomp and luxury that had surrounded her cradle while she was treated as the heiress of England. The first public act of Elizabeth's life, was her carrying the chrisome of her infant brother, Edward VI., at the christening solemnity of that prince. She was borne in the arms of the earl of Hertford, brother of the queen, her step-mother, when the assistants in the ceremonial approached the font; but when they left the chapel, the train of her little grace, just four years old, was supported by lady Herbert, as, led by the hand of her elder sister, the princess Mary, she walked with mimic dignity, in the returning procession, to the chamber of the dying queen.

All Henry's matrimonial schemes for his children were doomed to
remain unfulfilled, and Elizabeth, instead of being sacrificed in her
childhood in some political marriage, had the good fortune to complete
a most superior education, under the auspices of the good and learned
Katharine Parr, Henry's sixth queen.

During the reign of Edward, her life was tranquil enough—the most
exciting incident during it being the attempt of lord Seymour, the
brother of the duke of Somerset, the protector, to induce her to marry
him, when she was only sixteen years of age. Certainly the celibacy of
the sovereign was not in consequence of a want of suitors; excepting
Penelope, never lady was so pursued with matrimonial proposals.
Courtenay, earl of Devonshire, was a second pretender to the possession
of her hand; and then followed a proposition that she should unite herself to the king of Sweden. Subsequently, she was successively importuned to wed Philip of Spain, the earl of Arran, the dukes of Alençon
and Anjou, the archduke Charles a son of the Elector-Palatine, the
duke of Holstein, the earl of Arundel, sir William Pickering, and, at
last, *any body;* her parliament promising, in their own name, and that of
the people, to serve, honor and obey him faithfully, "whoever he might
be." But Elizabeth rejected all their propositions, and asserted and
verified in the sequel her intention to die a spinster. For this strange
determination, various and contradictory opinions are given. By many
writers it is attributed to political objects, not very obvious or intelligible; while others, with more appearance of probability, affirm it to have
originated in a conscious corporeal disqualification for the contingencies
of matrimony and childbirth.

During the reign of Mary, her whole life was one ceaseless peril
and adversity. These harsh trials, however, which are generally so
beneficial and mollifying to the heart, made no permanent impression on
the unfeminine mind of the energetic princess; and when, in her turn,
she obtained the power of persecuting and oppressing, she manifested to
another Mary a far greater extent of hate and cruelty than she herself
had ever experienced.

The circumspection of this princess during her long term of trial, was great and admirable. To all the machinations of her enemies to entrap her into some act which might serve as a pretext for her condemnation, she opposed an invincible prudence and discretion. When, thinking that she would have been eager to purchase escape from personal danger at any cost or sacrifice, a marriage with the king of Sweden was suggested to her, instead of precipitately accepting the proposal, she cautiously demanded whether her sister had been made acquainted with it? This inquiry receiving an unsatisfactory reply, she desired that the matter might be formally communicated to Mary, who, though doubtless previously possessed of the knowledge, feigned to thank her for her loyal and dutiful information, and to permit her to decide according to her own inclination. Afterwards, when subjected to the more perilous ordeal of an examination into her religious principles, she was undaunted and self-possessed; and being desired to state her sentiments respecting the doctrine of the real presence, she replied, after a momentary consideration—

> "Christ was the Word that spake it,
> He took the bread and brake it,
> And what the Word did make it
> That I believe and take it.'

This ingenious subterfuge and jargon seems to have completly perplexed and confounded her interrogators for we do not hear that they renewed their attempts to entrap her into some avowal which might have conducted her to the stake.

We are indebted to the lively pen of Giovanni Michele, the Venetian ambassador, for the following graphic sketch of the person and character of Elizabeth at this interesting period of her life. "*Miladi* Elizabeth," says he, "is a lady of great elegance both of body and mind, though her face may be called pleasing rather than beautiful. She is tall and well made, her complexion fine, though rather sallow." Her bloom must have been prematurely faded by sickness and anxiety, for Elizabeth could not have been more than three and twenty at this period. "Her eyes, but above all her hands, which she takes care not to conceal, are of superior beauty. In her knowledge of the Greek and

35

Italian languages, she surpasses the queen, and takes so much pleasure in the latter, that she will converse with Italians in no other tongue She is proud and dignified in her manners; for, though she is well aware what sort of a mother she had, she is also aware that this mother of hers was united to the king in wedlock, with the sanction of the church and the concurrence of the primate of the realm. The queen, though she hates her most sincerely, yet treats her in public with every outward sign of affection and regard, and never converses with her but on pleasing and agreeable subjects."

Upon the death of Mary, November 17th, 1558, Elizabeth, being then only twenty-five years old, succeeded to the throne. A deputation from the late queen's council arrived at Hatfield to apprise her of the demise of her sister, and to offer their homage to her as their rightful sovereign. Though well prepared for the intelligence, she appeared at first amazed and overpowered at what she heard, and, drawing a deep respiration, she sank upon her knees and exclaimed, "It is the Lord's doing, it is marvellous in our eyes."

Eight-and-twenty years afterwards Elizabeth, in a conversation with the envoys of France, spoke of the tears which she had shed on the death of her sister Mary, but she is the only person by whom they were ever recorded.

Her first public acts were temperate and generous, for though determined to restore the Protestant religion, she showed no animosity to the Catholics, or vindictiveness to her own previous persecutors. Her toleration was general,—all the bishops she received with kindness and affability, with the sole exception of Bonner, from whom she indignantly turned with too well merited manifestations of her abhorrence and disgust. She then recalled her ambassador from Rome, prohibited preaching without license, and the elevation of the host, and in other ways displayed such an unequivocal determination to suppress the Catholic religion, that her ministers found great difficulty to obtain the assistance of a prelate to crown her. When, however, that ceremony had been performed, and her title to the throne confirmed by act of parliament, she confirmed all Edward's statutes relating to religion, appointed herself governess of the Church, and abolished the Mass, and restored the Liturgy. Those great and hazardous changes, the least of which in unskilful hands might have

created a civil war and overthrown a dynasty, were effected by Elizabeth without any resort to violence on her part, or any agitation amount
ing to disturbance on the part of her Catholic subjects. To complete
fully his estimate of the difficulty of this vigorous and dexterous deed,
the reader must call to mind the years and sex of the perpetrator of it;
and then, however distasteful may be the character of Elizabeth as a
woman, he will readily admit that, as a ruler, she must have been endowed with many eminently appropriate qualities and talents.

Lord Bacon relates that on the morrow after her coronation, "It
being the custom to release prisoners at the inauguration of a prince,
Elizabeth went to the chapel, and in the great chamber one of her courtiers, who was well known to her, either out of his own motion or by
the instigation of a wiser man, presented her with a petition; and before a great number of courtiers besought her with a loud voice, 'That
now this good time there might be four or five more principal prisoners
released; those were the four Evangelists and the Apostle St. Paul, who
had been long shut up in an unknown tongue, as it were, in a prison, so
as they could not converse with the common people.' The queen
answered very gravely, 'That it was first best to inquire of them whether they would be released or no.' "

This was the character of all her alterations and amendments at the
present and during a long subsequent period; she did nothing precipitately or capricicously; but before the enactment of any important measure, was always careful to learn whether the people "would, or no."
This commendation, however, is very far from being intended to apply
to the whole of her career, for many were the despotic acts she afterwards committed; and she burthened the action with the most distress-
ing monopolies and patents, which was far more injurious to them than
the heaviest taxes, and certainly without previously demanding their
"yea or nay." Camden mentions, "that after the death of John Basi-
lides, his son Theodore revoked the privilege which the English enjoyed
as sole possessors of the Russian trade. When the queen remonstrated
against this innovation, he told her ministers that princes must carry an
indifferent hand as well between their subjects as between foreigners,
and not convert trade, which by the laws of nations ought to be common
to all, into a monopoly for the private gain of a few." To which state-

ment Hume subjoins the following judicious remark:—"So much juster notions of commerce were entertained by this barbarian than appear in the conduct of the renowned queen Elizabeth!" But this impolicy originated in no want of circumspection or deliberation, but in the detestable egotism of her character. She felt that a frequent application to parliament for subsidies would give to that body an influence in her councils; and selfishly, therefore, she resolved to sacrifice the nation's interests to her own haughty and arrogant love of independence, even when disastrous and illegitimate.

In the year 1559 occurred the commencement of Elizabeth's tyrannical intercourse with the unfortunate Mary queen of Scots. Originally, scarce foundation existed for an animosity which was afterwards, and for so many years, sustained by a sorry feminine spite and vanity. Mary had tolerated, if not encouraged, the asseverations of her partisans, that her claim to the throne of England was preferable to that of her masculine and powerful rival. She had also been weak enough to commit the still greater offence of assuming the arms of England, and quartering them upon all her equipages and liveries, and maintaining and justifying this act when remonstrances were addressed to her. Elizabeth clearly saw that it was personal to herself, or else, why had it not been perpetrated during the reign of her sister? consequently, it could only be viewed as an indication of an intention to question the legitimacy of her birth, on the first favorable opportunity, and to dispute her right to the throne.

Thus, by personal rancor, public policy, and religious bias, she was incited to interfere in the affairs of Scotland, and to give her strongest support to the Protestants of that country. When, therefore, emissaries were dispatched to her by the leaders of the Congregation, to solicit from her succor, she gladly granted it, and equipped a fleet, which she ordered to co-operate with Mary's rebellious subjects. The result of this alliance was the defeat of the Scottish and French Catholics, and the execution of a treaty of peace, in which, among other important concessions, Mary was made to stipulate to abstain from wearing the arms of England. But Mary, as long as her husband Francis II. lived, refused to ratify the proceedings of her ambassadors, and though, after his death, she desisted from assuming any longer the arms, she refused to forego her claim to them.

Our purpose is not historical, we merely select for narration such public acts as seem most suited to elucidate the intricate and inconsistent character of this anomalous princess.

The affair of Raleigh and his cloak is universally known, and we shall therefore prefer to relate some incidents connected with her partiality to Leicester, which are not equally generally notorious.

Sir James Melville, the ambassador of Mary at the court of Elizabeth was an observing man, well skilled in the world, and an accomplished courtier. How competent he was for observation the following extracts from his works will show:

"The ceremony of creating lord Robert Dudley earl of Leicester was performed at Westminster with great solemnity, the queen herself helping to put on his robes, he sitting with his knees before her with great gravity, but she could not refrain from putting her hand in his neck, smilingly tickling him; the French ambassador and I standing by." He subsequently adds, "The queen, my mistress, had instructed me to leave matters of gravity sometimes, and cast in merry purposes, lest otherwise I should be wearied, she being well informed of that queen's natural temper. Therefore, in declaring my observations of the customs of Dutchland, Poland, and Italy, the buskins of the women were not forgot, and what country weed I thought best becoming gentlewomen. The queen said she had clothes of every sort, which every day thereafter, so long as I was there, she changed. One day she had the English weed, another the French, and another the Italian, and so forth. She asked me, which of them became her best? I answered, in my judgment, the Italian dress; which answer I found pleased her well, for she delighted to show her golden colored hair, wearing a caul and bonnet as they do in Italy. Her hair was more reddish than yellow, and curled, in appearance, naturally. She desired to know of me, what colored hair was reputed best? and whether my queen's hair or hers were best? and which of them two was fairest? I answered, the fairest of them both was not their worst faults. But she was ever earnest with me to declare which of them both was fairest? I said that she was the fairest queen in England, and mine in Scotland; yet she appeared in earnest; I

answered that they both were the fairest ladies in their countries, that
her majesty was whiter, but my queen was very lovely. She inquired
which of them was of higher stature? I said, my queen. Then, said
she, she is too high, for I myself am neither too high nor too low."

In sir Walter Scott's "History of Scotland," is a passage which
records her vanity with such whimsical gravity, that it must be transferred to these pages in his own words:—

"Throughout her whole reign, queen Elizabeth, pre-eminent as a
sovereign, had never been able to forbear the assertion of her claims as
a wit and a beauty. When verging to the extremity of life, her mirror
presented her with hair too gray, and features too withered to reflect,
even in her own opinion, the features of that fairy queen of immortal
youth and beauty, in which she had been painted by one of the most
charming poets of that poetic age. She avenged herself by discontinu-
ing the consultation of her looking-glass, which no longer flattered her;
and exchanged that monitor of the toilet, for the false, favorable, and
pleasing reports of the ladies who attended her. This indulgence of
vanity brought, as usual, its own punishment. The young females
who waited upon her, turned her pretensions into ridicule; and if the
report of the times be true, ventured even to personal insult, by mis-
placing the cosmetics which she used for the repair of her faded charms,
sometimes daring to lay on the royal nose the carmine which ought to
have embellished the cheeks."

Scarcely can it be believed, that the individual exhibited in forms at
once so ridiculous and repulsive, can, under another phase, have ex-
torted from even a Jesuit, the following exalted praise:—

"Elizabeth is one of those extraordinary persons, whose very name
imprints in one's mind so great an idea, that the noblest descriptions
that are given of her are much below it. Never crowned head understood better how to govern, nor made fewer false steps during a long
reign. Charles the Fifth's friends could easily reckon his mistakes; but
Elizabeth's foes were reduced to invent them for her. Elizabeth's design was to reign, govern, and be mistress; to keep her people in
obedience and her neighbors in awe; affecting neither to weaken her
subjects, nor to encroach on foreigners, yet never suffering any to lessen
that supreme power, which she equally knew how to maintain by

policy or by force; for none at that time had more wit, management, and penetration than she. She understood not the art of war; yet knew so well how to breed excellent soldiers, that England had never seen a greater number, or more experienced, than those which existed during her reign. Her conduct in relation to the marriage of herself with the two successive dukes of Anjou, was in complete accordance with the determination she expressed to Melville, and so many others, "that she was resolved to die a virgin." It is evident that she never had the smallest intention to unite herself to either of them; with regard to the elder duke, the whole negotiation was equally a stratagem both on the part of Catherine and Elizabeth; but with regard to the second, her affections were involved though the object of them was a "very ugly man." The most amusing feature of this grand contention of will between two such illustrious practitioners as the queen-mother of France and the maiden ruler of England is, that each being far too clever to fail, only succeeded by each cheating the other. The purposes of both the arch-deceivers were attained, and both therefore were mutual dupes.

It was observed that after the death of Essex, the people ceased to greet the queen with the demonstrations of rapturous affection with which they had been accustomed to salute her when she appeared in public. They could not forgive the loss of that generous and gallant nobleman, the only popular object of her favor, whom she had cut off in the flower of his days; and now, whenever she was seen, a gloomy silence reigned in the streets through which she passed. These indications of the change in her subjects' feelings towards her are said to have sunk deeply into the mind of the aged queen, and occasioned that depression of spirits which preceded her death.

A trifling incident is also supposed to have made a painful and ominous impression on her imagination. Her coronation ring, which she had worn night and day ever since her inauguration, having grown into her finger, it became necessary to have it filed off; and this was regarded by her as an evil portent.

In the beginning of June, she confided to the French ambassador, Count de Beaumont, "that she was a-weary of life," and with sighs and tears, alluded to the death of Essex, that subject which appears to have been ever in her thoughts, and, when unthought of, still the spring of thought. She said, "that being aware of the impetuosity of his temper and his ambitious character, she had warned him two years before to content himself with pleasing her, and not to show such insolent contempt for her as he did on some occasions, but to take care not to touch her sceptre, lest she should be compelled to punish him according to the laws of England, and not according to her own, which he had always found too mild and indulgent for him to fear any thing from them. His neglect of this caution," she added, "had caused his ruin."

One of the members of Elizabeth's household gives the following account of the state of the queen's mind, in a letter to a confidential correspondent, in the service of her successor "Our queen is troubled with a rheum in her arm, which vexeth her very much, besides the grief she hath conceived for my lord of Essex's death. She sleepeth not so much by day as she used, neither taketh rest by night. Her delight is to sit in the dark, and sometimes with shedding tears, to bewail Essex."

These fits of despondency occasionally cleared away; and we find Elizabeth exhibiting fits of active mirthfulness, especially at the expense of her dwarfish premier, Cecil, who habitually played the lover to her majesty. She sometimes so far forgot the dignity of her age and exalted station as to afford him a sort of whimsical encouragement by making a butt of him. A ludicrous instance of her coquetry is related by one of her courtiers, in a letter to the earl of Shrewsbury:—"I send your lordship here inclosed," writes he, "some verses compounded by Mr. Secretary, who got Hales to frame a ditty to it. The occasion was, I hear, that the young lady Derby, wearing about her neck and in her bosom, a dainty tablet, the queen, espying it, asked, 'What fine jewel that was?' Lady Derby was anxious to excuse showing it; but the queen would have it. She opened it, and, finding it to be Mr. Secretary's picture, she snatched it from lady Derby's neck, and tied it upon her own shoe, and walked about with it there. Then she took it from thence, and pinned it on her elbow, and wore it some time there also. When Mr. Secretary Cecil was told of this, he made these verses, and caused Hales to sing them in his apartments. It was told her majesty that Mr. Secretary Cecil had rare music and songs in his chamber. She chose to hear them, and the ditty was sung." The poetry was not worth quoting; but the verses, it seems, expressed "that he repines not, though her majesty may please to grace others; for his part, he is content with the favor his picture received." This incident took place when the royal coquette was in her seventieth year. Strange scenes are occasionally revealed when the mystic curtain that veils the penetralia of kings and queens from vulgar curiosity is, after the lapse of centuries, withdrawn by the minuteness of biographical research. What a delicious subject for an " H. B." caricature would the stately Elizabeth and her pigmy secretary have afforded !

Cecil was, however, at that time the creature of the expecting impatient heir to his royal mistress, with whom he maintained almost a daily correspondence. One day, a packet, from king James, was delivered to him in the presence of the queen, which he knew contained allusions to his secret practices with her successor. Elizabeth's quick eye, doubtless, detected the furtive glance which taught him to recognize that it was a dangerous missive; and she ordered him instantly to open and show the contents of his letters to her. A timely recollection of one of her weak points saved the wily minister from detection. "This packet," said he, as he slowly drew forth his knife and prepared to cut the strings, which fastened it—" this packet has a strange and evil smell. Surely it has not been in contact with infected persons or goods?" Elizabeth's dread of contagion prevailed over both curiosity and suspicion, and she hastily ordered Cecil to throw it at a distance, and not to bring it into her presence again till it had been thoroughly fumigated. He, of course, took care to purify it of the evidence of his own guilty deeds.

The next anecuote, however, goes far beyond all our present discovery in optics:

" Afterwards, in the melancholy of her sickness, she desired to see a *true* looking-glass, which in twenty years before she had not seen, but only such a one as on purpose was made to deceive her sight, which true looking-glass being brought her, she presently fell exclaiming at all those flatterers which had so much commended her, and they durst not after come into her presence." Her attendants had doubtless left off painting her, and she happened to see her natural face in the glass.

36

A fearful complication of complaints had settled on the queen, and began to draw visibly to a climax. She suffered greatly with the gout in her hands and fingers, but was never heard to complain of what she felt in the way of personal pain, but continued to talk of progresses and festivities, as though she expected her days to be prolonged through years to come.

All contemporary writers bear witness to the increased dejection of her mind, after visiting her dying kinswoman, the countess of Notting-ham; but the particulars of that visit rest on historical tradition only. It is said that the countess, pressed in conscience on account of her detention of the ring, which Essex had sent to the queen as an appeal to her mercy, could not die in peace until she had revealed the truth to her majesty, and craved her pardon. But Elizabeth, in the transport of mingled grief and fury, shook, or, as others have said, struck the dying penitent in her bed, with these words, "God may forgive you, but I never can!"

The death-bed confession of the countess of Nottingham gave a rude shock to the fast-ebbing sands of the sorrow-stricken queen.

It is almost a fearful task to trace the passage of the mighty Elizabeth through the "dark valley of the shadow of death." Many have been dazzled with the splendor of her life, but few even of her most ardent admirers, would wish their last end might be like hers.

Robert Carey, afterwards earl of Monmouth, was admitted to the chamber of his royal kinswoman during her last illness, and has left the following pathetic record of the state in which he found her:—

"When I came to court," says he, "I found the queen ill-disposed, and she kept her inner lodging; yet hearing of my arrival, she sent for me. I found her in one of her withdrawing chambers, sitting low upon her cushions. She called me to her; I kissed her hand, and told her it was my chiefest happiness to see her in safety and health, which I hoped might long continue. She took me by the hand, and wrung it hard, and said, 'No, Robin, *I am not well.*' and then discoursed to me of her indisposition, and that her heart had been sad and heavy for ten or twelve days, and in her discourse she fetched not so few as forty or fifty great sighs. I was grieved, at the first, to see her in this plight, for in all my lifetime before, I never saw her fetch a sigh, but when the queen of Scots was beheaded. Then, upon my knowledge, she shed many sighs and tears, manifesting her innocence that she never gave consent to the death of that queen. I used the best words I could to persuade her from this melancholy humor, but I found it was too deep-rooted in her heart, and hardly to be removed. This was upon Saturday night, and she gave command that the great closet should be prepared for her to go to chapel the next morning. The next day, all things being in readiness, we long expected her coming.

"After eleven o'clock, one of the grooms (of the chambers) came but, and bade make ready for the private closet for she would not go to the great. There we stayed long for her coming; but at the last she had cushions laid for her at the privy-chamber, hard by the closet door, and there she heard the service. From that day forward she grew worse and worse; she remained upon her cushions four days and nights at the least. All about her could not persuade her either to take any sustenance or to go to bed."

Beaumont, the French ambassador, affords a yet more gloomy picture of the sufferings of mind and body, which rendered the progress of the "dreaded and dreadful Elizabeth" to the tomb, an awful lesson on the vanity of all earthly distinctions and glories, in the closing stage of life, when nothing but the witness of a good conscience, and the holy reliance on the mercy of a Redeemer's love, can enable shrinking nature to contemplate, with hope and comfort, the dissolution of its earthly tabernacle.

On the 24th of March, Beaumont made the following report of the state of the departing monarch:—"The queen was given up three days ago; she had lain long in a cold sweat, and had not spoken. A short time previously she said, 'I wish not to live any longer, but desire to die.' Yesterday and the day before she began to rest, and found herself better after, having been greatly relieved by the bursting of a small swelling in the throat. She takes no medicine whatever, and has only kept her bed two days; before this she would on no account suffer it, for fear (as some suppose) of a prophecy that she should die in her bed. She is, moreover, said to be no longer in her right senses; this, however, is a mistake; she has only had some slight wanderings at intervals."

Carey reports the last change for the worse to have taken place on
Wednesday, the previous day:—"That afternoon," says he, "she made
signs for her council to be called, and, by putting her hand to her head,
when the king of Scotland was named to succeed her, they all knew he
was the man she desired should reign after her." By what logic the
council were able to interpret this motion of the dying queen into an
indication that such was her pleasure, they best could explain.

The spirit of the mighty Elizabeth, after all, passed away so quietly,
that the vigilance of the self-interested spies, by whom she was surrounded, was baffled, and no one knew the moment of her departure.
Exhausted by her devotions, she had, after the archbishop left her, sunk
into a deep sleep, from whence she never awoke; and, about three in
the morning, it was discovered that she had ceased to breathe. Lady
Scrope gave the first intelligence of this fact, by silently dropping a
sapphire ring to her brother, who was lurking beneath the windows of
the chamber of death at Richmond Palace. This ring, long after known
in court tradition as the "blue ring," had been confided to lady Scrope
by James, as a certain signal which was to announce the decease of the
queen. Sir Robert Carey caught the token, fraught with the destiny of
the island empire, and departed, at fiery speed, to announce the tidings
in Scotland.

This great female sovereign died in the seventieth year of her age,
and the forty-fourth of her reign. She was born on the day celebrated
as the nativity of the Virgin Mary, and she died March 24th, on the
eve of the festival of the annunciation, called Lady-day. Among the
complimentary epitaphs which were composed for her, and hung up in
many churches, was one ending with the following couplet:—

"She is, she was: what can there more be said?
On earth, the first, in heaven, the second maid."

ANNE OF DENMARK.

QUEEN-CONSORT OF JAMES THE FIRST, KING OF GREAT BRITAIN AND
IRELAND.

ANNE OF DENMARK was undeniably inferior, both in education and
intellect, to most of the royal ladies. Her political position was, nevertheless, more important than any queen-consort of England, since she
was the wife of the first monarch whose sovereignty extended over the
whole of the British islands.

She was the first queen of Great Britain ; a title which has been
borne by the wives of our sovereigns from the commencement of the
seventeenth century to the present era. Before, however, she attained
this dignity, she had presided fourteen years over the court of Scotland
as consort of James VI.

The crowns of Denmark and Norway were, by the people, during
the lifetime of Christiern II., bestowed on his uncle Frederic I., whose
reign, and the change of religion from the Catholic to the Lutheran
creed, commenced simultaneously in 1524. The son of this elected
king was Christiern III., who completed the establishment of the
Protestant religion in Denmark. His eldest son, Frederic II., suc
ceeded him; he married Sophia, the daughter of his neighbor, the
duke of Mecklenburg, and had by her six children. Anna, or Anne,
the second child and subject of this biography, was born at Scander-
burg, December 12, 1575.

It was the opinion of the French ambassador, that Frederic II. was one of the richest princes in Europe, for he possessed the endowments of seven bishoprics in Denmark and Norway, which his father, Christiern III., had appropriated to his own use.

"Our king, this year, (1585,)" saith a queer old chronicle of delectable quaintness, "was become a brave prince in bodie and stature, so weel exerciset in reading, that he could perfitlie record all things he had either heard or read. Therefore that noble king, Frederic II. of Denmark, who had then twa doghters, was willing (gif it suld please our king) either to give him the choice of thaim, or that he would accept the ane of thaim, as it suld please the father to bestow *quhilk* suld be the maist comely, and the best for his princelie contentment." King James received the Danish ambassadors, who brought this civil offer, at Dunfermline, but advised them instantly to depart for St. Andrew's, as the plague was raging in the palace. The Scotch government did not relish the idea of a naval war with the powerful king of Denmark for the possession of the Orkneys; they had, as well, a shrewd idea that his daughter would have a "rich tocher," and therefore sent Peter Young, the king's old schoolmaster, to inquire all needful particulars in Denmark.

The Scotch ambassadors from Denmark returned, bringing with them the portrait of young Anna, which James received. How lovely the little miniature was may be seen to this day among the Scottish regalia, at Edinburgh. There is likewise a whole-length portrait of her, in a corner of the royal bedroom at Hampton Court, as a dark-eyed girl, with a very delicate ivory complexion. The dress is entirely white; the youth of the portrait, the queer costume of the high head, shoulder-ruff and immense farthingale, (the same worn at the court of France in 1589,) authenticate the tradition that it was another of Anna's portraits sent at this time to king James. Both the miniature of the Order of the Thistle, and this young portrait at Hampton Court, give the idea that Anna of Denmark, at sixteen, was a very pretty girl.

King James compared the portrait of the youthful Danish princess with that of the mature Katharine of Navarre, and then entered into a long course of prayers for guidance on the subject of his marriage. At the conclusion of his devotional exercises, he called together his council, and told them "how he had been praying and avisen with God for a fortnight, and that, in consequence, he was resolvit to marry the Danish princess."

The ceremonial of the marriage by proxy was delayed till the 20th of August that year (1589), because a noble fleet, the pride of the maritime and flourishing state of Denmark, had to be prepared to carry the young queen to Scotland to her future home. The earl-marischal of Scotland received her hand as proxy for his king at Corenburg, a strong fortress-palace in the isle of Zealand, built on piles, overhanging the sea, very richly furnished with silver statues and other articles of luxury.

Twice the Danish squadron, with the bride-queen, made the coast of Scotland, so near as to be within sight of land, and twice they were beat back by baffling winds, which blew them to the coast of Norway.

King James had previously heard that his wife was upon the sea, and had, from that time, exerted himself to his utmost for her honorable reception in Scotland. He busied himself greatly in the appointment of the ladies and gentlemen who were to compose the household of his bride; and it may be observed that he preferred those who had been faithful to his unfortunate mother in her long adversity.

Just after the woful catastrophe of poor lady Melville, arrived Steven Beale with the tidings of the distresses of the royal bride, who remained storm-bound on the desolate coast of Norway. He delivered her letters to king James, at Craigmillar castle. The king read them with great emotion. The very next day the king declared in council, that it was his intention "to send the earl of Bothwell (Francis Stuart), with six royal ships, to claim the Danish princess as his bride, and bring her home." In the afternoon Bothwell made his appearance, with a handful of monstrous long bills, containing the calculations of the expense of such a voyage, which cast the king into great perplexity.

From this moment, James took the resolution of going himself on this errand. It was an undertaking of some danger; for the best ship the chancellor could furnish was one of but 120 tons—a mere bauble for enduring the wintry seas, which rage between Scotland and Norway, and which had so seriously discomfited the powerful Danish fleet.

Fortune favored the brave, for a prosperous breeze succeeded the frightful storms, which had nearly shipwrecked his bride; and in four

days he neared the Norwegian coast, but he was not to land without a
sharp taste of the dangers he had voluntarily encountered; for, on the
fifth day, a furious tempest sprung up. For four-and-twenty hours the
king's little bark was in great danger of wreck. At last she ran safely
into one of those sounds which open their hospitable arms for tempest-
tossed mariners on the northern Atlantic, and the adventurous monarch
landed at Slaikray, on the Norwegian coast, October 28th, 1589; yet he
must have been many days travelling to find the village of Upslo, the
doleful abiding place where Anne of Denmark had, in great tribulation,
established her head-quarters since October the 19th.

"She," continues our annalist, "little looked for his majesty's com-
in gat sic a tempestuous time of the year." James certainly did not
discover his queen's place of retreat till the 19th of the following month,
according to all dates of their time of meeting ; when he at length discovered her abode among the Norwegian snows, he, with the *bon-hommie*
which marked his character as much at two-and-twenty as in his more
mature career, waited for none of the ceremonies of his rank and station,
but leaving his train to seek their lodgings as they might, he marched
directly into the presence of his bride, and, booted and spurred as he
was, he frankly tendered her a salute. Our annalist's words are, " Immediately at his coming, the king passed in quietly, with *buites* and all,
to her highness; his majesty minded to give the queen a kiss after the
Scottish fashion, quhilk the queen refusit, as not being the form of her
country. But after a few words, privily spoken, betwixt his majesty
and her, familiaritie ensued."

James VI. married Anna of Denmark, on that wild and stormy coast,
the Sunday after he met her, Mr. Davie Lindsay, his favorite chaplain,
performing the ceremony in French, a language mutually understood by
the bride and bridegroom. The banquet was spread in the best manner
the time and place permitted, and the harmony of the royal wedlock
would have been complete, excepting for a fierce wrangle for precedency
between the earl marischal and the chancellor of Scotland, which called
forth the utmost eloquence of the royal bridegroom to pacify.

The wild winds sung the epithalamium of this singular royal wedlock in so loud a tone, and the winter-storms, which had intermitted for
king James's arrival at Upslo, renewed their fury in a manner which

rendered all hopes of return to Scotland that season abortive. Mean time, king James sent an adventurous messenger, over the mountains, to Denmark, to inform the queen-regent of his safe arrival, and his marriage with his betrothed princess.

King James and his young consort sailed from Cronenburg about the 21st of April, escorted by a stately Danish fleet, commanded by admiral Peter Munch.

The royal fleet safely arrived at Leith, on May-day, 1590, and all Edinburgh came forth to meet their king, and see their new queen; both were received with the most extravagant demonstrations of joy. To the king's credit, the first thing he did, on landing, was to return thanks to God for the safety of himself and his wife.

The superabundance of gravity imputed to the young queen of Scotland is, by no means, in accordance with the general tenor of her conduct, during the first years of her marriage, which, in truth, rather indicated the levity natural to a girl of sixteen than the dignity becoming her exalted rank. She manifested more gayety than was consistent with prudence, and, at last, raised no little jealousy in the mind of her husband, by her commendations of the beauty of the earl of Murray.

Queen Anne brought her first-born son into the world, at Stirling Castle, February 19, 1594. The king determined to give him the name of his own unfortunate father, and the name of the queen's father, and Henry-Frederic the boy was named, with the first protestant baptismal rites that had ever been administered to a prince in this island.

The heart of the young queen was alive to the most passionate instincts of maternity, and these were painfully outraged when she found it was her husband's intentions to leave her young son in the royal fortress of Stirling, to the care of his hereditary guardian, the earl of Marr. The old countess of Marr, the king's former gouvernante, was to be inducted into the same office for the infant Henry, to the queen's extreme grief. She earnestly pleaded to have him with her during his tender infancy, instead of being restricted to occasional visits. It was in vain that king James explained to her that it was part and parcel of the law of Scotland for its heir to be reared in Stirling Castle, under of an earl of Marr, and that he owed his own life and crown

37

vidential arrangement, and that the Erskine family were most worthy of this high trust; but the queen would not be content.

When the news was brought to king James, that the queen had presented him with a second son, on the 19th of November, he made the following speech: "I first saw my wife on the 19th of November, on the coast of Norway; she bore my son Henry on the 19th of February; my daughter Elizabeth on the 19th of August; and now she has given birth, at Dunfermline, to my second son, on the anniversary of the day on which we first saw each other, the 19th of November, I being myself borne on the 19th of June."

There had certainly been some coolness between the king and queen before this auspicious event put him in good-humor. He immediately went to visit her at Dunfermline. He found her very ill, and the new-born prince so weak and languishing, that his death was hourly expected. The king, therefore, ordered him to be baptized immediately, according to the rites of the episcopalian church of Scotland; giving him the name of Charles, which was, in reality, his own first name, and at the same time that of his uncle (lord Darnley's brother), lord Charles Stuart.

At last, the hour sounded which summoned queen Elizabeth from this world, and which, at the same time, united the British islands under one sovereignty. King James had, long before, established spies at the court of England, who, by a system of concerted signals, were to give him the earliest intimation of this great event, which was communicated to him by a near and favored kinsman of queen Elizabeth.

King James commenced his journey to England, April 5, 1603. He bade farewell to his queen in the high street at Edinburgh. They both were dissolved in tears. The whole population of the metropolis of Scotland witnessed this conjugal parting; and now, anticipating all the tribulations of absenteeism, from which they afterwards suffered very long, the people lifted up their voices, and loudly mourned the departure of their sovereign, and joined their tears to those of his anxious consort.

It has been shown, that [...] mean to trust his volatile partner with the least p[...] that a minority had occurred; and he was e[...] admirable education he was giving prince He[...] Newton, should be interrupted by her fondness and caprice. She had, however, her own peculiar plans in cogitation, which she acted upon directly her husband was at a convenient distance. She was, at that time, in a situation which required consideration ; but it was hoped that her journey might be safely accomplished before her accouchement, which was expected in June. When the king bade her farewell, he appointed her to follow him in twenty days, if affairs in England wore a peaceable aspect.

No queen-consort had been crowned since the days of Anne Boleyn; yet no king and queen had been crowned together, since Henry VIII. and Katharine of Arragon; yet the dreadful state of the pestilence restrained public curiosity so much, that the august ceremony of the double coronation was almost performed in private. The royal party went by water the short distance between Whitehall stairs, and privy stairs of Westminster Palace, on the morning of the procession; their only processions were, therefore, the short distance between the abbey and the hall. A describer of the scene mentions, "that queen Anne went to the coronation with her seemly hair down-hanging on her princely shoulders, and on her head a crownet of gold. She so mildly saluted her new subjects, that the women, weeping, cried out with one voice, 'God bless the royal queen ! Welcome to England, long to live and continue!'" This coronation took place on St. James's day. A promise was made, that after the pestilence had abated, the king, the queen, and prince Henry, should visit the city, and share in the high festival the civic authorities were to prepare for them; and this took place with great splendor in the succeeding spring.

A foreigner, who visited England at the accession of James, draws an unfavorable portrait of the queen. He says, "she has an ordinary appearance, and lives remote from public affairs. She is very fond of dancing and entertainments. She is very gracious to those who know how to promote her wishes; but to those whom she does not like, she is proud, disdainful—not to say insupportable." Another Italian, cardinal Bentivoglio, is in ecstasies at her grace and beauty, and, above all, her fluency in speaking the Italian language, of which he was an undoubted judge. It would be difficult to ascertain what sort of persons Anne and the king, her husband, were, from the descriptions of contemporaries, so strongly did prejudice imbue every pen. There is no reason to suppose that Cardinal Bentivoglio was inclined to flatter James I., for he mentions, with much displeasure, his hostility to catholics; yet he describes his person in very different colors from the sectarian authors of the same century. " The king of England," says he, "is above the middle height, of a fair and florid complexion, and very noble features; though, in his demeanor and carriage, he manifests no kind of grace or kingly dignity."

One of the proudest and happiest periods of queen Anne's life was that in which her eldest son was created prince of Wales. This august ceremony had been delayed till the noble-minded boy could enter into all the historical interest of the scene. It was celebrated not only with the splendor of state pageantry, but heralded with all the glory of poetry.

The queen, the princess, and king James, and the little prince Charles, stood in the privy-gallery, at Westminster Old Palace, to see prince Henry's arrival from Richmond, his own private residence, whence he came, in state, down the Thames, escorted by the lord-mayor and city authorities, in their gay barges. London, as usual, contributed its thousands, who, floating in their pleasure-boats on the Thames, rendered their voluntary assistance in the gay aquatic procession. The prince landed at the Queen's Bridge, Westminster, May 31, 1610, and was received by his delighted mother in the privy-chamber; but the grand festival prepared by her did not commence till some days after, when the prince of Wales was introduced, in state, by his father, to the assembled houses of parliament, and his solemn investiture took place June 4th. The next day the queen appointed for her *second* grand masque, in honor of her darling son, in which she personally took a part, with her ladies and her little son, prince Charles, who had, by this time, overcome the weakness of his early years, and grown a very beautiful boy.

It was a beautiful idea in this masque, to cause the court ladies to personate the nymphs of the principal rivers which belonged to the estates of their fathers or husbands. The queen represented Tethys, the empress of streams; her daughter Elizabeth, princess-royal, was the nymph of Thames; lady Arabella Stuart, the nymph of Trent; the countess of Arundel, the Arun; the countess of Derby, the nymph of Derwent; lady Anne Clifford represented the naïad of her native Aire, the lovely river of her feudal domain of Skipton; the countess of Essex, then a girl-beauty of fourteen, unscathed as yet by the blight of evil, was the nymph of Lea; lady Haddington, as daughter of the earl of Sussex, represented the river Rother; and lady Elizabeth Gray, daughter of the earl of Kent, the Medway. The little prince Charles, in the character of Zephyr, was to deliver the queen's presents, attended by twelve little ladies, to his elder brother, the newly created prince of Wales. This was the ostensible business of the masque, which was thus mingled with historical reality. Eight of the handsomest noblemen of the court performed as Tritons, and were the partners and attendants of the river-nymphs.

The ante-masque commenced with the appearance of little prince Charles and his young ladies; they were all of his own age and height; they were the daughters of earls or barons, and personated the naïads of springs and fountains.

Prince Charles was dressed as Zephyr, in a short robe of green satin, embroidered with gold flowers. Behind his shoulders were two silver wings, and a fine lawn *aureole*, which Inigo Jones is much puzzled to describe. On his head was a garland of flowers of all colors; his right arm was bare, on which the queen had clasped one of her bracelets of inestimable diamonds. His little naïads were dressed in satin tunics of the palest water-blue, embroidered with silver flowers; their tresses were hanging down in waving curls, and their heads were crowned with garlands of water-flowers. The ballet was so contrived, that Charles always danced encircled by these fair children. They had been so well trained, that they danced to admiration, and formed the prettiest sight in the world. This infant ballet was rapturously applauded by the whole court. When the first dance was ended, the scene of Milford Haven was suddenly withdrawn, and the queen, as Tethys, was seen seated, in glorious splendor, on a throne of silver rocks; round her throne were niches, representing little caverns, in which her attendant river-nymphs were grouped. Her daughter, the princess Elizabeth, as the nymph of Thames, was seated at her royal mother's feet. There were dolphins in every shade of silver, and shells and sea-weed in every colored burnish that could be devised.

Glittering waterfalls and cataracts, gleamed round the grotto, in which the noble river-nymphs were grouped about the throne of the queen. Her head-dress was a murex shell, formed as a helmet, ornamented with coral, a veil of silver gossamer floated from it; a bodice of sky-colored silk was branched with silver sea-weed; a half-tunic of silver gauze, branched with gold sea-weed, was worn over a train of sky-colored silk, figured with columns of white lace, of sea-weed pattern. All this would have been elegant, and appropriate enough, only it is to be feared, that it was rendered ridiculous by being worn with a monstrous farthingale: for, whether arrayed in courtly costume, or in a hunting-dress, Anne of Denmark was never seen without that appendage, in its most exaggerated amplitude. As Inigo Jones mentions the high ruff she added to the costume of the river-goddess, Tethys, there is little doubt that she likewise afflicted the classical contrivers of the masque, by assuming a farthingale, as large as a modern tea-table.

As the poem, which explained the motive of the masque, proceeded, the reciter put into the hands of prince Charles, the trident, which he gave to his father, and the queen's splendid present of the sword and scarf, which he gave to his brother the prince of Wales. His next office was to court her majesty to descend from her throne, and dance her ballet with her river-nymphs. The little prince having performed all appointed *devoirs* with much grace and self-possession, returned to the middle of the stage, where he and all his little ladies went through another dance of the most intricate changes. They then gave way for the queen's quadrille; "and by the time that was finished, the summer sun showed traces of his rising and the courtly revellers retreated to bed." So closed a festival which was probably the happiest in the life of Anne of Denmark, if we may judge by the acute sorrow with which her memory, in after days, recurred to it.

The queen retained her girlish petulance after she had been for years a matron, and even when she was the mother of a grown-up son; that son, the joy of her heart, and pride of her existence, sometimes used a little playful management to obtain peace in the circle of royal domesticity, where occasional outbreaks of temper, on the part of her majesty, produced, at times, considerable disquiet.

The queen's bad taste in dress led her to exaggerate, rather than banish, the hideous costume prevalent in all the courts of Europe for half a century. This style of dress would have caricatured the Venus de Medicis herself, had she assumed farthingale and *tête de mouton*. There is a picture of this queen dancing merrily, with a very self-satisfied smirk, in a corner of one of the rooms at Hampton Court. A little, absurd, white beaver hat is perched at the top of her elaborately curled hair, and three little droll feathers peep over the summit. No one can look at the portrait without laughing, yet the face is rather handsome, and the design very animated; the figure seems as if it meant to dance into the midst of the room. The dress is white, with a waist five inches longer than any natural waist, and withal she wears a farthingale so enormous that her hands, which are certainly beautiful, just rest on it, with the arms extended, and hang over the extreme verge of its rotundity. Think of a dress that would not let a woman's arms hang down by her side, if she chose! In fact, a farthingale must have been a habitation, rather than a garment, and must have been as troublesome to carry about as a snail-shell is to its animal. The inconvenience attending this ridiculous dress at last exhausted the patience of king James, who issued a formidable proclamation against the whole costume, declaring that no lady or gentleman clad in the farthingale should come to see any of the sights or masques at Whitehall, for the future, because "this impertinent garment took up all the room in his court."

It was about the time of the king's return from Scotland, that apprehensions were first entertained that the queen's life would be a short one, and the expression used would indicate that her loss would be felt as an evil. "The queen is somewhat *crazy* (sickly) again; they say it is the gout, though the need of her welfare makes the world fearful." Soon after, "the queen continues still indisposed, and though she would fain lay all her infirmities upon the gout, yet her physicians fear an ill habit through her whole constitution."

The court intelligence, at the new year, 1617–18, thus spoke ominously of the queen's health: "Her majesty is not well—they say she languisheth, whether with melancholy, or sickness, or what not; yet is she still at Whitehall, being scant able to move." Three years previously, her physicians had treated her for a confirmed state of dropsy, and now this disease made an attack upon her which threatened to be fatal.

Like many persons who have declined long, she was carried off suddenly, at last. Notwithstanding all the jealousies regarding her attachment to the Catholic church, she died in edifying communion with the church of England, as distinctly specified by an eye-witness.

All her attendants were most desirous for her to make her will, but she prayed them to let her alone till the morrow, when she would. She was cold and pale, but her voice was strong; none durst come into her chamber, for fear of offending her, it being against her will; yet all stayed in the antechamber, till she sent a positive command for it to be cleared, and all to go to bed, forbidding any watch to be held. Her physicians came to her at twelve o'clock; when they were gone, she called to her maid, Danish Anna, that sat by her bed, and bade her fill some drink to wash her mouth; she brought her a glass of Rhenish wine. The queen drank it all out, and said to her woman, "Now have I deceived the physicians." She bade Danish Anna lock the door, and keep all out that were out. "Now," she said, "lay down by me, and sleep, for in seeing you repose, I shall feel disposed to sleep." Scarcely a quarter of an hour had passed, when she roused her woman, and bade her bring some water to wash her eyes; with the water, Danish Anna brought a candle, but the darkness of death had invaded the eyes of the queen, and she saw not the light, but still bade a candle be brought. "Madam," said Danish Anna, "there is one here—do you not see it?" "No," said the queen. Then her confidential attendant, finding that death was on her royal mistress, was terrified lest she should die locked up alone with her. She unlocked the doors, and called the physicians, they gave the queen a cordial, and sent for the prince, and the lords and ladies of the household. The clock then struck one. The queen's hand was then placed on prince Charles's head, and she distinctly gave him her blessing. The lords presented a paper to her, which she signed as she could. It was her will, in which she left her property to her son, likewise rewards to her servants. The bishop of London made a prayer, and her son, and all about her bed, prayed. Her speech was gone, but the bishop said, " Madam, make a sign, that your majesty is one with your God, and long to be with him." She then held up her hands, and when one hand failed, held up the other, till both failed. In the sight of all, her heart, her eyes, her tongue was fixed on God; while she had strength, and when sight and speech failed, her hands were raised to him in supplication. And, when all failed, the bishop made another prayer; and she laid so pleasantly in her bed, smiling as if she had no pain, only at the last, she gave five or six little moans, and had the happiest going out of the world, that any one ever had."

The poets in England offered many tributes to her memory. Camden has preserved two elegiac epitaphs, which possess some elegance of thought:

EPITAPH OF ANNE OF DENMARK.

" March, with his winds, hath struck a cedar tall,
And weeping April mourns that cedar's fall;
And May intends no flowers her month shall bring,
Since she must lose the flower of all the spring:
Thus March's winds hath caused April's showers,
And yet sad May must lose her flower of flowers."

HENRIETTA MARIA,

QUEEN-CONSORT OF CHARLES THE FIRST, KING OF GREAT BRITAIN AND IRELAND.

WHEN the beautiful daughter of Henry the Great became the bride of Charles I., two centuries had elapsed since France had given a queen-consort to England. The last was Margaret of Anjou—that queen of tears. Perhaps the crowned miseries of Margaret had offered an alarming precedent to her countrymen of high degree, for though several French princesses had been wooed by English monarchs, not one had accepted the crown matrimonial of England; till, in 1625, Henrietta Maria wedded Charles, and at the same time became the partaker of a destiny so sad and calamitous, that she, in the climax of her sorrows, surnamed herself *La reine malheureuse.*

The father of this princess was the most illustrious sovereign in Europe: she was the youngest child of Henry IV. of France and of his second wife, Marie de Medicis.

Henrietta was just five months old when all the preparations for the long delayed coronation of her mother were completed at the abbey of St. Denis.

Henry IV., from the first moments of their existence had, with his own hands, severally consigned his infants to the care of madame de Monglat, a lady who was distantly related to the queen. The beautiful daughter of madame de Monglat, who was about the same age with the elder princesses, had an appointment in the nursery of Henrietta; she exercised through life no little influence over her mind.

Of all persons that ever reigned, Marie de Medicis was the worst calculated to train a future queen-consort for England, and the sorrows of her daughter in future life, doubtless were aggravated by the foolish notions of the infallibility of sovereigns which had been instilled into her young mind.

Henrietta, and her young brother Gaston, received the practical part of their education from M. de Brevis, a very learned man, who had been attached to several embassies. How this nobleman managed the princess is not known; he controlled her brother Gaston, by tying a rod to his sash when he deserved punishment.

The first idea of a marriage taking place between Henrietta of France and Charles, prince of Wales, was suggested to him by her eldest sister, Elizabeth. This princess, as the young queen of Spain, wife of Philip IV., was greatly admired by Charles, while at Madrid.

After some diplomatic manœuvring on both sides, Marie de Medicis drew from the English envoy an admittance that the Spanish engagement was wholly broken, and that king James was desirous of matching his heir with her daughter. The queen-mother observed, "That however agreeable such union might be to all parties, yet as no intimation of such desire had been sent to the court of France, she could not consider the matter seriously," adding, significantly, "the maiden must be sought, she may be no suitor."

The ambassador then owned that he was authorized in what he said, and that his mission, though at present secret, was direct from his king and the prince of Wales.

The object of lord Kensington's visit to the French court soon became public there. Of course it occasioned very earnest discussion among the ladies of the royal household, who eagerly crowded round the handsome Englishman, and questioned him regarding the person and acquirements of the prince of Wales. The ambassador wore a beautiful miniature of Charles inclosed in a gold case, hanging from a ribbon at his bosom. Often when he entered the circle at the Louvre, the French ladies used to petition him to open the miniature, that they might look at the resemblance of the future husband of their young princess. Charles's portrait had been seen by every one but the lady most interested in it. But Henrietta of France was forbidden by the laws of etiquette to mention a prince who had not yet openly demanded her hand. She complained "that the queen and all the other ladies could go up to the ambassador, open the miniature and consider it as much as they liked, while she, whom it so nearly concerned, could hardly steal a glance at it afar off." In this dilemma she recollected "that the lady at whose house the English ambassador sojourned, had been in her service, and she begged of her to borrow prince Charles's picture, that she might gaze on it as much and as long as she chose." This was done, and when the lady brought it to her, Henrietta retired to her cabinet, and ordered her to be called in, and to remain alone with her, "where," continues the ambassador, "she opened the case in such haste as showed a true indication of her passion, blushing at the instant at her own guiltiness. She kept it an hour in her hands; and when she returned it, gave many praises of your person. Sir, this is a business so fit for secrecy as I know it shall never go farther than unto the king your father, my lord duke of Buckingham, and my lord of Carlisle's knowledge. A tenderness in this is honorable, for I would rather die a thousand times than it should be published, since I am by the young princess trusted, who is for beauty and goodness an angel."

He says, in one of his letters to the prince at this period—"She is a lady of as much beauty and sweetness to deserve your affections as any woman under heaven can be; in truth, she is the sweetest creature in France, and the loveliest thing in nature. Her growth is little short of her age, and her wisdom infinitely beyond it. I heard her, the other day, discourse with her mother and the ladies about her, with extraordinary discretion and quickness. She dances—the which I am witness of—as well as ever I saw any one; they say she sings most sweetly; I am sure she looks as if she did."

When Marie de Medicis and her daughter gave audience to the English ambassadors, letters and a portrait of Charles were offered by them, in form to the princess, who, turning to her mother, requested permission to receive them. Leave being granted by the queen-mother, Henrietta took the portrait she had so earnestly desired to possess, and

according to the testimony of the ambassadors, read the letter of the
prince with tears of joy, and when she had perused it twice, put it
in her bosom, and placed the epistle of the king, his father, in her
cabinet.

Lord Kensington requested the queen-mother to authorize a private
interview between the princess and him, because he had a message from
his prince which he wished to deliver in person. The queen-mother,
perhaps for the purpose of eliciting a lively dialogue with the handsome
ambassador, appeared to demur as to whether the interview ought to be
granted. "She would," writes lord Kensington, "needs know what I
meant to say to her daughter."

"Nay, then," quoth I, smiling, "your majesty would needs impose
on me a harder law than they in Spain did on his highness" (alluding
to the visit of the prince made to court the Spanish infanta). "But the
case is now different," said Marie de Medicis, "for the prince was in
person there; here you are but his deputy." "Yet a deputy," answered
I, "who represents his person." "For all that," returned the queen,
"what is it you would say to my daughter?" "Nothing," I anwered,
"that is not fitting the ears of so virtuous a princess." "But what is
it?" reiterated the queen-mother. "Why, then, madam," quoth I, "if
you will needs know, it shall be much to this effect, that your majesty
having given me liberty of freer language than heretofore, I obey my
prince's command in presenting to your fair and royal daughter his
service, not now out of mere compliment, but prompted by passion and
affection, which both her outward and her inward beauties have so kindled in him, that he was resolved to contribute the uttermost he could
to the alliance in question, and would think success therein the greatest
happiness in the world. Such, with some little more amorous language,
was to be my communication with her highness." "*Allez—Allez!*"
smilingly exclaimed the queen-mother of France, "there is no great
danger in that." "*Je me fie en vous,*" she continued; "I will trust
you."

"Neither did I abuse her trust," continues the elegant ambassador;
"for I varied not much from what I said in my interview with madame
Henrietta, save that I amplified it a little more. She drank it in with
joy, and, with a low courtesy, made her acknowledgments, adding, that

she was extremely obliged to my prince, and would think herself happy in the occasion that would be presented of meriting a place in the affections of his good grace." The flattering courtier had previously informed Charles "that his reputation, as the completest prince in Europe in manners and person, had certainly raised in the heart of the sweet princess, madame Henrietta, an infinite affection."

The duke de Chevreuse, a prince of the house of Guise, and (through the mother of Mary queen of Scots) a near kinsman of Charles I., on that account was appointed to represent his person, and give his hand by proxy to Henrietta. This ceremony took place May 21, 1625.

Scarcely was the marriage over at the door of Notre Dame, when the duke of Buckingham arrived, quite unexpectedly, with a splendid train of English nobles, in order to escort the young queen of England home.

Charles I., meantime, had travelled to Dover, where he was waiting impatiently the arrival of his queen. After a stormy passage, she arrived before Dover on Sunday evening, at seven o'clock, where she stepped from her boat on "an artificial bridge" the king had ordered to be constructed on purpose for her accommodation.

The king came to Dover castle to greet his bride at ten o'clock the following morning. His arrival was unexpected—she was at breakfast—she rose hastily from table, although he wished to wait for the conclusion of the meal. The royal bride hasted down a pair of stairs to meet the king, and then offered to kneel and kiss his hand, "but he wrapt her up in his arms with many kisses." The set speech that the princess had studied to greet the royal stranger, whom she had to acknowledge as her lord and master, was, "*Sire, je suis venue en ce pays de votre majesté pour être commandée de vous.*" "Sir, I am come into this, your majesty's country, to be at your command." But the firmness of the poor princess failed her, she finished the sentence with a gush of tears; and very natural it was that they should flow. The sight of her distress called forth all the kindness of the heart of Charles; he led her apart, he kissed off her tears, protesting that he should do so till she left off weeping; he soothed her with words of manly tenderness, telling her "that she was not fallen into the hands of enemies and strangers, as she tremblingly apprehended, but according to the wise disposal of God, whose will it was that she should leave her kindred and cleave to her spouse;

on their personal freedom.   They were deceived, for the parliament sent
a circular to all the nobility to arm and prevent the king from going
further.

Nothing could be more calamitous than the queen's prospects in her
approaching time of pain and weakness.   Ill and sorrowful as she
already was, she sought refuge in the loyal city of Exeter, where, amidst
the horrors and consternation of an approaching siege, she was in want
of every thing.   She took up her abode at Bedford House, in Exeter.
The king had written to summon to her assistance his faithful household physician, Theodore Mayerne; his epistle was comprehended in
one emphatic line in French.

King Charles I. to Dr. Sir Theodore Mayerne.

" Mayerne,
    " For the love of *me*, go to my wife!   C. R."

The queen likewise wrote an urgent letter in French to Dr. Mayerne,
entreating him to come to her assistance.

There is great generosity of mind in this letter.   The queen does
not say, as many a one does who requires impossibilities in this exacting
age, " Help me now, or all you have hitherto done will be of no use."
But, in a nobler spirit, " If you cannot come to me in my extreme need,
I shall still remain grateful for all your previous benefits."   Such, we
deem, offers a good instance of that ill-defined virtue, gratitude.

The faithful physician did not abandon his royal patrons in the hour
of their distress; he obeyed their summons, though we have reason to
believe that he looked not with affection on the queen, deeming her
religion one of the principal causes of the distracted state of England.

Perhaps the best trait in the character of queen Henrietta occurs at
this juncture; she reserved a very small portion of the donation of the
queen of France for her own use, and sent the bulk of it to the relief of
her distressed husband.   Boundless generosity—a generosity occurring
:n the time of privation, was a characteristic of Henrietta.

The queen gave birth to a living daughter, at Exeter, June 16, 1644,
at Bedford House, and in less than a fortnight afterwards, the army of

the earl of Essex advanced to besiege her city of refuge. On the approach of this hostile force, the queen, who was in a very precarious state of health, sent to the republican general, requesting permission to retire to Bath for the completion of her recovery. Essex made answer, " that it was his intention to escort her majesty to London, where her presence was required to answer to parliament for having levied war in England."

The daughter of Henry the Great summoned all the energy of character which she had derived from that mighty sire, to triumph over the pain and weakness that oppressed her feminine frame at this awful crisis. She arose from her sick bed, and escaped from Exeter in disguise, with one gentleman and one lady, and her confessor. She was constrained to hide herself in a hut, three miles from Exeter gate, where she passed two days without any thing to nourish her, crouched under a heap of litter. She heard the parliamentary soldiers defile on each side of her shelter; she overheard their imprecations and oaths, " that they would carry the head of Henrietta to London, as they would receive from the parliament a reward for it of 50,000 crowns." When this peril was passed, she issued out of her hiding-place, and, accompanied by the three persons who had shared her dangers, traversed the same road on which the soldiers had lately marched, though they had made it nearly impassable. She travelled in extreme pain, and her anxious attendants were astonished that she did not utterly fail on the way.

The rest of her ladies and faithful attendants stole out of Exeter, in various disguises, to meet her. Their rendezvous was at night in a miserable cabin, in a wood between Exeter and Plymouth.

Queen Henrietta did not reach the shores of her native land without a fresh trial to her courage. The vessel in which she had embarked was chased by a cruiser in the service of the parliament. Several cannon-shot were fired at the vessel in which she was embarked; and the danger of being taken or sunk seemed to her imminent. In this exigence, the queen took the command of the vessel. She forbade any return to be made of the cannonading, for fear of delay, but urged the pilot to continue his course, and every sail to be set for speed; and she charged the captain, if their escape was impossible, to fire the powder magazine, and destroy her with the ship, rather than permit her to fall

alive into the hands of her husband's enemies. At this order, her ladies
and domestics sent forth most piercing cries, she meantime maintaining
a courageous silence, her high spirit being wound up to brave death
rather than the disgrace to herself, and the trouble to her husband, which
would have ensued, if she had been dragged a captive to London.

Queen Henrietta trusted that the air and waters of her native land
would restore her to convalescence, and repair the constitution shattered
by the severe trials, mental and bodily, which she had sustained.   The
springs of Bourbon, indeed, somewhat ameliorated her health ; but her
firmness of mind was greatly shaken.   She wept perpetually for her
husband's misfortunes ; she was wasted almost to maceration, and her
beauty was for ever departed.   This loss she bore with great philoso-
phy ; she did not even suppose that it was caused by her troubles.

Père Cyprian Gamache, who was afterwards the tutor of the little
princess, details the story of her escape, and the simple man seems to
believe, in his enthusiasm, that Providence had ordained all the troubles
of king Charles, in order that his youngest daughter might be brought
up a Roman Catholic.

"Queen Henrietta," he says, " separated from her husband and children, living in loneliness of heart at the Louvre, had thought intensely
of this babe, and earnestly desiring her restoration, had vowed that if
she was ever reunited to her, that she would rear her in her own religion.

" Can a mother forget her child ?" repeats Père Gamache; "a hun
dred times each day did the thoughts of the bereaved queen recur to her
little infant ; as many times did her prayers, accompanied with maternal
tears, ask her of God ; nor did he refuse the just request.   His goodness
inspired the countess of Morton to divest herself of her rich robes and
noble ornaments to assume the garb of poverty, and disguise herself as
the wife of a poor French servant, little better than a beggar.   She likewise dressed the infant princess in rags, like a beggar-boy, and called her
'Pierre,' that name being somewhat like the sound by which the little
creature meant to call herself, 'princess," if she was asked her name."
Lady Morton was tall and elegantly formed, and it was no easy matter to
disguise the noble air and graceful port of the Villiers beauty. She, however, fitted herself up a hump, with a bundle of linen.   She walked with

the little princess on her back in this disguise nearly to Dover, giving out that she was her little boy. Subsequently lady Morton declared that she was at the same time alarmed and amused at the indignation of the royal infant at her rags and mean appearance, and at the pertinacity with which she strove to inform every person she passed on the road "that she was not a beggar-boy and Pierre, but the little princess." Fortunately for the infant Henrietta, no one understood her babblings but her affectionate guardian. Lady Morton had arranged all things so judiciously, that she crossed the sea from Dover to Calais, in the common packet-boat, without awakening the least suspicion. When once on the French territory, the royal child was no longer "Pierre" but "princess;" and lady Morton made the best of her way to the queen at Paris. "Oh, the joy of that meeting!" exclaims Père Cyprian—"oh, the consolation to the heart of the mother, when her little one who was lost was found again! How many times we saw her clasp her round the neck, kiss her and kiss her over again."

The queen remained in ignorance, not only of the death of her husband, but of every particular relating to his trial, until February 18, 1648-9. She was beleaguered in the Louvre, in double circles of siege and counter-siege. Thus was all intelligence cut off, since it was not without the greatest personal risk that any agent of queen Henrietta could pass both circles.

The actual truth had been communicated to the Père Gamache, who thus had nothing to distract his observation from the effect of the authentic tidings on the mind of the hapless queen; but what words can we find so forcibly to delineate this climax of a royal tragedy, as those of him who drew it from the life? "At this grievous intelligence," says the Père Gamache, "I felt my whole frame shudder, and was forced to turn aside from the royal circle, where conversation went on for an hour on divers matters, without any subject being started which had the effect of diverting the mind of the queen from the dire inquietude under which it was secretly oppressed. At last, she complained piteously of the tardiness of her messenger, and said 'that he ought to have returned before with his tidings.' Then lord Jermyn spoke: 'The gentleman dispatched on this errand,' he said, 'is known to be so faithful, and so prompt in executing all her majesty's commands, that, if he had had aught but very disastrous tidings, he would have been in your presence ere this.'

" 'Whatever they may be,' replied the queen, 'I see that you know them full well.'

" 'I do indeed know somewhat,' replied lord Jermyn. Then the queen, dreadfully alarmed, entreated him to speak less darkly, and, after many circumvolutions and ambiguous words, he at length explained the horrid truth to her, who never expected such intelligence."

Oh, the cruel kindness of those who undertake to break calamitous tidings by degrees! And yet sudden death has been known to follow such a tale too bluntly told, and indeed the communication, as it was, almost stopped the springs of life, when the widowed queen at length was brought to comprehend her loss.

"She stood," continues Père Gamache, "motionless as a statue, without words and without tears. A great philosopher has said that ordinary griefs allow the heart to sigh and the lips to murmur; but that extraordinary afflictions, terrible and fatal, cast the soul into stupor, and, by locking up the senses, make the tongue mute, and the eye tearless." If the good father had been, like Charles I. himself, a reader of Shakspeare, he would have described the state into which the royal widow was plunged, by that exquisite quotation:—

> " The grief that cannot speak,
> Whispers the o'er-fraught heart, and bids it break."

"To all our exhortations and arguments," the Père continues, "our queen was deaf and insensible. At last, awed by her appalling grief, we ceased talking, and stood round her in perturbed silence, some sighing, some weeping, all with mournful and sympathizing looks, bent on her immovable countenance. So we continued till nightfall, when the duchess of Vendome, whom our queen tenderly loved, came to see her. Weeping, she took the hand of the royal widow, and tenderly kissed it; and at last succeeded in awakening her from the stupor of grief into which she had been plunged since she had comprehended the dreadful death of her husband. She was able to sigh and weep, and soon expressed a desire to retire from the world, to indulge in the profound sorrow she suffered. Her little daughter was with her, and her maternal love found it hard to separate from her; yet she longed to withraw into some humble abode, where she might weep at will. At last, she resolved to retire, with a few of her ladies, into the convent of the Carmelites, Fauxbourg St. Jacques, in Paris."

Directly she entered into the convent she gave herself up to prayer, to mortification, and a course of meditation on the inscrutability of the decrees of God, the inconstancy and fragility of human life, and of the riches, grandeur, and honors of this world. Too soon was she roused from the holy calm which such salutary exercises give to sorrow. The affairs of the king, her son, and of her own family and household, being in so bad a state that they demanded her utmost care, her wisest counsel, and even active exertions, and I was obliged to seek her, to urge her to leave her peaceful retirement with the nuns, and return to the Louvre."

The queen resided upwards of six years in France, and all her habits and feelings began strongly to return to their original channel. A certain degree of liberality and political wisdom, which the strong pressure of calamity had forced into her mind, vanished after the war of the Fronde was pacified.

Reresby, who was rather better acquainted with the state of the public mind in England than the French prime minister, remained a close attendant on queen Henrietta's court, and was actually there when the news of the Restoration arrived. He affirms that the queen expressed extravagant joy; and that the whole French and English court might rejoice with her, she gave a magnificent ball, to which every courtier of note, belonging to either country, was invited.

" Our queen," says father Cyprian, " was not destined to see the end of the year 1669. Ever since her return from her last sojourn in London, she had laboured under complicated maladies, which caused her perpetual insomnolence, and intense suffering. From time to time the baths of Bourbon softened these pains, but could not cure them. She permitted the most able medical men in France to hold a consultation on her case; and M. Valot, the first physician of Louis XIV., M. Espoit, first physician to the duke of Orleans, and M. Julien, to the duchess, all met at the château of Colombe, where M. d'Aquin, physician to our

queen, introduced them into the chamber of her majesty. She explained
to them her symptoms with great clearness, and desired her physician
in ordinary ' to tell them the remedies he had applied for the shooting
pains which deprived her of rest.' Then M. Valot said, 'that, by the
grace of God, nothing very serious ailed her; that her malady was
inconvenient, but not dangerous; and that to the prescription of M.
d'Aquin he should add but three grains, which would give her majesty
sleep, and cure her disorder.'

"When the queen heard him talk of grains, she immediately suspected that he meant to prescribe opium, and she said, positively, that
she would not take them, ' for she knew by experience how noxious it
was to her, and how ill it made her.' "

Her repugnance was, however, overruled by the united arguments of
M. Valot and his medical brethren.

"When she went to bed she immediately fell into a sweet sleep."
Nothing can be more absurd than to wake a patient for the purpose of
administering a sleeping potion, yet such was the case; " the lady who
slept in her majesty's chamber roused her at the hour indicated, and
gave her the prescription. A few minutes after the queen again sunk to
sleep, and her attendant left her for repose, with the intention of
awakening her by daybreak to give her a draught, as directed by Dr.
Valot."

"Accordingly, the lady approached her bedside in the morning, and
asked her majesty 'how she had passed the night?" There was no reply. She spoke again louder; still no answer. The affrighted lady
leant down to her royal mistress, and fancied she heard low murmurs,
sighs, and labored respiration, upon which she flew to rouse the *valet de
chambre*, to seek for medical and spiritual aid, to fetch priests and physicians." "We came first," continues the sorrowful father Cyprian;
"the doctors soon followed."

"The physicians affirmed that she still breathed, and was even sensible; but that a dull vapor, mounting to the brain, prevented all
speech, that it would soon dissipate, and that she would manifest con
sciousness, and speak. I believed them at first," continues the Père;
"but seeing that her awful quietude still continued, I sent in haste for
monsieur le curé of Colombe, and the sacrament of extreme unction

being performed, she received the host without any difficulty, or the least convulsion of countenance, and soon after her slight respiration ceased, and she rendered her soul to God, undisturbed by a struggle."

The cause of the death of Henrietta Maria is mentioned by mademoiselle de Montpensier, her niece. She says, in her usual flippant style, " she could not sleep, the doctors gave her a pill to cure her wakefulness, which it did so effectually that she never woke again."

40

CAROLINE.

QUEEN OF GEORGE II.

CAROLINE WILHELMINA was the daughter of the margrave of Anspach, and was born in 1688. She lost her father when very young, and her mother, a princess of the house of Eysenbach, marrying afterwards the elector of Saxony, the young Caroline was confided to the guardianship of Frederick of Brandenburg, subsequently king of Prussia, and derived the inestimable advantage of receiving her education under the superintendence of her aunt, his wife, the accomplished Sophia Charlotte, sister of George the First. No less amiable than intellectually gifted, the queen of Prussia was honored and beloved for her patronage of literature, science, and art; and her death, when only thirty-seven, was universally lamented. This melancholy event occurred in 1705, the same year in which her niece gave her hand to George, then electoral prince of Hanover.

There is no doubt the electoral prince was as truly and warmly attached to his bride as it was possible for a nature essentially coarse and phlegmatic to be; and abundant evidence also proves that his affection increased with years, as did her influence over his mind and actions. Caroline must have been eminently discreet in her conduct, or she could not have steered her difficult course as she did, through the different cabals which began early in her married life. Long before the accession of George the First, the misunderstanding between him and his son took place,—originating, probably, from several causes, not the least being that the electoral prince doted on his mother, the unfortunate Sophia of Zell.

On the accession of George the Second to the throne, it was the influence of Caroline which retained sir Robert Walpole in office. The king had inclined towards sir Spencer Compton, "who, so far from meditating to supplant the premier, had recourse to sir Robert, and besought him to prepare the draught of the king's speech. The new queen, a better judge than her husband of the capacities of the two candidates, and who had silently watched for a moment proper for overturning the new designations, did not lose a moment in observing to the king, "how prejudicial it would be to his affairs to prefer to the minister in possession, a man in whose own judgment his predecessor was the fittest person to execute his office."

The queen also took another opportunity of declaring her sentiments. Walpole says, "Their majesties had removed from Richmond to their temporary residence in Leicester Fields, on the very evening of their receiving notice of their accession to the crown, and the next day all the nobility and gentry in the town crowded to kiss their hands, my mother among the rest, who, sir Spencer Compton's designation, and not its evaporation, being known, could not make her way between the scornful backs and elbows of her late devotees, nor could approach nearer to the queen than the third or fourth row; but no sooner was she descried by her majesty, than the queen said aloud, 'There I am sure I see a friend.' The torrent divided and shrunk to either side; 'and as I came away,' said my mother, 'I might have walked over their heads if I had pleased.'"

It may be that the penetration of Walpole early discovered that influence really lay with the queen, and that he paid his court accordingly; or some more honorable feeling may have originated the cordiality between them. Caroline appears to have taken great pleasure in the society of sir Robert and lady Walpole, and frequently dined at their house at Chelsea. On these occasions, however, the rigor of etiquette was maintained. Sir Robert did not sit down to table with his royal guest, but stood behind her chair, and gave her the first plate, and then retired himself to a separate table." Lady Walpole took her seat at table in company with the lady-in-waiting; but when we call to mind that in those days it was esteemed the indispensable duty of a hostess to *carve*, the exception in her favor may perhaps be explained!

Caroline had been esteemed handsome in her youth; but her beauty was subsequently marred by that pitiless scourge, the small-pox, and later in life an exceeding stoutness destroyed the symmetry of her figure. Her hand and arm were greatly admired for their whiteness and beauty of form, and her countenance is reported to have had that best beauty, the beauty of expression. A poet has lauded her smile as " celestial." She must have been a good conversationist, possessing the rare and delicate tact of adapting her discourse to the character and acquirements of those she addressed. At her toilette, " learned men and divines were intermixed with courtiers and ladies of the household, and the conversation turned on metaphysical subjects, blended with repartees, sallies of mirth, and the tittle-tattle of the drawing-room." She corresponded with Leibnitz, and delighted in abstract science.

Caroline was the friend and patroness of many celebrated divines and men of learning. Her intercession saved the life of the unfortunate Richard Savage, when condemned to death for the life he took in a tavern brawl; she settled an annuity of fifty pounds upon him, which was withdrawn after her death.

Her death took place on the 20th of November, 1737. The queen had suffered for years from a painful and dangerous disease, unwisely concealing her calamity from her physicians, who, had they known the truth, might have alleviated her anguish. It is difficult to reconcile with her general behavior, her refusal to see Frederick, prince of Wales, on her death-bed. In his youth she had shielded him, on many occasions, from the anger of his father; and in later years it is remarkable that, while his letters to the king were full of all the deferential expressions due to majesty, those to the queen abounded in the simpler words "madame," and "vous;" a familiarity that seems to tell of freedom and affection between them, rather than of want of respect. Nevertheless she refused him admission on that last awful occasion, though she sent him her blessing and forgiveness. Perhaps the mind of the poor queen—helpless and suffering in the last dread hour, as the meanest of her subjects—wandered in its judgment. Certain it is,

also, that she died without receiving the last sacrament. Whether con-
fused by her controversial readings, she hesitated, or whether archbishop Potter desired her personal reconciliation with the prince her
son, is not known; but the prelate had a wily answer ready to meet all
questioners. When a crowd eagerly asked, " Has the queen communicated?" he replied, evading a direct denial, " Her majesty is in a most
heavenly disposition."

With the death of the queen the king soon surrounded himself with
fresh faces, and probably forgot the superior woman with whom he had
been associated, in the society of his new and acknowledged favorite.

A number of laudatory effusions appeared after the death of Caroline, but not one of sufficient poetical merit to deserve a re-appearance
in modern type. But a few lines may be admitted from the eulogy of
Stephen Duck, which was probably a sincere tribute of gratitude. With
not a hundredth part of the talent of Burns, and of birth still more obscure, the self-taught versifier, the humble " thresher," found friends and
patrons, and royalty at their head, to give him that help, a tithe of
which, bestowed upon the Ayrshire Bard, might have enriched our
literature beyond all conjecture, and rendered his life honorable and
happy. Yet the thresher's fate points its moral most tragically. Conscious
at last that his powers were less than the world believed, existence
grew intolerable, and poor Stephen drowned himself in a fit of despondency :—

> " In every state her goodness has been proved,
> When ruled obedient, and when ruling loved ;
> Securely blest beneath her gentle sway,
> 'Tis happiness to serve and pleasure to obey.
>
> Nor fewer charms adorn her private life,
> The tenderest mother, most submissive wife ;
> Who never yet her consort disobeyed,
> By honor, duty, love and virtue swayed ;
> In virtue's path she constantly proceeds,
> By virtue's rule she measures all her deeds."

VICTORIA.

QUEEN-REGNANT.

THE name of Victoria is on every lip, and imprinted on the heart of each of her subjects, yet would the memoirs of English royalty be incomplete, without a brief outline of the life of the reigning sovereign.

The duke and duchess of Kent were united in the year 1818, and after spending some months on the Continent, returned to England, prior to the birth of their daughter, which took place at Kensington Palace, May 24th, 1819. The prince regent became sponsor at the christening of his little niece, on whom were bestowed the names Alexandrina Victoria; the emperor of Russia and the queen of Wirtemburg, also stood by their proxies.

The death of the duke of Kent at Sidmouth, when the princess was but seven months old, and that of George the Third, which happened a few days after, rendered her presumptive heiress to the throne, after her three childless uncles, George the Fourth, and the dukes of York and Clarence. The education of the princess became therefore a matter of momentous importance, and so conscious of this was the duchess of Kent, as well as scrupulously anxious in the undertaking, that it is said she never quitted the side of her child even for ten minutes together, until the period of her accession to the throne. The princess, under suitable preceptors, was instructed in every branch of learning that could adorn the monarch, or render the woman charming; ancient as well as mod-

ern languages, history, geography, mathematics, besides music, drawing,
and dancing, were by degrees ingrafted with complete success, upon the
mind of the young princess, until it soon became evident that her learning and talents, however little desire or occasion their might be to parade them, were really superior to those which any other queen regnant
of England had possessed.   Her preceptor, in the more solid branches
of education, as well as in religious instruction, was the Rev. Mr. Davys,
afterwards bishop of Peterborough, and dean of Chester, and her governess was first the baroness Lehzen, and afterwards the duchess of
Northumberland.   Parliament had early granted the sum of £6,000
per annum, for her educational establishment, and this sum was afterwards augmented to £16,000.   It is impossible for the nation to acknowledge in too high terms its debt to the duchess of Kent, for her
excellent management of the education of the heiress to the crown;
doubtless the liberal tendencies of the mother's mind found an easy impress on that of the only daughter, but that even balance of power with
which Victoria has swayed these realms during fourteen years, that
self-control over a mind of more than adequate capacity, which has not
given cause for a single complaint against her personal interference in
the affairs of the nation, must be traced in its germs to the constant example and supervision of the duchess of Kent.

They resided together at Kensington Palace, until the period of her
accession, making from time to time progresses through the country, in
order that she might obtain a practical and intimate knowledge of those
who were in time to be *her* people.   Most of the cities of importance
were visited at different periods, and the princess gained on the affections of all who knew her, by her genuine goodness of heart and
benevolence.

When she attained her twelfth year a juvenile ball was given by
queen Adelaide, who was always much attached to her, and the return
of her birthday was from that time marked by a similar demonstration
of their majesties' attachment to their youthful successor.

An intimacy had been fostered, as children, between the princess
Victoria and her cousin the prince Albert of Saxe Coburg, who had
been placed under the care of the duchess of Kent.   He resided alter-
nately at Kensington and at Claremont, with his uncle, prince Leopold,

to whom the princess and her mother were frequent visitors, and had been accustomed to share the lessons of the royal pupil. Thus a similarity of taste and feeling ripened into affection at an early age. This occurred previous to the year 1830, at which date, much to the regret of the duchess and her daughter, the amiable prince Leopold was called to the throne of Belgium.

Victoria was confirmed by the archbishop of Canterbury on the 30th of July, 1835, their majesties, her mother, and the rest of the royal family being present. In 1836, the duke of Saxe Coburg Gotha and his two sons visited England, and were royally entertained at Windsor; the duchess of Kent and the princess Victoria accompanying their relatives on their return as far as Portsmouth.

On the princess attaining her eighteenth year, the period of her majority, a state ball was given at St. James's Palace, at which, on account of the illness of both the king and queen, she presided in person. On that day many addresses of congratulation were presented to her, and, among others, one from the city of London, to which, she herself made a short but interesting reply with her accustomed grace of manner and delivery. At a drawing-room somewhat later, in honor of the king's birthday, the princess also appeared in public.

On the death of William the Fourth, June 20th, 1837, the archbishop of Canterbury waited immediately upon the new sovereign at Kensington with the melancholy tidings. The dignified demeanor of queen Victoria at the first council held after her accession, will never be forgotten by the eye-witnesses of the interesting scene. The events which followed are fresh in the minds of the English people. The first Chapter held for installing knights of the Garter, the prorogation of Parliament in person by a young maiden sovereign, her first thronged drawing-room, her triumphal entry at Windsor into the Castle of her ancestors,—these, on which space permits us not here to dwell, are all become matters of history. So, also, is the state visit she paid to Guildhall, which was the grandest pageant of those days. The Parliament was re-opened by the queen in person, when a crowded House had an opportunity of admiring the excellent address which is so particularly enjoyed by her majesty.

Among the many noble traits of character exhibited by queen

41

Victoria since the time of her accession, may be mentioned her kind attentions to the late queen dowager, and the last wishes of king William respecting the family of Mrs. Jordan, as well as the delicacy with which she caused the debts of her own lamented father, the duke of Kent, to be paid. These acts, among numberless others, cannot be sufficiently admired.

The day of her present gracious majesty's coronation was a holiday in the entire metropolis. It was such a time of public rejoicing for the multitude as has not been seen for many years. The numbers of all nations, who thronged into London constituted an unusual sight in themselves, independently of the splendors with which the occasion was celebrated. Among other novelties peculiar to the event, was a grand fair held for several days successively in Hyde Park.

For nearly three years her majesty ruled this empire alone, but although her own mind had probably decided long before in its choice of a fitting consort to share her exalted station, the importunities of her ministers at length prevailed upon her in the year 1839, to announce that her selection had fallen upon the playmate of her childhood, prince Albert of Saxe Coburg. She had been already frequently subjected from her peculiar position to many intrusions and annoyances from pretended aspirants to her hand. The prince had visited England in 1838 and again in 1839, prior to the formal intimation of the high destiny which awaited him.

In the spring of 1840 the royal marriage was celebrated, which, in the course of the ensuing ten years has been productive of seven children. The prince of Wales, Albert Edward, was born on Lord Mayor's day, 1841; there is a daughter older than him, and two sons and three daughters younger. In the same year, 1840, Oxford made his dastardly attack on her life; several other malicious persecutions of the same nature were suffered by her, with exemplary courage and truly regal dignity, at frequent intervals in the early years of her reign, but it was hoped that this mania for popularity and easy method of obtaining a sustenance during life at the hands of the nation, had been thwarted and extinguished, until in 1850, another wretched candidate for transportation for a like crime, presented himself in the person of a retired subaltern of her army named Pate. On the 16th of July, 1842, a bill passed through Parliament expressly for better protection of the queen's person, in consequence of these despicable assaults.

Her majesty has testified during these later years her predilection for pleasure excursions in her yacht during the parliamentary recesses, besides various progresses inland to the seats of the nobility. The most splendid reception of all the latter, was provided on her visit to the duke of Buckingham at Stowe. When the treacherous *entente cordiale* between England and the late king of the French was supposed to be the most firmly based, Queen Victoria made a visit to Louis Philippe at the Château d'Eu, in Normandy. The entertainments which she there met with, quite equalled general expectation; and notwithstanding the family intrigues which that monarch was even then prosecuting, her majesty's attentions to him since his expulsion to this country, by the French Revolution of 1848, betray her lively sensibility to past kindness. She has several times made an autumnal tour in Scotland, and once has been hailed with glad acclamations through the whole length of Ireland.

England has not been without its internal commotions during this reign. There was a Chartist rebellion, headed by Frost in Wales, almost at its commencement; there were disturbances in 1842; there was insurrection in Ireland and attempts at insurrection in England, consequent upon the foreign revolutions of 1848, but perhaps the many are not so happy under England's greatness as they might be made. Great victories have added to our territory in India during this period, and for the principal part of the time, a masterly foreign minister has preserved our interests abroad in peace with other nations. The grand political event of queen Victoria's reign hitherto, has been the Repeal of the Corn Laws, or the boon of cheap bread for the multitude at large.

We conclude—and what millions of hearts and lips will swell the proud chorus!—with the words of our national anthem,

"GOD SAVE OUR GRACIOUS QUEEN!"

THE END.